; BONES

DARRELL BRYANT

ENCHANTED INDIE PRESS

GERONIMO'S BONES

a novel by

Darrell Bryant

ENCHANTED INDIE PRESS

Austin

PUBLISHER'S NOTE

Copyright © 2018 Darrell Bryant
Cover design and interior formatting for digital and print editions:
Tosh McIntosh
Cover photo: Travis Neely, travisshoots.com

Published in the United States of America

Print Edition (v1.7.1)
ISBN-13: 978-1-938749-42-1
ISBN-10: 1-938749-42-1

Digital Edition (v1.7.1)
ISBN-13: 978-1-938749-43-8
ISBN-10: 1-938749-43-X

The minstrel boy to the war is gone,
In the ranks of death ye will find him;
His father's sword he hath girded on,
And his wild harp slung behind him;
"Land of Song," cried the warrior bard,
"Tho' all the world betrays thee,
One sword, at least, thy rights shall guard,
One faithful harp shall praise thee!"
—Thomas Moore

I wish I had never given up. I wish I had kept
fighting until I was the last man alive.
—The dying words of Goyaałé,
known to his enemies as
Geronimo.

Waŋzi okíčhize waš'ákA kiéi kiŋ Lakota ('A fierce fighter for the Human Beings').
—for Russell Means (1939–2012)
—and for Wilma Mankiller (1945-2010)

GERONIMO'S BONES

A Native American warrior journeys through the towns, train depots, and wilds of the early-20th-century West in this debut historical novel.

Young Chaco only knows the prisoner-of-war camp in Fort Sill, Oklahoma, where he hears stories about his people's old ways at the knee of his uncle, the famed Apache chief Goyaałé, known to whites as Geronimo. But Chaco is soon forcibly taken to an "Indian school" in Pennsylvania—leaving behind Goyaałé; his adoptive mother, Aná; and his sister, Bui. He joins the Marines after he graduates, and during a stint in Cuba fighting the 1906 Pacification Campaign, he receives terrible news: Goyaałé is dead. Shaken, he returns to Fort Sill, where he cares for his aging mother and finds out that Bui has ended up in the local whorehouse. His mother also tells him Goyaałé is actually his father and wanted his bones to be taken to the mountains he called home. Shortly after she delivers this revelation, she dies. Chaco is filled with a steely resolve: to break Bui out of the brothel (owned by an unscrupulous proprietor named Alton McDonnell) and to bring Goyaałé's bones to the mountains. His quest to do so will take all of Chaco's tactical skill and courage— and a few daring car chases and shootouts—as the resulting manhunt draws lawmen from all over the region. For a story that's equal parts rollicking adventure and a sensitive account of a Native American's odyssey in a particular era, Chaco is an ideal protagonist: intelligent, battle-worn, quick on his feet, and occasionally philosophical ("As he stared at the young wolf, it occurred to him that the Indian school had never been about education. It had been about domestication"). Bryant also clearly depicts the extreme racism Chaco faces, which makes his successes all the more satisfying. The book is full of historical details, deftly deployed so that they heighten the action instead of impeding it: People hop on trains, cut telegraph lines, and wrestle with high-maintenance automobiles. Add in a few colorful, nuanced characters along the way, like the cancer-stricken, former Civil War surgeon dwarf Doc Kale, and the novel shines.

A thought-provoking tale about an Apache's struggles as well as a rousing romp.

— *Kirkus Reviews*

"Geronimo's Bones is both evocative and rich in history. Bryant's U.S. marshal steps off the pages. The ending haunts me still."

—Jodi Thomas, bestselling author
of 48 novels set in Texas

EPILOGUE AS A PROLOGUE

Geronimo's Bones is based on an Apache legend, a story I came across on a hot August day at Fort Sill, in western Oklahoma, where I'd driven a few days before to do a bit of research. Under a cloudless sky, in a historic graveyard near the fort's main post, I had been taking photos of Comanche and Kiowa headstones and scribbling notes in a spiral notebook for about an hour when I was approached by a groundskeeper. He was a strong-looking, friendly fellow—a throwback to the sixties, with a graying ponytail, full mustache, and earthy manner. He had bright, curious eyes, and asked what I was doing. I told him I'd driven up from Austin to gather all information available on the Comanche Nation. Why? For a pre–Civil War novel I was writing. It was at that point he asked me if I knew anything about Apaches, which I did, and he then asked if I'd ever heard a local legend about Geronimo, an event that he claimed had taken place a few short months after the old warrior's death in 1909.

I hadn't.

The legend of Geronimo's bones had come to him by way of an Apache buddy, with whom he'd played football in high school. The buddy, in turn, had the story by way of an uncle, a surviving elder whose parents remained in Oklahoma after the U.S. government's resolution of the Apache prisoner-of-war issue in 1928—four years after Native Americans were finally granted citizenship in their native country, and a full nineteen years after Geronimo's death.

His story so intrigued me that I asked him for directions to the Apache Prisoner-of-War Cemetery, where Geronimo's grave was located. I found the graveyard in an isolated area on the military reserve, several miles from Main Post on a narrow, winding road. It was quiet there, save for the distant and once-familiar *whunk* of impacting artillery rounds.

Geronimo's grave was singular in that it alone of all the Apache graves there lay beneath a low mound of gray stones, bound together with black mortar. There was a small bronze plaque affixed to the mound that addressed the Apache wars and Geronimo's ultimate defeat by the U.S. Army. But on that day I had learned that the book of Geronimo's life had not ended with his death, and as I stood at the foot of that heap of stones, surrounded by the headstones of Geronimo's long-forgotten kinsmen, I knew that I would write that final chapter. I wanted the legend to be true then, just as I want it to be true now, and if it is not the truth, it ought to be.

—The Author

1

He was born a prisoner of war at Mount Vernon Barracks in Alabama, where under the harsh conditions of the camp many of the People died. His mother, Lozen, famed shaman-warrior sister of the great Victorio, in the fading hour after her infant's birth, looked up into the watchful eyes of Aná Liluy and, with trembling hands, lifted him from her breast. "Take him," she whispered. "See that he lives."

Aná Liluy accepted the newborn, tied his birth cord, and, claiming him as her own, she walked out into the sun and held him up to the sky for Usen to see. A red hawk cried high in the sun-split blue. It was a good omen, a sign from Usen, given when a great spirit enters or leaves the world.

She named him Chaco for the mystic canyon in which her daughter, Bui, was born, in that time when she and Lozen had fled from a bad place together. She gave him this name against the orders of the chief soldier over them, who told her that the boy's name on the paper would be Frank Kidd and that she must call him by that name. Bui, who became Chaco's sister, was also given a whiteeye name: Sally Liluy, a name to be used when dealing with the soldiers.

Chaco's first memory was of digging beside his sister in their mother's garden behind a sun-scorched shack. On that hot, humid day of first memory, as Chaco moved along the rows of vegetables, he roused a rattler coiled among the beanstalks. He froze as the snake's tail quivered. An instant later Aná's hoe flashed between him and the snake, severing its raised head.

"*Learn from this,*" Aná hissed in his ear in the tongue of the N'dé, the Apache. "*This snake is dead because he warned his enemy.*"

The People died almost as much at Mount Vernon Barracks as they had at Fort Marion. In fact, so many died that in 1894, in Chaco's sixth summer, the head soldier over the prisoner-of-war camp received a new order: the N'dé were to be moved to yet another place, a place called Fort Sill in Oklahoma Territory.

And so, on the appointed day, soldiers came with rifles to the camp. Aná had made up two bundles, one for her and the other for Bui. Many of the People were apprehensive, some were confused, but Aná remained calm. Out of caution, she kept both Chaco and Bui close to her. She was not afraid of the soldiers. *"What can they take from us that they have not already taken, but our lives?"*

It surprised Chaco that his sister was afraid. He, for his part, felt only curiosity. He liked the soldiers' oiled rifles and their crisp uniforms. Liked their upright bearing, their fearless arrogance while escorting the People to the train station. The N'dé would travel in boxcars, and one of the soldiers with stripes on his arms pointed to one of several open cars and said, "Get in," and Aná lifted him through the opening, climbed aboard herself and pulled Bui up into the car after her.

Chaco stared down unblinkingly into the soldier's eyes as he closed the cargo door, the sound of the lock latching, sharp in the gray gloom.

Within the hour the train rumbled westward, the car hot and drafty by day, chill and drafty by night. The little water they carried dribbled out into the mouths of the youngest, and the air soon reeked of sweat and the fetid odors of the slop jars. Two days of uninterrupted travel brought the train to a final, rumbling halt at Lawton Station.

Chaco heard orders being shouted outside the car. The sort of orders he'd often heard being given to soldiers. He came to his feet as those around him stood. The lock on the car door rattled. And a moment later the door slid open. In the sudden morning glare, a soldier stared at him and those standing in the car about him, the soldier level with them on the station's rough-plank platform near a yellow building a short distance to Chaco's left.

"Get out," the soldier shouted, and Chaco, squinting against the sun, weak from thirst, saw the soldier's face pucker as he stepped back, waving his hand back and forth in front of his face. "Jesus, stinking gut-eaters," he growled, and moved down the platform to the next car.

As Chaco's vision cleared he saw other soldiers, some seated on the benches of a waiting line of open mule-drawn wagons, most of them mounted on well-groomed horses, the butts of their shiny carbines at rest on their thighs. An impressive number of armed men under the command of a young officer, now shouting, "Out of the cars, into the wagons," as he strode back and forth along the rough planks of the station platform, a riding crop slapping rhythmically against the top of one of his highly polished boots. Chaco heard an undercurrent of fear in the lieutenant's voice, was surprised by it. What had he to fear with so many well-armed soldiers under his command?

Chaco stepped from the car to the platform ahead of Aná and Bui. Fell in beside his mother and the three of them made their way down a set of plank steps and crossed the gravel road toward the nearest wagon. The wagon filled before they reached it. They moved on to the next. He used the wheel hub for a step, climbed aboard, and made room for his mother and sister. Aná sat on her bundle, wrapped her arms around him. Chaco leaned against her and studied the mounted soldiers. Liking the look of their oiled carbines, liking the sleek, well-cared-for horses they rode. They looked fast, and the men mounted on them sat smartly upright, carbines at the ready, the horses arranged in a cordon midway between the line of wagons in front of the station and a gathering of angry whiteeyes from the town, who had come to watch.

When the last child had settled in beside her mother, the officer gave an order to an older soldier with many stripes on his sleeve.

The soldier saluted, stepped into the saddle, and shouted, "Move out."

Whips cracked. Drivers called to their teams. The driver in charge of their wagon clucked up the mules and the wagon jerked out of its tracks and fell in behind the others.

An angry shout, "Red niggers," and Chaco turned toward the sound as their wagon rumbled past the whiteeyes from the town. A scar-faced old man, livid with anger, the old man shaking a clinched fist, shouting, "Red hide niggers as ever was."

The wagon rolled past the old man and moved away.

"Why does the old Indah hate us, Mother?"

Aná drew him closer. *"It is enough that you know he does."*

The wagons lined out and rumbled away from Lawton, dust drifting back toward the town from the wheel-cut ruts of the road. They passed between a brace of rock columns that marked the boundary entrance to the military reserve. And within the hour their train of wagons rumbled into view of an unwalled quadrangle of single-story stone buildings situated on a low hill that was Fort Sill. At the base of the hill, near a number of recently constructed barracks, a group of soldiers was playing at ball. A soldier in rolled-up shirtsleeves threw the fist-sized ball at another soldier who swung at it with a heavy stick . . . and missed. Another soldier yelled, "Strike," as the soldier with the stick pointed toward the approaching wagons and the game stopped. All the soldiers playing at ball raised their hands, shaded their eyes, and watched the line of wagons move by.

They rolled past other newly constructed barracks, with wheeled artillery pieces arranged in precise rows on neatly mowed grass in front of the structures. Seeing it all, Chaco imagined how wonderful it must be to live the life of a soldier. He leaned over the side of the wagon, looking back until the soldiers and then the stone buildings of the fort itself faded from view.

The day wore on, hot and dry, dust drifting from the wheels of the wagons and the hooves of the horses and the mules. In time he spied a series of peaks off to his right, mountaintops made up of reddish rock, hash marked with greenery.

"*Look, Mother.*" He pointed.

"*Yes, those are the Wichitas,*" she whispered.

He stared up at the mountaintops, their tan peaks rising above the green tree-grown landscape, and for a moment his mind filled with possibilities. There was so much space here, it seemed to him they must certainly have more freedom here, and for a few heartbeats it seemed possible the wagons might go on forever; an endless journey, with stops at night only, a time to eat and to sleep before going on. If they could keep going, he thought, what a wonderful life that would be to live, just going on toward horizons without end.

The wagon road meandered between low hemlock- and

tamarack-covered hills, across shallow vales into the late afternoon, and yet well before sundown they came in sight of the Apache POW camp, a barbed-wire enclosure situated amidst a scattering of spruce near a slow-flowing creek.

"*This is where we will live now,*" Aná whispered into his ear.

Bui's owllike eyes widened as they approached. While Chaco, for his part, took in the barbed-wire enclosure, and the manned watchtowers, much like those at Mount Vernon Barracks. Yet as their wagon rumbled through the open gate, he saw that weeds had grown up around the gates since they'd last been closed, and noted several gaping holes in the wire enclosure.

Many N'dé already lived in this camp, and it seemed to him that all of them had turned out at their arrival. Among them were relatives and friends who had not seen one another in years. Many happy faces; brothers greeted sisters; friends greeted friends. Yet with so many dead left behind after the long separation, there was grief also.

Chaco's eyes were bright with happiness, yet the joy and sorrows of the People remained subdued until the mounted soldiers had ridden away behind the wagons that had brought them. As evening settled over the camp, fires were lit and the N'dé, the People, began to chant, and food was brought out and shared, and the People celebrated under the rising moon.

That evening Aná's friend, Olivia Yanozha, led Aná, Bui, and Chaco to a small two-room shanty, the rooms divided by an eight-foot wide dogtrot. And told them they would share one of the rooms. This would be their new home.

On that first night, as Chaco lay on his back looking up at dancing shadows cast by wind and firelight across the board ceiling, in his heart he felt they had come to a good place.

The days that followed were good. He helped his mother and sister spade up and plant a fresh garden, using seeds Aná had brought with her. In both Florida and Alabama, there had never been enough food, and the government rations they were supplied here proved to be no better than those supplied at the other camps.

Even so, the conditions were better here. The women of the camp explained to Aná how things went at Fort Sill. The sentries in the towers were no longer strict in their duties. "*They allow us to go out to gather our own firewood. That way they don't have to cut the wood or bring it to us.*"

"*So they are lazy.*"

"*What else? They are men, are they not?*"

And so when Aná and his sister went out to gather wood for their cook fires, Chaco went along with them. He had never known such freedom. Life here was easier. The days drifted by. White clouds floated across the blue sky. The summer sun was warm, and in the evenings it sometimes rained. He loved the sound of rain on the tin roof of their room, especially at night.

One day Aná pulled him away from digging in the garden and pointed to a group of boys.

"*Go,*" she said. "*Make friends.*"

It seemed that here there was even time enough for him to play at games with the other boys. Everything was good and in his mind seemed to be settled until the afternoon Aná summoned him to her.

"*Come,*" she said. "*There is someone you must meet.*"

She led him across the camp to a shanty where an old man sat on the porch-like edge of a dogtrot, whittling long white slivers from a willow stick onto a growing pile kindling. The old man looked up as they approached, folded the knife, and slipped it into his pocket. He stood and with a lift of chin called out, "*Yatasay.*"

"*Da go te', Goyaałé,*" Aná answered, and stopped in the dusty yard a polite distance away. She pulled Chaco around from behind her and gripped his shoulders. "*This is Goyaałé,*" she whispered into the boy's hair, and then, in a louder, strangely defiant voice, she said to the old man, "*This is the son of Lozen. Before she died she gave this one to me. I say he is mine now.*"

The old man's hard gaze fixed on Chaco, and for several heartbeats the boy stared wordlessly back. He swallowed in a dry throat and was afraid, for he recognized the old man. The other boys had pointed him out. This was the one the Indah, the whiteeyes, called Geronimo. He sensed terrible purpose in this old man, sensed the smell of bullets and of horse sweat, of leather and of camp smoke—the smell of blood and war and power. No bullet could kill this one, it was said.

"*Yes,*" Goyaałé answered, his gaze fixed on Aná again. "*You are right to make this one your own. It is as it should be.*" He drew a ragged breath and for several heartbeats stared at the watchtower nearest his shanty.

Chaco looked at the tower. The sentry in the tower stared back; his rifle slung carelessly over one shoulder. Chaco felt Geronimo's gaze, turned, and met the old man's stare, and was surprised when the hard old eyes wavered, seemed to soften.

"*I am Goyaałé, your uncle. And I have waited long for this day.*" He turned to Aná. "*Can he run? Does he have the strong legs of his father?*"

"*I brought him to you. It is for you to say.*"

Goyaałé shook his old head. "*They watch me. He is yours. Teach him what he must know in this world. Teach him that his legs are his best friends. That they will carry him where he must go in this life.*"

"*He will sit at your fire, and you will talk to him of these things,*" she insisted.

"*He is young. They will not allow it.*"

Aná's frown deepened. "*I have watched. The whiteeyes at this place are lazy. They will say 'Don't do that,' and say it again, but if you do it a third time and there is no trouble, they will shrug.*"

After that Chaco sat at Geronimo's fire, and as Aná had predicted, he was sent away twice. But after his third attempt the soldier said, "Well, you better not make any trouble," and after that nothing more was done to keep him away.

In the evenings Chaco would sit with Goyaałé and a few old men from the old warrior's free days. They would stare into the flickering depths of his uncle's fire and, with Chaco listening, talked of the old ways and of the time before, when the Apache were feared men and free to ride where they willed across their sacred lands.

One evening Goyaałé said, "*The Indah promised to let me go back to my own country in two years, but they lied.*" There was a long, embarrassed silence before he sighed and looked up at the moon. "*At least the People do not die so easily here.*" His chin dropped, and he stared across the fire into Chaco's watchful eyes. "*I thought I could run them off, but there are too many of them. Usen always knew I could not win, but he told me in a dream that I had to fight them. That my name would outlive the last Indah. But now I am too old to fight.*"

"*You're not too old, Uncle,*" Chaco said fiercely.

The easy laughter of the other men brought a flush to Chaco's cheeks and silenced him.

"*Do not mock the boy,*" Goyaałé muttered.

"*No, Goyaałé,*" said Yanozha, *Goyaałé's* brother-in-law, and one of the warriors who had fought to the last at his side. "*We laugh because his heart is good. We see his father in him.*"

There was a silence. Goyaałé nodded, looked at Chaco. "*Yes.*"

"*He has the hawk eyes of his father,*" said Yanozha.

"*Did my father fight beside you?*" Chaco asked.

Yanozha considered the question for a moment. "*Yes.*"

"*Was he a great warrior like you?*"

"*Some say he was as great as Mangas Coloradas.*"

The other men nodded in agreement. Chaco's heart soared like a hawk. "*What happened to him?*"

Goyaałé turned to the others. All of them stared back; waited for his answer. "*He was betrayed by the Indah.*"

"*He was shot?*"

"*No . . . he was tricked and captured . . . and then killed.*"

3

The dusty days of summer faded into the first chill nights of autumn, and life seemed as good as it could be to Chaco. He was happy in this place. But then came the bad day when a fat, gray-haired army lieutenant, who gave his name as Richard Henry Pratt, rode into the camp, accompanied by armed soldiers. The lieutenant had written orders that gave him the power to take Chaco and all other children his age far away to the whiteeyes' Indian school.

His uncle Goyaałé confronted the old lieutenant.

"Leave this one," Goyaałé said, as he placed a war-scarred hand on Chaco's shoulder. "I ask that this boy not be taken away from his mother with the others that you take to this school."

The old lieutenant frowned. "There will be no exceptions, Geronimo. Not even for you."

Wagons arrived from the main post. The shouting soldiers grouped the children in the center of the camp. There were wails of anguish and a struggle. A mother would not let go of her child. A soldier struck her with his rifle. The woman's father leapt forward and cut the soldier with a knife. Another soldier shot the father. Then came angry shouts, and Chaco thought there would be a fight. But then his uncle Goyaałé rushed forward, arms and hands waving.

"*Nəʊ*," he shouted, yelling a warning *No* in the tongue of the People, and thus forestalled the young men now moving toward the soldiers who waited, rifles raised and ready to fire. The old men held back their angry sons, and in the end the battle-tested wisdom of the aged prevailed.

"This is a lawful order," the lieutenant shouted. "You will comply or be fired upon."

The memory of Wounded Knee was fresh in everyone's heart; it was submit or die. And so the children were gathered, and Chaco, confused and afraid, witnessed the coming apart of his world. He was frightened and very much wanted to cry, but Aná gripped his chin, turned his face up to her, and, with eyes ablaze, whispered, "*No. Do not cry. Be strong.*"

For love of his mother, he swallowed his tears. He did not cry, as did so many of the others, even some of the boys with whom he'd played, although the urge in him was strong.

He was placed in a wagon with the other children and there sat looking back into the unflinching eyes of his mother and his sister, who looked older than her fourteen summers, as the camp filled with the wails of the women.

At the train station in Lawton township, he and the other children were given sack lunches, were put into coach cars and from Lawton traveled through the long day and longer night well into the following day.

The Indian school was in a place called Carlisle Barracks in a faraway country one of the soldiers called Pennsylvania. The barracks was an old cavalry post that the fat lieutenant, a former cavalryman who'd fought in the Indian wars, had helped convert into a school for Indian children.

Upon their arrival the boys were immediately separated from the girls. Chaco and the other boys were shepherded into a building where they were told to strip off their clothes. Once naked they were doused with buckets of water and given bars of yellow soap and ordered to scrub themselves head to foot. There were men inside the building who saw to it that everyone did as they were told. Afterward, after everyone had rinsed the soap away with more cold water, Chaco and the others were given towels, told to dry themselves and to wrap the towels around their waists. After which their hair was sheared off, in a few instances done so by force. The men with the shears dusted their heads with a smelly white powder, and the towels were then taken back and each boy was given a school uniform and ordered to put them on. Some sneezed from the lingering odor from the powder, a few became ill and vomited. Chaco didn't like the smell and didn't like the new clothes, which itched, nor did he like the shoes, which felt odd on his feet—they were the first shoes he had ever worn.

Chaco was herded out of the building along with the other boys. And there were rejoined by the girls, now wearing dresses made of the same material as he and the other boys now wore. The girls' hair, wet from washing, was full of the same white powder, but most still had their hair.

At that point, the men stood back and several whiteeye women took over. There was a big woman the other women called Warden. The women moved among them, shoving and pushing until they had grouped everyone into a kind of square. At that point the Warden made a head count, and after the count the boys were separated from the girls again and divided into small groups. A woman led Chaco's group to one of several two-story buildings. They climbed a set of external stairs and went in. The room was long and narrow. There were almost as many windows in the room as there were bunk beds. The woman positioned herself just inside the entrance and as they shuffled past her they were each given bedding and told to pick out their own bunk.

"Everyone must know how to make their bed," the woman announced, and ordered them to gather around her. She picked a bunk and demonstrated how it should be made.

Chaco spent the next hour making and remaking his bunk, but neither he nor any of the other boys seemed able to make a bunk well enough to satisfy the woman. On his tenth attempt to do it right, Chaco noted the way the woman kept checking her watch and realized she was merely keeping them busy until time for the next foolish thing they would make them do. That turned out to be the dinner hour. Not so foolish—the sack lunches were the only food they'd been given since leaving Fort Sill. The woman formed them into a group and walked beside them from the dormitory to a place she called the mess hall, a building with a kitchen at one end and a very large room with many tables and benches at the other end.

"We're having a late lunch," the woman said, somewhat apologetically.

Lunch was a watery bean soup ladled into shallow bowls and served with poorly made corn bread. After a few spoons full, some of the girls began to cry and even some of the boys. The women in charge came forward then and moved from child to child, asking what was wrong, asking didn't they like the soup? Almost all of the children spoke a little English, Chaco too, and he noted that when a boy or girl answered in English, the woman who asked would copy the number affixed with a pin to the collar of the child into a little black book they all carried. When the woman in charge of Chaco's group asked, "Don't you like the soup?" Chaco looked up at her blankly and said nothing.

Goyaalé had warned him about the whiteeyes and their tricky ways. And so it proved. For once the children had finished eating everyone was reassembled outside. The Warden reappeared and each of the women gave her a list of numbers and the Warden moved among the children, located and separated all of the children who had answered when questioned and wrote down the name of every child in her own little black book. The Warden smiling benignly as she affixed a yellow ribbon to each child's clothing with a safety pin. These English speakers were grouped together and told that henceforth they could speak in no other tongue but English and if they failed to obey they would be punished. "Here you must speak only English."

"*What they cannot take by force they take by guile,*" his uncle had warned.

That evening as Chaco lay awake amidst the muffled sobs of others, he studied on the purpose of this place. And in the end knew he wanted no part of it, knew he must run away and that now would be easier than later. He expected the Warden to look in on them at some point. And so it proved. For near the hour of midnight, she entered the dorm. Passed down its length, heels clicking against the floor planks, paused at the opposite door and went out.

He swung out from under his blanket. Stood and went to the window and, hidden in shadow, watched the big woman climb into a waiting surrey. The driver flicked the reins and drove away.

Night winds stirred among the trees. Moon shadows moved over the ground like dancing spirits. He studied the other buildings. In some, lights still flickered. He might be seen. Yet now was the time if he would go. He rolled the blanket they'd issued, tied it over his shoulder.

"*You will make trouble if you go.*"

It was Kuruk in the bunk next to his, a burley boy taken from his mother, the same as he.

"*Come with me.*"

"*It will make trouble,*" Kuruk whispered, easing up onto an elbow.

Chaco studied Kuruk's dim shape. Like his namesake, he was strong like the bear, and yet timid, even at games. "Go back to sleep."

"There will be trouble," Kuruk whispered in final warning as Chaco made his way quietly to the exit door at the end of the dorm, slipped out, and descended the stairs.

He studied the rows of well-ordered buildings as he moved from shadow to shadow, a shadow himself, until beyond the last building he set out at an easy mile-eating gait, running as he had been taught, run for a while, walk for a while, then run again.

Dawn found him many miles west of the school, trotting along a dusty road within sight of the iron tracks over which he believed he had traveled the previous day. In the first clear light, he recognized a faded two-story building he remembered passing, and from that point onward, certain of his direction, he abandoned the road but never drifted more than a mile or so from the rails. He jogged steadily westward across fields and meadows, over ridges and through stands of hemlock and spruce. The shoes they'd given him began to bother his feet, so he discarded them. For food on his first day he stole several ears of corn from a half-harvested field, and that night he slept without a fire. In the morning he killed a rabbit with a throwing stick, skinned it with his teeth and strong, capable hands, and ate its flesh raw. He ran all the following day, pausing at the streams he came to only long enough to slake his thirst before crossing and moving on. He was completely on his own for the first time in his life and afraid, but he was also happy. As he ran, he thought about his mother and sister and even his uncle. He wondered what they would say when they saw him again. They would be surprised, and for his part he would be happy.

At the end of the day, jogging along a rocky ridge toward the setting sun—a red, pulsing coal at the edge of the world—he came upon another brook. He flopped down on his belly and drank, felt the flow of renewed energy in his weary limbs. The sun would be down soon. He needed rest, but as he cast about for a place to lie down for a few hours rest, he spied a flicker of light. Lamplight near the base of the ridge, perhaps a farm like the one he'd come upon with its patch of sweet corn. At the thought of food, his stomach growled, and he descended through the trees in the fading light. He came to the forest's edge and for a time stood concealed in leafy shadow, looking out on a small cabin, its windows lit by the flicker of a lamp. Beyond the cabin was a shedlike barn with an attached split-rail corral off one side. There was a chicken coop, a hog pen from which grunts could be heard, and a shadowy garden.

He stepped into the open. But as he did, a dog ran out to the end of a rope leash, was snapped around, and began to bark. Chaco retreated into shadows as the cabin door swung open. A shirtless man rushed out, in one hand a lantern held above his head, in the other a shotgun. The man rushed toward the chicken coop but then stopped short, and with eyes searching he walked around the coop and finally looked back at the hound. The dog had retreated to the narrow porch, where it now sat watching the man, tail thumping the boards, tongue lolling.

"That's another false alarm," the man accused, and, looking around again, walked past the dog into the cabin and slammed the door.

For several heartbeats Chaco stared longingly at the garden and the chicken coop. The dog was on its feet again, standing in the yard at the end of its leash, sniffing the air in his direction. The grumble in Chaco's stomach was so loud he felt certain the dog must hear it. The dog didn't bark any more. But even so, he knew he must go hungry. He retreated, climbed to the ridge, and pushed on. That night he covered several more miles before stopping to sleep on a moon-washed hill.

When his eyes snapped open, it was daylight. Dogs bayed in

the near distance. It had been their baying that woke him. He sat up and for several moments listened to their mournful bugles. The sound was getting closer. He scrambled to his feet. Ran to the nearest tree, climbed up, and looked back. There were mounted men, two of them, leashed hounds out front moving in his direction, their noses to the ground.

Trackers.

He descended the tree by quick bounds, missed his footing near the bottom, and fell the last few feet. Hit the ground rolling and came up, cast about for some sort of weapon, grabbed a length of deadfall, and ran. He was angry. Why had he stopped? He should have kept going. It was the school—the school must have sent these men with dogs, and now they had his scent. They were mounted while he was afoot. But he couldn't give up. He wouldn't give up. The fire in his heart would not let him. And so he ran. They would have to kill him.

An hour he ran, then two; he was crossing an open meadow, running toward another tree line with the promise of thick underbrush beyond, when one of the galloping riders came up from behind and dabbed a rope over him. The horse set down in a skid; Chaco kept running to the end of the loop and was snapped off his feet. The rider hit the ground laughing and ran down the lariat as the horse backed in an effort to keep the line taut.

"Got you, you little bastard."

Chaco came to his feet, swung the stick. The man's eyes went wide as the blow landed with a meaty smack. The man yelped, staggered back, a hand covering his bloody face.

"You little shit. Hit me, will you?"

The other rider was laughing as he loped around to block Chaco's retreat.

"I told you, Wally."

"The little bastard." Wally's hand came away bloody from his face. He growled.

"Don't kill him," the other warned. "They won't pay for a dead one."

The man called Wally extended his blood-smeared palm toward his partner. "Look," he complained, but his partner only laughed the harder, slapping his thigh gleefully. Wally doubled the end of his lariat and swung it whiplike at Chaco, who dodged and swung the remains of his club to deflect the man's blows. The rope snatched Chaco's weapon from his grip. Wally, despite a big gut, proved to be quick; he stepped in fast and swung, and the last thing Chaco saw, before the world went black, was the man's big fist coming at him.

4

When Chaco woke some time later, he was breathing through his mouth, his nose clogged full of drying blood. They'd tied him belly-down over a pack animal, his head throbbing and both eyes swollen nearly shut, and for two days they carried him like that, strapped over a packsaddle. Two days with no food or water. At night Wally bound him to a tree and left him shivering, staring through a partially open eye at the Indah, the men eating and joking and drinking whiskey by their campfire. As he watched them, he felt the first stirrings of hate.

The trackers delivered him to the guardhouse at the Indian school just before sundown the following day. The one called Blandon pulled him off the horse and stood him on his feet, but Chaco was too weak to stand.

"Lend a hand," Blandon called to Wally. "This is your doing, asshole."

Wally dismounted, and together they dragged him by his collar into the guardhouse.

The turnkey stood up, came around a scarred oak desk. "Caught him, I see."

"Busted Wally in the mouth," Blandon said.

"Screw you."

The turnkey laughed and followed the men back to the cellblock. He opened a cell door. Blandon cut Chaco's bonds, and the two trackers tossed him into the cell. The turnkey locked the door, and the three walked back through the cellblock door into the small guardhouse office.

Chaco, lying on the cold stone floor, had heard the heavy key turn in the lock, had listened as the men walked away, and now could hear them talking beyond an open doorway. The cold of the stone floor tugged at his pain. There was a bunk. He needed to move, to get up onto the bunk, but he lacked the strength. I have to move, he told himself. And after what seemed a considerable time, by an act of will, he managed to drag himself to the narrow bunk and pull himself up and onto the mattress. It stank of mold.

The two men who'd caught him left. Then there was silence except for a single sound through the barred window, the cry of a hawk. The dim light through the window faded. He slept. When he woke again, he saw that the turnkey had brought a water bucket. Summoning strength, he moved across the cell and drank from it. He felt the flush of moisture under his parched eyelids and kept drinking. He drank until he could drink no more. The left side of his face still throbbed. He couldn't see out of the eye on that side. It had swollen completely shut. The flesh hurt when touched, but not as much as before, and when he parted the swollen eyelid he could make out the blurred bars of the cell door. So he still had the eye.

When the turnkey came back, maybe to see if he was still alive, Chaco pretended to be asleep.

"Are you okay?"

Chaco didn't answer.

"I sent for the school nurse."

Nurse? He had no idea what that was. But it didn't matter. Nothing mattered.

A few moments passed. The turnkey sighed and walked back toward the door.

Chaco opened his one good eye. Time passed. He waited for whatever came next. He thought about dying and wondered if they would kill him. Maybe. His mind fogged, and he faded into a dream. In the dream he was flying, his arms extended, yet somehow they worked like wings despite the absence of feathers. He was flying among a great circle of strange-looking hawks. He knew he was dreaming, but it was such a powerful dream, the strongest of all dreams. He was happy, part of the sky, and in the sky he was free.

But then the other hawks faded into mist and the mist vanished, replaced in his awareness by loud voices. He was waking, although he had no wish to wake. Yet the pull of the voices was stronger. They were angry now, at least one of them was, and he felt that anger pulling him down from the sky, and then he was awake. He became aware again of the pain. It hurt to move, hurt even to lie still. He opened his good eye, listened to the voices. It was one angry voice; the answering voice defended itself.

He managed to sit up, though it hurt, and placed his bare feet on the floor. The stone floor was cold. He stood and, on unsteady legs, got to the cell door, where he looked between the bars through the open door into the room beyond. An angry man, tall with red hair and bright-brown freckles that made his very white skin look even whiter, was yelling at the turnkey, whom he had backed up against a wall. The turnkey was clearly afraid.

"You would do well to pray to whatever mongrel god you worship that the boy recovers," Red-Hair shouted. He turned and strode to a battered desk, where he snatched up a ring of keys.

"He attacked Wally," the guard complained. "Hit him in the face with a stick."

"Not another word, Mr. Collette. Not another word. Now get out of my sight."

"I got to fill out the bounty papers. Wally said—"

"Go. As God is my witness, Mr. Collette, there will be no bounty. Now go."

The guard sidled from view. A moment later Chaco heard a door slam. The red-haired man leaned against the desk, his breath heavy. He straightened, lit a lamp, and, carrying it at eye level, passed through the door into the cellblock.

Chaco stumbled back to the bunk. Sat on the edge and waited. The big brass key rattled in the lock. The door swung open, and the red-haired man stepped through. Chaco stood. He would have backed away had there been room. Red-Hair had fierce eyes. But then the fierceness faded and he smiled. He left the cell door open and advanced slowly toward Chaco. For a moment Chaco wondered if he might be able to dodge around him.

"I'm not going to hurt you."

The anger was gone from his voice. Replaced with kindness. Yet, though Chaco had not known it before, he knew it now: you could not trust the Indah.

"What those men did, and what the guard allowed, was unconscionable." Red-Hair frowned for a reflective moment, then, rephrasing, added, "What they did was wrong."

Chaco blinked. There were tears in the man's eyes. The boy hardened his heart. The tears meant nothing. The Indah were tricky.

"Why don't you sit down, son? You must be weary . . . You must be tired."

Red-Hair gestured to the bunk. Though Chaco wanted to sit, needed to sit, he stayed on his feet. He needed to be ready in case he had to move. The man advanced another step. Chaco sidled away. Red-Hair's expression changed, from concern to curiosity. For a lingering moment he studied Chaco. Then nodding as if in agreement with whatever he was thinking, the red-haired man hunkered down and looked across the space between him and Chaco, eye to eye with him now.

"The nurse will be here shortly. She'll do something about your nose and eyes," he said. "She'll give you something for the pain. But before she gets here, you and I need to talk." He cocked his head slightly. "I pray to God you understand enough English to understand this. But one way or the other, here it is. You can't run away, son. They'll break you, or they'll kill you."

With that admission he drew an angry breath, wagged his head side to side, and scrubbed the palm of his hand over his face. He blinked back tears and studied Chaco. "Do you understand? The unvarnished truth is this: they're looking for an excuse, any excuse . . . and if you run away again, they *will* kill you. There are people out there, awful people, powerful people, who would very much like to eradicate all Indians . . . That means kill all red men. These people see the Indian races as bloody vermin. It's what they think you are, and, if allowed, they would rub out all Indians . . .

"Those two men who caught you? They'd be quick to kill you, except they have to bring the runaways back alive or they do not get paid. This school is your only hope. Believe me, son, there are actually good people here at this school, and good people out there in the world, people of conscience who are willing to and want to help you. I left the church to teach here, and I will help you, if you'll let me. But you can't run away again. Do you understand any of this?"

"Yes."

He sighed. "Good." When he straightened, his knees cracked a little.

Red-Hair's eyes were so blue Chaco couldn't understand how he could see out of them. Turning, Red-Hair crossed to the cell door, paused, and looked back.

"I'll do what I can," he said, and then smiled. "I promise. Okay?"

Chaco nodded, though he did not believe him.

The redheaded man closed the cell door, left it unlocked, walked away. Chaco wondered if it was a trick, a test to see if he would run again. He sat on the bunk. He thought about his mother and sister, and about Goyaałé, his uncle. The world was on fire. It had come apart. He felt water come from his eyes. Blinked. Wiped at the tears and looked at his wet fingertips as he remembered his mother's final words to him: "*Be strong.*"

5

In the winter of 1905, Chaco was seventeen when the soldiers brought his uncle Goyaałé to the Carlisle Indian Industrial School, along with American Horse and Hollow Horn Bear and Little Plume and the Ute chief Buckskin Charlie and the Comanche war chief Quanah Parker—all warriors of different tribes on their way to Washington to ride in the inaugural parade of President Teddy Roosevelt.

Ten years had passed since he had last seen the old man—a time so far into the past his life before Carlisle seemed like a dream. On the day Goyaałé was brought to the school, classes were suspended and everyone was ordered to assemble in the gymnasium, where his uncle was to give a speech. Chaco crowded through an entrance door with his fellow students, and they, knowing that he, too, was Bedonkohe of the Chiricahua Band, discreetly made a place for him on the floor in front of the assembly.

He sat cross-legged among his fellow students and when Goyaałé entered the gymnasium, Chaco, like the others, stood and applauded, as they had been instructed.

Goyaałé mounted the platform and walked to the lectern. He

stood in front of it and looked out at the assembly. And Chaco, seeing him after so many years, was saddened. Absent was that quickness of movement he remembered. The old man had gone to fat. Nevertheless, soldiers with guns still watched him at all times. Chaco saw that even in old age they still feared him.

The applause died, the assembly took their seats again, and slowly the shuffling and whispers faded until there was almost complete silence. He sensed the backbones of those seated around him begin to straighten, and then Goyaałé, looking out at them, nodded and his features softened.

"My friends," he began, and Chaco remembered that once-familiar voice. "I am going to talk to you a few minutes. Listen to what I say. You are all just the same as my children to me, just the same as if my children are going to school when I look at you all there. You are here to study, to learn the ways of the white men. Do it well. You have a father here and a mother also. Your father is here. Do as he tells you. Obey him as you would your own father. Although he is not your father, he is a father to you now."

Goyaałé paused as his intimidating gaze passed over the assembly. He looked directly at Chaco, and, as he did, Chaco sensed that his uncle's words were meant for his ears above all others, and so he straightened and nodded slightly, wanting his uncle to know that he understood.

"The Lord made my heart good. I feel good wherever I go. I feel very good now as I stand before you. Obey all orders. Do as you are told all the time, and you won't get hungry. He who owns you holds you in his hands like that," he said, and extended his hands together, palms turned upward. "And he carries you around like a baby. That is all I have to say to you."

Chaco came to his feet with the others and applauded as his uncle Goyaałé left the platform and walked ahead of the soldiers out through a side entrance.

Everyone around Chaco was talking about the speech as they

shuffled shoulder to shoulder toward the main exit. He heard his name called and turned. It was Mr. Smith, one of his shop teachers, waving for him to come over. Chaco changed direction, shouldered his way back through the thinning crowd.

"Yes, sir?"

"He wants to see you." Mr. Smith jerked his chin toward a side exit and led the way out into the gray afternoon. The snow that had fallen during the night had crusted over during the day. His uncle stood apart from the soldiers, who huddled watchfully and shivering, hugging themselves and stamping their feet against the frozen ground.

"Make it quick," Mr. Smith said, and hurried back through the door out of the cold.

The snow crunched underfoot as Chaco walked toward his uncle. He stopped a polite pace away and waited as the old man's rheumy eyes moved over him. Chaco remembered him as taller, remembered his eyes as fiercer.

"*You look like her,*" Goyaałé said. Meaning Lozen, Chaco supposed, and fell in beside Goyaałé as he set off along the footpath. "*They broke your nose, I see.*"

"Yes," he answered in English. "A long time ago."

Winter-blackened trees bordered the path, skeletal against the backdrop of snow and the freshly painted white dormitories to their left. Behind them Chaco heard the soldiers complain of the cold, the crisp sound of their boots crunching against the frozen ground. Ahead was a line of snow-dusted motor carriages that would take his uncle and the others back to the train. Goyaałé asked about Chaco's life at the school, and Chaco asked about Aná and Bui.

"*They are well,*" his uncle said.

"Do they still live in the camp?"

"*Yes, we all do.*"

Goyaałé paused and stood silent for a moment, Chaco

studying the aged profile of this man who had been a great warrior and who was now an old man staring at the icy ground. An unexpected yearning welled up in him, battered against the interior walls he'd so carefully built up over the lonely years. He remembered the evening fires and the stories his uncle had shared. And now, after all the lonely years here he was again. He would listen.

"*I have nothing. No people. I hate this place. I want to leave it. Take me with you.*"

Goyaałé's gaze swung momentarily toward the unhappy soldiers, then back to Chaco. A fleeting kindness lit his hard old eyes, revealing a hint of the pain he carried in the dark stone of his heart, and in that moment Chaco knew that in this they were much alike.

"I did not want this for the People. Or for you." Goyaałé's eyes were implacable again, the hard slash of his mouth tight. He placed a hand on Chaco's shoulder, much as he had on the day they took him from his mother. "In this there is no choice," he said, and, looking up into the cold, gray sky, his lips moved silently, sending to Usen an unuttered plea. He looked at Chaco again and frowned. "I am going to ask this president Teddy Roosevelt to let my people go. I am too old to fight now. I want to go home to the mountains. I want to be buried where the earth knows my name." Then, under his breath and in the tongue, he said, "*I wish I had never given up. I wish I had kept fighting until I was the last man left alive.*" He sighed then and, in English again, said, "I don't think this Roosevelt will let the People go."

"Maybe he will, Uncle."

Goyaałé shook his head, said, "No," and they walked on.

6

In June of that year, Chaco graduated. He was eighteen and would leave the industrial school a cooper, a wheelwright, and a journeyman carpenter. In his uncommitted time he'd learned as much of the blacksmith trade as the shop teacher knew. And during the "outings" of summer, when he and the other boys were hired out as farmer labor, he, for his part, had learned as much as he could about farming and livestock. He had put in the hours needed to learn all that his teachers knew of arithmetic. And he had read every book and magazine in the school's meager library, and even the commentaries of Caesar in Latin from the more extensive private collection of his English instructor, Hiram McGregor—the redheaded man who had visited him in his cell the day they brought him back after he'd run away.

In the beginning, Mr. McGregor—who had taught him that dead tongue with the same fervor the school employed in the eradication of Chaco's own—had asked, "Why the Latin?"

"That I might more fully understand the teachings of the Bible and the words of our Lord Jesus Christ," Chaco had answered, and, by this subterfuge, advanced his purpose. It was a harmless if cruel deception, but it had pleased Mr. McGregor greatly, who was deeply religious, and to Chaco's credit he had never recanted the lie. But the answers he sought from Caesar were not to be found within those ancient texts.

Affixed to the wall at the foot of the stairwell in his dormitory were two side-by-side photographs of an Indian inside a single frame. The first photograph showed the Indian with long hair, dressed in traditional clothes, and the second photo showed him with his hair cut short and dressed like a white man. Below the photographs in bold block letters were these words: "Kill the Indian and Save the Man." At every passing of those photos, at every reading of those words, he remembered his mother's last instruction: "*Be strong.*"

He had early on, as a means of escape, set himself to learn the white man's way. But what he had not foreseen was the seductive power of the white way. The magic of the white man's written word, that binding together of knowledge in books, the recorded wisdom of their ancestors, all there free for the taking. In his heart he remained true to his blood and to his mother and sister, yet the more he learned, the more it altered him. Over time he became precise, self-contained, quietly isolated within the integrated outward agreeability of form and action. He learned to live within himself—externally functional, inwardly alone. In class he never spoke but to ask or to answer questions. And the questions he posed and the answers he gave he framed in words intended to satisfy his instructor's expectations. While others played, he studied. More and more he lived inside his mind. Days passed in which he spoke hardly a word. He knew that he was no longer Apache, but neither was he what the Indah school would have made of him. The years had transformed him into a creature divided against itself, cut off from the world of the Indah by his blood and yet alone among his own kind.

The day he graduated, an official from the Bureau of Indian

Affairs arrived by train from Washington to give the commencement address. The BIA man had, in reality, come to honor the old lieutenant, who had resigned the previous year in protest over the poor rations being supplied to the school. There were a few newspapermen in attendance, and at the hour assigned, the old lieutenant, the faculty, and the BIA man from Washington mounted the podium ahead of Chaco and the two girls who were his fellow graduates.

The Washington man approached the lectern. He cleared his throat and looked out at the student body, seated on folding chairs in their freshly pressed school uniforms.

"Good morning. My name is Marcus Seal." He drew an uncomfortable breath and commented on the gorgeous weather they were having. "I am most heartily pleased to be present on such an important day," he said, and then turned and summoned the old lieutenant.

Pratt rose from his folding chair and with some reluctance crossed to the lectern.

Physically the men were similar enough in stature and facial features they might have passed for father and son. Chaco read the mutual loathing behind their smiles as Marcus Seal gripped Henry Pratt's hand and congratulated him for his years of loyal service. Seal drew a folded sheet of paper from inside his coat, shook it out, and read off the long list of Superintendent Henry Pratt's accomplishments.

As he droned on, Chaco looked up at the sky and wondered whether the school administration would actually allow him to leave Carlisle today—or any day, for that matter. Mr. McGregor harbored hopes of finding a place for him at Yale for the fall term, but that required money, and there was no money. Chaco thought it possible the new superintendent might send him back to Fort Sill. He was, after all, a ward of the state and in legal terms still a prisoner of war. He longed to see his mother and sister again, but not as a prisoner. He'd been a prisoner his entire life.

There was a smattering of applause; the Washington man was summing up, and Chaco, lowering his gaze, saw Marcus Seal clap Henry Pratt on the shoulder, grip his hand again, and call out for more applause. Pratt pulled his hand free and limped back toward the line of folding chairs. He sat in the vacant seat adjacent to Chaco.

"Good to see you again, Mr. Kidd."

"Superintendent Pratt." Chaco looked at him. Gone from the old lieutenant's lumpy face was the ever-present sternness he remembered.

"God, how I hate that pompous windbag," Pratt muttered under his breath. "The truth is, Mr. Kidd, I only consented to this travesty in order to be here for your graduation." He hesitated. "You may be my greatest success or my greatest failure. Time will tell." He looked out at the students seated on the rows of folding chairs arranged on the green lawn. "I am not unaware of the wrongs I have done, my boy. They were necessary cruelties. Nor am I forgetful of the children who lie buried here. You should know, however, that the path I charted was far less cruel than the extermination policy that was being run up the flagpole by some in the administration back in my day." A ripple of emotion touched his eyes. He sighed again, his gaze focused on the student body in their fresh uniforms, hundreds of brown faces dutifully gathered on the lawn. He wagged his head from side to side. "I am fully aware that most of those young people out there hate me, and they have a right to, but at least they are alive to hate me, and that is my solace, Mr. Kidd."

Chaco stared into the man's self-condemning eyes. What was there to say? He faced forward, and they sat together in silence through the last of the Washington man's speech. There was dutiful applause as Marcus Seal left the lectern and was replaced by Mr. McGregor.

McGregor recognized everyone who required recognition. Next, he told an anecdotal story about each of the two graduating girls—Dianna Wilson, a Choctaw from Gotebo, Oklahoma, and Adelia Janese, a Lakota Sioux from South Dakota. He then recounted a story about Chaco, telling how he had run away on his first day at the school and managed to cover more than fifty miles before being overtaken by the mounted trackers who had returned him.

Finally, Mr. McGregor summoned the three of them forward individually and presented each with a certificate of graduation. When he placed Chaco's diploma in his hand, there were tears in his eyes. They shook hands, and Chaco returned to his chair. McGregor thanked everyone for coming, declared the proceedings closed, and that was that.

The student assembly began to disperse. The platform cleared and Chaco, the last to descend the stairs, was met at the foot of the steps by a marine sergeant in summer dress.

The sergeant smiled. "Frank Kidd?"

"Yes, sir."

"They tell me you are a smart lad, Mr. Kidd. The Corps is looking for smart lads."

"Which 'they' would that be?"

"Why, Lieutenant Pratt, for one."

Chaco looked past the marine and saw Pratt and McGregor engaged in an argument, McGregor apparently pleading his point as Pratt noticed Chaco staring at them and flipped him a casual salute. McGregor hesitated, turned, and the bright anger in his eyes quailed into a look of despair.

"So you are here to recruit me?" Chaco asked.

"Why, that I am, Mr. Kidd," the marine said, his scar-etched face crinkling in a grin.

"Can the Marine Corps teach me to fight and how to shoot?"

The sergeant laughed. "I like that one. Hell, son, the Corps makes heartbreakers and widow makers out of hayseeds. Teach an Apache how to fight? Mr. Kidd, I got a feeling you and the Corps are going to go together like rifles and bullets."

7

That afternoon Chaco raised his hand and swore an oath, and that evening he boarded an eastbound for South Carolina. Mr. McGregor came to the station to see him off.

"You've made a life-altering choice, Frank. I hadn't exhausted all hope of getting you into Yale, had you been willing to wait. But you've chosen a path, and now I'm afraid you must see it to the end. I wish you all the best. I mean that from the heart."

"You helped me, Mr. McGregor. I'll not forget you, sir."

"You did all the work, son. I merely indicated the way. And it's Hiram. Call me Hiram. You are now officially a scholar, my boy. Hardly six Americans in a hundred graduate high school, and today you've become one of them."

The engine whistle sounded, and the conductor stepped aboard the rearmost Pullman and swung his lantern side to side. They were out of time. Mr. McGregor pressed an envelope into Chaco's hand. "Take this. It contains all my contact information, including my parents' address in Bangor. Write me once you've settled in."

The wheels of the engine spun on the rails, and the linkages between the cars tightened. The train jerked forward and slowly advanced along the platform as Chaco climbed the iron steps to the vestibule, turned, and waved farewell. "Thanks for everything, Mr. McGregor." He wanted to say more—there was so much he had left unsaid—but in the end he simply couldn't.

"Good luck, son. Remember, the world is a fine place. Try to find some happiness in it. It is out there. I believe that, as I believe in God."

8

H e spent three days aboard the cars before his arrival at Port Royal Sound at the Parris Island naval refueling station, midway between Savannah and Charleston on the Carolina coast. A marine sergeant and four red-faced shouting corporals met him and several other recruits. What followed were weeks of training, intended to toughen them. Some of the recruits complained of the hard conditions, and maybe the conditions were hard, but they did not seem so to Chaco. He thrived, and a few short months later, at Guantánamo Naval Station, he found himself standing in company formation as their commanding officer, Captain Weekly, announced that Cuban anarchists had risen up against their American liberators.

"We've got us another shooting war, boys," the captain shouted.

The company sent up a cheer.

The rebels were in the mountains, and Chaco's company, in coordination with regimental command, went into the mountains after them. In the months and years that followed, the fighting was good. At least it was good for Chaco. He liked being in the field and detested garrison duty. From his first day in combat, his platoon leader, Lieutenant Attila Reeb, assumed that Chaco, being Apache, must know how to track and scout, and so he put Chaco on point. Of course, having been raised by white men in a white man's school, Chaco knew no more about war than any other schoolboy, but somehow he survived, and, in surviving, he learned.

The longer the guerilla war lasted, the better he got at the business of it. Time and again fellow marines were wounded, others were killed, yet no bullet ever found him, and he began to believe that he, like his uncle Goyaałé, might have the 'power.' That he, too, might be invulnerable to the bullets of his enemies.

Then on a Tuesday afternoon, 12 January 1909, it happened. His platoon was in close pursuit of rebel saboteurs who had blown a bridge in the mountains, sending a truckload of supplies crashing into a river gorge. Chaco, on point as usual, led his platoon to the edge of a clearing in the mountains. He signaled a halt, went down on his belly, the platoon deploying in a skirmish line as Gunny Hinojosa bellied forward.

Lieutenant Capshaw, their new officer fresh out of the academy, came jogging forward and stood with fists on hips, surveying the meadow. "Have we made contact, Sergeant?"

Hinojosa rolled over and looked up at him—this young man who had replaced Lieutenant Reeb, killed by a rebel bullet. Tall and blond and as pretty as a girl, the lieutenant exuded the self-confidence of inexperience. "Sir, you might want to get down before you get yourself shot."

The lieutenant squinted across the clearing into the diffused glare of the sunset. "I detect no activity."

"Could be they've moved on, sir. We'll know for sure in a minute."

"If you aren't sure, why have we stopped?"

"To prefire the tree line, sir. It's SOP—"

"Not any standard operational procedure they taught at the academy. Reassemble the men, Sergeant. We're losing the light." The lieutenant's gaze shifted to Chaco. "On your feet, Corporal. You'll lead the attack."

"Yes, sir." Chaco stabbed the butt of his rifle into the ground and came to his feet as Hinojosa shouted the order to move out. Chaco noted the other riflemen's worried glances as he freed the safety on his '03 and set out across the clearing.

Lieutenant Capshaw followed him, an act of bravado that proved as foolish as the order to advance, for midway across a machine gun opened up on them. And Chaco dove for the ground, landed, and rolled, the sod around him spitting up in chunks. He looked back. The lieutenant was down. Chaco snugged the rifle to his shoulder, aimed at the shiver of leaves that marked the *tat-tat-tat* position of a Hotchkiss gun, and squeezed off a shot. The gunny shouted, "Open fire," and the air crackled with the passage of marine bullets as they hammered the opposite tree line. The Hotchkiss was momentarily silenced, but then it spoke again, this time from another position. Chaco pressed his face into the dirt as bullets from the Hotchkiss zipped like thunderclaps above and around him, and then he felt a numbing punch.

He was hit.

Behind him Hinojosa shouted, "That clump of el-da-rita bushes, that's his position. Aim for that, boys," then yelled for the lieutenant to stay down for Christ sake.

Chaco gasped in an effort to suck back the wind the bullet had knocked out of him; he blinked against a spinning dizziness and knew he had to move, that he was inside the kill box and it was move or die. He gritted his teeth and waited for the next break in the *tat-tat-tat*. The Hotchkiss was fed by a thirty-round magazine that required time to remove and replace, time to jack the bolt, and time to get back on target—all measurable in moments, but it was all he would get, and when the break came, he shouted "Hold your fire I'm coming back," struggled to his feet, and lurched back toward the firing line. The call passing from man to man, "Hold your fire, it's Powwow, he's coming back," as he staggered over ground that seemed to tilt this way and that. The exacting order of his mind was scrambled, and seeing the lieutenant on his belly, blubbering, "Please, God, don't let me die," it took him a moment to remember who he was, but then he grabbed the LT by the shirt collar and somehow managed to drag him back toward the safety of their firing line. The Hotchkiss opened up again, and as the bullets chopped up the ground toward them, Harrison dashed forward and grabbed one of the lieutenant's flailing arms. Bullets from the Hotchkiss kicked up the dirt around them as they staggered rearward, and then somehow they were behind a tree on their bellies with bark and splinters flying from the tree's trunk.

Gunny shouted, "Fire, fire at will," and the air quaked with counterfire.

Harrison rolled over and rested his head against the base of the tree. "That was the dumbest thing I ever did," he gasped.

They were both out of breath, both grinning. Chaco saw that the lieutenant had pissed his pants. Harrison saw it, too, and averted his eyes, muttered, "It ain't that big a deal," and lifted his chin toward Chaco. "Looks like they tagged you."

"Looks like."

"You're leaking pretty good."

The counterfire had quieted the Hotchkiss, and this time apparently ended the fight, for they could hear the rebels moving off. The gunny shouted, "Cease fire, cease fire," and slowly in the ringing silence the men got to their feet again.

Chaco used his rifle like a crutch as he stood up. The inside of his head was still turning. He stared across the clearing, the air smelling of cordite, the leaves still falling from the bullet-splintered trees in the aftermath of battle.

Harrison yelled, "Hey, Doc, you best get over here before Powwow bleeds out."

"He should take care of the lieutenant first," Chaco said. Lieutenant Capshaw's face and neck were covered with blood.

A private fired blindly into the forest in the direction of the retreating rebels.

"Save your ammo, Private," Hinojosa barked. "It's a long hike back, and if we meet up with any more of them, you'll want something besides spit to fight with."

A fire team was sent out in a flanking move. Within the half hour, Corporal Byre called out from the far side of the clearing and was acknowledged. He emerged from the covering underbrush and signaled the all clear. Then walked across and reported to Gunny. They'd found blood sign in several places, but the rebels had left none of their wounded or dead. Byre extended a handful of spent brass from the Hotchkiss. "From the blood on the ground," he said, "I'd say the gunner got nominated."

The gunny grinned. "Good."

All of this Chaco heard through a fog, for by that time Doc Kale, their corpsman, had him shot full of morphine, and a wounded or killed rebel machine gunner was of no interest. His thoughts had gravitated toward poetry, and toward that stupid, heartrending line from the play he had seen in Havana, "O happy dagger, This is thy sheath," and Juliet, the Spanish beauty who played her, and he wondered what it must have been like to see that play in London the first time those words were spoken before an audience? He squeezed his eyes shut as Doc Kale mopped his wound with iodine and told him he was lucky, that the bullet had traversed just under the skin.

"It don't feel lucky," he said.

"It raised a nice welt along your flank. It's turning purple and spreading out."

"Don't hold back, Doc," Harrison joked. "Powwow can take it, can't you, pal?"

"This'll be an easy fix, Kidd. You'll be back in a month."

"Thanks, Doc." Chaco swallowed. He liked the corpsman. Everybody did. "Think I can walk out of here on my own?"

"It's okay by me, if you're up to it."

With the morphine working, he felt able to do about anything. The lieutenant had ceased his blubbering. But Chaco thought maybe that had to do with the shot Doc Kale had given him. The way the morphine made you feel, or rather not feel, Chaco could see how easy it would be to become a hophead. "How bad is the LT?"

"They nicked him twice, but neither wound's bad as yours, and yours ain't bad. He'll have a lovely scar, though, like a dueling scar. Give that pretty face of his some character."

Harrison grinned. "Probably get him a promotion."

"He took them in the front, didn't he?" Chaco said. "He gets my vote."

Harrison shrugged. "He didn't have time not to," he said, but then nodded in agreement.

The corpsman gripped Chaco under the arm and helped him to his feet. For a moment Chaco wobbled unsteadily, but then he waved Kale off. "I've got it," he said, and smiled against an eddy of blackness. What he wanted, maybe needed, was another shot of that wonderful morphine, but he didn't ask. He'd seen what the drug had done to others—knew that along that path lay ruin.

"Here, drink some of this." Harrison offered him his canteen.

Chaco accepted it and drank a couple of swallows.

"Go ahead, finish it," Harrison said. "I'll refill it down the trail."

He drank the last of it, handed the canteen back, and felt the coolness of the water in his empty stomach. His vision seemed to clear as he swayed and looked around. The gunny was forming up the men, getting ready to move out. Doc Kale rested a hand on Chaco's shoulder.

"It's okay if you can't walk."

"I walked in, I'll walk out."

Harrison grinned. "They can kill him and cook him, but he's too tough to eat, huh?"

Chaco's gear and the lieutenant's gear got divided up among the men for the march back. The gunny ordered a litter made for the LT, who was staring into the distance with that farseeing look Chaco had seen in others after a hard fight. The platoon moved out, one man on point close ahead, and no flankers.

Gunny Hinojosa dropped back and fell in beside Chaco. "The LT, he doesn't look too good."

"Doc says he'll be okay."

"Captain Weekly told me to look after him, told me his pappy is a rich senator."

"If he was so worried, he should have put him in a tent at headquarters."

The gunny shrugged his massive shoulders. "There'll be hell to pay."

"If his daddy's so rich, what's he doing in the middle of all this?"

"Maybe his daddy was fixing it up so people would vote for his kid later on. But a bullet, it don't know your daddy is too important for you to die. You really think he's okay?"

"He's not dead."

"*No nació para la guerra*, eh?" Gunny muttered.

"No," Chaco agreed, "this one is not made for war."

"I want you to stay close to him, okay?" Gunny's frown deepened.

"I can do that."

"You know we should be carrying you, too?"

"I can walk."

"We got to keep this quiet, the way the lieutenant took it, I mean."

"Keep what quiet?"

"Good. You understand what I'm saying, then?"

"Understand what?"

"You have no idea what I'm talking about, do you?"

"Get back to the head of the column, Gunny. I've got this end covered."

The platoon followed a trail, a practice the gunny had long since abandoned, since it was on the trails the rebels set their ambushes. It annoyed Chaco, who thought it a foolish risk, but he knew they followed the trail because of the lieutenant, the gunny's concern for him. Privates Hugh and Clark were in charge of the lieutenant's makeshift stretcher. The sun went down, and the forest darkened along the descending trail. Above them was triple canopy. And in darkness Chaco moved along beside the litter. The moon rose, and shafts of gray slanted down through openings in the leafy canopy, and this helped light the way. At one point the trail passed directly through one of these ghostly shafts and Chaco, looking down, studied the lieutenant's moonlit face, noted his vacant stare.

Night birds called, and hunting bats flittered like black butterflies through the rays of moonlight. They were three hours into their return march when Chaco heard the first rumble of thunder. A cloud drifted under the moon and was soon followed by others, and then the moon disappeared. Flickers of lightning and the rumble of thunder became constant, and through it all the gunny kept the platoon moving. The moon briefly reappeared, a ghostly eye seen through an aperture in the oncoming storm. And then came the first heavy drops of rain. They splattered against the broadleaf plants around them.

The lieutenant caught hold of Chaco's wrist and pulled him close.

"You saved my life," he whispered, his voice raw with emotion.

"Not really, sir." Chaco gently freed his wrist.

The storm swept over in earnest then. The rain fell in torrents. Lightning etched the night sky. Within minutes Chaco's clothes and boots were soaked through. The trail twisted and turned as they trudged steadily downward. Five hours into the march they came to a stony, all but treeless ridge. The gunny called a halt and sent scouts forward. Chaco sat down in his own muddy footprints. He was weary, much of the vitality he had always taken for granted sapped from him. He wanted to lean against something and close his eyes for a while, but then word passed down the line: one of the scouts was back with the all clear.

They moved on, the trail twisting downward along the barren, narrow spine of the ridge, the platoon fully exposed to enemy fire in the constant flash of lightning, and then they were into the trees again, descending into the inviolable darkness. The lightning now faded to ghostly glimmers above the triple canopy. And high above, the force of the wind seemed to increase. High up the limbs of the trees hammered against themselves. Chaco heard a sharp crack and looked up as a limb snapped off and rattled on its way down, shearing off lesser limbs before it struck unseen into the flank of the mountain somewhere off to their left.

A marine a few yards ahead cursed under his breath.

They kept going. From time to time the lieutenant would reach out for Chaco's hand. It bothered Chaco, embarrassed him. In some ways the LT reminded him of the little ones whose hands he'd held during their first frightened nights at Carlisle. Back when he'd been hardly more than a child himself—and full of silence. The words in there somewhere, the true words of his heart, words he never let out. But this thing with the lieutenant was different, this unmanning of him, and he felt nothing for him. Not even pity.

Every hour or so the gunny called a rest halt. And during one of these the lieutenant sent an FNG over to Chaco from second squad with a request. "He wants to talk to you." Chaco suppressed a sigh, extended his hand for Huge to pull him to his feet. He crossed the trail and knelt beside the stretcher as Huge resettled himself a few paces away.

"Sir?"

"Have we gotten away from them yet?"

The lieutenant's hand extended toward him, and, reluctantly, Chaco took it. "We have, sir. We're in the clear." But, of course, they were far from being in the clear. You were never in the clear in this kind of war, but the lie seemed to give the LT comfort.

They moved on, and soon enough the trail brought them to a stream they had forded the previous day, a stream that was now rain swollen and far too swift and deep to risk crossing. They turned and followed the flow of its rushing course toward the rumble of plunging water, a lip of rock over which the river plunged into the misty darkness of its own thunder. There was a rain-slick ledge of stone they edged along where it skirted the sheer drop. Someone flicked on an Eveready, and the gunny sent word back to kill the light. The risk of being spotted by a rebel patrol was too great.

Lieutenant Capshaw was mumbling to himself now, complaining of responsibilities, of people at home who depended on him, of not having the luxury or the right to run such risks.

They were well below the falls when Gunny called the next rest halt. The corpsman came back to give the lieutenant another injection and, before putting away his needle, looked at Chaco. "How about you, Kidd? You look like you could use a booster."

"Maybe later, Doc," he said, breathing slowly against the pressure of the tight field dressings. He wanted the shot, but chose instead to endure that which could be endured.

9

By the time they reached the road, the storm had eased to a steady rain. The commandeered trucks that had carried them forward were still in place. The perimeter guards were called in as the platoon climbed into the canvas-domed truck beds. The drivers cranked the engines and climbed back into their cabs. Doc boosted Chaco aboard the last truck and sat next to him by the tailgate, rain pattering against the canvas as the truck growled down the winding mountain road toward regimental command.

An hour after their arrival at camp, Chaco and the gunny found themselves standing at attention inside Captain Weekly's tent.

"There goes my gawddamn career."

Weekly scrubbed at the stubble on his chin with the palm of his blunt-fingered hand.

"Sir, no sir," Hinojosa said, looking straight ahead.

"Marine captains who get the sons of U.S. senators killed in action don't get to be majors in this man's corps, Gunnery Sergeant Hinojosa. You two can count yourselves lucky he wasn't."

The captain ordered an ambulance for Capshaw, but when it arrived the lieutenant insisted that Chaco be evacuated to the hospital at Guantánamo with him.

"He saved my life. If Corporal Kidd's wound can be treated here in the field, then my injuries can be treated here as well."

It might have been a bluff, but Captain Weekly folded and gave the order.

I n the weeks that followed, Chaco got enough rest and recovery for an entire squad of wounded riflemen. The surgeon who had worked on Lieutenant Capshaw—a top man in his field —had also sewn Chaco up. The incision he'd made along the course of the bullet had left a centipede-like scar from his shoulder blade to his midsection, and as it healed it itched relentlessly.

As for hospital life, it wasn't half bad. These past few weeks were the only real luxury Chaco had ever known. The lieutenant saw to it that he lacked for nothing. His meals came from the officers' mess, and when the lieutenant was finished reading his copies of the _Times_ he always sent them over to the enlisted ward.

By the end of the fourth week, Chaco believed he was healed up and haired over enough to be sent back to his platoon. He'd grown weary of the ease of hospital life and sent a request asking for reassignment to full duty.

Three days later, while taking the sun, he looked up in time to see Gunny Hinojosa push through the screen door, step out onto the ward's veranda, and look around.

"Nice view."

The bay lay off to their left, and to their right, beyond several buildings, was the parade ground, where a marine in full combat gear was walking a punishment tour.

Hinojosa sat in the adjacent rocker. "Looks like you got it made here, Kidd."

"I've had all of it I want."

"The captain's recommended the lieutenant for a medal."

"Not a court-martial?"

"RHIP, bub. Rank do have its privileges. The bad part of it is, Capshaw put you in for one, too."

"Me?"

He shrugged. "Take any medal they'll give you but a posthumous one, I always say."

Chaco traced the tips of his fingers back and forth over the part of the bandage he could reach, in an attempt to relieve the itch. "What exactly did I do to earn it?"

"The worst sin of all, *'mano*: you saved a lieutenant. The captain says you're to sit tight, says to tell you your duty station is here in this hospital until he gets Capshaw safe on a boat headed back to the good old U-S-of-A. The lieutenant's been voted out of the Corps. The captain, he called in some favors, got the LT a disability discharge."

"A ticket home."

"Yeah, home," Hinojosa said, like a man remembering a time when he had one.

"Tell the captain I got the message." Chaco leaned back and looked up into the branches of the overhanging banyan tree. Its oddly shaped limbs shaded the veranda and kept it tolerably cool even on the hottest days. Bradley, the day-shift corpsman, had told him this type of tree was like no other on earth. This particular one had a large cavity at its base, and, at Bradley's urging, Chaco had stepped into the cavity and, looking up, had seen the tree was hollow as a chimney all the way up to the open sky.

"The tree is actually a vine," Bradley explained, once Chaco stepped out. "At least it begins as a vine. What it does is take root at the base of a tree and over time the vines surround the host tree as they grow toward the sun. By the time the banyan vine reaches the sky and spreads out to form treelike branches of its own, you can no longer see the trunk of the host tree. The vines by that time have grown together and look very much like connected muscle, like what you see now. It's at that point the banyan crushes and kills its host. In time the host tree decays and falls away, leaving only the banyan, a tree of great strength but hollow at its core."

"You okay, Kidd?" The gunny was looking at Chaco, his head cocked a little.

"Just thinking."

"You know, the lieutenant, he ain't a half bad kid. He's just yellow and, except maybe for anybody who ain't a Marine, that ain't no crime."

11

A few nights later Chaco awoke with a fierce pain in his chest. He at first attributed the pain to his wound. But then his ears filled with a kind of muffled silence, as if something had gotten inside his head, something that also filled the air all around him, a kind of presence. He blinked up at the wind-stirred shapes of trees, the shadows moving back and forth across the ceiling, and a prickle of gooseflesh moved across his scalp. The pain was so intense he rose on one elbow, ready to summon the duty corpsman. But the guy was gone at the station where he usually sat out the midnight shift reading by lamplight. Chaco lay back, thinking the corpsman had probably gone to the latrine. He waited for him. What else could he do? But as the minutes passed, the pain in his chest began to subside and gradually it went away. For a long time he lay sweat soaked in the dark, listening to the steady patter of rain against the ward's iron roof. He felt strange, but it was a strange night.

Over the next few days, there was no recurrence of chest pains and his memory of the incident faded. And then one morning while sunning himself on the veranda outside the ward, Seaman Marco, the lieutenant's Filipino steward, brought him a rumpled copy of the *New York Times* along with his breakfast. While Marco filled a porcelain coffee cup to its gold rim, Chaco unfolded the newspaper, shook it out, and read the headline: "Geronimo Dead."

He froze.

Below the block-letter banner was a photograph of his uncle Goyaałé, his hard black eyes staring out from the cheap pulp of the newspaper. He was on one knee, holding a rifle in a posed photograph taken months after the surrender. A pang of unexpected grief went through him. He drew a ragged breath and, holding on to his nerve, thanked the steward and waited until he was gone before he read on, his vision hazy—his long years of absolute discipline broken.

The report said his uncle had died of pneumonia on Wednesday, the seventeenth of February. Chaco folded the paper, and, carrying it, he rose and walked to the screen door. He entered the ward, looked at his bunk, and remembered the pain in his chest on that rainy night. The long, narrow building, much like the school dorm where he'd lived out his lonely childhood, was lined with mostly empty bunks. The ward was as shipshape and as sterile as his life.

What have I been doing? he wondered. He had joined the marines to avoid being sent back to Fort Sill as a de facto prisoner of war. But even so, he could have returned home. He could have made that choice. He could have been there for his uncle, and for his mother and sister. But instead he was here in Cuba. Four years of tracking rebels, hunting them down, and killing them. And for what? He blinked, and thought: I have done terrible things to a people who were never my enemy, for a people who were never my own.

He raised the paper and shook it open again. Studied the photograph of his uncle. The lean, toothless, oddly youthful scowling face, fit and strong at sixty, despite the four-decade war he had fought against the Mexicans and the Americans.

A war he could not win.

A war he did not win.

The newspaper said his uncle had gotten drunk on a rainy night, that he'd fallen off his horse or out of a buggy on his way home, and that he'd not been found until the following morning. Reading this, Chaco frowned.

Where were the soldiers who guarded him?

The paper said his uncle had been buried in the cemetery at Fort Sill. That would be the Apache Prisoner-of-War Cemetery, situated several discreet miles from the main post on the military reserve.

His scowl deepened. A passing corpsman paused and looked at him.

"Are you okay, Corporal? In pain?"

"No."

"I'm authorized to give you morphine."

Chaco simply stared at him.

The corpsman shrugged. "Lieutenant Capshaw, he's got more pull than a bird colonel."

"No shot, but thanks."

The corpsman nodded and continued with his rounds.

Chaco thought about his mother. More than a year had passed since he'd last written her. Not that it mattered; she never wrote back. But then, how could she? She hardly spoke English, much less read or wrote it.

I will send her a letter today, he thought.

He turned and pushed through the screen door and stepped out onto the veranda again.

In the near distance the Stars and Stripes snapped against the lanyard of the flagpole on the parade ground. He sat in the chair again and stared out across the harbor, seeing everything and nothing. His uncle Goyaałé was dead. Strange that his death should move him so—it was as if the news of his passing had wakened something within him.

I will go back to Fort Sill, he thought. I will take my mother and sister out of their prisoner-of-war camp and out of Oklahoma.

And thinking this, he felt good in his heart again.

12

Word came down from the admiralty: the fighting in the mountains was over. American military forces would be vacating the island. For the first time since the outset of the Spanish-American War, there would be no military presence in Cuba, other than the naval station at Guantánamo.

Chaco's wound had long since healed, and he was fit to rejoin his company, but the hospital held on to him until the day the lieutenant's discharge came through. On the morning Lieutenant Capshaw was scheduled to depart, he came around to see Chaco. They were about the same age, although the lieutenant seemed younger, despite his handsome new scar.

"I'd like you to be there to see me off, Corporal Kidd."

Chaco donned a set of dress khakis for the occasion. The lieutenant wore dress whites with gloves. His grandfather had sent the *Eurotas*, his personal steam yacht, to collect the LT. She was an elegant white vessel with dark teak handrails, upper decks shaded beneath white canvas, and she lay at anchor alongside a heavy cruiser—a grand yacht overshadowed by the iron warship with its modern turreted batteries. They stood on the quay as a motorized dinghy, launched from the yacht, crossed the harbor. When the craft swung alongside the quay, the lieutenant took Chaco's hand and held it, in his eyes a question he clearly wanted to ask. But, unable to say whatever it was he wanted to say, he simply nodded. Then realized he was clinging to Chaco's hand and let go. He turned abruptly, descended the stone steps, handed his seabag to the coxswain, and stepped aboard. He took a seat as the coxswain shoved off.

The *putt-putt* of the engine quickened and, as the dinghy moved away, the lieutenant abruptly stood and looked back at Chaco, a hand placed against the engine cowling for balance. The scar on his cheek lent him a heroic air. Neither of them waved, and finally the lieutenant turned and sat again.

13

L ater that afternoon Chaco was discharged from the hospital and given written orders to rejoin his company. He reported to the orderly tent at battalion command, and after being processed he sought out Gunny Hinojosa. The gunny took him around to meet their new lieutenant, fresh from a tour in the Philippines. The new LT asked Chaco a few perfunctory questions and then welcomed him back to the platoon.

The gunny and he made their way to the gunny's tent, where Hinojosa produced a bottle of rum and two glasses. He topped off the glasses, extended one of them to Chaco, and raised his own in salute. "Absent friends."

"Absent friends."

Gunny took a long drink. Chaco sipped off the top off his. And then watched as the gunny finished off his drink, belched, and looked at Chaco, watery eyed and happy.

"It's good to have you back, Kidd."

"It's good to be back."

"Now maybe we can get some of this shit done around here."

He took up the bottle, refilled his glass, and drank again. "You're falling to the rear, Kidd. You're always about four drinks behind."

"My enlistment is up in a couple of months," Chaco said. "I'm going to get out."

Hinojosa lowered his glass and stared at Chaco as if maybe he'd misheard him. "You mean get out of the Corps? It ain't on account of that little scratch you got. I know that."

"No."

"It's that damned lieutenant. That rich bastard offered you a job, didn't he?"

"No, I think maybe he wanted to, but he didn't. It's something else."

The gunny's eyebrows bunched together. "What could make a man give up the Corps?"

"I'm going back to help my mother and my sister. My mother is getting old."

"Oh." Hinojosa looked down at his boots. Then leaned back and stared at Chaco. "I didn't even know you had a mother and a sister." He worried his lip with his tobacco-stained teeth. "Hell, Kidd, you've got a world of leave on the books. Never took a day of it, as far as I can tell. Why not take an extended one? Go home for a while. Hell, I'll put you in for it today. You go home and see your mother and sister. Take three months. You got four on the books. I can't believe you never went home in all this time. Dammit man, it ain't human. A man's got to see his mother once in a while. I wish I'd seen mine more, but it's too late now."

Chaco set the glass on the dirt floor. "If I've got four coming, put me in for the four."

"I'll do it. Four years is a long time for a man not to see his mom."

"It's more like fifteen," he said. "I was seven when they took me away to the Indian school."

"And you ain't seen your mother in all them years?"

"No."

Gunny drew one of his pawlike hands over his face. "I got to ask: Why now?"

"My uncle died. My mother's about his age, and it got me thinking about time."

"How old was your uncle?"

Chaco shrugged. "I don't know, eighty, maybe ninety."

The gunny stared into his glass. "Eighty seems like a long life, till you get to be seventy-nine, I guess."

Chaco grinned. "I'll miss your jokes."

Hinojosa raised his glass and drank. "Who's joking?" He topped his drink off again and placed the bottle on the ground. "Answer me this, Kidd. What difference is it going to make after all this time?"

"Did it make any difference to you?"

The gunny blinked. "I don't understand."

"That you didn't go see your mom."

The gunny thought about that and nodded. "I'll say this one thing, Kidd, and then no more. The Marine Corps is where we belong. There ain't no place else in this world for likes of you and me. I don't know much, but I know that. And if you don't know it now, you'll know it soon enough."

"There's got to be more to life than killing."

The gunny drank, made a face, and shook his head. He looked down at the bottle a long moment and then stared at Chaco, a big man seated on a canvas cot inside a canvas tent at the end of a failed war. "This is all there is for the likes of us, Kidd. All there is."

14

He shipped out of Guantánamo for the States aboard a cargo vessel bound for Tampa, four days and three nights at sea. In the evenings he walked the weather decks and watched the changing face of the moon mirrored off the restless waves. Nights at sea sucked away by the dawns, and, leaning against the starboard rail, he greeted the sunrises. Around him a wilderness of water, a desert of waves upon which a kind of liberty could be had at the price of absolute risk.

In Tampa he presented his terminal-leave papers to the port authorities, and the following day, dressed in freshly pressed khakis, his hair cut close beneath a new campaign hat purchased at the post exchange, he boarded the northbound for Atlanta. He was on his way home—if a prisoner-of-war camp could be thought of as home.

In Atlanta, while waiting in the station café for a westbound connection, four men confronted him. The tallest of them said, "What part of colored don't you understand, boy?"

Chaco stared at him.

"I don't think he speaks American," one of the others said.

"Let's drag his little ass out to the yard," another said. "Give him an education."

The fight was brief and one-sided. Chaco left them on the floor, hurt but alive. He took up his seabag, and, with a woman screaming "Help, police," he left the station and in the rail yard located a suitable hide.

Uniformed police officers arrived, their Eveready torches flashing here and there as they searched the yard. He watched from his hide until the westbound sounded its whistle and moved away from the station, and as it rolled by he took up his seabag, jogged across the yard, tossed it up onto the forward platform of a sleeper, and climbed the iron steps. As the train gathered speed, he stared back at the seeking flashlights of the Atlanta police and watched until the last of them faded from view.

15

Three days and several train changes later, he stepped down from the baggage car. The sun had burned away most of a hoarfrost that had formed during the night, and passengers were debarking from the Pullmans. He lowered his seabag to the platform. Lawton had grown. There were more buildings now. Even so, the town seemed somehow smaller than he remembered. The platform had been extended, and the original wood-frame station was now a brick building with a tiled roof.

He was taking up his seabag when he saw a man hurrying toward him along the platform.

"Hello there. Please tell me you are Corporal Frank Kidd?"

The man was slender, hatless, and wore a dark suit, and Chaco, thinking this might be connected to the difficulty in Atlanta, looked beyond him at the men milling about outside the station building. No apparent threat there, and behind him the platform lay empty. He saw no threat from the street beyond the station. And so he lowered the seabag.

"Yes?"

The man was about Chaco's age, had neatly cut hair parted

down the middle, with cheeks that were smooth and clean-shaven.

"Corporal Kidd?" He extended his hand.

Chaco shook it briefly. "What do you want?"

"It *is* you, then? Oh, wonderful. I'm here to interview you for my newspaper, sir."

"Why?"

"The name's Halliburton Phillips, but, please, it's Hal for short." He produced a pencil and notepad. "I'm a reporter with the *Kansas City Star*. Actually more a cub reporter." He smiled apologetically. "If you wouldn't mind the inconvenience too terribly, I would very much like to ask you a few questions."

"Why?" Chaco asked again, genuinely puzzled.

"Obviously because I am a reporter for the *Kansas City Star* and—"

"I get the reporter part, but why me?"

Phillips had the same eastern, upper-crust accent as Lieutenant Capshaw.

"Why, sir, because you are a war hero, and people want to read about war heroes. You are of course aware of the medal and commendation you are to receive during your stay here?"

"Medal?"

"Yes, the one you're to be presented for valor during the Battle of Gomez Heights."

"Gomez Heights?" Now Chaco was genuinely confounded but then remembered the gunny saying something about him being put in for a decoration. "You mean in Cuba?"

"As depicted in at least four feature articles in the *Times* this week. How Lieutenant Capshaw and you held out against three rebel machine gunners long enough for your fellow marines to withdraw to safety."

"Three machine gunners?"

"I was sent down by my editor to interview you, if possible."

"How did you know I'd be here?"

"The article in the *Times*—it said you would be staying here on extended leave while recovering from your wounds. Actually I expected to meet a man on crutches."

"I'm trying to get along without them." He looked past Phillips and saw the crowd outside the station had thinned somewhat. Porters, moving along the platform, were collecting the wooden stools from under the bottom steps of the Pullmans. The conductor shouted, "All aboard," and the great wheels of the engine spun and caught. Chaco stepped away from the cars, the couplings slamming tight as the train moved ahead. He looked at the reporter.

"You got a buggy, Mr. Phillips?"

"I have the use of a Ford motorcar. That's it parked over there." He pointed.

"If you'll give me a ride to the Apache prisoner-of-war camp, you can ask your questions on the way."

Phillips frowned. "Why, that place is almost cleared out. I was out there only yesterday with a Captain Alexander Banyan. He oversees provisions for the camp. The captain tells me that with Geronimo gone and only a few old derelicts still living out there, it's been decided that the last of the aborigines will be evicted soon. All I saw out there was a bunch of old women."

"Yeah. One of them old aborigines is my mother."

"Sorry. No offense intended, Corporal. It's kind of sad, if you consider the circumstances. I mean, where will they all go?" Phillips shrugged matter-of-factly. "I can carry that for you," he said, and pointed to the seabag.

"I've got it."

Chaco followed the newsman across the street to his motorcar. It was a new-looking Model T Ford that had been repainted a bright, shiny red that gleamed under a highly polished coat of wax. The car belonged to a local doctor, Phillips said, one of his father's college chums.

Chaco placed the seabag on the back seat. "I'll give you a hand with the engine."

"I've got it," Phillips declared, hurried around to the front of the motorcar, engaged the crank handle, and gave it a hard upward pull. The engine coughed and sputtered and then ran as he rushed back and got in behind the wheel. He adjusted the levers on the steering column, worked the throttle, and, once the engine smoothed out, he winked at Chaco.

"Here we go."

They lurched away, rolling past buggies and horses, and soon enough were motoring past a sign that announced they were entering the Fort Sill military reserve.

There were more trees than Chaco remembered. Some of them were in early bud. The military road was better maintained than he remembered, and the Ford clipped along at a rate of speed equal to a high gallop. Phillips appeared to enjoy driving fast, and he talked above the wind and the putter of the engine as they rolled along. He told Chaco that his job with the *Star* had been his father's idea—intended, his father claimed, to keep him out of mischief until the fall. Phillips's editor, like the doctor who owned the Ford, was one of his father's college chums. Phillips was enjoying his time out West. So far he had interviewed a former gunfighter, and an ex-cavalry trooper who had been wounded with the Seventh under Captain Benteen on that fateful day back in '76. Phillips's editor was always more than glad to have him interview historic figures—especially since he paid all his own expenses. "The frontier may officially have closed out eleven years ago," he said, "but I am glad to be a witness to what is left of it, before I assume a situation with my father's firm."

"What kind of situation?" Chaco asked.

"Oh, I'll start from the bottom. Work the floor to begin with. The exchange, you know?"

"The exchange," Chaco said, as if he did know.

"I'm to marry my cousin as soon as I've settled in. We'll live in the brownstone my mother is having fixed up. It's all arranged. Angelia, my mother, hired a decorator while she was in Paris last season. He's redoing everything. From what Mummy writes in her letters, it's going to be a smash-up job." Phillips dipped a hand inside his coat and brought out a leather wallet he extended toward Chaco. "There's a likeness of my fiancée inside."

Chaco took the wallet, opened it, and looked at the tintype of a corseted girl with large bosoms, demurely concealed beneath the white lace of a long-sleeved blouse; she had light-colored hair done softly up under a wide-brimmed straw hat, a lovely oval face, and a forthright expression. Chaco closed the wallet and handed it back. "She's beautiful."

"She is, isn't she?" Phillips laughed and shook his head. "Look at me. I've been doing all the talking. Apparently I'm not as good at the newspaper game as I was beginning to think. Look." He gestured with his chin. "There's the camp. Tell me something about the battle?" he said, and shrugged apologetically. "I have to write something."

"Whatever the lieutenant told the *Times*, you can say that's exactly what happened."

"Can I quote you on that?"

"Why not?"

The road curved past a cluster of skeletal trees, and there was the camp. Phillips drove through the open gate and braked to a stop just outside a weed-grown cluster of faded clapboard double-pen cabins. The lack of paint made the buildings seem shabbier and older than they were. There was no glass in the window openings, nor doors in the doorways. Chaco studied the equally weathered sentry towers, stationed at intervals around the camp, and realized they were all vacant. No guards.

The People began to come out of the tiny clapboard dwellings. Phillips killed the engine. Chaco saw, as he stepped out of the car, that they were mostly sun-withered old women with mostly white, gray-shot hair. He extended a hand toward Phillips. They shook briefly.

"Thank you for the ride."

He retrieved his seabag from the back seat, turned, and looked for his mother among the curious faces. Then he saw her. She was shorter than he remembered, and much altered by the years. He walked toward her as she hurried across the grassless ground to meet him, her withered face bright as sunlight on autumn leaves. They stopped a polite pace apart, and he dropped his seabag, and, against the dictates of tradition, he closed the space between them and embraced her. He felt her ribs beneath the thin fabric of her dress, felt the frailty of this woman of iron. Then, stepping back, he held her at arm's length, and, in the language of the People, so long in disuse by him, he said, "*I see your face,*" the words forming on his tongue like the half-forgotten verse of a once-familiar poem.

"*I see your face,*" Aná Liluy said, her dark eyes shining up at him.

He turned and looked back at Phillips, still standing beside the Ford, notepad and pencil in hand, and waved and watched Phillips's eyes cloud with disappointment as he waved back.

"I'll see you again at the ceremony, then," Phillips called, and Chaco watched as he cranked the Ford's engine and drove away.

He turned back to his mother. She was smiling toothlessly up at him.

"*I thought I would never see you again,*" she muttered, her fierce eyes like rain-wet flint in her shrunken face.

"*I have come back to take you away from this place.*"

Her toothless smile broadened, and in that moment he knew the long years had changed nothing. They were as they had been before in their solitude together. The others were smiling as they turned away and Aná took his hand in hers, pressed it against her cheek, and Chaco looked around.

"*Where have all the People gone?*"

"*Many are dead now. Others have gone away. Come,*" she said, and led him to the tiny room with its connecting dogtrot that he still remembered well. She lived alone now, she told him. The other room was empty.

"*Where is my sister?*"

"*It is not like before, when they took you,*" she said. "*Much has changed.*"

He tossed his seabag on the porch end of the dogtrot and noted the dust that rose from the boards. He sat beside her on the weathered planks of the dogtrot and answered her questions as he waited for her to tell him about Sally Liluy, the sister he had always thought of by her true name, Bui. The tongue of the People was as sweet to his ears as water to thirst. A neighbor brought them a tin can of boiled coffee and with it a plate of flatbread and a pot of red beans.

"*You want something to eat?*" the woman said.

Chaco touched her shoulder. "*Thank you, little mother.*"

Aná asked him if he remembered the woman, Olivia Yanozha. He had no memory of her, but he smiled at the woman and said, "*Yes, of course.*"

Olivia Yanozha nodded. "*You look like her,*" she said, and, with a glance at Aná, turned and walked away.

They ate the food and drank the coffee, and he sat with his mother as she grinned toothlessly into the fading day. "*I am glad I lived long enough to see your face again. I feel very good now. Now I can fulfill my promise and go to Usen with a clean heart.*"

"*Not for a long time, Mother,*" Chaco said. "*Now tell me, where is my sister?*"

In English Aná said, "Sally went to Lawton two years ago." She hesitated for several heartbeats, then said the rest of it. "She is in the saloon of Mr. Alton McDonnell."

"Saloon?"

Aná's chin sagged; she sat exactly still.

Finally he said what she could not say. "She is a whore?"

Aná's chin bobbed almost imperceptibly.

"Why would she do such a thing?"

"*Who knows why anybody does anything?*" Aná's gaze turned fierce as she looked up.

"I will bring her home," he said.

"*Good,*" Aná said. "*But not tonight. As for me, I have promises to keep. Things I must tell you about Lozen, your mother. But I will not speak of these things tonight.*"

She entwined her fingers with his and cradled his hand close under her chin, the way she had when he was a boy and her hands seemed so large and she and his sister had meant everything to him.

16

He lay awake late into the night, thinking about Bui, thinking he should have come home after graduation. A drop of water spilled from his eye and slid down his cheek; he wiped at it, looked at the shadow shape of his fingertips in the dark. None of this should have happened. The Corps had been a mistake, something he'd done before he knew better. He felt an anger he could not reason away.

In the morning he woke early, full of the need to be doing, angrier now than before. He must do something about this thing with Bui. If it came to trouble, he knew that others at the camp would suffer. That was the burden of his anger, the price that his people would pay.

He borrowed one of the three buckboards in the camp, harnessed an old horse to it, and drove out across the military reserve. By day's end he had gathered several loads of deadfall for firewood. That evening he cleaned the weeds from his mother's garden and freshened up the rows. That night they ate the last of the red beans and afterward sat together staring into the pulsing coals of the fire pit. He listened as she talked on, his hands kept busy sharpening the narrow blade of her rusty hoe.

Late in the night Aná paused and fell silent. He stopped what he was doing and looked at her. "What is it, little mother?"

"*I am glad you came back. Truly, I feared I might not fulfill a promise.*"

"*What promise?*"

She stared silently into the pulsing coals, gathering her thoughts and the words she must say. "*I knew your mother, Lozen, long before the Indah took us to Fort Marion. Lozen was your mother's war name. She was the sister of Victorio. As children she and Victorio played at warrior games, and as a young woman she chose the warrior road. She was wise in battle, and for this she was given other names. She was called Gouyen, the wise woman, but also she was called Biyaneta. That was the name she gave to the soldiers the day Goyaałé surrendered. She used that name so that they might not know the greatness of their victory. She was the wife of Perico and for a time the wife of Kayatennae. She was my friend.*

"*Upon this earth on which we live, Usen has power. This power Usen shared with Lozen. She used it to locate the People's enemies. She used it to help her brother Victorio in battle. She fought beside him in every battle he won. The Mexicans would never have defeated Victorio had she been with him that day.*

"*When I left my husband, Chatto, the betrayer, it was Lozen who came for me. It was she who guided Bui and me past the enemy and over the mountain. In saving Bui and me, she lost her brother. Few know that it was Lozen whom the Mexicans could never defeat. That it was Lozen in those last years who guided Goyaałé in battle. And that it was she whom the great whiteeye general could not defeat in war. She saw in a vision the iron horse that would carry us to a faraway place where they would break the People. She saw the final betrayal of the Indah, and she told me it was for this she lay with Goyaałé to get a child by him. A child for a purpose known only to Usen.*"

Chaco blanched and stared at her flickering outline. "*Goyaałé was my father?*"

"*Yes,*" she whispered, her eyes cast down. A heavy silence hung between them.

"*Why did he not tell me? Or you?*"

Aná gazed quietly into the fire pit, still silent. Finally she looked at him. She could see the anger in his eyes. His clinched fists trembling against his knees.

"*I never told him you were his son. But I know he knew . . . and that is why he never asked.*"

Chaco thought about that a moment. What did that mean? Why *hadn't* he asked? Geronimo had other children, Chappo and Doh-say, and he acknowledged them. And in many ways Geronimo treated him like a son . . . but then never told him he was. There was something missing. Something Aná wasn't telling him. Chaco looked down, noticed his trembling fists. He unclenched them, slid his hands under his legs.

"*I don't understand. I asked him about my father, and he told me he'd been killed. Now you tell me he lied? That he made it up? That all the elders went along? That you were all lying to me? Why?*"

"*If the whiteeyes had known who you were, what do you think they would have done?*"

"*I don't care. You should have told me the truth.*"

Aná's eyes softened. She studied him for several heartbeats. "*Goyaałé had other children. I know you know this. But they were born free. Not like you.*"

"*What difference did that make? I had no choice where I was born.*"

"*Did Goyaałé ever talk about his first wife, Alope? And their three children? Do you know what happened to them?*"

Chaco studied her, his eyes somber, as he shook his head.

"*He was young, about your age. His daughters were three and four . . . his son was eight—about your age when they took you*" *away.*" Aná folded her hands, looked into the fire. "*One day some Mexicans from Chihuahua came to the camp. They invited Goyaałé to their town to trade with them. They said they had many good things to trade—they had horses and guns, and ammunition and food. They said they wanted to trade for our blankets and jewelry and buffalo hides. So the next day Goyaałé and the other men left for Chihuahua to do the trading. Only about twenty men stayed behind to guard the camp . . . but it was a Mexican trick planned by Colonel Carrasco. He planned it. And after Goyaałé and the others left, this Colonel Carrasco and four hundred Mexican soldiers attacked the camp and killed everyone. The men, the women, the children, over two hundred of them. And Goyaałé's wife and children, his girls and his son—this Carrasco, he knew who they were. The soldiers scalped them and stabbed out their eyes and mutilated their bodies and hung them from trees so that when Goyaałé came back, he would see them first.*" Aná's jaw clinched, and for a time she sat silent. When her eyes rose, they met Chaco's, and she whispered, "*Your father did not trust the soldiers. He loved you and wanted to protect you. I think, had he lived, he would have told you someday. He waited to let you grow into a man who could protect himself.*"

"He waited too long," Chaco said in English.

"*Yes,*" she said, and, not wanting to shame him, looked away from his tears.

17

That night Chaco dreamed dreams, and in the morning, when he sat up on the thin mattress of his hammock, he knew what he must do. On the other side of the tiny room, he heard his mother's slow, steady breath. He pulled on his boots, laced them, and got to his feet. For a time he stared at Anâ's slumbering form. That strong face, long remembered, now half-hidden by the weblike ravages of time.

I will take Bui out of this McDonnell's Saloon. This I do for you, Mother.

Doubtless there would be consequences. Yet he must find a way to get her out of that place or make one.

Through the window opening he saw sunlight on the upper reaches of the Wichitas. A skim of ice had formed in the water bucket. He shivered. It was cold enough to warrant the wearing of his field jacket this morning. His jacket hadn't seen much use in Cuba but had served well enough as a cache for the more than six hundred dollars he'd managed to save during his four years in the Corps. Easy enough, if you didn't drink or shoot dice.

That first month in Cuba, a barracks thief had stolen money from an unsecured footlocker. There had been a shakedown and the thief had been caught, sent to the brig, and given a Bad Conduct Discharge. But in the interim, Chaco had slit an inner seam in his field jacket and carefully stitched the pockets of three discarded fatigue shirts into the inner liner—thus creating his personal bank. Now he would spend some of that money.

He didn't really need an excuse to drive into Lawton, although he thought he ought to have one. And he did have one: his mother's meager larder was in need of resupply.

He went out into the chill morning and borrowed the buckboard again. By the time he got back with it, Aná had a blaze going in the fire pit behind the cabin.

"*You want to eat?*"

"*I go empty during the day.*" He stepped down from the buggy, went to her, and hugged her. "*I am going into the town.*"

Her eyes hardened. "*Do you remember the things I taught you?*"

"*I remember everything.*"

"*You know what you are doing?*"

He nodded. "*Yes.*"

"*Then everything is good.*"

The sky had brightened to a clear blue by the time Aná followed him out to the buckboard and watched after him as he drove away. Chaco let the horse pick its own pace. He looked around, and seeing there was no one in sight, he slipped a hand inside his field jacket, slid it through the slit in the liner, and plucked a few bills from one of the cache pockets. He glanced at the denominations and, satisfied, folded the bills and slipped them into his trouser pocket, took up the reins again, and drove on.

The flag was up and fluttering from the pole on the main post quadrangle by the time he came in sight of the line of barracks and drove by a battalion formed up by company, the sergeants issuing orders of the day. He noted the loathing gaze of some of the soldiers, the way they tracked his progress. Such looks shouldn't have surprised him, but they did.

When he came to the stone pillars that marked the boundary of the military reservation, he pulled to a halt and stared ahead at the town. He had come prepared to make inquiries, but such inquiries would be unnecessary; he could see McDonnell's Saloon shouldered between other saloons and businesses on a muddy street that faced the tracks not a hundred yards ahead.

He flicked the reins and sent the skinny horse across the tracks, pulled to a halt at the water-trough in front of McDonnell's, tied off to an iron hitch ring, and mounted the four plank steps to the boardwalk. The faded white clapboard building had garish advertisements painted across its face, offering everything from five-cent beer to a free lunch—but there was no mention of girls. He was about to go in when a soldier lurched through the batwing door, bumped into him, and staggered back a step.

"Apologies, apologies." The soldier blinked as he ran his tongue around inside his mouth. "Ah, a marine. Top of the morning to you, Mr. Marine. And it's a long way from the ocean-sea you are." His brogue was as thick as his grin was broad. He gave Chaco a jovial salute and wobbled, unsteady on his feet. "The name's Duffy, Niall Duffy, and for your information, Mr. Marine, you're looking at the best damned artilleryman in this man's army. That includes the Marine Corps, too, if you don't mind me saying."

"Not at all."

"I can put a twelve-pounder up a gnat's ass at five thousand yards. A month's pay on it, anytime there's a taker, but, more's the pity, there's not a soul who'll wager me anymore." He squinted myopically at Chaco. "Say, I know you? Ain't you that marine in the newspapers, the one that's to get the medal?"

"Is Mr. McDonnell in there? I'm here to see him."

"Alton McDonnell in there? No, lad, you'll never catch Alton McDonnell in that saloon, or in any other, for that matter. His wife won't allow it, so they say. Can you imagine? The man owns the best whorehouse in Lawton, maybe in the whole of Oklahoma, and he can't even get him none. No sir, if it's Alton McDonnell you're seeking, you'll find that gentleman next door, right there at the AM Mercantile." The soldier jerked a thumb toward the adjacent building, a clapboard two-story structure much like the saloon, but with a gallery that extended out over the boardwalk.

"Nose-to-the-grindstone kind of a feller, so they say, and friendly enough, if you got money." He winked, then came to attention and snapped another awkward salute. "I'm starved. Got to get something to eat. Best of luck to you, Mr. Marine. And, oh, by the way, you best not go in there." He jerked a thumb toward the batwing doors. "No Injuns, niggers, and hardly no Irishmen allowed—except for whores, of course. McDonnell is liberal in his thinking when it comes to Irish whores. He's got all the colors in there, even a Chinawoman—if she ain't a Jap-o or a Filipino." The soldier leaned toward Chaco, his breath foul as kerosene, and whispered, "Just between you and me, they're wrong about what they say—it don't go sideways." He winked merrily and hurried away along the boardwalk and, a few doors down, opened the door of a café, shouted hello to someone inside, and disappeared.

Chaco turned back and stared at the batwing doors. If Bui was in the saloon, in all probability she'd be upstairs asleep at this hour. He could go in and get her, but if he did, there would be trouble. How much trouble depended on circumstances, but if blood were spilled, the soldiers would come to the camp. And there was no guarantee she would want to come away. Some liked the life, and he hadn't seen Bui in fifteen years. She would be close to thirty now. He had to consider that.

He turned toward McDonnell's store and descended three board steps to a lower section of the boardwalk. Stopped out front and stared through a dingy plate-glass window at a dusty display of goods. The store's interior was dim. The entrance doors recessed. He turned the knob and pushed the door. A tiny bell rang above his head as he stepped through and rang again as the door closed behind him. Electric fans hung from the stamped-metal ceiling, their blades turning slowly. The air was redolent with rich smells of coffee, leather, flake tobacco, and other exotic aromas. At the far end of the center aisle he saw two men and walked toward them. The taller of the two faced the entrance from behind a glass display case and was hefting a Sharps .50; he was florid faced with graying red hair and wore a dirty white shirt and black trousers. The other was a soldier. He stood with his back to Chaco, listening to the older man brag about the good old days and doing his best to appear interested.

"That's some rifle, Mr. McDonnell. Ten thousand buffalo, you say. Wow."

"She's a fifty-caliber," McDonnell said. "Best damn long-range killer ever made. Not as fancy as one of these newfangled thirty-calibers my brother-in-law is always bragging about, but this one's killed many a buff. That's how I got my start when I first come out to this country in '65, sixteen I was, with a year in the fight before we licked the Johnny Rebs."

"Yes, sir, so I'm told. She's one heck of a rifle," the soldier admitted. Then, with an almost-embarrassed shrug, he said, "About that six dollars, Mr. McDonnell?"

"Oh, sure, son, sure. When I get to talking about the old days, I sometimes lose track." McDonnell placed the Sharps on the glass display case and dug a roll of bills from his pocket. Peeled off six singles and counted them out one at a time into the soldier's outstretched hand. The money disappeared into the soldier's pocket.

"You drive a hard bargain," McDonnell said.

"Thanks, Mr. McDonnell. Thanks a lot. Listen, I hate to rush, but . . . I just got this one little thing I need to—"

"Sure, sure, go on ahead."

The soldier turned, saw Chaco, and his grin faded into a frown. He bulled ahead, bumping Chaco deliberately with his shoulder as he went by and hurried on. McDonnell watched him go. The entrance bell rang, and a moment later McDonnell grinned. Chaco turned, saw the soldier through the display window as he hurried in the direction of McDonnell's Saloon. He turned back in time to see McDonnell pull a long-barreled Colt from his pants pocket, presumably the item he'd just bought for six dollars. Watched him retrieve a ring of keys from behind a file cabinet, then unlock the sliding door of the display case and place the heavy revolver on the top shelf among several other handguns.

McDonnell straightened and looked at him. "What can I do for you, chief?"

Chief, Chaco mused. He'd intended to ask about Bui straight out and go from there, but he took that one disdainful word for the warning it was. He looked around, stalling for the moment he needed to readjust. Then noticed a pyramid of five-gallon buckets of paint.

"I want some paint."

"What kind of paint, war paint?"

McDonnell cackled at his own joke. And ended any notion Chaco might have had of doing this in a straightforward manner. "House paint, white Seroco ready-mixed, like that." He pointed.

"You can have all you can pay for, chief. But I do a cash-on-the-barrelhead business here, and that Seroco brand goes for a dollar a gallon. I got to pay shipping."

McDonnell lifted the Sharps .50 off the glass display case, placed it in one of the empty slots in the gun rack attached to the back wall. He swung an iron security bar into place and affixed a brass padlock, glanced in the direction of the cabinet, and slipped the key ring into his trouser pocket. "How much paint you got money for, chief?"

"I'll take five gallons of the white to start. I'll need a four-inch brush, and I'll want some other things, too."

"Like what?"

"Like six bars of Armour's Tar Soap. Four wool blankets from that shelf over there. And four flannel sheets."

McDonnell's expression altered from one of disdain to avarice. He reached for a notepad and began to scribble with the stub of a pencil.

"I'll take fifty pounds of dried beans, a twenty-five-pound sack of corn flour, a five-gallon tin of lard, a measure of salt and pepper. Toss in one of those hundred-pound sacks of potatoes, and add a five-pound can of Arbuckles' coffee, five pounds of sugar, and a dozen cans of condensed milk. I'll take a slab of side meat, too."

Chaco looked around like a man trying to remember something else he needed. Noted the set of stairs that led to a landing where a woman sat at a writing table adjacent to the handrail, a beautiful, haughty woman. Likely the wife the artilleryman mentioned. Behind the woman was a decoratively papered wall with two bright white doors, a stand between with a vase full of flowers—a woman's touch in stark contrast to the functionality of the store itself. There was a counter beneath the landing on which sat a device for weighing things, and there were shelves behind the counter loaded with goods. A blanket covered a cased opening between the shelves—the storage room would be back there.

He turned to McDonnell, said, "That ought to do it for this trip." But then he noticed a brush-comb-and-mirror set in a red jewelry-box-like case, covered with hand-brushed gold scrolls. He closed the lid and placed it on the glass counter. "Add this to the bill. Wrap it carefully, and tally up what I owe."

"You got a way to carry all this stuff?"

"I have a buggy out front."

"Drive around back. We'll load you back there. But let's settle up first."

McDonnell added up the total, and when he was done he looked up solemnly. "That comes to eighteen dollars, fifty-six cents. You got that much?"

Chaco pulled the folded bills from his pocket and saw the concern in McDonnell's eyes alter to greed as he peeled off two ten-spots and placed them on the counter.

"I don't recall seeing you before," McDonnell said.

"I've been away for a while."

"Those your fatigues, or did you buy them?"

"I earned them."

The merchant nodded. "I own this place. The name's Alton McDonnell."

"Frank Kidd."

McDonnell stuffed his hands in his back pockets. "Well, *Mr.* Frank Kidd, if you need anything else, I'm open six to six, seven days a week, every day but Sunday." Again he cackled at his own joke.

Chaco went out to the buggy, drove past the saloon to the corner. Turned left onto the cross street and left again into the alleyway. McDonnell stood waiting on a small porch by the rear entrance as Chaco pulled to a halt by the porch steps. He noted a set of carriage doors to the right of the porch, one of them ajar, and inside the black fender of a motorcar. He tied off, went up the steps, and followed McDonnell through the screen door into a cluttered office. They moved through another door, past a wall-mounted telephone, and on to his waiting goods. He tucked the handle of the paintbrush into his boot and carried the five-gallon bucket by its wire handle. McDonnell picked up the blankets and sheets and followed. There was a closed door that would be the entrance to where the automobile was kept. The heavy bucket in hand, Chaco turned sideways going through the office and noted the etched-glass panes in the upper half of the rear door. He shouldered through the screen, went down the steps, and placed the bucket in the buckboard. As McDonnell put the blankets and sheets in back beside the bucket of paint, Chaco gestured toward the carriage door. "Where do you buy gasoline for a machine like that in this country?"

"Why, at a drugstore, of course. Where else would you buy gasoline? Come on. I'll help you haul out the rest of your plunder."

18

On the drive back he kept going over the things McDonnell had said and the things he hadn't. Without question he could take Bui out of McDonnell's place. But if it came to that, they would have to run. It would be better if he could get her out without force. Maybe a letter sent to her in the saloon, although a letter would serve as a clear warning to McDonnell.

"He is dead because he warned his enemy."

Chaco blinked and frowned, shook his head. He'd heard Aná's voice; the words had just popped unbidden into his mind. It is not that simple, he thought. Warning or no, he would write her, and if a letter could get her out of that place without trouble, so much the better. He would write, and she would come back to the camp, and the three of them would leave this country.

Chief, he thought, thinking about McDonnell, a man who looked tougher than the few whoremasters he'd known in Cuba. He remembered Bui's silent tears on the day Lieutenant Pratt took him away, but the anger in him was under control now. He had a plan.

He was nearing the place where the road divided and curved

off toward the POW camp when a column of troops rode into view. The sergeant at the head of the column signaled a halt, and as the column reined in, he aimed a finger at Chaco. "You in the buggy," he shouted.

Chaco pulled up, and the sergeant rode forward. He came up even with the buckboard and glared down at him—a ruddy-faced, clean-shaven man, his eyes hawked by the sun.

"How is it you're dressed like a marine?"

"Because I am one."

"That so?"

Chaco stared up at the sergeant.

"You've got quite a load there, Corporal."

"Supplies for my mother."

"You're from the Apache camp?"

"I used to be."

"I bet you got some whiskey in there."

"I don't drink. And you'd lose the bet."

"An Injun that don't drink," the sergeant scoffed. "You know, you got an attitude, Corporal. Anybody ever tell you that?"

"If I do, it's a marine attitude, Sergeant."

"You got leave papers?"

Chaco pulled the forms from his shirt pocket and held them out.

The sergeant leaned out of the saddle, took the forms, shook them open, and read, his lips moving and his brow furrowed.

"Oh yeah, I heard about you." The sergeant leaned and handed the papers back. "How long you plan on staying, Corporal Kidd?"

"To the end of my leave. I'm here to see my mother."

"A soldier ought to visit his ma ever so often. Don't overstay your welcome, though. And stay out of trouble."

"What trouble?"

"Getting drunk, getting in fights, the usual shit. Hear me?"

"Loud and clear, Sergeant."

"Good."

The sergeant brought his mount around, waved to the column, and rode on.

Chaco waited until the last trooper had ridden past before he clucked up the horse and drove on.

When he reached the camp, he found his mother planting in the new rows he'd turned for her. She got up and brushed off her knees and came over to help. He gave her the blankets to carry; they were light, and soon enough he had the buggy unloaded. Aná's eyes glowed as she lifted the bag of Arbuckles' Ariosa from the new stores.

"I will make us some coffee," she said.

"Good."

He changed into his oldest fatigues and boots. Went out again and carried a number of old planks back to the cabin—lumber that had been pried from the walls of abandoned shacks. It had been done for the nails in them, a toothless old woman explained as she offered him a canful of salvaged nails, some of which had been hammered into crude bird points. He hunkered down by the flat rock Aná used for a back step and, one by one, straightened the nails with the hammer end of Aná's hatchet.

Aná brought him coffee.

"*What are you doing?*"

"Straightening nails."

"*Why?*"

"To build a ladder," he said. "I am going to paint this house."

"*Why?*"

He answered with a shrug and worked on. In fact, he had no answer, other than an urge to be doing something for her. He straightened nail after nail until he'd straightened them all. Then he picked out the best of the old lumber and built a ladder. He leaned it against the cabin and took up the brush and started painting.

By nightfall he'd applied paint to all the external walls. There was enough left in the bucket to paint the splintery planks of the dogtrot, but he decided to hold off on that. He stepped back and studied his work and decided the cabin now looked out of place among the others. He hadn't considered that.

He stripped to the waist, washed his face, hands, and upper body out of a bucket, and used his shirt to dry off. Dug a clean shirt out of his seabag and pulled it on.

They ate in silence and afterward sat staring into the remnants of the dying fire. Aná's eyes glowed with pleasure. He could see how weary she was. Whatever questions she might have about Bui, she kept them to herself. There were things he would tell her about this McDonnell: how the man's hard-edged contempt and greedy eyes had warned him against any direct questions about his sister.

When Aná's eyelids drooped, Chaco set his cup aside. He said, "*I am going to lie down, little mother. I am weary.*" Saying this because he knew she would not lie down until he did.

They went in, and she lay down on her new sheet and pulled her new blankets up under her chin. She smiled up at him as he extinguished the paraffin lamp. He sat in the dark, unlaced and removed his boots, stretched out on the hammock pad, and stared at the dark ceiling.

"*Tell me about the school,*" she said, her voice sleepy.

"*They took me there to learn the white way, to walk the white road, and I learned it.*"

"*Tell me . . . is the white way good for anything?*"

"*For some things, yes. For others . . . maybe not.*"

She asked him other questions, mostly about the Corps and the war in the mountains.

"*I liked being a Marine, but the* Cubans *were never my enemy.*"

"Did you kill many of them?"

"Yes, too many, I think."

Her silences lengthened until at last she slept. He lay in the dark listening to the steady sound of breath and thought about Bui. Would they let her walk away? He hoped so. He hadn't considered the difficulty of her life over the years, or the life of his mother. He grimaced and rubbed the rough surface of his palm over his face. He'd been a child, but he was a child no more. One thing he knew: he would take Bui out of McDonnell's whorehouse. And once he had they would all go away from this place. He had enough money to buy a few acres somewhere. A parcel of land by a stream, like in the dream he'd dreamed during his first lonely years at Carlisle, before something changed in him, before he hardened his heart.

I should have come home, he thought.

He was a year into the war with twenty confirmed combat kills before his first time with a woman, a Cuban whore he'd mounted again and again, on fire for her and convinced he was in love, until the madam beat on the door and yelled that his time was up. The whore had sat up in bed, smiled at him, and in a cheerful voice said, "Just for fun, I want to look at it," and gave his member a friendly squeeze. Later he returned to the cantina, but he never saw her again. He had known two kinds of whores in Cuba: the very stupid and the very brave. The brave ones were possessed of the sad bravado of the balladeer who sings of lost love in the midst of flying bullets. But always, inside of them, an inner solitude he recognized far too well.

He felt a stirring in his heart, a teetering sense of having come to the periphery of a kind of barrier beyond which all questions would be answered—but then nothing, no answers. He passed his hand over his eyes in an effort to bring whatever it was back, but the stirring sense was gone. He questioned whether it was the white man's way or his own blood that stirred in him at this moment, but he did know that being a whore was the cruelest kind of existence. And thinking this, thinking about Bui's life in that place, he felt the banked fires of his long-dormant childhood hatred rekindled. And at the core of that flame burned the face of Alton McDonnell, merchant and whoremaster.

19

At first light Chaco left Aná asleep and went out into the morning. Rather than wake someone to borrow their buggy, he set out for Lawton on foot. He encountered another mounted patrol near the main post and again was required to show the sergeant-in-charge his leave papers.

The morning had warmed by the time he crossed the track into Lawton. He located the post office, crossed the busy street, and walked in. High ceilings, a wall of lockboxes to his left, a marble counter straight ahead, behind which a postman stood sorting letters. His heels clicked across the waxed terrazzo, the postman looking up from his letter sorting as Chaco reached the counter. Soft eyes in a middle-aged face, rounded shoulders inside a blue uniform shirt, bushy gray eyebrows that arched toward a receding hairline.

"May I help you?"

"I want to write two letters."

"Will you need paper for these letters?"

Chaco nodded.

"Will you need stamps?"

"Yes, two."

The postman opened a drawer and tore a couple of stamps from a purplish sheet and placed them on the counter.

"How many sheets of paper?"

"One for each envelope."

He sorted out two sheets of paper and two envelopes, and placed them on the counter.

"Anything else I can do for you?"

Chaco shook his head.

"You got a dime?"

He dug a handful of coins from his pocket, placed a dime on the counter. "Do you have a pen or a pencil I can borrow?"

"You'll find one over there, against the wall."

Along the wall behind him were several chest-high writing tables situated between the floor-to-ceiling windows. He nodded thanks and crossed to the nearest. Arranged the sheets of paper and envelopes on the table's marble surface and took up a pen, attached to the table by a length of beaded chain, and dipped its nib into the inkwell. Leaned over one of the sheets and only then realized he had no idea where to begin. There was so much he wanted to say, and yet, despite all the books he had read and all the poems he'd memorized, he had no words of his own for her. He blinked. What he had, he realized, was discipline and the patience with which he had filled the years of his own wordless longings.

He wanted to touch the air Bui breathed, wanted to take away everything that had been done to her. Yet these were not words that would serve his purpose. The words he must use should be simple and to the point. He had one sheet of paper on which to write—the other he would include with the letter alongside a self-addressed stamped envelope to facilitate her quick reply. There would be time enough to speak of these things later, after she was free of that place.

He wrote:

Dear Sally,

I got out of the Marine Corps and came back to Fort Sill to take you and Aná away from this place. Aná wants to see you. Come back to the camp in a hurry.

Your brother, Corporal Frank Kidd

It wasn't much of a letter. But it would have to do. He folded the sheet of paper, slipped it into the envelope, and crossed the lobby to the postman, who set aside a fresh batch of letters he was sorting.

"Anything else?"

"Do you have a directory? I need an address."

"You're mailing that to somebody in Lawton?"

"Yes, sir."

"You could as easily have paid a visit and saved yourself a dime, son." The postman grinned, reached under the counter, brought out a slim brown volume, and slid it across.

Chaco nodded his thanks and thumbed through it, located McDonnell's Saloon, walked back to the writing table, and wrote: "Miss Sally Liluy, c/o McDonnell's Saloon," and under that carefully wrote the street address and "Lawton." He reread her name and hesitated as it occurred to him that Bui might have taken up some other name. In Cuba he had known whores with different kinds of noms de guerre: Lulu, Cherry, Paris, Salomé, and even one who called herself Desdemona, like in the play. But Sally Liluy was all he had; it would have to do. He stamped the extra envelope, wrote his name, and below that wrote, "General Delivery, Lawton, Oklahoma." He folded the envelope and extra sheet of paper and slipped them in with his letter, sealed the envelope, and affixed the stamp. He crossed to the postman's window, slid the directory and letter across the counter.

"When will this be delivered?"

The postman glanced at the address. "Tomorrow. You didn't write in a return address, in case they refuse delivery." He placed a pencil on the counter.

Chaco wrote, "Frank Kidd, General Delivery, Lawton" in the upper left-hand corner and slid the letter and pencil back.

"If they refuse delivery, you can pick this up day after tomorrow."

"Why would they refuse to take delivery?"

The postman's eyes softened. "It's a hard world, son."

20

In the days that followed, as he waited for Bui's answering letter or her return home, Chaco busied himself gathering firewood for the old people. He spaded their gardens, sharpened or repaired their worn tools. He built a forge and refurbished the iron tires of their rickety buggy wheels. He replaced a splintered board in the bed of a light wagon. He reshod the few horses the People were allowed. And in the evening he sat with his mother and listened to the stories of her life and the stories she knew of Lozen, the mother who had died giving him birth. Aná told him of the lasting friendship between Lozen and her, told him of the men Lozen had killed in battle, and of her grasp of the mysteries that guide men to their ruin.

The days slipped away as he waited for Bui's letter, but no letter came. Nor did she. He had hoped she would at least write. Every few days he would tell Aná he had something he needed to do in town. Each time she would simply nod and smile. She was leaving it up to him to do what must be done.

He would take the buggy and drive it into town. The mounted patrols were accustomed to seeing him now and ignored him. In town he would park outside the post office, go in and ask whether a letter had come for him. But no letter came. And then, toward the end of the second week, an artillery officer named Captain Alexander Banyan—the officer Hal Phillips of the *Kansas City Star* had mentioned—rode out to the camp from Main Post. He found Chaco laying up a rock rubble wall along one side of the root cellar he'd dug behind his mother's shack.

"Corporal Frank Kidd?"

Chaco looked up at the captain, wiped sweat from his face with a bandana. "I used to be."

The captain, a supercilious expression on his face, shifted his gaze from the freshly painted shack to the garden with its well-turned rows; he looked at the fire pit Chaco had dug and at the considerable collection of rocks he'd gathered for other projects, and finally looked at Chaco. "You're wasting time and money, Corporal. Unless I miss my guess, this camp will be vacated within a year or two."

"So I've heard." Chaco placed another stone, troweled away the excess mortar that squeezed out around its edges, and tossed it onto the mortarboard. He looked around as he came up out of the pit, and knew the captain was right. Every improvement he'd made here was pointless. And yet the work had satisfied a need in him he couldn't wholly explain. Even to himself. Why would anyone else understand? "It's something to do," he said.

The captain shrugged dismissively. "It's your money. I'm here on orders of division command. You're to receive the Navy and Marine Corps Spanish Campaign Medal one week from Saturday. You're to attend in full dress summers. You must report to the main post quadrangle no later than oh nine hundred hours."

"I thought the Corps would mail the citation."

"There will be a parade. You are under orders to be there. Field-grade officers will be in attendance. I'm instructed to ask if you require transport."

Chaco looked into the captain's hard eyes. Another Indian hater. He had never been able to understand how the Indah, who, having defeated his people, still hated them so. But maybe it was best that way. At least there could be no misunderstanding between them. "I'll get there on my own, sir. If I am to do this, my mother will be with me."

The captain frowned disapprovingly but finally said, "I suppose that'll be acceptable."

21

The following day Chaco borrowed the best of the three buckboards and drove Aná into Lawton. He located a ladies' apparel and bought her a blue dress with white ribbons, undergarments that included a corset, a pair of white silk stocking, and to go with the stockings a pair of low-heeled high-button shoes. He also bought her a pair of white gloves, and a lady's hat. He preferred Aná in her own clothes, but the glow in her eyes told him that the new dress pleased her.

"I never had anything this nice before."

"After they give me the medal, *you can wear this dress all the time if you want."*

"Oh no," she whispered. *"This is the dress I will wear when I go to the other side."*

On the day of the ceremony, he borrowed the buckboard again. He wore his best dress summers, and when Aná came out of the cabin in her new dress, she was smiling.

"You are as pretty as a flower."

She hadn't worn the corset but was so terribly thin it hardly mattered. He helped her into the buggy, walked around and climbed up beside her, and drove toward main post. The sky was clear—a perfect day for the ceremony. He knew this day was not about him, but about a belief system. He had wanted to learn war, and he had learned war; he'd learned that, at its heart, war was more about power and wealth than freedom or justice. And more than that, he had learned that men loved war more than peace. And yet with Aná seated erect beside him as they clipped along, her face bright with pride, he was glad he'd decided to take the medal. This day pleased her, and that pleased him.

They were met by a sergeant in dress uniform, who led them across the green to a podium draped in flags and bunting. The sergeant went up the steps ahead of them and guided them across the podium to a brace of chairs that had been reserved.

As soon as they were seated, the post band struck up a tune.

Aná looked around, her chin held high.

Soldiers in tight formation marched up one side of the quadrangle, passed in review, unit by unit, and marched away along the opposite side of the quad. Finally all the units formed up facing the podium and stood marching in place until the command to halt passed down the ranks. There was a whispered rumble of boots. Guidons fluttered and snapped in the abrupt silence.

A colonel rose from his seat, walked to the lectern, and shouted, "Parade rest," and again a whisper of boots drifted up from the ranks. The colonel summoned a Marine Corps major forward. They saluted, and the colonel handed the proceedings over to the major and returned to his seat. The major placed a document on the lectern and read from it. "Attention to orders: Corporal Frank Kidd will step forward now to be recognized."

Aná stiffened as Chaco stood; he rested a hand on her shoulder and smiled. The major frowned as he quickstepped forward, snapped to attention and saluted, and was saluted in return. He was left at attention while the major read the citation. The major's voice carried out across ranks of soldiers, flags fluttering and popping in the hands of the company guidons. The citation was a brilliantly crafted piece of fiction, and when the major finished reading it he affixed the decoration to Chaco's tunic and shook his hand. They saluted then, and the colonel came forward, and the three of them stood shoulder to shoulder between a set of flags that fluttered in the morning wind as the battalions came to attention, drums rolled, and the post band struck up a martial tune. The battalions broke up by company, and the companies maneuvered and marched past the podium one after the other, the sergeants shouting "Eyes right," as they passed in review. And when the last company had marched past, the major shook Chaco's hand again and then the colonel shook his hand, and the ceremony was over.

There was a reception afterward at the officers' mess that Chaco was required to attend. Lace tablecloths, finger sandwiches on silver trays, cake served on gold-leaf china, lemonade dipped from cut-glass punch bowls. Chaco stood beside Aná in the reception line beside the colonel and his wife. He shook the hands of the arriving officers and noncoms and their respective wives. When Captain Banyan arrived, he was all smiles as he shook hands with the post commander and the major. And he smiled as he took Chaco's hand and introduced his wife.

"Melissa, my dear, allow me to introduce Corporal Frank Kidd, the reason for today's festivities."

"Corporal." She extended a gloved hand.

Chaco gripped it briefly. "Ma'am." She smiled, batted her eyes, and moved ahead.

There was wine and lobster fresh from the gulf, and dancing through the afternoon. Chaco stood beside his mother the entire time. Of course they had to stay to the last. The sun had set by the time Chaco lifted Aná into the buckboard and started for the camp. She rode in silence for a time but finally looked up at him.

"*What did it all mean?*"

22

Over the unseasonably warm week that followed, he drove into Lawton to check the mail three times. The postman would dutifully check and recheck, but no letter from Bui arrived, nor was his letter to her returned. He wrote her another, more urgent letter. Another week passed and still no response.

"*They withhold them from her,*" Aná said, staring into the fire one evening.

Even knowing this, his mother appeared to be happy. In the mornings she woke smiling her toothless smile. She would ask whether he wanted sugar in his coffee, and he would say, "No, little mother, black with no cream." She knew he drank his coffee black, but it pleased her to ask, now that she had sugar and cream to spare.

Her withered cheeks blossomed like a rose in autumn.

But now that she had seen his face, now that she had told him the stories she had sworn to tell, now that he knew who he was, and now that he was here again with her after all the absent years, "Now," she said, one night as they sat up late, staring into the pulsing embers of a dying fire, "everything is good."

Her gaze rose from the glowing coals, and he felt her words like cold wind in the stillness.

They sat up night after night, his mother retelling the stories of her life, of her own days before the People lost the long war. She told Chaco of her own father's life and of her mother's life, and of the happy times and of the sad. She told him of another son born of her flesh, killed by the Indah. She told him the creation stories of the People. And in the telling of all this, he recognized the depth of his aloneness before this time. She would touch his cheek and tell him her heart was glad. And when she did this, his heart, too, was glad. She seemed more like a grandmother to him now than the mother he remembered.

One evening, as they sat together, she fell into a long silence.

Finally Chaco asked, "*What is it, little mother?*"

Aná looked at him, the fire reflected in her flint-black eyes. "*You should take Goyaałé home. Your father's spirit is not happy here.*"

He studied the shape of her in the dark, the outline of her features against the lighter darkness of the painted wall behind her. "*I will take the bones of my father with us when I take you and Bui back to our own country.*"

She shook her head. "*The earth here knows me. It would miss me if I took the long rest in that other country. But you should take Goyaałé back. He never belonged here. He belonged to the mountains.*"

She stared into the fire again. And he waited, sensing she had something more to say. After a time she sighed and looked up at the stars. "*It was good in the time before, back when we were free.*"

23

Befor first light, Chaco rose. He looked down at Aná, her still form faced away from him, asleep on her side. He laced his boots, buttoned his shirt, and left her there. He built up the fire and boiled some coffee. Poured some into the two bean cans they used for coffee cups, added sugar and condensed cream to hers, the way she liked it, and, with a can in each hand, he went back into the cabin and knelt by her pallet to wake her.

Only then did he realize that she wasn't breathing.

He set the cans of coffee on the floor. Gently rolled her toward him, touched her throat, and felt no hint of pulse; her body still warm, not yet stiffened. He chaffed her hands. Placed his mouth over hers and blew breath into her several times. Nothing. He tried again. Nothing. He had seen a lot of death. Too many dead. She was gone. He drew a long denying breath. Her eyelids half-closed above an unfocused stare. All eternity in that stare as he placed a gentle hand against her cheek. In death reposed she looked younger than in life. His gaze swept the tiny room, her enforced world. The sun, peering through the window casement, brushing her withered brown cheeks with the rose light at dawn as he sat beside her on the floor. For a long time he held her fragile old hand, a hand that had seemed so strong in that time before they took him away, now tiny and shriveled in death. The world, of a sudden, felt empty. Sorrow and wordless longings, silent questions without answer.

He lost touch with time, and the day warmed. And when he looked out the window again, the sun lay in the west. The day had slipped away as quietly as her irreplaceable life.

He retrieved Aná's blue dress, unbuttoned the back, slipped her arms into the sleeves, tucked the skirt around her night clothes as he wrapped her in one of the new flannel sheets, and, finally, wrapped her again in a new blanket.

But they knew. They stood waiting outside.

Olivia Yanozha came to him, touched his face.

"*She is with Usen now, beyond the sun.*"

He carried Aná out to the buggy, and with Olivia Yanozha and four others he drove the buggy under the pale moon out to the Apache Prisoner-of-War Cemetery.

Tall grass grew under the willows that shaded the plot of ground. Over the years many of the People had been buried here; their graves unmarked in this place of the Indah's choosing, where dead enemies could be buried and forgotten. He did not want to bury Aná here, but this was where she wanted to be.

He carried her body from the buggy.

Olivia Yanozha walked ahead. "*Over here, this way.*" She stopped and stamped her foot. "*This is where she told me.*"

He placed her body gently on the grass, went back to the buckboard, and retrieved the pick and shovel. The ground was soft and in short order he had a grave dug to shoulder depth. He set the shovel and pick aside and nodded to Olivia Yanozha. She and one of the other women lifted Aná's body and placed her in his arms. He lowered her into the grave, stretched her out, adjusted the folds of the blanket, and then straightened and looked up at the women. They had brought things to be buried with Aná. Things they believed would travel with her spirit to the land beyond the sun. They stoically passed the items to Chaco: a new sewing awl with a ball of twine; a good steel cook pot with a wooden spoon; a hatchet, a knife, an emery stone, flint and steel for making fire—no one believed that the matches of the Indah would work on the other side. They passed him other things meant to comfort her in the other world, and when he had arranged them around her and over her, he came up out of the grave. He stared at her tiny form for a long time. And finally took up the shovel and buried her.

When he finished, he looked around. He wanted to remember this place.

Moonlight winked off the water of a narrow, meandering creek that flowed inaudibly a short distance from the grave. The grave was located under a tree that would shade her from the sun in the hot days of summer.

Do the spirits of the dead linger? he wondered.

From where he stood he could see Goyaałé's grave in the moonlight—fresh dirt mounded above the father he had always thought of as an honored uncle. He remembered the day his father had walked with him out to the waiting motorcars. "*You look like her,*" Goyaałé had said.

Lozen. He meant Lozen. Of course he knew. He should have told me.

In his mind he heard his mother's final instruction: "*You should take Goyaałé home.*"

Did she know that would be the final thing she'd ask of me?

He looked up at the moon and felt a chill.

Olivia Yanozha began to sing. The others took up the song, a death chant to Usen mixed in with thanks to Jesus, the good son of God.

Chaco left them singing and went to his father's grave. For a time he looked at the leaf-littered mound, his mother's words echoing in memory: "*You should take Goyaałé home . . .*"

His lips tightened against his teeth. He thought about Bui, about what he must do next, and then the echo of words again: "*It was good before, back in that time when we were free.*"

He looked up at the moon.

"*You should take Goyaałé home.*"

He could no longer live as he had lived.

"*It was good before, back in that time when we were free.*"

He saw it clearly now in this place of death: living among the Indah could not be done.

"*You should take Goyaałé home.*"

He had come to that point he'd seen in others: that point at which life and death cease to matter.

The women had stopped singing and now waited for him. Olivia Yanozha came forward and stood beside him.

"*Let's go back. I will fix you something to eat.*"

Chaco blinked, and he was back again. He looked at her.

"*I will take Goyaałé back to his own country.*"

"*Good,*" Olivia Yanozha said. "*You are his good son, and she would want you to do this thing that he cannot do for himself.*"

The old women gathered around Goyaałé's grave and under the waning moon sang a war song that was old before the rocks were hard.

24

In the morning he borrowed the buckboard and drove into Lawton. He went to the post office and wrote Bui a final letter, told her that Aná had died and that he'd buried her, and urged her to come back to the camp. There was more gesture than purpose in the act. He did not expect a reply, but no matter. He would not idle away the time.

He walked out of the post office and drove the buckboard out of Lawton, followed the rails westward across the seemingly flat prairie toward the featureless horizon, the tall winter grass yellow where it swayed in the sun and softly brown beneath the shade of the drifting clouds. That night he camped beside a trickle of water in Devil's Canyon, and the following morning he started back.

A few miles before he came to Lawton, there was a crossroad that cut north across the tracks. He swung the buckboard over the tracks and angled northeast, away from the road through the tall grass into the military reserve. Before sundown he was back at the camp.

He returned the buckboard to its owner. Then walked across the camp to Aná's cabin and had a fire started in the pit and was peeling potatoes when Olivia Yanozha came over with a bowl of chili and beans and several pieces of flatbread.

Chaco accepted the food and thanked her, said, "*There's a lot of food and other stuff here. I think you'd better take it all. It'll just go bad.*"

Olivia Yanozha sat quietly on the other side of the fire and watched while he ate. After a time she cleared her throat.

He looked up from his bowl.

"*When will you go?*" she asked.

"*Soon.*"

She nodded and stood up. "*For what they did to us, do it to them . . . only better.*"

25

On the morning of the third day after Aná's death, he drove the buckboard into Lawton and purchased some of the gear he would need. That evening he carried four tins of gasoline, a shovel, and several other items out to the Apache cemetery and cached them. He spent the next two evenings watching the saloon and McDonnell's mercantile. On the fifth night, as Olivia Yanozha stood beside him under the winking moon beside Aná's garden, he pressed a roll of money into her gnarled hand.

She looked at the money and tried to give it back. "*You will need this.*"

"*I have more.*"

"*What will you do?*"

"*Take her back.*" He could see his breath in the icy moonlight. A cold front had swept out of the northwest that morning. Ice skim was forming in the water bucket.

"*They will not give her up,*" she said.

"*I know.*"

Olivia Yanozha nodded.

"*Goodbye, little mother.*"

The pony whiffled softly at his approach. He stroked its nose, blew his breath into its nostrils. He hunkered down and checked the gunnysacks he'd wrapped about the pony's feet. Night birds called, but they were only birds. A dog barked, but it didn't worry him. Goyaałé was dead, and the soldiers no longer watched from the low towers around the camp.

He moved away at the double time, the pony close behind on lead. An hour's jog brought him to the shallow ford below the main post quadrangle. He crossed the creek and moved up through the cottonwoods, past the walking sentries. From previous observation he knew the soldiers were most vulnerable to deception here. Living as they did in garrison, they had grown careless. He moved, a shadow within shadows, and soon was beyond the last of the barracks. The pony followed on silenced feet. It whiffled softly when he lifted a foot into the stirrup and mounted. Beyond this point there was no return. By this time tomorrow he and Bui would be dead or free. And with that thought he rode ahead into the dark and away from all his yesterdays.

26

W alking the pony between the stone pillars that marked the boundary of the military reserve, Chaco swung west and followed the rails to a point beyond the last lights of Lawton. He rode across the tracks and reined up beside one of the shorter telegraph poles, stationed at regular intervals along the railroad right-of-way. Dismounted and snubbed the pony to the pole, remounted, and stood on its saddle. He pulled Aná's hatchet from his belt and chopped at the telegraph wire. Parted it on his second swing. The wire pinged and shot away into the dark. He looked around, tossed the hatchet into some brush beyond the right-of-way. Dropped to the ground, untied the pony, stepped into the leather again, and rode back toward town.

The chill air smelled of burning oak, and in the moonlight smoke rose from the chimneys of the houses as he rode past, the smoke swept away on the wind. Ahead was the business district. The icy wind whistled and he turned up his collar against it as McDonnell's Saloon came in sight. A commotion in the street up ahead, a fistfight: two soldiers in the freezing mud outside the

Cock and Bull, both of them swinging and ducking one another's punches with the drunken adroitness of vaudeville performers. Other soldiers formed a circle about the two, laughing and shouting encouragements. Chaco rode past the combatants, and ahead rode past McDonnell's saloon and store. Light from the streetlamp in front of the store intermixed with light that spilled through the windows of the saloon. But there was no visible light from the store. At the intersecting street he swung right and midway down the block swung right again and rode into the alley.

He reined to a halt behind the mercantile and stepped down as scudding clouds raced under the winking moon. The air was sharp, and he was certain the temperature was still falling. The curtains over the second-story windows of the saloon were all drawn. It bothered him to know that Bui might be in one of those rooms. He clenched his teeth, drew a slow breath, and refocused on the business that had brought him here.

He studied the window of the room where McDonnell and his wife slept. The faint flicker of what might be a night candle glowed beyond its frilled white curtains. McDonnell would be up there, hopefully alone and hopefully asleep. From the saloon came the sound of breaking glass and the startled laughter of a woman.

That's not her. She never laughed like that.

He thumbed open the blade of his clasp knife and ran his free hand down the pony's leg. One at a time he lifted its feet, cut the bindings, and tossed the frayed gunnysacks away. He removed the makeshift halter, hung it over the saddle horn, and slapped the animal on its rump. It went away at a trot and would hopefully find its way back to the camp.

He went up the back steps and tugged on the screen door. It was latched. He cut the screen close to the frame, slid a hand through, and freed the latch. The hinges squeaked softly as he pulled the door open. He closed the knife and dropped it into the side pocket of his field jacket. Pulled the Eveready he'd purchased at the drugstore from his other pocket and switched it on. Its narrow beam passed through the door glass and lit the connecting door. The door stood ajar. He heard muffled noises from inside and switched off the electric torch and stood listening for several moments. Whatever it was, the sound was not repeated.

A snowflake drifted between him and the door. He looked up into ghostly swirls of snow falling out of the darkening sky. The moon disappeared as a flake touched his face and melted. It was late in the season for snow; this was an unexpected thing. For a moment he considered postponing, but he'd already snipped the telegraph wires and cut the door screen, and the pony was gone. He was committed.

What was it the gunny used to say? Nut up or shut up?

From his coat he drew a roll of adhesive tape, purchased the same day he bought the Eveready and the tins of gasoline, and peeled off a strip. He smoothed the tape against the pane of glass that was closest to the door lock. Peeled off another and applied it adjacent to the first, and kept stripping off tape and applying it until the square of glass was entirely covered. He used the heel of the Eveready to strike the taped glass a sharp blow: a muffled shatter. He pushed the shards inward, reached through, ran the deadbolt, and the door groaned softly inward. He stepped through, relatched the screen, closed and locked the door, and removed the last telltale shard from the mullion. He waited for his eyes to adjust to the deeper dark. The office smelled of mold and old paper. Muffled saloon noises penetrated the walls. He could make out the shapes of things well enough now, and he skirted the small desk and stepped through the office door into the rear area of the store.

The aisles and shelves were better lit than he'd expected. Light from a streetlamp out front spilled through the display windows, casting misshapen shadows against the store's back wall. He leaned against his palms on the glass surface of the rear counter, his breath making fog in the chill air and, in a reflected wedge of light, studied the revolvers and semiautomatics arrayed on the top shelf under the glass—but first things first.

His listened for a moment—the noise from the saloon was louder here—then left the counter and made his way up the center aisle to the front entrance. Outside, the slowly falling snow slanted through the electric halo of the streetlamp. An icy dust of white had formed across the boardwalk and on the saddles of the horses standing hipshot at the hitch. Snow was beginning to collect in the street. He lowered the door blinds and the blinds above the display windows and retraced his steps up the aisle to the display case.

The light was far dimmer now. But with the blinds down, it was less likely a passerby would notice the goings on inside. He stepped around the display case and went to the rifle rack. It was locked, as he'd expected. He went to the cabinet and reached behind, and his fingers closed around a ring of keys hung from a peg. It surprised him, finding them there. Evidently McDonnell wasn't as cautious as he'd assumed. But the keys saved him a bit of hacksaw work.

He went back to the rack. The third key he tried turned, and the padlock snapped open. He swung the iron bar aside and lifted a twelve-gauge Winchester Model '97 "Takedown" from the rack, passed the tips of his fingers over the outer machined parts of the action to verify integrity, then placed the weapon on the glass countertop. He went back to the rack and took down the heavy Sharps .50. He hefted the big-bore rifle and reluctantly replaced it in the rack. He needed a rifle, but there were several others more suitable to his purpose. There was a Winchester

Model '95 lever-action thirty-caliber and also a Winchester Model 1907 self-loader that fired a .351 smokeless cartridge— those two just for beginners. The self-loader was certainly a fast shooter, but replacement ammo might be difficult to come by in the territories. In the end he settled on a '93 Marlin .30-30 lever action, took it from the rack, and placed it beside the shotgun.

Ammunition was next on the list. He hunkered down in front of the ammo shelf, flicked on the Eveready, and read the labels. Then pulled a box of twelve-gauge slugs from the shelf, set the box on the floor, and stacked two boxes of double-aught and a box of number fours on top. He added five boxes of .30-30s to the stack and, almost as an afterthought, pulled a fifty-round box of forty-fives from the shelf; he picked up all the boxes then and carried them to the display case and lined them up on top.

He located the key that opened the display case, slid the flat panel aside, reached in, and by feel located the U.S. Army .45 Colt single action—the revolver the soldier had sold McDonnell the day Chaco first came to the store. The pistol was an officer's model and almost certainly was stolen. The fact that its black grips had been replaced with something lighter in color, possibly bone or ivory, all but validated his suspicion. There were several modern pistols in the display glass case: a nine-millimeter Luger, a new-model Colt .38 semiautomatic, and a couple of others. But he was familiar with the army model and could shoot a consistent five-inch group at fifty yards with this particular handgun.

He opened the loading gate, drew the hammer to quarter cock, rolled the cylinder around, and dropped the long, heavy cartridges into the chambers one after another before tucking the pistol under his belt near his spine and taking up the shotgun. He opened a box of double-aughts and thumbed six shells into the tube, jacked one into the chamber, lowered the hammer to quarter cock, and was shoving another into the tube when he heard a noise he recognized. The rhythmic squeak-bang, squeak-bang of bedsprings. The sound came from the head of the stairs. McDonnell's bedroom was located up there. It wouldn't be his wife up there with him. Yesterday he'd watched as McDonnell walked his wife to the station, watched as he'd kissed her indifferent cheek before she stepped aboard an eastbound for Kansas City. That was the moment he decided tonight would be the night. Of course it was possible McDonnell was suffering some kind of fit, but it was odds on there was a woman up there with him now other than his wife.

He gripped the shotgun pistol-fashion and laid it across his shoulder, tipped back his campaign hat, and remembered the drunken artilleryman, what he'd said about McDonnell's wife and the man's untouchable whores. Apparently his covey of soiled doves was not so untouchable after all. Chaco made his way to the foot of the stairs, stared up at the dimly lit writing desk. It stood against the handrail, where it was supposed to be, half-lit by a vertical strip of light to the right—light that flickered from behind a partially open door. No movement on the landing. No sound up there other than the rhythmic complaint of bedsprings.

He climbed the stairs, testing each tread before rising to the next. Near the top he stared across the waxed floorboards. Heard muffled voices drift out from the room. He mounted the last few steps. Eased toward the door and heard a woman's deep-throated moan. He touched the door with the muzzle of the shotgun; it swung silently inward, and he stepped through.

On the bed a naked woman rose and settled on top of the thrusting body of a man. The man he'd come for. The light from the open grate of the potbelly stove flickered against the fluid ivory of their bodies as Chaco moved farther into the room. A floorboard groaned, but neither of them noticed, and he edged along the wall, in no hurry now. The woman's face came into profile, a strand of firelit hair undone and her features drawn and intense, but even so he recognized her—remembered her beautiful face from their brief encounter in the greeting line on the day he was given the medal: the calmly elegant Melissa Banyan, Captain Banyan's wife.

McDonnell grabbed her hips, muttered, "That's it," and Melissa Banyan leaned forward and their mouths came together.

Chaco shook off his momentary surprise, turned the shotgun, and stepped toward the bed. Melissa Banyan saw him, and her eyes widened, but before she could scream he thumped her behind the ear with the butt of the gun. Not too hard, though; he didn't want to kill her.

She sighed and rolled away, and McDonnell muttered, "What the . . ." and the next moment he was looking into the business end of the shotgun. The dullness in his eyes resolved into fear. "Sweet Jesus, don't shoot." His hands came up to his face, palms outward.

Chaco stepped back. "I need you to be quiet, understand? Don't talk."

McDonnell nodded, his eyes flicking from Chaco to the shotgun and back again. The man was no coward, but neither was he stupid, and Chaco gave him a moment to compose himself. There was no need to humiliate him, and he wanted McDonnell to get his mind around what he needed to do to get through this situation alive.

"You need to be very careful. You understand? You don't have to get shot over this. Keep your hands where I can see them at all times. Don't move unless I tell you to move. And when I tell you to move, you better move slow. You do what I say when I say, and you won't get shot. You don't want any of this." He tilted the barrel of the shotgun up a little, to make his meaning clear. "But remember: I will shoot you if I have to."

McDonnell nodded.

"Good. Then we understand each other. Right now everything depends on how smart you are. I don't see you as a foolish man. Don't prove me wrong. Now, carefully get off the bed."

Chaco backed off yet another step as McDonnell sat up and swung his legs over the side. Light from the open grate played across the puckered hieroglyphs of old bullet wounds and crudely stitched knife scars—records, written in his flesh, of this man's life before he became a merchant and a whoremaster. McDonnell stood up naked, his neck and forearms as dark as the rest of him was white: hard muscles under old skin, large work-seared hands at the end of strong wrists, a man to step aside for even now, despite his gray hair.

"I'd like to pull on my pants, if that's okay?"

"We'll get to that. First I want you to rip that bedsheet into strips four inches wide."

"Why?"

"You don't get to ask. You get to do what I tell you when I tell you."

Reaching, McDonnell pulled the sheet from the bed, started a rip with his teeth, and tore off a strip. The naked Melissa Banyan lay on her side, turned away from them. The sound of the ripping sheet mixed with the crackling of the fire in the stove. McDonnell worked slowly, careful in his movements, alert and watchful for any mistake on Chaco's part. He finished with the sheet and looked at Chaco.

"If it's okay with you, I'd like to cover her."

"Use those strips to tie her wrists behind her."

McDonnell drew an angry breath. He grabbed one of the strips off the bed and pulled Melissa Banyan's wrists behind her and quickly bound them, then straightened and faced Chaco. "Can I cover her now?"

"Now bind her ankles and her knees together."

"It ain't right you looking at her nakedness."

"Do what I tell you."

Resentment burned in his eyes as he reached for another strip of bedsheet, shifted his weight, and abruptly lunged for the shotgun. Chaco sidestepped, brought the weapon around, and came down with the stock across McDonnell's extended neck and send him sprawling. He stepped back and waited, and after a few moments McDonnell groaned and rolled onto his back. The move had been well calculated, a good trick that might have worked but hadn't.

"That was foolish. I might have hit you the wrong way and accidently killed you. You don't want to get yourself killed for no reason, okay?"

McDonnell rolled up onto his knees. Shook his head. "Whoa. Jesus."

Chaco gave him a little more time, raised and lowered the shotgun's hammer to let him hear the clicks. "Crawl back to the bed. You can pull yourself up."

McDonnell wiped the back of his hand across his lips, and then on hands and knees he moved to the bed, took hold of the bedpost, and pulled himself up. He swayed a little, looking at Chaco as he massaged the back of his neck. Then reluctantly he finished tying up the woman.

"Now tie a strip around her mouth."

McDonnell frowned but did as he was told. Chaco backed him away and then checked the knots. He stepped back.

"Now you can cover her."

McDonnell pulled the bunched quilt from the foot of the bed up over the naked Mrs. Banyan and tucked in the quilt's edges with surprising care. He then straightened and looked at Chaco. "What next?"

"Where are your trousers?"

"On the floor at the foot of the bed."

"Move over to that wall and face it."

A pulsing oak coal slumped audibly on the grate as McDonnell skirted the stove and stood, face to the wall, beside a framed portrait of his wife. The painter had captured his wife's accusing eyes, and Chaco wondered if she'd always been angry, or if marriage to this naked man had hardened her. He hooked the man's trousers with the muzzle of the shotgun and dropped them on the bed. Patted down the pockets and removed a folding knife, which he slipped into his own pocket before stepping back.

"You can turn around now."

McDonnell turned.

"Put your trousers on." He gestured toward the foot of the bed with the shotgun, and McDonnell crossed to the bed, grabbed his trousers, and stabbed his legs into them one after the other.

"What about my shirt?"

"Pick it up." Chaco watched as he retrieved the shirt and pulled it on.

"Can I sit down to put on my socks and boots?"

"No footgear. I don't want you to get too comfortable yet. Let's go downstairs." He gestured toward the door, and without being told McDonnell elevated his hands and led the way. As they went out onto the landing, Chaco pulled the Eveready from his pocket and switched it on. He kept the beam centered on McDonnell's back as they descended the stairs. So far everything had gone according to plan, except for the woman upstairs and the snow. But unexpected factors always popped up during military operations, and he'd planned this the same way he would have planned a combat mission. The snow was still a factor; but as far as the captain's wife went, she no longer factored into the equation.

At the foot of the landing, McDonnell turned and squinted into the flashlight.

"What now?"

"Walk ahead of me to the telephone. And be careful."

"I'm not stupid."

"If you want to prove it, stop acting stupid."

McDonnell walked gingerly across the cold floor ahead of him. They passed the glass case with the Winchester on top beside the boxes of ammo, and McDonnell, seeing the rifle, hesitated.

"It's not loaded," Chaco said, to save him the trouble.

McDonnell looked past the display case at the open gun rack against the wall. "I see you've been shopping." He came around and faced Chaco accusingly.

"Over there." Chaco gestured toward the wall-mounted telephone and followed him over.

He shined the Eveready's beam on a paraffin lamp located near the phone and then lit up a whiskey glass full of matches located on the barrelhead beside it.

"Light it up."

McDonnell plucked a match from the glass, raised the chimney, struck the match against the wall, and lit the wick. He adjusted the flame, and as he lowered the chimney, yellow light pushed back the darkness. McDonnell shook the match out, turned, and looked at Chaco, and as he did so his eyes filled with recognition. "You," he muttered with the first hint of fear.

"Good, you remember me. Then we can get straight to it."

McDonnell swallowed. "Straight to what?"

"You're going to try to play games here?"

"Okay, okay, look, Kidd, if you're here about those letters—"

"Not the letters. We're past that, friend—"

"Wait, whoa. Listen, it weren't . . . It wasn't me. It was Cecil —he's the one that held 'em back. He's—"

"Cecil? Who is this Cecil?"

"His name's Collins. Cecil Collins. He manages the saloon." McDonnell's gaze flicked nervously between the shotgun and Chaco's face. He fidgeted. "What's it going to take to make this right?"

"What do you think it's going to take?"

"Your sister. Okay, this is about your sister, right? So listen, we can do a deal. I can—"

"Where are the letters?"

McDonnell swallowed, shook his head. "I don't have them. Cecil might. He's the one that read them."

"You read them, too. No games, okay?"

"Look, Kidd, it's not like that. This can be fixed."

"Yes. I am here to fix it. You've got one way to come out of this. What you're going to do now is ring up the saloon. You're going to get this Cecil Collins on the telephone, no one else. You're going to tell him to bring Sally Liluy over here—"

"Sally who?"

"Whatever name it is she is using, you know who she is. You tell this Collins to bring her over here. Say the right words to get him here with my sister. If he doesn't bring her, I'm going to hurt you like you've never been hurt before, and after that I go there and I kill everybody. You tell him to bring her here—him, and no one else. Look at me. Good. Now listen. Any tricks—if this Collins brings anybody else, if he causes any trouble—I shoot you first; I shoot him next. After that I burn down this place with you in it. Do you understand?"

McDonnell swallowed audibly and nodded. "I believe you."

"Good. I know you are a man of courage. Just so you know, I didn't come here to do the things I told you, but I will if I have to. This is about your business, not about courage. Don't confuse the two. Think about the money. Do you want to risk your life and everything you have for one woman?" Chaco shrugged. "It's up to you."

"I'll make the telephone call." McDonnell's tongue passed over his lower lip.

"Good. How many bags of salt do you have?"

The question elicited a startled expression. McDonnell blinked. "Salt?"

The question had thrown him, as Chaco intended. A bead of sweat, glistening on McDonnell's forehead, broke free and furrowed down the hard contours of his face. His shallow breath was visible in the chill, lamplit air. "Yes, salt. How much of it do you have on hand?"

"Maybe five or six fifty-pound bags, I'm not sure."

"That will do. You'd better ring up the saloon now."

"You want me to have him bring the letters along?"

Chaco suppressed a smile, said, "No," and for the first time questioned whether this man was as smart as he'd assumed.

"So you just want the girl?"

"That's right."

Reaching, McDonnell lifted the receiver off the hook and cranked the ringer—two long cranks and one short. Then held the black bell-shaped device to his ear. A muffled voice answered on the other end, and McDonnell leaned close to the mouthpiece. "It's me. Put Cecil on." He stared at Chaco until a garbled voice finally came through the receiver again. McDonnell stiffened and leaned toward the mouthpiece. "Cecil, it's me. I need you to bring Lulu over here. No, not later, bring her over right now . . . I don't give two shits who she's with. Get her away from him and get her over here . . . Well, get him somebody else, then. Anybody else, give him the best we got, three at once if that's what it takes, but get her ass over here right now. And I want you to bring her over here, you hear me . . . That's right. You. And get yourself over here right quick . . . Well, throw a blanket around her. Jesus. It ain't snowing that bad . . . No, no problem. I'll explain later. I got something going on is all." He listened. "No, I want you to bring her by yourself, not nobody else, by Gawd. And be quick about it . . . No, everything's okay, Cecil. Hurry it up. I'll be waiting."

McDonnell hung the receiver on the cradle and looked at Chaco. "How was that?"

"Which way will he bring her, front or back?"

"It's snowing. He'll come by the front way."

"You better unlock the front door, then, huh?" Chaco tossed him the keys.

McDonnell caught them, frowned in the direction of the filing cabinet, then walked ahead of him to the front entrance. He sorted out the right key and inserted it into the lock, turned it, and the deadbolt slid back with an audible click. He opened the door an inch. Snow flurried through before he shoved it closed.

"What now?"

"Move away from the door a little."

McDonnell took a step back.

"More than that," Chaco said, and backed him up the aisle about twenty feet, and then positioned himself near the entrance. McDonnell had raised his hands again. This time Chaco did smile. "Lower your hands."

McDonnell lowered them with a shrug, allowed his hands to hang at his sides.

"What now?"

"We wait."

He would have to allow McDonnell to put on some boots soon. His own feet were numb from the cold. The man continually lifted one foot and then the other as they waited.

"My feet are freezing."

"Don't talk."

Maybe he wanted to say more, but he held his tongue, and they waited. Ten minutes extended into fifteen minutes before the shadow of two figures interrupted the light from the streetlamp. "Get along with you," a gruff voice said, and a moment later a fist hammered against the entrance doors.

With a jerk of chin, Chaco signaled for McDonnell to answer.

"It's open," McDonnell called. "Come in."

The door swung inward.

"What in hell's going on, Boss?"

A paw-like hand shoved a woman, stooped and blanket wrapped, through the opening into the aisle. Swirls of snowflakes followed, and Chaco glimpsed bare legs, sandaled feet. A man followed close behind—six and a half feet tall, massive in an old buffalo robe coat. "This better be good," he said, turning to close the door. His eyes went wide as the shotgun butt hammered him in the face. Bone shattered. He staggered back a step, went down like a felled tree. Rolled over and came up on hands and knees. Chaco stepped in, drove the shotgun against the base of his skull, and he slumped to the floor as McDonnell muttered, "Jesus wept," and backed away. He froze as Chaco leveled the shotgun on him.

"Remember what I said about doing stupid things."

McDonnell's hands went up again. "You killed him."

"No, but he'll wish it when he wakes up." He turned to the blanket-wrapped woman, gripped her chin, and elevated her face, switched on the Eveready. It was Bui, his sister Sally, although the years had not been kind. Gone was the sparkle he remembered. She squinted dull-eyed at him, a hand raised against the Eveready's beam. Her exposed arm was blackened with needle tracks, and for a long moment Chaco clamped down on a killing rage. He swung the Eveready's beam toward McDonnell, said, "Turn around," his voice raw with emotion.

"I done everything you told me, didn't I?"

"Show me your back."

Reluctantly McDonnell turned away. "Take it easy, okay?"

The bell above the door rang as Chaco closed it and ran the bolt. Bui stood beside Collins, staring down at him, the man on his belly snoring. Chaco placed a hand on her shoulder and brought her around to face him.

"*Sister, it's me, your brother. I have come to take you away from this place.*" She blinked up at him, searched his face, but he saw no hint of recognition. "*It is time for us to leave.*"

"*My brother is dead,*" she said, her voice a harsh whisper.

"*As you see, I am alive. We will talk of this and other things when there is time, but at this moment I need you to be strong.*"

She blinked up into his face, confused, disbelieving.

"*There is much that must be done, and we must travel far.*" There was, he knew, no time for further explanations. He faced McDonnell, whose back was still to him, and said, "Lower your hands and look at me."

He lowered them and came around, his gaze locking on Collins, sprawled on the floor.

"Walk ahead of me to the back of the store."

McDonnell nodded and limped on cold feet ahead of him up the aisle as Chaco gave Bui a gentle nudge to get her started. The way she was, he assumed she was drugged. In Cuba he had seen whores in this condition, seated like blind beggars outside the blanket-covered doorways to their hovels, alive in no meaningful sense of that term. For the present he must think for them both. This thing was never going to be easy, but it had just gotten harder.

They came to the gun case. "Stop here."

Bui stepped into the yellow glow of lamplight. She looked at him, leaned closer.

"*Truly, it is you?*"

The blanket slipped from her shoulders. Under it she wore a partially buttoned bodice and a cotton skirt. One of her breasts was exposed, and she covered it as she stepped back and leaned against the gun case, with a hand raised to her mouth. "*They said that you and Mother were . . .*"

"*I see your face,*" he said.

She looked down at herself and tried to cover her face. "*Don't look at me.*"

"*I have come to take you away,*" he said.

"*They said you were killed in the whiteeye's war—*"

"*Listen to me. We can talk later. For now we must get away from here. Be strong.*"

"*But—*"

"*You will need better clothes. It is cold. Dress warm.*"

Again she looked down at herself, but this time to button her blouse. "*What kind?*"

"*Men's* jeans—*they are over there—and the* flannel *shirts are over there.*" He pointed. "*Take a heavy coat, even if it is too big, and put on wool socks, more than one on each foot, and find low-heel boots like the walking soldiers. Find some that fit your feet.*"

She nodded and moved off.

He looked at McDonnell, said, "Lower your hands," and when McDonnell's hands came down to his sides, he nodded. "Good. Now about that salt—let's see exactly how much you have. I'll need that heavy canvas tent over there, the brown one, and that spool of five-eighths manila. How many feet on a spool?"

McDonnell blinked. "About five hundred, I think."

"That'll do."

"What you aiming to do to me?"

"Right now I'm robbing you. Let's take a look at your motorcar."

"You're taking my Locomobile?" McDonnell flushed, but then he said, "Sure, okay."

Chaco grinned, the look on McDonnell's face telling him that the man thought he'd finally caught a break. That he was in fact dealing with just another dumbass Indian about to steal his car. Come morning he'd have the sheriff follow their tire tracks through the snow, arrest him, and cart him off to prison. "Walk ahead of me. Let's take a look-see at that motorcar."

The beam of the Eveready jiggled against McDonnell's back as they crossed to the doorway. The air inside the carriage room reeked of gasoline and burned oil. McDonnell switched on an electric light device. They were on a landing. A set of steps went down to a dirt floor, where the motorcar sat facing the carriage doors. It was black and highly polished, a 1904 Type C Locomobile, almost identical to one Chaco had seen in Cuba—the motorcar that Lieutenant Capshaw had the use of during their convalescence at Guantánamo, a car the lieutenant claimed was capable of an incredible sixty miles per hour. That speed had been achieved under ideal conditions: at sea level on a stretch of sandy shore somewhere in England. The radiator and the acetylene headlamps, the horn, the steering column, and the hand levers were made of highly polished brass. Affixed to the motorcar's rear mudguards were two heavy wicker baskets whose wicker lids were held shut by buckled leather straps. Access to the back seat was through a rear door that once closed became part of the back seat. All the seats were black tuck-and-roll leather. The wheels were of the wooden-spoke gun-carriage type and mounted with Goodyear tires. Adjacent to the passenger seat was an exposed drive chain that looped back to the rear axle in a way that lent the car the appearance of power and speed.

"How much gasoline in the tank?" Chaco said.

"I keep it full."

They went back into the store, and Chaco walked behind

McDonnell as the man carried the bags of salt out to the car and placed them in the rear footwell. The tent went in next and the spool of rope after that. As they came back into the store, Chaco saw Bui seated on a keg of nails she'd overturned near the gun case. She was wearing a checkered shirt and jeans and thick socks and was pulling on a pair of low-heeled boots. She noticed Chaco as she stood up and stamped her feet into the boots.

"*What can I do to help?*" she asked.

"*Can you load a rifle?*"

"*Yes.*"

"*Load that one.*" He gestured toward the lever action on the glass case. "*And find something to carry those boxes of bullets in.*"

Chaco dumped apples out of a shipping crate and tossed the wooden box to McDonnell. "Sit on that," he said, and watched McDonnell place the box long-end-up on the floor and sit. He tossed him a pair of woolen socks off the shelf, said, "Put those on," and read the relief on McDonnell's face as he pulled the socks on, one after the other. Chaco then ordered him to take up the apple box and had him back along the aisle ahead of him as he dropped in canned goods plucked off the shelves: peaches, beans, roast beef, spinach, and other foodstuffs. They carried four crate loads out to the car. On one pass Chaco picked a twenty-power, marine-type expandable telescope off a shelf, which he slipped into his coat pocket, and on another pass a ten-inch set of improved combination fence pliers went into the other side pocket.

Meanwhile Bui had used a sheath knife to cut a length of harness leather, with which she'd fashioned a sling for the Marlin, and was now stuffing the boxes of ammo he'd stacked on the counter into a set of leather piñon.

"You're cleaning me out pretty good," McDonnell said.

"Keep the crate level, and keep backing up. We're not done yet."

"You load much more in that car, you'll get her stuck in the snow."

Bui slung the saddlebags over her shoulder and came toward them with a coffeepot and several one-pound bags of Arbuckles' Ariosa coffee and a coffee-bean grinder. She looked at McDonnell as she dropped the items into the crate, pulled the saddlebags off her shoulder, and set them on top. There was a look like defiance in her smoky eyes.

The ammo-stuffed saddlebags made a load, and Chaco followed McDonnell out to the motorcar, the man limping on cold feet despite the wool socks. For the time being he wanted McDonnell a little uncomfortable. It gave the man something to worry about besides the sort of mischief that might get him killed, but this next part would be tricky. Every man had his limits, or what he believed were his limits, and he was about to test McDonnell's.

When they got back from the garage, Bui was placing a case filled with dusty green pre-1903 bottles of Coca-Cola on top of the gun case.

"That's no good for you," he said.

"*I know*," she said. Then in English, added, "I filled my pockets with laudanum, too."

"Did they do this to you, or did you do it to yourself?"

She shrugged and gestured toward the aisle where Cecil Collins lay sprawled on the floor. "*He did it to me at first. Later I did it to myself.*"

He let that part of it go, another question for another time. What mattered for the present was that she do all she could do now. The next few days would be hard on her. There was just enough coca in those bottles to increase energy, like chewing the leaves, and that might make all the difference. He refocused on McDonnell, who now balanced on one foot with the other hooked over his knee while he massaged it through a dirty sock.

"Sister, I want you to load anything else you want in the car, and then wait for me there."

"*If you are going to kill this one, I want to watch.*"

"*I did not come to kill,*" he said, reverting to their own language.

He read disappointment in her eyes as she glanced at McDonnell.

"How about a few bottles of whiskey," McDonnell said, "to go along with that Coca-Cola?" Saying it in a way that he meant to be taken for a joke.

Up to that point Chaco hadn't thought about whiskey. But it might be just what he needed. "That's a good idea," he said, and read a flicker of hope in McDonnell's eyes.

"I keep a stock of it in the storage room."

He waited until Bui disappeared through the carriage-room door, staggering under the weight of the case of Coca-Cola. Then gestured toward the storage room. "Let's get that whiskey."

When they came to the blanket that hung in front of the doorjamb, he told McDonnell to yank it down.

"Why?"

"Just do it."

The last thing he needed was more foolishness—allow McDonnell to push through the blanket, then spin around and have another try at him. One corner of the blanket ripped audibly as it came away. McDonnell reached through and switched on the electric light. Then he walked to the shelves where he kept the whiskey. There were several brands in unopened crates.

"Got any preferences?"

Chaco shrugged. "The stronger the better."

McDonnell took down a crate of Old Corn and turned with it for Chaco's approval. "You might as well take the whole case," he said. "Gawd, my feet are cold. If it's okay with you, what do ya say we pull a cork?"

"Sure," Chaco said, then gestured with the shotgun. "Right after you open that safe."

"What safe?" The tip of McDonnell's tongue passed across his lips.

A blanket hung in front of the vault, concealing the safe's door from view, but the safe's side could be seen through the storage shelf it sat adjacent to. Chaco said, "The poorly hidden one over there in the corner."

"Oh, that one," he said. "I forgot. There's nothing in there but some of my wife's papers. I can't even open it. It's her safe. She's the one who keeps up with the combination."

"For your life, I hope that is not true," Chaco said, and gave McDonnell a moment to consider the implication. The man was an ex–buffalo hunter from the old days and would remember stories about men tied upside down by Kiowas to wagon wheels with their heads above slow fires. Staring at him, McDonnell kept raising one foot and then the other, his breath visible as puffs of fog in the raw electric light of the single bulb. Too cheap to keep his place of business heated after work hours, and too cheap or too stupid to adequately hide the safe Chaco would not have noticed had it been better concealed. There was fear in McDonnell's watchful eyes, and there was avarice. Chaco clicked the hammer of the shotgun back a notch. "We'll start with your feet. Warm them up for you. Put the whiskey down. I don't want you to drop it."

"Don't shoot." McDonnell bent over and placed the case of Old Corn on the floor. "Okay, I'll open it for you."

"I knew you were smart," he said, and gestured with the shotgun.

He followed McDonnell to the vault at the far end of the storage room. McDonnell pulled the blanket aside. The safe was a big Vulcan on iron casters. McDonnell lowered himself onto one knee, worked the combination, turned the handle, and the locking lugs thudded as they withdrew. He came to his feet and pulled the heavy door outward and reached inside the safe.

"Stop," Chaco said, and thumbed the hammer on the shotgun back another click.

McDonnell froze. Then slowly turned his head toward Chaco. "What?"

"Bring that hand out slow and empty."

There were calculations going on in McDonnell's eyes, a man weighing his chances.

"Even if you beat me, this thing goes off. You'd better think about it."

There was anger in him. He wanted to try it, but finally he withdrew his hand empty from the safe.

"Get up and turn around. I want you to lean on your hands against those shelves." Chaco gestured with the shotgun and stepped back.

McDonnell got to his feet, placed his hands against the shelves.

"Move your feet farther back, and spread your legs apart a little more."

McDonnell complied.

"You look straight at that shelf, and don't move until I say different."

"Kidd, I think you got this shit worked down to an art. You and me, we could do business. It's something to think about . . ."

"Don't talk, either."

Chaco hunkered down and shone the Eveready into the safe. He reached in and retrieved a small revolver out of a cubbyhole—a nickel-plated .32 Bradley and Wesson. He dropped the small piece into the side pocket of his field jacket and rifled the contents of the safe. The vault was indeed filled with documents, but there was also a small metal lockbox.

He carried the box to a fifty-gallon barrel of molasses and placed it on top. Opened his clasp knife and popped the lock, then raised the lid. Inside he found several banded packets of new-looking paper money: five packets of twenties, two packets of tens, one packet of fifty-dollar notes, and three packets of crisp one-hundred-dollar bills. He'd never actually seen a hundred-dollar bill before, but they looked real enough.

He looked at McDonnell, and asked, "Why here and not in the bank?" as he tucked the packets into his field jacket.

"I don't trust banks."

"We'll call this partial compensation for what you did to my sister."

"Compensation? I like that. You mean stealing."

"Pick up that whiskey, and carry it out to the automobile. Move it."

McDonnell pushed away from the storage shelves, glanced at the open safe and the empty lockbox. He moved toward the door, and Chaco followed him out of the storage room. When they came to the boot display, Chaco told him to stop, then reached up and pulled a pair of size-twelves off the shelf.

"Set the whiskey on the floor."

McDonnell put the case down, and as he straightened Chaco tossed him the boots.

"Pull those on."

The boots were too big for him, but that was okay, too. McDonnell stamped his feet a couple of times and looked at him.

"Pick up the whiskey and keep going."

Bui was leaning against the glass display case, wiping the blade of her new knife on a bath towel. The reflective look on her face faded, and she dropped the towel as they approached and slid the knife into its sheath.

Chaco said, "Hold it a minute," studied the bloody towel, and looked down the aisle, saw Cecil Collins, a great lump on the floor near the entrance doors, with blood spreading blackly over the waxed boards. He looked into his sister's dark eyes. This had never been part of the plan. He was not morally opposed to this outcome, but killing made for complications he'd hoped to avoid. But it was done now.

"Here," he said, and gave her the Bradley and Wesson. "Keep this in your pocket. You're going to need it."

Bui climbed into the back seat and began rearranging and stacking. McDonnell heaved the case of whiskey up to her, but as he did she edged away from him, eyes feral as a barnyard cat. McDonnell set the case on top, adjusted it, and pulled out one of the bottles. He broke the seal, pulled the cork, and extended it toward Chaco.

"You want the cherry off this?"

"Go ahead. I don't drink."

A look of puzzlement passed shadowlike across the man's face.

"But I want you to take a drink," Chaco said, and watched as McDonnell pulled on the bottle, lowered it, and after a moment took another long pull. He grimaced and recorked the bottle and replaced it in the case.

"Anything else you want?"

"Crank the motor."

"This machine is a little tougher to start than you might think, chief. You have to fiddle with the spark and set the throttle. You'd best let me do it."

"I drove a car like this in Cuba. You turn the drip knob on the acetylene generator before you crank it."

"An educated Injun." McDonnell scowled. He activated the acetylene generator located on the left side of the car and stepped around to the front, opened the hinged glass of the lamps, struck a match, and lit the headlamps. Closed and fastened the glass windshields, then bent over and gripped the crank handle as light from the lamps painted his shadow against the doors behind him.

"Ready," he called.

Chaco adjusted the levers. "Give her a turn."

McDonnell yanked up on the crank handle as Bui stepped over the front seat and settled in next to Chaco. The engine sputtered and Chaco worked the levers, adjusted the spark, but it died.

"Give her another crank."

McDonnell reengaged the handle, gave the engine another hard pull. It caught, bucked with a tin-pot clatter, and ran. Chaco adjusted the idle until the motor smoothed out. Then took up the shotgun and stood on the driver's seat. "Open the doors. Push them back far enough to drive out."

McDonnell removed the plank crossbar and, one at a time, shoved the doors outward. There was a buildup of snow he had to push against, and flakes drifted into the carriage room like cotton lint, alighted on the warming hood, and melted. But the snow collecting on McDonnell's hair didn't melt, not right away.

Chaco gestured with the shotgun as he stepped over the driver's seat and stood atop the load, said, "Come here," and watched as McDonnell came around and stood beside the car, shivering. He grabbed one of the blankets they'd taken and tossed it to him. "Wrap that around your shoulders."

The man shook it out and wrapped it around himself.

"Get in behind the wheel. You're driving."

"Hold on there, chief. I ain't going nowhere with you."

"I didn't kill the woman, but if I kill you then I have to kill her. You understand?"

McDonnell chewed at his lower lip a moment. "The smart thing would be to tie me up, like you did her. Right now it's just robbery. They won't do much to you for that when they catch you—and they will catch you. But you take me hostage they'll hang you for sure. You were a marine. You know how it works."

"Yes. I know." Chaco studied him a moment. McDonnell had either failed to notice the bloody towel and Collins, or was playing dumb. "What you have to ask yourself is: am I going to be there to watch this Injun hang?"

For a worried moment McDonnell looked up at him, more fear in his eyes than hatred. His underlying confidence was shaken, this man who had bullied, bribed, and reasoned his way through a lifetime of difficulties. "Think about it like this," Chaco said. "Without you driving this thing, if somebody sees us going away in it they're going to say, 'What're them damned red niggers doing driving Mr. McDonnell's motorcar?'"

McDonnell's gaze flicked to the shotgun, then settled on him again, and he shrugged.

"Good," Chaco said. "You see how things are. Let's get." He drew the Colt and sat down and rested the shotgun across his knees. "When you drive out, turn to the right."

Bui was twisted around in her seat, looking up at him, her eyes luminous in the electric light as McDonnell settled in behind the wheel. The motor accelerated, he engaged the transmission, and they rolled out into the snow-altered alleyway. The car swung to the right, and Chaco glanced up at the saloon, the honky-tonk clink of the out-of-tune piano muffled by the falling snow as they rolled by.

"Turn right when you come to the street. And remember, don't do anything stupid."

"I don't plan on it."

The car's back tires fishtailed as he swung into the street.

"At the next corner you turn left."

"*Where will we go?*" Bui asked.

"*To a better place,*" he said.

"*What about Mother?*"

This was the question he'd come prepared to answer, but that had been before he saw her. Maybe she was strong enough to take it, but then maybe not, and he needed her strong.

"*We will be with her soon enough,*" he said.

"Listen, chief," McDonnell said. "I'm just a man trying to make my way in the world, the same as any other. I meant no hurt to you or yours. For Gawd's sake, I'm on the city council."

"Don't talk."

"What I'm saying is I'm a civic leader, a leading citizen. You cain't take me hostage."

Someone behind them called out, and Chaco turned. A soldier was standing on the boardwalk outside a saloon, pissing into the horse trough and shouting up into the night. "Hey, it's snowing. Hey, boys, come on out for a look-see—it's snowing."

Chaco faced forward, and snow swirled in the headlights. The edge of town was just ahead, and the snow-covered road ran away into the dark. "You'd better make this motorcar go faster."

28

McDonnell adjusted the throttle, and the engine pulled harder. They followed a construction road that ran parallel to the tracks, moving west out of Lawton. A few miles beyond the town, they came to the solitary oak Chaco was looking for. Snowfall had covered the intersecting road, but the tree marked the turn.

"Slow down. Turn right before you get to that tree up ahead."

The headlights swept a yellow arc across the snowy field, and the luminous eyes of nocturnal animals were reflected back at them. They went under the telegraph wires and up and over the tracks. The headlamps marked the double depression in the snow that was the wagon road, but Chaco gestured with the Colt in a northeasterly direction. "Go that way."

"Ain't that the road straight ahead?"

"It is but we go that way." He pointed again. "This car can make it."

They left the road and rolled away across an open, snow-covered pasture, the Goodyear tires crunching through the crust of half-frozen snow, the engine running well and true. He directed McDonnell by memory rather than by the stars. At one point they crossed a grassy, bread-loaf ridge he remembered, and beyond the ridge was a tree-dotted swale. There were more trees on the military reserve than in the surrounding country, and he supposed that had to do with the reserve being spared the settlers' ax.

The snow stopped falling. And soon after, the sky began to lighten and the first gray brushstroke of day painted the snow-dusted peaks of the Wichitas. He judged by the relative position to the peaks that they were north of the Apache camp, and then he saw the road and realized how close they were to the cemetery.

"That's a road up ahead. When you come to it, you turn left and stay on it."

They angled down a slope and rolled up onto the road. The ride smoothed out. Heat from the engine blew back over them, mixed with the bitter cold. Ahead the road curved gently off to the right. Chaco saw the grove of willows he was looking for.

"Those trees over there," he said, pointing. "That's where we're going."

McDonnell swung the car and rolled off the road and through the grass and in among the willows.

"Stop here," Chaco said, and McDonnell braked to a halt.

Bui, who had dozed off, sat up and looked around.

"*Where are we?*"

"Kill the engine."

McDonnell turned the switch, the engine sputtered and died, and, in the ringing silence, Bui gripped the windshield and stood up, erect and tense.

McDonnell looked around. "This is a graveyard," he muttered. "Sweet Jesus, why a graveyard?"

"Sister, I want you to close the valve to the headlamps."

She climbed out of the car, studied the valve a moment, then turned its stem a few times, and the headlamps faded. The engine ticked as it cooled. Chaco jumped to the ground, tucked the Colt away, and, with shotgun in hand, ordered McDonnell out of the car.

"Did you bring me all the way out here to kill me?"

"I brought you here to dig up a grave."

"You mean to dig myself one? Because you'll have to do that work yourself."

"No, to dig up someone who didn't want to be buried here."

McDonnell studied Chaco a long moment. "The dead don't care where they're buried."

"How would you know?"

29

C haco might have had difficulty locating the shovel under the blanket of snow had it not been for the tins of gasoline, his seabag, and the other things they would carry. He knocked the snow from the shovel and tossed it to McDonnell.

"You planned this pretty good, I see."

"You've got some digging to do."

"Whose grave am I digging up, if you don't mind me asking?"

"I mind," Chaco said, and moved McDonnell ahead.

There was a wooden marker at the head of Goyaałé's grave, a plank with the whiteeye's name "Geronimo" carved deep into its weathered surface.

"You're digging up Geronimo? Are you crazy?"

"Get to work."

McDonnell shook his head. The ground was frozen, but the blade of the shovel cut through the crusty surface readily enough, and McDonnell made steady progress, sinking the shovel with his booted foot and laying up the dirt. It had gotten light enough now they could see, and soon the odor of death began to taint the chill air.

"Jesus. You sure you want to do this?"

"Keep digging."

Bui, standing a few feet away from the grave, wrinkled her nose and backed away.

McDonnell leaned out of the grave and gagged. "Jesus, man, I can't—"

"You're almost there. Keep at it."

He spaded out several more shovelfuls before the point of the shovel thumped with a hollow sound. Chaco moved around to the foot of the grave. "Clean the lid off."

It took as much time for McDonnell to scrape the last of the dirt off the coffin as it had to dig down to it. He shoveled out a place to stand adjacent to the coffin. Stepped off the lid onto the standing place and began to probe with the shovel along the coffin's rough-plank edges. He located a purchase and worked the blade of the shovel in under the edge, then pried down. Nails groaned, the lid came up, and the trapped gases inside rose into the cold morning. McDonnell gagged, turned, and leaned against the soil he'd mounded beside the grave.

Chaco reckoned he was putting on an act. After all, he'd hunted buffalo. But he allowed him a moment, just in case. Then said: "Push that lid all the way back."

McDonnell passed the sleeve of his shirt across his mouth. Bent down and gripped the lid with his big hands and wrestled it all the way over.

An unexpected knot formed in Chaco's throat as he moved to the foot of the grave and looked at what was left of his father. The worms had done their work: the flesh of his face was gone; only patches of shriveled skin and a coil of hair yet clung to his skull. The skull rested in the moldered remains of a feathered headdress Chaco had never seen. His father's bones protruded through his rotted shirt and a ceremonial vest of bones and beads. The vest was something else Chaco had never seen. A saddle and bridle had been buried with him, and there were other death gifts.

He gestured with the shotgun. "Lift that saddle and the other stuff out, and set it aside."

McDonnell held his breath and, as quickly as he could, removed the saddle and bridle. He straightened and scooped a handful of dirt and used it to scrub his palms, then slapped them against his trousers to knock off the dirt. He scowled up at Chaco. "What now?"

"Come out of the hole."

McDonnell climbed out of the grave, got to his feet, and stretched his back as he looked around, about to try something stupid with the shovel trailing in his hand.

"Drop the shovel."

He looked at Chaco, all innocence. "What?"

"Just let it fall."

The tool slipped from his grip.

"Walk over to the motorcar," he said, jerked his chin to get him moving. Then glanced in Bui's direction. "*You need to move back a little, sister.*"

Even in her condition she'd seen it, the fake behavior of this bad actor. She backed out of the way as McDonnell moved past her and limped up to the Locomobile and stopped.

"Everything in the back seat comes out except the canned goods."

"Why?" McDonnell asked.

"Just do it."

The job didn't take long. Standing in the back seat, McDonnell tossed things out like a petulant child, but soon enough the last bag of salt flew out of the footwell and landed in the snow beside the tent. McDonnell was panting a little, and sweating despite the cold, a palpable anger and fear in his eyes. "What now?"

"Get out of the car, and carry the tent over there. Spread it out beside the grave."

The tent unfolded readily enough into a rectangle of double-stitched canvas panels.

"Stand over there." Chaco indicated where he wanted him.

McDonnell backed away, and when he was far enough, Chaco said, "That's good," and took two quick steps out to the center of the canvas. He stood with his feet close together, and, taking small, side-by-side steps, he walked out a shoulder-width-by-body-length depression, flattening the snow under the canvas. He then retraced his steps off the canvas, walked away from McDonnell, and leaned the shotgun, butt-down, against a willow. Then drew the Colt and slid it into his pants pocket for quicker access, and looked at McDonnell. Now came the tricky part.

"Back to the grave," he said, and walked toward it. McDonnell followed. Chaco pointed to the head of the grave, said, "Stand at that end," and took the position at the opposite end. "We're going to step down together and, if we can, lift him out in one piece. When I tell you to lift, take hold of his shirt at the shoulders. I'll grab his trousers. We'll lift together when I say and set him out on this side of the grave, okay?"

McDonnell nodded he understood.

"We get him out, we step out of the grave together, and then carry him over there and place him in the depression I walked into the canvas. Understand?"

"What happens then?"

"Then you refill the grave, and we're done. You get to walk back to Lawton."

McDonnell's frown deepened, his eyes dark with disbelief.

"Okay, both together now, let's step down. And don't be foolish. You're close to the end. You're going to get out of this okay, understand?"

McDonnell nodded. "Let's get it over with."

They stepped down into the grave from opposite ends, and McDonnell lunged, cat-quick, an uncoiling of sinew and muscle. He grabbed Chaco's gun hand in a viselike grip, his other hand clawing for the pistol in Chaco's pocket as he leaned his greater weight against Chaco, wedging him against the side of the grave. Chaco twisted to one side, wanting to keep the pistol out of reach, but McDonnell was too strong. Then a sharp crack, a pistol, and Chaco looked up into McDonnell's hard eyes and watched as they blanked out. He looked past McDonnell and saw Bui. She stood beside the grave, smoke curling from the muzzle of the nickel-plated pistol he'd given her. He shoved McDonnell off him and looked down. They'd trampled his father's body, had broken several of his bones. McDonnell, still alive, had recovered some; he ripped open his shirt and stared at the blood-weeping hole in his chest. Fatally wounded and aware of it, he blinked in disbelief as he looked up at Bui.

"I would have let you go. I wanted to kill you, but it was never part of the plan."

McDonnell opened his mouth as if to speak—no words came. Chaco climbed out of the grave. He took the pistol from Bui's limp hand, lowered the hammer, and gave it back. He went back to McDonnell and hunkered down, his forearms on his knees, hands hanging loosely. "Lean back and take it easy. It won't take long."

McDonnell blinked and swallowed and looked up at him. "I'm a rich man." There was blood in his mouth. "This ain't supposed to happen."

"All the buffalo you killed, all the whiskey you used to make my people foolish, all the women you whored to make money— these things are what brought you to this. If not my sister, then some other woman or man would have done this. This is the end you were moving toward from the beginning."

McDonnell looked at him, the disbelief gone and in its place the sneer Chaco remembered. "I hate a preachy killer," McDonnell said, coughed, and for several moments struggled for breath. And then was still—whatever had been alive in him uncoupled in a heartbeat from everything he was or would ever be.

Bui tilted her head as she stared down at the slumped body.

"I killed him," she said, in English.

"No, he killed himself. I told him I would let him go. He didn't believe me."

"*I cut the throat of the other one,*" she said, voice scarcely above a whisper.

"Yes, I saw. I think maybe he did, too." He jerked his chin toward McDonnell.

"*He said he loved me . . . The other one. And I believed him.*"

He studied McDonnell, slumped bare-chested at the opposite end of the grave; in death his eyes as clear and guiltless as an infant's. Maybe that's how it is, he thought. Maybe it is in death we retrieve the innocence taken from us in life. He turned back to Bui. "I'll need your help now to do this."

"*It is better this way. He would have come after us.*"

"They'll all come after us now."

30

On a shift in the wind, he heard the faint reverberations, from the direction of main post, of reveille being blown. The duty detail would be raising the flag on the quadrangle. This business at the grave had taken too long. It was time to move.

With his sister's help he dragged McDonnell out of the grave. He told her to wait there and went back to the motorcar, shouldered a sack of salt, and carried it back to the depression he'd walked into the canvas. He dumped the contents into it. Then returned to Bui at the grave, stepped down, and slid his arms under the rotted garments of his father's skeletal remains. He lifted him out, amazed when the bones hung together. Then stepped out of the grave, took up the body again, and walked toward the salt-lined depression. A forearm slipped from one of the rotting leather sleeves, and a moment later the skull plopped softly onto the snow. He kept going, hoping to get the bulk of his father into the depression. He managed it, and once he'd arranged his father's bones properly, he hurried back to retrieve the arm and skull. He placed them with the body, stepped away, and joined Bui. For a long moment they stared at the remains.

Worms squirmed through the rancid holes in his father's clothes and from the sockets of his once-fierce eyes.

"*We should clean his bones and take them apart,*" Bui said. "*It will make him easier to carry.*" She gestured toward the automobile. "*That thing will not last.*"

"Do it," he said, switching out of long habit to English. He walked over to the crate of Old Corn, lifted it, and relocated it on the canvas. Pulled out the bottle McDonnell had drank from, discarded the cork, and poured the contents carefully over the body, opened another bottle, and continued pouring. Worms began to writhe out of the desiccated remains, and by the time the last bottle gurgled empty, the odor of death had mostly dissipated. In its place a kind of morning-after-payday cantina reek hung in the chill air as he opened another bag of salt and emptied the contents into the brownish slurry.

"*Let the salt and whiskey work while we reload the* car," he said.

"*Where will we take him?*"

He looked west. "*Back to his own country.*"

"*Do you know where that country is?*"

"*The Gila River or the Sierra Madre; I will know the place when I see it.*"

Bui pursed her lips. "*I was too young to remember, but Mother will know.*"

"It was she who told me to do this thing."

"*Good. Do we go back to the camp? Or does she wait for us somewhere?*"

He looked at her, a yes on the edge of his tongue. She does wait for us somewhere, he thought. "She told me she would not leave this place. She said that the earth here knows her name. That it would miss her if she went away."

In his last letter to her, he'd told her of their mother's death, but of course the saloon men had withheld his letters. Although Bui had this night killed the two men, she seemed to him like cracked glass, and he feared the blow of their mother's death might shatter her—he needed her to be strong.

"*It was her wish to die and be buried in this place,*" he said, reverting to their tongue.

"*We cannot leave her behind. How will she live?*"

"*How did she live before?*" It was a cruel thing to say, and he saw the shadow of guilt in her eyes. He shook his head. "*No, sister, in this we must obey her.*"

He stared in the direction of Aná's grave and wondered how he would tell his sister when the time came. Would she hate him, as she'd hated Cecil Collins and McDonnell?

"*I must see her,*" Bui said.

"*If we do not go away from this place quickly, we never will.*"

He placed three of the four cached tins of fuel into the back seat; the fourth he poured into the car's tank. There was a little left over, and the can went into the back seat beside the others. He returned to the grave, rolled McDonnell into the coffin, stepped down, and straightened his body. He settled the saddle and the bridle and the other death gifts they'd removed back in the coffin. For several heartbeats he stared down at McDonnell, wondering if his father's death gifts would travel with McDonnell to the other side—if there was another side. He hoped there was. Hoped there was more to life than life itself.

When the time comes, I'll buy my father a better saddle, he thought.

And leaned forward and gripped the coffin lid, ready to close it on the dead merchant, but then hesitated. There was something wrong with McDonnell's mouth. The man's teeth were skewed. A stab of shame went through him. He leaned down and worked a set of false teeth from McDonnell's slack mouth. Studied them for a moment before he angrily tossed them away—aware that the shame he felt was a white emotion. Yet even so, it was deeply felt. They had killed an old man—tough and fit, but an old man nevertheless. He closed the lid, stood on it, and stomped it down. Stepped out of the grave, took up the shovel, and sunk the blade into the half-frozen earth. The first several shovelfuls thumped hollowly against the lid. It took a while to refill the hole. Time enough for the long morning shadows cast by the willows across the snow to have shortened. Mounted patrols would be out by this time. It was past time for them to be gone.

He stuck the shovel in with the rest of the gear. Saw that Bui had stripped the rotted clothes from Goyaałé's bones, had used the whiskey-soaked salt to scrub away the last remnant of decayed flesh, and had walked down another smaller depression in the canvas and arranged Goyaałé's bones in it. Did a man's spirit inhabit his bones? The question nagged at him as he helped Bui cut the canvas to shape and fold the laps over his father's remains. Here was all that was left of the Goyaałé he had known and honored. His question was rhetorical; a man's spirit did not reside in bones, but in the world, in the things he did while he lived. When they had his father's remains neatly encased, he went to the rope spool, cut several ten-yard lengths from it, and used one of them to bind up the canvas bundle with a diamond hitch. When done, he lifted the bundle. Though it looked heavy, it was in fact light enough for Bui to carry, even in her weakened state.

"You did well, sister."

He placed the canvas bundle in the back seat. And together they collected everything and piled it in the car. Nothing could be left behind that might indicate what happened here. He looked around. Only tire tracks in the snow, and a few spots of blood, all of which would vanish once the snow melted. The trees were already dripping coldly from their snow-dusted branches.

"Let's get," he said.

Bui settled into the passenger seat as he adjusted the starting levers. He walked to the front of the car, and on the third vigorous crank the motor caught and ran. He slipped behind the wheel, adjusted the magneto. The engine smoothed out to a purr. He looked over at his sister, the early sun warm against her cheek in the cold, crisp air, and the snow rapidly melting everywhere.

"Let's hope the ground stays frozen long enough for us to get back to the tracks."

Her eyes darkened with concern. "And if it doesn't?"

"Then I'll deal with it." He shouldn't have shared that with her. Not yet. That look in her eyes—he remembered it from when they were children, the look she took on when she knew he was holding back some part of the truth.

31

M ort Pope grumbled under his breath as he climbed the stairs behind Deputy Sheriff Jim Travis, Trav more or less ignoring him. The deputy reached the landing, paused, and looked around, and Pope craned his neck in an effort to see past him.

"What in hell you looking for?" Pope demanded.

"For anything out of place."

"Ain't nothing out of place out here, it's what's in the bedroom that's out of place. That's what you need to be looking at."

"You going to let me do my job, or do you want to do it for me?" Jim Travis had never cared much for the saloon man. For that matter, he'd never cared for any of Boss McDonnell's bullyboys. Pope was a pig-eyed thug, minus a pig's intelligence, and this morning, as usual, his breath smelled like an unwashed spittoon. It was Mort who'd discovered Cecil Collins lying in the coagulated brown paste of his own dried blood, Mort who'd telephoned the jail to report the killing. With Cecil Collins, you couldn't rightly call it murder; at least not in Jim Travis's book. He looked down into the saloon man's whiskey-ravaged face. "The thing is, Mort, it's all the same to me. I'd as soon be back at the jail drinking coffee, if you'd prefer to wait on Ham and have him do this."

"I ain't saying you don't know how to do your job."

"Then leave me be while I do it, understand?"

"I done been in the boss's bedroom before I called you. That's all I'm saying."

Travis crossed the landing, pushed the door inward, stepped into the bedroom, and with slow deliberation ran his gaze over everything in the room. "What did you touch or move in here, Mort? And don't lie to me."

"Nothing important," Mort said, his voice going up an octave.

The barman, who had crossed the landing behind him, was standing just outside the door. Travis focused on the bed: the bedcovers were on the floor, and the cover sheet had been ripped into bandage-width strips for some purpose other than binding a wound—he saw no blood sign. Most of the linen strips lay loosely scattered. He moved farther into the room. The mattress sheet was marked by a series of dried narrow blemishes. Travis recognized them for what they were. He thought about McDonnell's wife and looked at Mort.

"When'd you say Miz McDonnell left for Kansas City?"

"I didn't say, but yesterday afternoon Boss took her to the train. He said something about her going to visit her mother."

"Hmm." There was a rumpled strip of bedsheet on the floor with a knotted loop that retained the semblance of its purpose. He bent down to retrieve it. "Did you touch this?"

Mort Pope shook his head dumbly. "No, I didn't."

"So what you're thinking is, Boss got himself tied up here by them that killed Collins?"

"It's the only thing that makes sense."

"Then he worked himself loose and took out after them in his motorcar—them that robbed him and killed Collins?"

"That's the way I got it figured."

"You say he called over to the saloon around one or two this morning?"

"That's right."

"He asks for Cecil Collins and then told him to bring over a certain Injun whore—"

"Lulu, that's her name."

"And all this took place in the big middle of that snowstorm and nobody asked why?"

"You don't ask Boss about his business if you want to keep a job. Or get into Cecil's business, either one, for that matter. What I figure, whoever it was kilt Cecil, they taken off after they tied the boss up. I figure when he worked himself free, he was hopping mad to get even, so he lit out after them."

"Because he knew who it was that robbed him?"

"Yeah," Mort said.

"And of course the fact he knew them, that's why they didn't slit his throat, too. Did it occur to you even once that maybe he might've been kidnapped, or just decided to light out with that Injun whore?" The baffled expression on Mort's face was all Jim needed to confirm that neither possibility had. "What happened to last night's take?"

"I took it back to the saloon. It's still there." Mort Pope scrubbed the palm of one of his big hands across his mouth. "The way the money usually gets delivered, about eight or nine of a morning, Cecil'd bring over the night's proceeds. But since Cecil never came back last night, I figured I'd better bring the cashbox over. I found the place locked up tight as a drum. The blinds was all lowered, and he never lowers them blinds. Plus he don't ever open much later than six. I knocked on the front door for a while but got no answer. So, like I told you, I went back to the saloon. I tucked the cashbox away and come out the back alleyway. The carriage-house doors was standing wide open, and Boss's motorcar was gone. I looked in through the back-porch winder and that's when I seen the screen was cut and the winder glasses knocked out. So I went in for a look-see, and that's when I found Cecil."

"And then you called me right off?"

"Not right off, no. First I looked around for Mr. McDonnell, in case he was kilt, too."

"Or in case he was the one who killed Cecil?"

"No, I never thought no such thing. But when I seen that he was gone along with his motorcar, and seen the gun rack left unlocked, and the store about half-ransacked, I reckoned it was time to call in the law. I didn't see that the safe had been left open until after I called you. But that's when I figured it a robbery for sure. Why ain't Ham here? After all the support Boss give him in the last election, you'd figure—"

"He'll be here shortly," Travis quipped preemptively. He lifted the knotted strip of bedsheet to his nose; sniffed in a lingering hint of perfume. "What kind of toilet water do you splash your whores with?"

"Lye soap is all they get. What the hell you think? This ain't Dallas."

"So this Lulu, this Injun whore, she wears eau de lye soap, like all the others?"

"Eau de lye?"

"Lye soap."

"I done told you, we don't baby our whores."

"Nor customers, either, as far as that seems," Travis said. "Miz McDonnell, when was it you said she left town to visit her mama?"

"Yesterday, she left on the CRI and P, like I done told you

once. The Boss done seen her off at the station. How many times you goin to ask me that?"

Travis crossed to the small vanity situated against the wall. Lifted the vials of perfume there to his nose, one after the other. None of the fragrances matched the scent on the strip of bedsheet. Interesting, he thought, as he replaced the last vial and turned back to Pope.

"When is Miz McDonnell expected back?"

"I don't know. That would be by way of Boss McDonnell's private business."

"Hmm."

Travis noted a pair of calfskin boots on the floor at the foot of the bed, wadded socks stuffed inside them. He picked them up and saw they were custom made, with McDonnell's name stitched in fancy lettering along the stovepipe tops.

"How many pairs of these does McDonnell have?"

"I didn't notice those," Pope admitted. "Far as I know, them's his only boots."

"There was a woman in this bed last night. Think it could have been the Injun gal?"

"Not likely. Boss hates Injuns, as you well know. And, besides, she belonged to Cecil."

Jim Travis studied on that remark. He had some ideas of his own.

"My question is," Mort persisted, "what'd you aim to do about getting him back?"

As far as Jim Travis was concerned, someone had just done the general public a service, and good riddance to Cecil and Boss McDonnell both. But he couldn't say that. Instead he shouldered past the saloon man and went down the stairs, Mort Pope close behind him all the way down. Travis studied the shelves as he moved down the center aisle past Collins's body, covered now with a brown woolen blanket.

He unlocked the entrance doors and stepped out into the morning. There were people out. Many of them shoveling snow off the walkways. A buggy moved up the street. No sign of the sheriff yet. The freak storm had passed, leaving the sky a cloudless blue. The cold morning air bit his lungs, despite the warming sun. The snow wouldn't last, and that was a problem. They needed to get started, but Sheriff Ham seemed to be taking his own sweet time.

He turned and studied the body through the open doors, thinking about the evidence upstairs, the rifled safe, the ransacked store. The missing Indian whore was part of this puzzle. Whoever had done the killing had taken her. The question was why. Answer that question, he'd probably be able to sort out the 'who' part.

Travis went back inside and made his way to the wall phone. Lifted the bell-shaped receiver off its cradle and cranked the generator handle, held the receiver to his ear, and waited. When Betty, the operator, came on, he leaned close to the transmitter.

"Hey, Betty, it's me, Trav. Listen, hon, you mind putting me through to the sheriff? Yeah, he should be at the office. Try there first."

Pope meandered up and, folding his arms, leaned a shoulder against the wall.

"Sheriff Jones here."

Travis straightened slightly. "Hey, Sheriff, it's Trav." Travis leaned toward the mouthpiece. He knew Betty would be listening in, the old busybody. So he kept it circumspect. "It's a mess over here. Somebody filled out Collins's dance card for him."

"So the son of a bitch finally bought it."

There was a soft click on the line. Betty had disconnected. Travis smiled. Ham had his own way of dealing with her puritanical inquisitiveness. "Yes, sir," Travis said. "He sure did."

"From what I'm hearing, you don't know who this killer is yet?"

"Not yet, sir. There's more to it. Probably we don't want to talk much about it over the telephone. The short of it is, either McDonnell was robbed or he slit his partner's throat and run off with an Injun whore."

"Alton McDonnell do something for love? Not in this life, by Gawd," Ham guffawed.

"There's evidence he or somebody else copulated with a woman in his bed last night."

"Humping some woman other than his wife, you mean?"

"Yeah."

Ham took a moment, then said, "Hang tight. I'll be there as quick as I can."

The line went dead. Travis hung the receiver on the hook, turned, and looked at Pope.

"This Injun whore, what's her real name?"

Mort's face went blank. "I never knew her Injun name. Cecil knew it."

"But Cecil is dead."

"Boss knows it, too. It was the boss who ordered Cecil to bring her over here. Told him to bring her himself and come alone. Cecil said he was pretty clear about it. Hey, now that I think on it, could be somebody had a gun on him, made him say all that stuff. What do you think?"

"I think you're a regular Sherlock Holmes."

"A regular who?"

32

Tendrils of mist rose like chill steam off the melting snow as Chaco and Bui motored off the military reservation. The tracks of the St. Louis and San Francisco spur appeared ahead. He swung back onto the road and into the tracks he'd left going in. The tires rumbled as they rolled across the rail. He glanced east, saw no sign of pursuit, and swung westward, the tires cutting through the irregular patches of rapidly melting snow. Telegraph poles marked the unswerving course of the tracks to the horizon—the line of communication out of Lawton. Though he'd severed that line last night, he had to assume that by now they would have located the break; he must sever the line again, but with greater care. He watched for a place where the snow had yet to melt, and when one appeared he slowed and pulled off the road, eased the car up close to a pole, and stopped.

"*What are you doing?*" Bui asked.

"*Using a little trick I learned from the Cubans.*"

With the engine idling, Chaco stepped up onto the back of the driver's seat and used the fence pliers he'd taken to twist a couple of loops into the wire about a foot apart. Bui got out of the car and stood squinting up at him, eyes shaded by her hands. He smiled down at her. He'd merely cut the telegraph line back in Lawton, and if they hadn't repaired it yet they soon would. This break would take longer to locate. He pulled a length of braided horsehair from his pocket, made for this purpose, and knotted the thin black length of it to each of the two loops. He then cut the wire in between. The telegraph line jerked apart with a humming ping. The loops stretched and flattened. He carefully nipped off the excess wire, and now the telegraph line between Lawton and points west was truly severed. A repair crew would locate this break, but it would be difficult to spot and would take them a day or more to locate. By that time they would be across Texas into the territory of New Mexico. He slipped the wire cutters back into his pocket and dropped into his seat behind the wheel. The world was changing fast: telegraphs, telephones, electric lights, automobiles, and aeroplanes. The new artillery could place a round in a fifty-foot circle two miles downrange. The Indah kept moving ahead faster and faster. And he knew one thing else about them: they could be killed, but not defeated.

"Get in," he said.

Bui scrambled back into her seat. He engaged the engine and continued west.

At Cache Creek he used the railroad trestle for a bridge to get across, the tires bumping against the crossties, and Bui staring down at the trickle of water far below. On the other side he swung off the rails, rolled down the gravel ballast to the road again, and drove on.

Fifty miles out of Lawton, he spied a water tower and stopped the car. He used the spyglass. There were several buildings near the tower, and the water tower itself was equipped with a downspout. The place looked deserted, but with that many buildings there would most certainly be people somewhere near about.

"*What is it?*" Bui asked.

"*A water stop for the iron horse. We'll have to go around.*"

He dropped behind the wheel again, swung left, away from the tracks, and rumbled out across the tall-grass prairie. Only a little snow had fallen in this country, and most of that had already melted. The land looked parched, and the yellowed winter grasses crunched dryly under the car as he drove. A mile out they came to a barbed-wire fence, and he cut through. The grazing cattle in the pasture scattered ahead of the car. He drove another mile before turning west again.

Bui opened a bottle of Coca-Cola and drank. He glanced at her and then looked straight ahead, frowning as he focused on the treeless prairie.

"*I am going to quit this thing,*" she said, "*but not until we get somewhere.*"

He let it alone. She was with him, and that was what mattered. He had gotten her away from McDonnell. As for the rest of it, that would take time. He thought about McDonnell and Collins. It bothered him that she'd killed them. It ended any possibility of a future for them in this country. There would be no place for them among their own people. No corner of an Apache reservation where they might disappear. For a foolish moment back there, after McDonnell opened the big safe and he discovered all that money, he'd imagined that future for them. But then she'd cut the throat of the one called Collins.

The money, he thought, remembering a line from one of the books in Mr. McGregor's personal library, a Bedouin proverb: "Too much water makes slaves of men." The Bedouin lived free in a distant, waterless land. They understood that water, like wealth, bound men to a way of living that in the end made them servants to the leisure of others. He had expected to find money in the safe, a few hundred dollars, but not thousands. Not enough to change everything.

"I've been thinking," he said.

Bui was staring at the rolling prairie ahead, the tall winter grasses slapping at the sides of the motorcar. She turned, looked at him. "Thinking what?" she asked in English.

"I have this money I took from McDonnell."

She cocked her head. "How much money?"

"Enough that we can do something with it."

"Like what?"

"Maybe go down into Mexico, buy some land down there. We wouldn't need much, only enough to live on. What would you think about something like that?"

"I don't speak Spanish."

"You can learn. I did."

"You know Spanish?"

He shrugged. "I picked it up in Cuba."

Her eyes filled with wonder, and she smiled—and he remembered that slightly crooked front tooth.

"Could I have some chickens?"

"Anything you want."

"I'd like a goat for milk. I prefer a goat to a cow. They are better company."

"Yes, of course."

She brightened, and with the prospect of a place of their own to consider she settled more comfortably into her seat. "Will we have a house?"

"Yes, absolutely. I can build you one."

"I will help you." She frowned thoughtfully. Then asked, "What kind of a house?"

"Like the ones they build down there. They use mud bricks, I think, but however they build them, that is the way I will build this house for you."

Bui drew a happy breath. "It must have three rooms," she said. "That way all the windows can let in the air. I would like us to have a water-well close by. You should build this house close to a spring so I won't have to carry the water far."

"We'll make that part of the plan."

"And a garden," she added. "We will need seeds for squash and corn and beans."

"Yes, of course."

The country through which he drove bore the marks of the Indah civilization. They rumbled across a few plowed fields, maneuvered around weathered tree stumps that marked the dusty course of dried-up stream beds, avoided the masses of transitory tumbleweed banked against the occasional east-west-running barbed-wire fence. He avoided the homesteads they came within sight of, their rooftops rising out of the seemingly level prairie. Smoke from the chimneys of other houses marked their locations in the distance. The Locomobile rumbled across an overgrazed pasture, and he braked to a stop at the barbed-wire fence. He got out and cut through, drove on, and, a short distance beyond the fence, crossed over a juniper-dotted rise and ahead saw a north-south-running set of tracks.

He slowed the car and eased it, with a couple of bounces, over the rails. Once on the other side, he stopped and set the hand brake. Engine idling, he climbed out, placed the Colt on the driver's seat, and walked an adequate distance from the car.

"*What are you doing?*" Bui called.

He held up a pocket compass. "This," he answered, lowered the device and read its quivering needle. It confirmed what he knew: the tracks ran north and south. A man might lose his way, but his compass never. Either the rails out of Lawton had swung abruptly south a short distance beyond the water station, or this was another set of tracks, entire.

He walked back to the car, stepped on the running board and up onto the driver's seat, and, from that elevation, glassed the country behind them.

"*Do you see them?*"

"No, but they're back there."

"*How do you know?*"

"I don't, but they're coming."

They drove on.

Over the next several miles, they crossed a number of wet-weather creeks. Piñon trees that were more like brush than trees rose along their dry and crooked courses. The land had taken on a downward tilt. He stopped the car on a rise and again brought the spyglass to his eye. He studied the country ahead, saw a series of piñon-choked gullies miles apart, all of them meandering southward. He lowered the glass and reckoned the last of long-grass country was behind them. This would be the short-grass country his mother had told him of.

He drove westward down the descending land and by chance happened upon an old game trail. The trail led to an ancient ford, and, crossing its sandstone bottom, the tires left clear prints in the powdery dust. He shifted to a lower gear, and as the car began to climb Bui stabbed a finger in the direction of a rock shelf.

"Look."

He saw the sun-bleached buffalo skull affixed to the barkless trunk of a long-dead tree.

The engine whined as the car climbed. They had ascended but a short distance before the motor sputtered, then clattered a few times and died. Chaco engaged the hand brake and glanced over his shoulder as Bui looked across the car at him.

"*Why has the* machine *quit?*"

"*It is nothing, sister.*"

He read the doubt in her eyes as he disengaged the transmission. Then, looking back over his shoulder, he used the hand brake to ease the car slowly back into the dry bottom of the ford. He got out and opened the hood. As he'd thought, the fuel supply was gravity fed. A problem he'd dealt with before. He primed the carburetor, lowered the hood. Engaged the crank and pulled up hard. On his second try the engine caught and ran again.

Bui, standing beside the car, asked, "*Why did it quit before?*"

"Fuel wasn't getting to the motor. When you climb a steep hill with this type of car, you must back it all the way, the way you have to with a Ford motortruck."

He wheeled the Locomobile around and, looking back over his shoulder, began to climb the car in reverse. It was a long way to the summit and took the better part of an hour before they rolled up onto the level prairie. The engine had overheated by that time, and they were forced to shut it down and wait for the water in the radiator to stop boiling before he was able to remove the cap and top it off again.

Bui aimed a finger at the ground underneath the engine. "Look."

Chaco frowned and shook his head. Beneath the radiator a tiny puddle of water had formed. He raised the cowling and located a needle-sized hole with steamy water trickling from one of the radiator's copper cooling coils. He took a moment to consider how best to deal with it, then went to Bui and plucked the sack of Bull Durham from her shirt pocket. He removed the radiator cap and dumped in the contents. Pulled a canteen from the back seat, poured water into the radiator, and replaced the cap. He cranked the engine, and within moments the flake tobacco gravitated to the leak and plugged it.

Bui blinked in amazement. "*You can do anything.*"

He looked east and saw a haze of dust on the horizon. With the engine idling, he topped off the fuel tank and tossed away the empty can and threw the other empty tins after it. He unraveled two additional thirty-foot lengths of rope from the heavy spool and discarded the spool as well. He tossed the ropes into the back seat. "Time to go."

Bui was staring eastward. "*They are coming.*"

"I know." He raised the spyglass to his eye. For them to be this close, this soon, they had to have a motorcar—probably more than one with the amount of dust they were raising.

So much for the advantage of a car, he thought, and lowered the glass.

33

S heriff Hampton "Ham" Jones tugged the brim of his Stetson down against the wind. He'd never gone this fast in his life, not even on a train. He glanced across the car at Trav, the deputy seated upright behind the Ford's steering wheel.

"I detest these damned contraptions," he shouted above the sound of the engine and the rumble of the tires. He seldom raised his voice—it detracted from a man's power—but he had to shout now, just to be heard. Travis leaned over the steering wheel, happily focused on the twin lines of bent grass that marked the direction of the motorcar they followed. "You don't slow this damned thing down," Ham shouted, "you'll like as not kill us both."

"I'm hardly doing forty miles to the hour, Ham."

"My point exactly. If God had meant men to go forty miles an hour, he'd have given him longer legs."

"Or horses," Travis yelled, and laughed at his own joke.

"What?" Ham cupped a palm behind his good ear.

"Never mind," Travis yelled again, and focused on his driving.

Ham knew his deputy considered him backward in his thinking, but unlike Trav he had read up on the latest scientific evidence. Evidence that Trav obviously hadn't acquainted himself with: namely, that speeds in excess of fifty miles an hour would kill a human being. The theory had been scientifically proven less than a month ago in downtown Oklahoma City when the Reverend L. L. Lewis, had, according to the newspapers, dropped a three-hundred-pound hog off the roof of a five-story building. Fifty miles an hour, killed him dead.

The Ford bounced again, and Ham's grip on the dashboard tightened. "The world's moving ahead too fast for the likes of me."

"You're doing just fine, Sheriff."

Ham craned around in his seat and studied the Model T racing along behind them: five of Boss McDonnell's thugs were jammed together in it, shoulder to beefy shoulder.

"You'd think the axle on that Ford would break, loaded down like it is."

Mort Pope was driving and at the moment seemed to be falling behind. Ham was tempted to tell Trav it'd be okay was he to go faster, but then he lost his nerve. Getting rid of that bunch was an encouraging prospect, but it wasn't to be, not if they had to go faster to do it. It had gone against his better judgment, deputizing Mort Pope and Budd Ryan and those other three bullyboys McDonnell liked to pass off as bartenders. Hard men, who in practice were actually enforcers for Boss's political machine. The same political machine that got him reelected this last go-around. He hated Boss McDonnell, but he also was indebted to him. Politics was a lot like war: you allied up with those who could help you win. And with Cecil Collins out of the picture, Boss missing, and Mrs. McDonnell out of town, Mort Pope had taken charge and for the present was the de facto boss of Boss's operation. So when Ham had motored up to the scene of the crime in Doc Carvalo's new Ford—with Slim, his other deputy, behind the wheel—Mort Pope had sent Budd Ryan straight across to Raymond Gaylonson's livery to borrow his '08 model.

"Me and the boys aim to come along with you, Sheriff," Mort said. "You'd best swear us in, 'cause one way or the other we're a-coming."

It was either give them badges or give up on any kind of control . . .

"Watch out for that rock," Ham yelped.

Travis swerved. "I saw it."

"Like hell you saw it."

There were only two things in this deal that surprised him thus far. The first being Mort Pope himself. It hardly fit the man's character to volunteer, much less insist on coming along. He'd have figured Mort for the kind to stay-behind-and-pilfer. The second surprise was the last-minute appearance of Captain Alexander Banyan and his lovely wife. The couple had driven up in a covered surrey as Mort and his boys were tossing blankets and canteens and cans of bean into the back seat of their borrowed motorcar. It wasn't Ham's first time to meet Melissa Banyan. They'd been introduced on a previous occasion —she'd strolled into Boss's store on a day he was there on law business. Boss McDonnell had introduced her as his stepsister. She'd smiled at him, cool and lovely as a spring morning on that day, but this morning she'd seemed more flustered than charming as she stepped from the surrey and hurried toward him, waiting just inside the open front door of McDonnell's pilfered store.

"What does all this mean, Sheriff Jones?"

"Why, just what you see, ma'am. There's been a mite of trouble."

"They killed Cecil Collins," Mort Pope blurted, rushing up

behind them from the muddy street and his borrowed Ford two-seater.

Captain Banyan caught up to her and took her arm as Melissa Banyan reached the boardwalk and stiffened as she noticed Collins's covered body through the open doorway.

"Is that my brother?"

"No, ma'am. That's his man Collins."

"He's dead?"

"Well. Got a slit gullet. So, yeah, he'd dead."

She looked up into Ham's eyes. "And Alton?"

"We don't know for certain, ma'am, but—"

"They kidnapped him," Mort interjected.

Ham had bristled at this second interruption. Luckily for Mort, at that moment Trav came galloping back from the west end of town, and sliding his pony to a halt, jumped down.

"They're headed west for sure," he called out as he came up the steps. "The telegraph line is down on the edge of town. Snow's melting fast; if we aim to get 'em we'd best get a move on."

Trav had stomped the mud from his boots, causing Miz Melissa to step back. She'd looked up at Ham, her eyes full of appeal, and, although he liked to think of himself as being too old to be affected by the beauty of women, when she asked on behalf of her stepbrother to be escorted through the store, the best Ham could manage was a nod followed by acquiescence.

A carpenter was at work on the back door and screen, but Miz Melissa's interest lay elsewhere. She'd gone directly into the storeroom, walked to the safe, and lifted the empty metal box off the top of the barrel. Turned and exchanged an unreadable look with her husband.

"We've seen enough," the captain said.

Miz Melissa turned toward Ham. "I assume you intend to pursue those who did this."

"We were preparing to head out when you all drove up, ma'am."

"Then let us not delay you further, Sheriff," she said, and touched his arm.

Ham had felt the electricity of that touch. No fool like an old fool. But knowing it hadn't helped much.

The Ford bounced again, and Ham blinked. This was no time for woolgathering. He swiveled around. Mort and the rest of that bunch were still back there. They had closed the gap.

He shook his head. "I'd rather have left that outfit behind."

"If there was one straight nose amongst them, they'd look like a bunch of hunters from back east."

Ham had to agree: they did look like a bunch of stylish dudes in their checkered suits and derby hats. "With all them semiautomatic rifles they're a-carrying, if they ever cut loose, it's Katy-bar-the-door."

"I really do love driving automobiles," Travis said. "I wish I could afford one. This here is the future. One day you'll see as many motorcars as buggies on the streets of Lawton."

"Gawd forbid."

"I wouldn't doubt that someday every town of any size will own at least one or two motorcars for the use of their lawmen. There might come a day when lawmen everywhere will drive around in a machine like this one."

"Thank Gawd I won't live to see it."

"Oh, you will, Ham. Trust me on that one." Travis's gaze went out of focus for a thoughtful moment. He blinked then and spared Ham a brief glance. "You know, I still think we should've followed those tire tracks down into Fort Sill."

West of Lawton they'd come to an intersecting road where the Locomobile had swung north over the tracks. On the other side the motorcar had angled off a little east, back toward the Fort Sill military reserve. Ham would have followed those tire tracks, too, had there not been another, fresher set left by the Locomobile when it returned more or less along the same route. This second set of tire tracks had recrossed the rails and continued west on the service road. Ham had ordered Trav to stop the car, had gotten out, and examined both sets of tire imprints. There was a deformity in the tread of one of the tires that showed up in both sets, and, though Travis disagreed, it made better sense to him to follow the fresher set.

"First we catch up to McDonnell or whoever it was that took him," Ham had said. "We can backtrack into Fort Sill later, if there's a need. I'm still not convinced that Boss McDonnell ain't taken the opportunity of his wife's absence to start off a new life with that missing Injun whore."

"You think it was Boss that cut Collins's throat?"

"I'd not put it past him. He'd cut his own mother's throat if there was a dollar in it."

"I don't see him going sentimental for an Injun whore this late in the game. Not sentimental enough to leave everything he's built up."

Ham pointed. "Pay attention to where you're driving, will you? You're headed straight for that hole."

Trav swerved the Ford a little, went around the old buffalo wallow, then straightened out again. "There's something I need to tell you, Sheriff."

"Tell me anything you want, but you bust a tire on this thing, it comes out of your pay."

"It's about Miz Banyan, the captain's wife?"

"What about her?" Ham straightened in his seat.

"The thing is, Sheriff, I got a whiff of the perfume Miz Banyan was wearing, and it's the same perfume I smelled on Boss McDonnell's bedsheets."

Ham blanched and turned in the seat. "You know what

you're saying, son?" He felt a tingle on his arm where she'd placed her hand.

"Yes, sir. But there ain't no doubt about it in my mind. It's the same perfume."

"Well, I will be damned," Ham said.

34

C haco turned northward and drove out of the breaks. Within the hour they came in sight of the westbound rails of the St. Louis and San Francisco again. He'd guessed right: the rails they'd crossed earlier had belonged to another line. He cut through a fence and swung left onto the service road. An hour's drive brought them to a trestle over the shallow flow of a river made up of a series of conjoining tributaries with reddish sand bottoms. Here again he used the trestle to get across. On the far side a crude sign nailed to a post read, "Salt Forks of the Red River."

He drove the car off the rails and down the ballast and back onto the wagon road. Stopped and set the brake and stood on the driver's seat and glassed the country behind them.

"*That dust, it's closer now,*" Bui said, belting her pants up after making water.

"*We need to go faster, I guess.*"

She gestured toward the front wheel. "*That tire is flat.*"

Chaco jumped from the seat, landed lightly on the balls of his feet, and saw the passenger-side front tire was indeed nearly flat. This was bad. It would cost them time. He broke out the tool kit, slipped the jack under the axle, and jacked up the front end. He removed the wheel, bled off the last of the air, and used the tire iron to pry the outer lip of the tire off the rim. He removed the tube, located the puncture, scuffed the rubber, and applied a hot patch. While the patch smoldered, he felt around inside the tire and located the point of a thorn. He used the pliers in the kit to remove it. Then reinserted the tube, worked the tire back onto the rim with the tire iron, and inflated the tire with the hand pump. The wheel went on. He lowered the jack and tossed the tool kit and jack into the back seat.

Only then did he allow himself to look east again: the pall of dust was considerably closer. They needed to make tracks. He gave the engine crank a quick turn. The motor caught and ran. Bui scrambled into her place as Chaco slid behind the wheel. She was looking at him, her eyes fierce.

"*Can this* automobile *stay ahead of them?*"

"Yes," he said with more confidence than he felt, the car accelerating along the dusty road. Behind them the peaks of the Wichitas had slipped beneath the turning curve of the earth, and now only the treeless prairie stretched before them. In all directions there was only the grassy land, as unforgiving as the unforgiving sea. Bui was bright-eyed with worry. They were moving at close to fifty miles to the hour, but if he could go fifty so could the men who followed.

"As soon as it's dark, I'll turn south," he said. "We might lose them if we travel all night."

"*Then we must do that, keep going all night,*" she said.

He hoped they had gasoline enough. The plan had been to follow the rails, because the rails would pass through towns where gasoline could be found. But now he must alter that plan. He studied Bui's profile. The day had worn on her. For all her courage, she clearly needed rest and food. But that meant stopping and building a fire. A risk he would not take, not yet—not while they were being pressed so hard.

I must learn how to conceal my tracks, he thought. There is so much I don't know. The road immediately ahead was good, and he risked a quick look back. They were still back there. If I can see their dust, then they can see mine. He checked the position of the sun. Three, maybe four hours until darkness, and then—

"I'm thinking now it should have more than three rooms," Bui said.

"What?" He glanced across the car at her and then quickly swerved to avoid a rock.

"The house you will build for us. I think it should have at least four rooms. What do you think about that?"

Chaco spared her a quick glance. Bui had reverted to English. She gripped the back of her seat, her worried gaze focused on the road behind them.

"Do you want four rooms?" he asked.

"Yes. One for you to sleep in and one for me, and I want one room for us both to live in. And another room to cook in," she said, almost as an afterthought.

"I can build a house like that."

"Yes, we should have at least four rooms, but there should be a dogtrot between the kitchen and the rest of the house."

"Yes. I agree. Kitchens get hot."

"Build that house. That house would be a good place for us," she said, her voice trailing off. She bit her lower lip, staring fixedly at the road behind them. Finally she said, "If I hadn't killed them, they wouldn't be back there, would they?"

"It's best not to look back unless you're planning to go that way," he said. "What's done cannot be undone."

She came around and studied him for a long moment; then she nodded and began to describe what the rooms would look like and what she would put in them. He listened to her as he drove, hearing that treble of urgent hope he remembered from the dying wounded. All the things they would do once they got home . . . At length she fell silent, turned around in her seat, and stared mutely back into the distance.

Time sped by to the rumble of tires, the clatter of the engine, the whine of the drive chain.

"*I don't see their dust now,*" she said. "*You'd better slow down before you kill us both.*"

He eased off on the throttle, and when the car slowed enough, he looked back. The dust of their pursuers no longer marked the horizon. He looked at her and remembered that smile from when they were children, and for a moment it seemed possible to him that she might be able to find her way back to herself.

They'd covered nearly fifty miles in the last hour, and focused as he'd been on driving he'd failed to notice the imperceptible southward swing of the road and the tracks. The position of the late-afternoon sun alerted him. They were in drier country here. Ahead the tracks cut through a low uplift of reddish sandstone. They approached, and Chaco slowed the car as they rolled up onto its hard surface. He braked to a stop and studied the ground around them. They were not likely to come upon a place to equal this, and he made a decision. He swung the car right and bounced it over the rails, drove fifty yards, stopped, and set the brake. He got out and yanked up a broomweed and hurried back to the tracks. He used the weed to dust away the faint imprint their tires left, working at it until he reached the car. Bui nodded approval as he slid behind the wheel again, engaged the engine, and drove on.

"Finding that place back there was a bit of luck," he said. "It'll be dark soon. If they miss where we turned off, it will buy us the time we need."

They traveled close to a mile before the shelf of sandstone gave way to the short-grass prairie again. The sun faded to a clear, true light, and Chaco looked for reference points—a lone tree, a point of barren rock—but there was only the seemingly endless prairie. He spied a windmill and near it a cluster of forlorn-looking cattle. He drove across a prairie-dog town, the burrowing rodents barking and diving into their tunnels as the car rumbled over them. Bui aimed a finger at a family of ferrets and then at a burrowing owl ripping at a luckless prairie-dog pup. Farther on they saw another windmill and more cattle grazing near it. They heard the squeak of the water well's sucker rod and the splash of water spilling from a rusty pipe into a stone stock tank as they rumbled by. The occasional barbed-wire fence blocked their way. At these he used such gaps as were in sight but otherwise cut through and drove on. The fading day had taken on shades of gray. Bui was mostly silent. At one point she turned in her seat and looked east toward the darkening sky as the sun slipped below the western horizon. It had been a long day. They needed to eat, and the car must be serviced if they were to drive on through the night. Ahead was a likely place, and as they came to it he rolled the car to a stop. Set the brake, stood in the driver's seat, and, with the engine idling, raised the monocular to his eye.

East of them the short-grass country rolled away toward the coming night. No evidence of pursuit back there, and yet he sensed pursuit. He lowered the glass, turned, and looked west. The horizon was black beneath a yellow sky. Again he scanned the country to the east, moving the glass slowly across the gray horizon: nothing. He slipped the spyglass into his pocket and jumped to the ground. The radiator was hissing—probably the flake tobacco had failed and the radiator was again low on water. He wondered whether Bui had another sack of Bull Durham. If not—

"*Look.*" Bui pointed to a flight of birds whirling blackly across the sky. "*There is water near. Birds will fly to the water for a drink at sundown.*"

Yes, of course, Chaco thought, aware of moisture in the parched air now, surprised that a man could smell water. Another first for me, he mused.

"Get in," he said, resituating himself behind the wheel.

He engaged the transmission and, guided by the flight of the birds, drove over the next rise. He stopped the car and looked down at a natural tank, a kind of hollow, a bit of low ground into which the surrounding country drained. He killed the engine and set the brake. The last true light fading fast now, and this as likely a place as any to refill their canteens and the water bladders, and while they were at it to refill the fuel tank, and eat something, and, once the engine cooled, to top off the radiator and dump in a little more flake tobacco to reseal the small leak.

"*I see rabbits down there,*" Bui said. "*Can you shoot one?*"

"*The gun will tell them where we are. We have food.*"

"*You fill the* gas tank," she said. "*I will use the empty* tin *to fetch water. It is better if you don't have to back up all that way from that water when it is time to go.*"

"Yeah. Good thinking."

Chaco was smiling inwardly as he refilled the tank. Bui was already telling him what to do, the way she used to when they were children. It was a good sign. He lowered the empty tin, and as he did he spied a solitary wolf among the cattails on the far side of the black-water tank. The wolf, silent and still amongst the cattails, staring back at them.

Bui hurried forward a few steps. "*Look,*" she said, pointing.

"Yes, I see it."

"*I thought the Indah had killed them all.*"

"I guess not," he said.

A whippoorwill called and as it did the wolf turned and slunk away, and Chaco, watching it go, spied a small herd of antelope as it crested a rise. The herd paused long enough to look back, as if in objection of both man and wolf for disturbing the herd's evening drink. Smiling now, Chaco brought out the glass, raised it to his eye, and studied the prairie to the south, west, and north. To the north a faint ribbon of smoke rising out of the prairie—possibly a ranch house or maybe even the night camp of some lone fence rider.

He lowered the glass. Said, "Looks like . . ." and the next instant yelled, "Get down," and dove for the ground, having seen the flash of a rifle to the east. While Bui, turning toward him with a flower she'd picked, jerked as the *whunk* of impact slammed to the ground, and his world emptied out behind the distant thunder of a rifle report.

He scrambled to his feet, scooped her up, and dumped her in the car as another bullet whistled by. He cranked the engine. The motor caught and ran and he vaulted in behind the wheel. The car lurched forward. A bullet slammed into the car with a hard ping. He swerved down toward the water hole, reached across, and grabbed Bui's arm to keep her in her seat. Then swerved again and drove along the slope above the tank, risking a stall but at least no longer in sight of the shooter.

His sister's eyes blinked once but rolled vacant, dark blood dribbling from her side.

35

M ort Pope squeezed the set trigger, took quick aim, and touched off another round. The Sharps bucked: flame and smoke and the heavy cough of report billowed from the muzzle.

Sheriff Hampton Jones, running toward him, yelled, "Damn you for a fool."

Mort rolled onto his side to reload, and Budd shouted, "I think you hit Boss's motorcar with that one," as Sheriff Jones came running and sank the toe of his boot into Mort's side.

The rifle went off, the saloon man grunted, and rolled away. Then rolled and rolled again in an effort to distance himself from the sheriff's kicks. Ham seemed like a man in a killing mood, but somehow Mort managed to get his hands and knees under him. He came up, fists raised, ready to fight, and as he did the sheriff caught him under the chin with the toe of his boot. It was a high kick and the blow sent Mort sprawling.

Budd put himself between the two. "Good Gawd, Ham, what the hell?"

Ham wheeled on him, black with fury. "You want some of it?"

Bud back-crawled fast. "Easy, Sheriff." He held his hands, palms outward, in a gesture of appeasement. "You gone completely off your rocker?"

The sheriff, in better control now, turned and glared at the others. "The rest of you want any of this?"

Cassel, who was standing close enough to be in danger, waved the lawman off. "We're on your side, Sheriff, in case you forgot?"

"I give the orders." Ham walked over to the Sharps and picked it up. He tossed it to Cassel. "You idiots are shooting at people when we don't even know for certain who they are."

"They're driving Boss's motorcar," Wesley White said plaintively.

"And what if that was Boss he just took a shot at?"

Wesley shrugged. "Pope was just doing what any lawman does."

"Not any lawmen I know." Sheriff Jones snorted. "Not this one, for sure." Wesley's answer was the sort of whiny nonsense a man usually got from his kind. "I told you all when we pulled up you was not to shoot unless I said shoot. And I didn't say shoot. When I give an order, it gets obeyed, you all understand?"

"Why sure, Sheriff, ain't nobody's saying no different," Cassel said.

"Any of you don't like how I run things, you best head back and take that trigger-happy idiot with you."

"Ain't nobody saying you ain't in charge, Ham," Budd said.

"It's Sheriff Jones to you, buster . . . and to the rest of you, too. From now on till we get back in Lawton, I'm Sheriff Jones. To every one of you, you got that?" Ham wheeled about on his heels and stalked off a way before he said something he might not be able to take back. He looked westward into the gathering dark. A faint red line marked the black horizon.

Trav came up beside him.

"You over being mad?"

"Yep," Ham lied, shook his head and grimaced. "They was stopped on that little rise, probably done traveling for the day. We could've slipped up on 'em in the dark. Now he'll likely drive all night." The light was all but gone now and Boss McDonnell's motorcar was on the move again—and getting farther away by the minute. Ham spit a stream of tobacco juice in Budd's general direction, shouted, "Mount up, boys. Let's get cracking. Whoever that is, he's done hightailed it."

"What about Mort?" Budd asked. "He's kindly bad hurt."

"Bring him or leave him lay," Ham growled. "I don't much give a damn."

36

Befor the second report faded, Deputy U.S. Marshal Tom Starrett had belly-crawled up to the high point above his camp. A quarter mile out he saw a motorcar on the move. He brought his binoculars to his eyes and glassed the vehicle: A lone driver in a heavily loaded motorcar. A third shot punched the car and sent it careening in another direction. The car disappeared into a swale. He swung the binoculars eastward. Refocused and saw the faint drift of gun smoke and several men milling about near two motorcars situated behind them. The shooter was on the ground, and it looked like one of the men was trying to kick him to death and was doing a pretty good job of it.

Tom lowered the binoculars. "Wonder what the hell that's all about."

He back-crawled off the summit, got to his feet, and walked back to his camp, and found Vernon Cotton seated more or less where he'd left him on the far side of his dying fire pit. His prisoner's wrists were raw from tugging at his handcuffs, which were padlocked to a steel ring affixed to the iron rod he'd driven into the ground.

"It's Hubert and the others, ain't it?"

Before the first report had faded, Vernon announced his brothers were there to rescue him, his gap-toothed face split by a fierce grin. "They're going to skin you alive, Marshal."

Now, walking back into camp, Tom was annoyed by his idiotic grin.

"It's them, ain't it? They'll kill you for sure if you don't let me go, Marshal."

Tom shoved dirt, with the side of his boot, back into the fire pit he'd dug earlier. The blue flames of the cow-chip fire sputtered and died. He left Vernon yelling, "Over here, I'm over here," and caught up his pony and pack mule. Neither had drifted far.

He led the animals back to camp, saddled Buck, and put the packsaddle on the mule and strapped on the panniers. He removed the hobbles from both animals, about out of patience with Vernon Cotton's yelling by that point, and then checked the loads in his Colt and the smaller double action he carried in a Texas shoulder rig under his vest. He pulled the pickax from the packsaddle and went over to Vernon, who was still yelling and yanking against the iron ring.

"Hubert's a mean he-coon. He's going to skin you, Marshal. And I aim to watch."

"Hold still."

"The hell I will."

Tom kicked him under his chin. Vernon stretched out and lay groaning. It was wrong of him to abuse a prisoner, but as Tom slipped the point of the pickax into the steel ring and leaned back on the handle, he experienced a deep satisfaction for having done it. The iron stake came up. He grabbed a handful of Vernon's hair and dragged him over to the mule. Hoisted him up and flopped him belly-down across the packsaddle, the mule hee-hawing in protest as Tom untied the dirty bandana from around Vernon's neck and stuffed it in his mouth. He tied the gag in place with his own bandana, then patted Mabel's neck. "I don't like him, either, girl." Mable snorted, and he swatted at her nose to distract her from whatever meanness she might be considering. "Hush up, we all got a job to do, and your bad luck was to be born a mule."

He worked the pickax into place under one of the pack-straps, then stepped up to Buck and tied his bedroll behind the saddle. He mounted, and with Mabel following on lead he spurred the gelding ahead.

He'd never entertained the notion that the shooters were any kin of Vernon's. The Cotton clan, despite their windy brags about loyalty, hadn't struck Tom as all that close-knit. In fact, it was Vernon's own wife, Delores, who'd sent for the law after Vernon had in a state of drunkenness tied their daughter to a wagon wheel and beat her to death with a bullwhip, then followed that barbarity up by rope-dragging one of his sons to death behind a horse as punishment for the boy's interference with the beating he gave his sister. He'd killed two of his own children and would hang for it.

Darkness had settled fully over the prairie by the time Starrett crested the rise and saw the distant headlights of two automobiles moving westward, one ahead of the other. In the silence of the evening, he could still make out the sputter of the gasoline engines. He pulled the binoculars from his coat pocket and glassed the motorcars—dark, advancing bulks behind the dim glow of their headlamps.

He swept the prairie ahead of the two cars but couldn't see the one they were chasing. Logically, the other motorcar would be running without lights. This situation had put him between a rock and a hard place. A part of him wanted to say this was none of his business, wanted simply to ride on, but, in point of fact, this was his business. He needed to know who the shooters were and who they were shooting at.

This far out in the middle of nowhere, it's a hell of a thing, he thought.

He slipped the binoculars back into his coat pocket and raised his collar against the quickening chill. Then pulled out the makings and built a cigarette, fired a match off the end of a ragged thumbnail. Cupped the flame, puffed, and shook the match out and rolled its blackened end between thumb and index finger until it cooled. He flipped it away and, still watching the progress of the motorcars, reluctantly nudged the gelding west after the retreating motorcars. He had no expectation he'd be able to overtake them.

37

Chaco glanced up into the star-spotted sky, a part of him not wanting to believe this bad thing had happened to Bui. He called out to the night, bargained with the God of the Indah, the one who had raised his son from the dead. I will be good, I will be quiet, I will follow the white way. He listened to the night. Looked down at Bui, then looked up again and called out to Usen. But knew as he bargained that if Usen had a plan for the People it was as an instrument of his own purpose. Maybe it was thus with all the gods.

As the last of the light faded, he turned north and drove about a mile before he crossed a rise, stopped the motorcar and set the brake. With the engine idling, he lifted Bui from the seat and placed her gently on the ground.

She gasped, and his heart leapt. She lived.

"*Sister,*" he muttered, voice raw with emotion. He undid her belt, pulled out the tails of the two shirts she wore, unbuttoned her trousers, and exposed the midsection of her body. The bullet had taken a chunk out of her side. It was a flesh wound of the sort he had come to think of as the luckiest kind, but she had lost too much blood. He thumbed open his clasp knife, cut away a large square of cloth from one of her shirttails, folded it into a compress, and placed it over the gouge in her side. Then used her belt to bind the compress bandage in place. The bleeding stopped.

He got to his feet and quickly rearranged a few things in the back seat. Then gently stretched her out back there. He leaned against the car, closed his eyes, a silent rage in him like nothing he had ever known. He looked at the sky. They had taken everything. Everything.

Now I will make a war against them, he thought.

The fiery arc of a meteor ran down the night sky.

"Usen," he whispered, a tingle of wonder quickening along his spine.

He turned toward Bui, his mouth hard-set as he moved around the motorcar. Raised the spyglass and studied his pursuers, his vision blurred momentarily. Frowning, he scrubbed at his face with a quick wipe of his sleeve and reconcentrated his attention on the two sets of headlights that marked the progress of the motorcars. They were moving west and in their haste had missed the place where he had swung north.

He reached into the back seat, located the half-empty box of buckshot, and stuffed the remaining shells into a front pocket of his trousers.

He checked his sister again. Her breath was shallow, but she was still breathing. He touched her cheek. "I am sorry," he whispered, aware of the whiteeye part in him that needed this act of contrition. Carlisle had changed him, but not as they had intended; the school had failed to kill the Apache. He checked the loads in the shotgun, slipped in behind the wheel again, and, engaging the transmission, set out.

A crescent moon lay low above the horizon, the sky star washed, and yet all was darkness except for the moving headlights of motorcars. He drove at reckless speed and soon was gaining on them; his pursuers now the pursued. The Locomobile rose and sunk over long, grassy swells, Chaco guided by dead reckoning and the occasional glimpse of their headlights. He drove toward a place where they would intersect and was confident the engine noise of their machines would cover the noise of his own. He would overtake them in the manner they'd managed to overtake him. He would end this now, one way or the other. In his heart life and death had become the same.

38

When Tom heard the rattle-pop of the approaching engine, he pulled the gelding to a halt. The motorcar that the others had fired on apparently had circled back and was absolutely headed in his direction, running without headlights.

He leaned back in the saddle and swatted at Mabel's nose with his hat, distracting her in the hope she'd keep quiet. He eased out his Colt. West of him the headlights of the other motorcars were moving away. His mustang Buck snorted and Tom patted his neck.

"Easy, boy."

The approaching motorcar was coming on fast—too fast. He had no idea what he faced, outlaw or honest citizen. But the problem solved itself. The pitch of the engine changed, and as he listened the sound of the motorcar faded. Tom put away his shooter and leaned on his saddle horn. Now that does surprise me, he thought. The car being chased was now in pursuit of the bunch who thought they were doing the chasing.

He eased Buck ahead and rode around a slight rise to avoid any chance of being skylined. His ears were telling him he wouldn't have long to wait for whatever was going to happen. He came around the rise. The headlights of the two motorcars were still going away. He could still hear the engines, but he could no longer distinguish between them. Then the cars went over a rise and dropped from sight.

As he trotted on, he drew a half-pint of whiskey from his inside breast pocket. Took a drink and was about to take another when the crack of a single gunshot drifted back. He saw the headlamp glow of one of the motorcars momentarily as it illuminated the summit of a rise, like maybe the car had veered after the gunshot. He pulled Buck to a halt, and a long moment later the silent distance filled up with the hammering of rifle fire.

"That didn't take long," he muttered and corked the whiskey, reached back and drew the Winchester from its scabbard. One man going up against better than a half dozen guns was no dogfall. He was considering his own long-term prospects once he rode over there, when the flat report of another gun drifted back. The shot was quickly followed by more rapid rifle fire. When the last report faded, Tom tilted his hat back, muttered, "What the hell." He could hardly believe the witness of his own ears when the second extended silence was broken by a third solitary report that was quickly followed by more rapid rifle fire.

By that point Tom figured all bets were off and this fight was going to be an all-night affair. He pulled Vernon off the mule, removed the gag, and rolled him onto his belly so he wouldn't choke on his own spit and blood. Hobbled his stock and left them to graze while he settled in to wait out events.

Over the next several hours, there were periods of extended silence followed by the single report and ever-briefer volleys of return fire.

"They must have brought along a shitload of bullets."

Tom built another cigarette, fired a match, and cupped the flame in his hands. Like a lot of men who spent too much time alone, he'd fallen into the habit of talking to himself. An hour after the last shot was fired, or at least what Tom hoped was the last, he retrieved Buck and Mable, removed their hobbles, led them back to his prisoner and poured a little water from his canteen onto Vernon's snoring face.

Vernon sputtered and sat up, shook his head, and groaned.

"Time to go," Tom said, and got him to his feet and back on top of the mule.

He remounted Buck and eased ahead, the eastern skyline showing hints of gray.

Vernon, grumpy after being knocked out for most of the night, said, "You shouldn't have kicked me, Marshal. You busted out a couple of my good teeth."

Tom turned in the saddle, looked at him. "A man who'd tie his own daughter to a wagon wheel and beat her to death with a bullwhip ought not to complain about a few teeth."

"I was drunk. Anyway, you don't know the whole story. What she did to—"

"Here's all you got to know, Vernon: don't give me any more excuses."

"That ain't fair treatment, Marshal, you kicking me like you done."

"It wasn't, but if you aim to hang on to the teeth you got left, shut your biscuit hole."

"Speaking of biscuits, when do we eat? My stomach thinks my throat's been cut."

Tom held up his hand for silence and stood in the stirrups. He cupped his hands behind his ears and heard the faint metallic clatter of an engine being cranked. Heard it catch and grumble to life. Then a set of headlights appeared over a rise moving westward and away.

39

The eastern horizon had brightened to light gray by the time Tom rode within sight of the black shapes he recognized as automobiles. There was one just ahead, and another maybe twenty yards farther on. He pulled to a halt, stood in the stirrups, and looked around with the familiar feeling of having come upon a dangerous place. He eased the .45-70 Winchester from its scabbard and nudged the gelding onward. Mabel jerked her head and snorted, and Tom pulled up again.

"I'm a federal marshal, and I have a ten-man posse behind me," Tom shouted. "So don't shoot unless you want to get hung."

He seldom used the ploy. Few outlaws in this country were that gullible. He clucked up the gelding and eased forward again, Mabel jerking against her lead rope as he eased up alongside the rearmost motorcar. The body of a man sat slumped against the steering wheel.

Vernon laughed nervously. "I ain't ever seen a man with his head blowed off before."

The back half of the dead driver's head was missing. Tom dismounted, tied off to the rear bumper, and swatted at Mabel's nose with his hat to distract her from the blood smell. The last thing he needed was her broadcasting their presence. He looked up at Vernon.

"Get down."

Vernon swung a leg over the mule's back and dropped to the ground.

Tom thumbed back the hammer on the Winchester and walked slowly around the motorcar. It was a new Ford that had been repainted fire-engine red. Flies hummed around puddled blood caked to the seat covers and the floorboard. The driver's forearms and neck were as sunburned and raw looking as what was left of his face.

"You got to respect a shotgun, eh, Marshal?" Vernon muttered.

"Hush."

"Yes, sir."

The dead man's pockets had been turned out. The killer had taken the time to do that. Interesting, Tom thought. The man's weapons were gone. There were tracks on the ground on all sides of the Ford. Actually three sets. First the tracks of the men who'd jumped from the car, gotten down on their bellies, and crawled away. The second set were boot prints made by a man with small feet. Tom glanced across the hood of the Ford at Vernon, his prisoner looking around apprehensively.

"I hope you're not getting any jackrabbit ideas."

"I'm not, Marshal."

"If you run, just so you know, I ain't digging no graves in this hard ground."

"I'll stay put, Marshal. It's just that I'm kindly agitated. Cain't say why."

Tom nodded. He hadn't thought Vernon had that much sense. He turned and followed the bent-grass trail left by the crawling men. He heard Vernon coming up from behind, stopped, and looked back at him.

Vernon halted and raised his cuffed hands. "I cain't wait back there with no gun, Marshal."

"Okay, but keep your distance and keep quiet."

"Yes, sir."

There was a sly, coyote-caught-in-the-henhouse way about Vernon Cotton—a quality, if you could call it that, Tom would have found amusing had Cotton been something less than dangerous.

He moved on and soon enough discovered the next body. It lay sprawled on a patch of beaten-down grass. Like the man in the car, this one had been shotgunned. The bunch from the car had crawled to this point and formed a defensive circle. From the position of the body and the corresponding shotgun wound, Tom calculated that the shooter had flanked them in the dark. The brass casings of spent cartridges littered the grass. The men had apparently fired in all directions. Tom went back to the dead man, lined up on his wound, and walked out a little way. Thirty steps brought him to a spent twelve-gauge hull lying in the grass. He hunkered down and picked it up and rolled it between his fingers. Whoever he was, the man who'd done this knew how to move, knew when to move, and he hit what he aimed to hit in the dark. Tom bounced the hull in his palm as he looked back at the dead man.

"I wonder if this bunch had any idea who they were up against."

"I got an ideal," Vernon said. "My ideal is, let's get the hell gone from here."

The survivors of this fight had, in an apparent effort to extricate themselves, crawled away again. Tom followed their belly-down, bent-grass retreat and soon enough came to another body. The crawlers had formed a circle again, had fired in all directions again. Their scattered brass, bright in the early sunlight, marked where men had lain. He walked out a little distance from the body and located another shotgun hull, this one on their opposite flank. Tom imagined the rising panic these men must have experienced. The desperation that clearly, at this point, impelled them to scatter, every man for his own life—probably it had gone quicker for the rest of them after that. Soon enough Tom was standing above what he supposed was the last of them. Like the bodies of the others, the man's pockets had been turned out, all his weapons and ammunition taken.

"How many do you figure was in on this killing, Marshal?"

"One man."

"Bullshit. Ain't no way one man could've kill all this many."

"Kind of draws your pucker string, don't it?" Tom gestured toward the second motorcar, a black, roofless machine with a lot of polished brass and a couple of wicker baskets mounted to the body above the rear wheels. "We're going over there next. Walk ahead of me."

"You wouldn't be aiming to get me shot before he shoots you, would you, Marshal?"

"The one that did this drove off before we rode up."

"How sure of that are you?"

"Enough to bet your life on it. Get going." Tom gestured with the Winchester, and Vernon, given no selection in the matter, led out.

They angled down the gentle rise toward the car, an oddly made machine, with a back-access door to the rear seat that had been left hanging open. One of its rear tires was flat.

"Hold up."

Vernon stopped as ordered and looked back at Tom.

Tom indicated a direction with the business end of his rifle. "Get over there out of the way, and stand still."

When Vernon was where he wanted him, Tom walked the last few yards to the car. A nameplate on the radiator said it was a Locomobile Type C, 1904 model. There was a bullet hole through the engine cowling, another through the radiator, and the ground beneath the radiator was damp. He checked the driver's seat and found no blood sign. But there was caked blood on the passenger seat and more traces of blood in the back seat. So there were three of them: the driver and two wounded passengers. Odd that the only tracks around the Locomobile were those of the one he presumed was the shooter. This had to be the vehicle that motored past him last night. He studied the boot tracks, the way they ran back and forth between the Locomobile and the spot where the other motorcar had been—the car the shooter had driven away.

"He moved his stuff from this car to the other," Tom said under his breath.

He followed the tracks to the spot where the other car had been and looked around. There were other large boot prints, all but obliterated by the shooter's. Two sets of size-twelve down at the heels doggers that went away in a different direction from where the second car had been. He hunkered down, picked up the casing of a spent cartridge, and rolled it between his fingers as he looked behind him to check on Vernon. His prisoner had scrunched down with his arms wrapped around his knees. He noticed Tom looking at him, stood up, and raised his hands.

"I ain't moved, Marshal."

"Get over here."

"Yes, sir."

Vernon came a-scurrying, his shoulders hunched, eyes darting this way and that. He reminded Tom more of a coyote than just about any felon he'd ever hauled in. It was a discomforting thought. Coyotes were survivors, and Vernon needed a good hanging. The man stopped a few yards away, like he was afraid to come much closer.

"I'm going to walk out these tracks." Tom gestured with the

Winchester. "You stick with me, but stay back. I don't want you too close."

"Yes, sir. I mean no, sir." Vernon frowned, then added, "I'll hang back."

There was nothing for it but to go out and locate the last of them, and Tom followed their sign and found them in an old buffalo wallow. This time their rifles hadn't been taken—they lay on the ground beside their bodies, muzzles angled outward. Both men rested on their sides, as if asleep. He approached slowly, mindful of their weapons, and stopped ten yards out.

"I'm a U.S. marshal."

Neither man responded.

"You might as well yell at a stump," Vernon whispered from a few yards back, then turned quick to look behind him, as if he expected to see somebody sneaking up.

"Stay there," Tom said, and walked over to the first man, thinking there had to be a reason the shooter hadn't taken these men's weapons.

He knelt and rolled the first body over, intending to check for a pulse—this man's pockets turned out like all the others—and froze as light reflected off a badge pinned to the man's shirt. He looked at his face and blinked. It was young Jim Travis, Sheriff Hampton Jones's deputy. No pulse. He grimaced, came to his feet, and crossed the wallow to the second man, not wanting to believe what his eyes were telling him. He knelt beside his old friend, pressed his fingertips against the artery in his neck, hoping for a pulse, and Ham gasped at his touch. The old man's eyes fluttered open, in them the wild look of a child wakened from a nightmare.

"Hold on, old friend, it's me. It's Tom Starrett."

There were cartridges piled on the ground for quick loading. Ejected hulls scattered to the side. They had put up a fight. But so had the others. The fact that Ham and Travis had stumbled across this old buffalo wallow had probably made the difference.

"Ham, can you hear me?"

He gripped his friend's hand, pressed the palm of his other against his forehead. No fever. Was that good? He didn't know. The sheriff's eyes fluttered open, looked from side to side full of wild fear. Then he looked at Tom and the wildness faded. The familiar grin took shape under his gray mustache.

"Why, hello, Tom. What in the world are you doing way out here?"

"What the hell, Ham . . ."

"It must have been you who scared him off?"

"Scared who off?"

"Something did," Ham said. "It sure wasn't us."

"How bad are you hit?"

The sheriff swallowed and blinked. "Forty years. Never seen the like of him . . ."

"We're going to get you patched up, Ham. You hang on, hear me? I'll get you to a doctor, he'll fix you right—"

"We never even seen him, never even heard him coming."

"Rest easy now. I'll take care of everything. You hear, Ham? Everything." Tom checked the old man for wounds. Ran his hands over his body—one hand came away bloody. He drew his sheath knife, gave Vernon a summoning wave. "Get over here."

Vernon sidled over. "What'd you aim to do with that knife, Marshal?"

Tom got to his feet. "Turn around. I need some of your shirttail."

"You ain't going to gut me, are you?"

"Vernon, would you please stop giving me such good ideas. Now turn around."

Reluctantly Vernon eased his back toward Tom, stretching his chin hard around in an effort to watch as the marshal pulled his shirttail out and used the knife to cut away almost the entire back panel.

"Get back to where you was standing, and stay put," Tom ordered.

"Yes, sir."

Vernon sidled away as Tom deftly ripped the material into a series of small squares. He then used the knife to cut Ham's shirt and ripped it, and then rolled him over. He folded one of the squares of faded sweat stained cotton over the end of his index finger and inserted the material into one of the shotgun pellet wounds. Moved on to the next, did the same, and soon enough had the rest of his wounds similarly plugged. A rough bit of doctoring but he'd more or less stopped the bleeding. Six pellet wounds in Ham's side. No exit wounds. They would fester if he didn't get those pellets out of him fairly soon. Not to mention the prospect of lead poisoning. Ham needed a surgeon, and that meant Tom had to take one of those automobiles. And that meant he'd have to abandon Buck and Mabel. They needed to travel fast, and neither of his animals would be able to keep up. Everything now was about time . . . Time was his enemy.

Ham groaned, swallowed, and choked on his spit.

Alarmed, Tom lifted his friend, propped his back against his own knee, and waited out the coughing fit. What Ham needed, after the loss of so much blood, was water. But his canteen was hanging on his saddle, and, of course, he couldn't send Vernon to fetch it.

Ham's sun-weathered eyelids fluttered open, teary and bloodshot. "What?" he muttered, his wild and frightened old eyes out of place in that craggy face. He grabbed hold of Tom's shirtfront and pulled. "I'm going to die," he said with raw conviction.

"No, you ain't, Ham. I ain't going to allow it."

"I'm going to die," he muttered again, voice trailing off as his eyelids fluttered and closed.

Tom ran a hand over his face. He caught Vernon eyeing Jim Travis's rifle, where he'd left it lying. It would be so much easier if he went for it. But it wouldn't be right. No, Vernon needed a hanging. It had to get written down that his daughter and son got justice. "Anytime you feel froggy, Vernon, go ahead and jump."

"I ain't done nothing, Marshal."

"You were pondering your chances. I ain't in a place to fool with you no more. So listen tight. You wobble left or right one step, you're going to get shot. I'll leave you for the buzzards."

"No call to get riled, Marshal."

"I know you ain't the sharpest tool in the shed, Vernon, but you ken my meaning."

Vernon swallowed audibly as he nodded.

The thing was, they had to move Ham. They had to get him into one of those motorcars back there. The red Ford—the other one had a flat tire and was shot half to pieces. He lowered Ham onto his back and crossed his friend's arms the way you might a dead man. Then thought better of it and straightened them out along his sides. He came to his feet and looked at Vernon.

"Sheriff Jones needs a doctor. We'll be taking that Ford motorcar."

"The red one's got a bullet hole in it."

"So does the black one, and it's got a flat tire and a bullet hole through the radiator," Tom said.

40

C haco rolled back on his heels. The sun well above the horizon now, he rested his chin against his knees and studied Bui's face. The laudanum still held her in deepest sleep. He'd given her an inordinate dosage and watched her drift away before he cleansed the terrible gash in her side. Then powdered the wound with sulfur and stitched the ragged edges together and, finally, bound the wound tight with a clean compress bandage. Would she survive his rough surgery? He grimaced, stood up, lifted her from the blanket he'd spread on the ground, and settled her on the bed he'd made for her in the back seat of the Ford. Her headrest was the canvas bundle that held his father's bones; the bed was made on top of the other things they carried.

For a time he studied the seemingly empty country around them. This was a lonely land inhabited by few people and well suited to the inner life he had known. And yet through all the lonely years, never until this moment had he actually felt utterly alone. Always in the back of his mind had been his mother and sister. He studied her face, reached out, and touched her gaunt cheek.

Why am I here? What did I hope to accomplish?

Around them as far as he could see was the short-grass prairie. He looked up into the shelterless sky and in his mind heard his mother's softly spoken words: *"You should take Goyaałé home. Your father's spirit is not happy here."* Her last instruction weighed on him. Words he had read somewhere echoed out of memory: *If you do not feel the obligation, then there is no obligation.*

He removed his campaign hat, wiped the sleeve of his shirt across his brow, pulled the hat on again. He lifted one of Bui's bottles of Coca-Cola from its pre-1903 case, opened it, and drank down the contents. He couldn't remember the last time he'd slept. But there was no time for sleep; he had to keep going.

There were tasks at hand. He lifted the tin of fuel he'd placed on the ground and topped off the tank. Checked the oil level in the engine, the water level in the radiator. The tires were in good condition. He studied the eastern horizon a final time, got in behind the steering wheel, and adjusted the levers, put the transmission in neutral. Then moved to the front end of the car and took hold of the crank. One hard pull and the engine sputtered and coughed as he jumped into the driver's seat and adjusted the controls. The engine smoothed out and ran.

All around him was an essentially waterless country, an empty land the Indah had taken, as they had taken everything. He wondered what good it had done them, and drove on, thinking maybe they had taken it simply because they were stronger and could.

He tried to keep his mind on what he must do next and not think about Bui. Live or die, he had done what he could. For a time back there, he had gone crazy. For the first time in his life, he had wanted to kill, and he had killed. He shook his head and refocused on the motorcar. The motor in the Ford seemed to run truer than the one in the Locomobile. He hoped the engine would hold up long enough to get them to the Gila River country.

I need to sleep, he thought, but the Coca-Cola will keep me going.

The driver's seat was high enough it allowed him a good view of the empty country ahead. He still saw the occasional finger of chimney smoke, and these he avoided as he continued west. He spied the infrequent antelope and once, motoring over a rise, came upon a small herd of them. The herd turned and raced away. The cattle he saw looked out of place in this crueler land. The grass here was sparse and appeared to be water starved.

In the early afternoon he came within sight of a thin green line along the horizon. The browning prairie gave way to the river breaks above the upper Red. He drove the Ford up a grade onto a low, mesa-like rise, the engine sputtering as he leveled out on top and braked to a stop. He killed the engine to conserve fuel, his supply critically low now. He got out of the Ford and glassed the distant line of green. He pulled the compass from his shirt pocket and verified north. The river flowed directly out of the west.

He strapped on the heavy cartridge belt for the Sharps .50. He'd taken it off the man who had likely shot his sister. The one whose eyes he had stuck the point of his knife into so he would enter the next world blind—in the event his mother was right and there was another side.

He was beginning to think there might be.

The heavy rifle in hand, he slung two canvas water bags over his shoulder and jogged the quarter mile down to the river. He refilled the water bags, and afterward stripped naked and sat in the cool flow of one of the shallow channels. He scrubbed clean every place he could reach, using handfuls of the reddish sand as an alternative to soap. Then stood and used one of the water bags to rinse and afterward hand-stripped the water from his limbs and body, the warm afternoon sun drying him as he dressed. He refilled the water bag and, with the bags slung over his shoulders, jogged back to the Ford.

Bui's forehead was cool to his touch; her breathing seemed regular.

He topped off the radiator, checked the oil level, filled the fuel tank with the last tin of fuel, and tossed the tin into a nearby gully.

The engine cranked on the first pull, and he turned west and followed the river.

Late in the day he motored across a dome of sparse ground and spied the rooftops of a small town and braked to a halt. Maybe a dozen buildings in the near distance; they were situated on the bluff above the river. He used the spyglass to study the town. One of the buildings might be a general store. Another was definitely a blacksmith's. It pleased him that he could see no telegraph poles, but it seemed unlikely there would be gasoline down there.

At this point it's either find gasoline or buy horses, he thought, turned and grimaced as he looked at Bui. I'd need a buggy, too.

The color he saw in her cheeks made him wonder whether that was a good sign. He didn't know. Her breathing was still okay. To reassure himself he pressed the tips of his fingers lightly against her throat. The pulse he felt was strong and steady.

He turned his attention back to the town. It looked like many others he had seen from the train on his trip back to Fort Sill: thrown up fast and largely left unpainted in the heady days of new hope and fresh beginnings. A place that had used itself up as it used up the land around it—and he noted with that thought the remaining cottonwoods along the river, stand-alone soldiers amidst the stump remains of their felled brethren. Off to his right a road curved down into the town from the dry plains above.

He collapsed the spyglass, studied Bui's sleeping face for a worried moment, then slid down behind the wheel and drove on until he came to the road: a set of ruts with a strip of weedy grass growing down the middle. He lined the Ford out in the road and followed it down to the cluster of buildings and swung onto the town's main street. People hurried out onto the porches of their houses to gawk; women in work dresses looked up from their vegetable gardens, shading their eyes against the afternoon sun; the smithy's hammer ceased its ringing, and the smithy stepped out of the livery in a black leather apron, carrying hammer and tongs.

Boys appeared from every direction, and by the time Chaco braked to a stop outside a wind-scoured building that was the town's only store, several of them were running along behind him. He switched off the engine and waited as the motor sputtered itself out and died. The boys were standing back from the car in a panting half-circle, eyes lit with wistful curiosity.

Chaco stepped down from the car. He adjusted the canvas pack into what seemed a more comfortable position under Bui's head and, for a moment, could almost see Goyaałé's withered face again. Among the People it was said that his father had the power —and that this power had protected him against all the Indah's bullets. Strange that, in the end, it had not been the whiteeyes' bullets that killed him, but whiskey—in a way the same kind of thing they'd used against his sister.

Some part of him hoped that the power his father once possessed remained in his bones, and that Goyaałé's medicine even now was seeping through the canvas into Bui's heart. That his father's power would go to his sister and overpower the damage the bullet had done. Bui must live and be strong again.

One of the boys ventured closer. "Say, mister, you mind if we touch it?"

Chaco blinked. He'd been woolgathering. He looked into the

boy's eager blue eyes. He had a freckled, sunburned face under a shock of curly, uncombed, reddish hair.

"Better not. I'm carrying a sick woman."

"Oh." The boy took a hesitant step back. "Is it catching?"

"Probably not for you, but it'd be better if she's not disturbed. Sorry."

"It's okay. It sure is a pretty motorcar. How fast will she go?"

"Faster than a racehorse, I can tell you that."

"Wow." The boy studied Chaco's clothes. "You're a marine, ain't you?"

"I used to be."

"Then you've seen the ocean. Is it big as they say?"

"Bigger than Texas."

"Wow. No kidding?"

The store's screen door slammed. Chaco glanced at the man, who stepped out onto the porch, a grungy white apron tied about his middle; he walked out to the edge and leaned against one of the support posts of the rusty awning. A skinny man in his mid-forties, he picked at his tobacco-stained teeth with the whittled end of a match stem, eyes shifting back and forth between the gang of boys and Chaco.

"How'd you get that motorcar, Meskin, steal it?"

For a half dozen heartbeats Chaco considered shooting him. It was the unspoken apology in the boy's eyes that saved this fool. No shield of law, of station, or right of rank stood between this one and death, save this boy full of dreams. He studied the man and wondered why he would say such a thing, or even think it, and looking back at him the man's eyes wavered.

He thought: This one thinks I'm Mexican. He decided to use the mistake to his advantage and, jerking his chin toward the Ford, said, "How do you like it, boss?"

The man snorted. "Something like that'd cost a man eight hundred bucks."

"Oh, this one, she don't belong to me, boss," he said, imitating the speech patterns of some of the English-speaking Cubans he'd known, the way they talked when they were putting the Indah on. "No, boss, this fine car, she belongs to my patron. I'm taking her to him, but I'm not sure where I am. Is this town Amarillo?"

"That's a good one," the man scoffed. "This here is the grand metropolis of Olympia. Your boss could probably buy this whole shebang for the price he give for that motorcar. I know I'd trade my part. If you don't know where you are or where Amarillo is, then I got just the thing you need: a map. Come on inside. I'll fix you up with one—that is, if you got any money."

"How about gasoline, you got any of that for sale?"

"I can't help you there. Might be they have some for sale in Childress. The rails go through there. Although your best bet is Clarendon. Say, is that a woman you got in back?"

"It's my sister. She's sick."

"Ain't got the yeller fever, has she?"

Chaco shrugged. "Who knows?"

The freckled boy took another step back, said, "We had a bout of that here last summer."

Chaco studied the worried expression on his face. "See that nobody touches this motorcar, and I'll give you a quarter, okay?"

"Wow. Sure, sure, mister."

Chaco adjusted the heavy cartridge belt about his middle, lifted the Sharps out of the Ford, and followed the man into the store.

"The name's Mr. Clark," Clark said, with an emphasis on the mister. "I bought this place from its original founder. It was a trading post in the old days. At the time I thought I'd make my fortune."

He shook his head, reached under a counter, and brought out a tattered map.

"This here is the only one I got, and I expect it's the only one in town. So I'll have to charge you a dollar for it, cash on the barrelhead. You got that much money?"

Chaco placed a silver dollar on the counter and nodded toward the map. "Spread it out, and show me where we are on it and where Amarillo is."

The dollar disappeared into Clark's pocket before he unfolded the map, a ragged, fading square of yellow paper. "This is where we are," he said, stabbing a finger at an X and the word "Olympia" neatly inked in beside a set of lines that represented the river below the town.

Chaco rested the butt of his rifle on the counter and pointed. "So all this part up here is all one canyon?"

"The Palo Duro," Clark said. "Charlie Goodnight's JA Ranch is up that way. Him and his partner, John Adair, Gawd rest him, they got about a million acres they say. Then there's the RO and the Quarter Circle Heart, the two other ranches in there. They ship a lot of cattle out of Clarendon. You can bet they'll have gasoline in that town, if it's to be had in this gawdforsaken country. What I'd do is drive to Childress; it's a water stop on the Fort Worth and Denver City."

He referred to the map.

"It's not drawn here, but if you follow the road you come in on it'll take you south on to Childress. If they don't have any gasoline, you can order some or just follow the tracks west on into Clarendon. You'll get you some gasoline there, and after that all you got to do is keep following them tracks right on into Amarillo. I could have told you that before, but then I wouldn't have your dollar. What kind of businessman would that make me?"

"Hardly any kind at all," Chaco said. "This Mr. Goodnight, he lives in Clarendon?"

"I believe he lives on the ranch. Near eighty years old and still alive. I heard his partner was a rich Scotsman. He died in '85 and being in the cattle business I won't take my oath on him still being rich, even dead. Anything else I can sell you?"

"No." Chaco folded the map, tucked it into his shirt pocket, and walked out of the store. More boys had gathered in the street. Most of them stood back from the Ford, but there were some who were circling close, their eyes full of admiration. The freckled-faced kid was saying things like, "There's a sick woman in that car. I think she's got something catching. Best keep back."

Chaco went down the steps and walked over to the car. He waved the freckled-faced boy over to him. "Like to help me crank this thing?"

The boy's eyes brightened. "Can I?"

He judged the boy was maybe ten or twelve years old, but already as tall as him. Chaco talked the boy through the cranking process, demonstrated how to draw the handle away at the top of the pull to clear the crankshaft when the engine caught, thereby avoiding the kickback and potential broken forearm.

"Wow," the boy muttered.

"You ready to try this?"

The boy nodded, and Chaco pressed a silver dollar into his hand and watched his eyes widen.

"You said a quarter."

Chaco winked, and the coin disappeared into boy's pocket as he climbed behind the wheel and got everything ready. "Okay, crank her."

The kid spit into his palm, rubbed his hands together, took hold of the crank handle, fitted the cogs into the crankshaft, and yanked up hard. The engine caught and ran. The boy moved off to one side and was instantly surrounded by the other boys, who began slapping him on the back and congratulating him.

Chaco eased the Ford down to the shallow crossing, most of the boys running along close behind him. They stopped at the water's edge and stood waving as he drove across, climbed the opposite grade, and drove on.

Although he'd studied the map only briefly, he had it in his head now. The road, if it continued south, would bring him to Childress. He saw cattle in the road up ahead. At the sound of his approach, they scattered and ran away. This was cattle country. It had been overgrazed and looked as used up as the brushy mesquites that littered the landscape like skeletal apparitions. When he'd driven far enough south of the town that his engine noise would no longer be heard, he swung west again. Soon enough he came to another fence, stopped and cut through. As he walked back to the Ford, he heard Bui moan. He hurried to her and saw that her eyes were open.

"Can you speak?"

She had worked her arms out from under the blanket and now raised a hand to shade her eyes. "*How long have I slept?*"

"Are you in pain?"

"*A little.*" She stretched and winced. "*I remember. Someone shot me.*"

"Yes."

"*It was by those who followed. How did you get away from them?*"

"*They no longer follow.*"

The corners of her mouth turned down with a look of harsh acceptance.

He reached across the driver's seat, retrieved one of the canteens, and held it for her while she drank. "Drink it all," he said. "When you lose blood, it is a good thing to drink plenty of water."

Reluctantly she finished off the canteen, closed her eyes a moment, opened them again and looked at him. "*Where are we?*"

"In Texas near the Red River," he said.

"*We have traveled far.*"

"Do you need anything?"

"Laudanum," she muttered, the dullness in her eyes touched by shame.

He pulled the cork on a bottle, with a couple of swallows left in the bottom, and gave it to her. She drank it down.

"Want some more water?"

She shook her head.

"Okay, then. We have to keep moving."

She nodded, and he got in behind the wheel and drove on.

The Ford's engine ran smooth, and the car covered ground well, and they made good time. Soon enough they came to another set of rails at a whistle-stop called Estelline—a few cattle pens and a yellow wood-frame depot, some houses. He asked the station agent if there was any gasoline he could buy, but there was none. Nor was there any at Newlin, the next water stop up the line. Both agents showed an inordinate interest in the Ford and in Bui, who despite her claims of being okay had grown feverish and occasionally mumbled in her sleep.

He drove on, the tires rumbling softly over the uneven ground.

"*I can smell him,*" Bui blurted out behind him.

The car slowed as he eased off on the accelerator. "*Smell who?*"

"Geronimo's bones," she answered in English.

"You're lying on them; on him."

"*I know,*" she said, and with a slight groan she sat up and looked around.

Chaco brought the Ford to a stop. "What are you doing?"

"*I've slept long enough. I need to sit up. I must see the country we're going through.*"

"I can give you some more medicine and something else to lean against."

"*The smell of death is nothing.*" She shook her head. "*I want to see this country.*"

There was no dissuading her. He nodded assent, and she moved, the pain in her eyes like a momentary reflection of candlelight. He hovered, ready to help. But she managed the move on her own and relocated in stages from the bed in back to the passenger seat. She settled in and looked at him, and he asked whether she was hungry.

"No." She shook her head.

There was another canteen, and this she accepted and drank deeply from.

He drove on.

The air was drier and the sun's heat sharper here. There were fewer cattle and fewer fences. Juniper-covered ground, reddish sandstone pillars, and distant uplifts under the seeming endless vault above the blue world marked the vast gateway into the Palo Duro.

Bui sat straight, her eyes taking in everything. She smiled at him when she noticed his worried glances. If she suffered, she hid it well. Or the drug hid it. But what else should he expect? The absurdity of what he was doing, of what now they were doing together, was not lost on him—he put at risk their lives to transport the bones of a dead man from one grave to another. And what did it matter, really? Yet it did matter. It had mattered to his mother and to Goyaałé, and now it mattered to him. He had read Cervantes and from that book had learned that without such seemingly pointless acts of defiance, a man was nothing. That mankind was nothing. What they did now was by far the greatest thing he had ever done and perhaps ever would. He must do this thing in defiance of the men in Washington, in defiance of that power that, over the centuries, had wiped the earth of his kind. It would change nothing, and at the end of all things it mattered only to him, to his mother, and, if the spirit of a man lingered in the world after death, to his father. He wondered if they were together now, the ghost of his father and the ghost of his mother, Lozen, the one who had given him life at the cost of her own.

The sun sank flame-red beneath a horizon gone black, and he halted long enough to light the headlights. An hour later and a few miles beyond Memphis, he came upon a signpost located near the rails: "Entering Donley County." Further on they bypassed Giles and other whistle-stops, not a drop of gasoline to be had at any. They overtook an ox-drawn freight-wagon a few miles on, and Chaco slowed to a crawl as they came abreast of the driver.

"How far to Clarendon, mister?"

"About another eight to ten miles, which I won't make tonight, but you might."

Chaco waved and drove on.

As the stars brightened in the early evening, Bui gripped the windshield, stood up. She extended her arm toward a cluster of lights on the featureless land ahead, the town they'd hoped to reach before they exhausted the last of their gasoline.

We made it, he thought as Bui sat down and smiled across the car at him.

A mile farther on he caught a whiff of ammonia: the smell of cattle urine and the signature odor of cattle pens. When they came to the edge of town, Chaco slowed to a stop. He could see the lights of the train station reflected dimly off the water tower just beyond the station. He studied the telegraph wires that preceded them into the town. By this time the telegraph service out of Lawton might very well have been restored, and he could be driving into a trap.

I should have planned better. I should have stationed horses a hundred miles west of Lawton and abandoned McDonnell's motorcar.

But he hadn't stationed horses, and in the end it didn't matter what he should have done, only what he had done. Right now he needed gasoline. He considered cutting the lines before driving in, but if the telegraph out of Lawton had been repaired, then cutting the line into Clarendon was pointless and, in fact, would serve only as a warning.

"*What troubles you?*" Bui asked.

"*The talking wire.*"

"*Cut it as you did before.*"

"No, not this time," he said, then reached down and turned the water drip on the acetylene generator to the off position. "You should respect the intelligence of an enemy enough never to risk the same trick twice."

"*We can go around.*"

"We must have gasoline," he said as the headlights faded and went dark. He swung the Ford left and drove out onto the prairie a little distance. Killed the engine, climbed out, and began unloading their gear.

"*I can help.*"

"I'll do it. All the guns and cartridge belts have to come out. And Goyaałé's bones and anything that came from McDonnell's store."

Bui began lifting things out of the back seat.

"You should rest. I can do this."

"*I am stronger than you think.*"

"That's the laudanum talking," he said. She grunted contentiously, looped several cartridge belts over one arm, grabbed a rifle, and moved off toward the growing pile.

"*How many did you kill?*" she asked.

"As you see, we have their weapons." He shrugged. "That's how many."

The work didn't take long, and when they were done, Chaco pressed the spyglass into her hand.

"You can watch me through this. Once I have the gasoline, I will come back for you."

"*I want to come with you.*"

He rested a hand on her shoulder and shook his head.

"I'll be back in an hour."

He removed the tattered map from his shirt pocket and placed it in her hand.

"Take this. If I'm not back in an hour, you'll know something went wrong. It will be for you then to see that Goyaałé's bones get to the Gila River country."

"*I cannot do it alone.*"

"There's no one else. *Be strong.*"

She studied the hard set of his face a moment, then nodded. "*I will.*"

"*You were always strong. You only forgot it for a while,*" he said in their tongue. Now was the time to tell her about their mother, if he was ever to tell her. If something happened to him, there was the possibility she might go back for Aná. "*I wrote* letters *and sent them to you before I came to get you,*" he said.

"*I never saw them.*"

"*I know. In the last one I wrote, I told you something that I need to tell you now.*"

She was looking at him, her dark eyes faintly luminous in the semi-dark. "*There's no easy way. Aná is dead. She is in that graveyard where they bury our people.*"

A low moan escaped her. He reached for her and held her to him, and she buried her face against his chest.

"*I'm sorry, but I couldn't tell you before. Now I have to. You cannot go back to that place, ever.*" He felt her head nod against his chest. Telling her had taken only a few words, but they were for him the hardest words he'd every spoken.

The engine cranked and ran on the first try. He slipped behind the wheel, turned the car around, and drove back to the road. He relit the headlamps and swung left and drove into the town, past several streetlamps and on toward the train station.

The ticket office was located adjacent to the tracks, and was a narrow, rectangular, boxcar-like building painted railroad yellow, inside of which he saw the flicker of lamplight—someone he could ask about fuel was probably on duty.

He throttled back as he came to the station, and the brakes squealed as he brought the Ford to a stop. As he killed the engine, the red ember of a cigarette arched from the shadows and sparked against the station platform. A man came away from the building and walked toward him, a hatless man in a black suit coat and dark trousers. He was about fifty, his black hair graying at the temples, a sun-ravaged face, his coat unbuttoned, and a silver star pinned to his white shirt. "Nice-looking T Model," he said, his smile friendly as he looked directly at Chaco. "Just so we're clear on what happens next, son, right now you're covered by four rifles. So don't make any sudden moves."

41

It had been the right thing to do, turning Buck and Mabel free on the prairie. It hadn't been easy. Buck had been with him going on ten years and Mabel somewhere around eight. Like riding away from two best friends, but at least by pulling their shoes before setting them free he'd given them an even chance.

Tom had made Ham as comfortable as possible in the back seat of the Ford. Which wasn't easy, seeing as he was over six feet in height and big, and the Ford's back seat was short and narrow. He'd driven a Buick for a week once while on federal business in Oklahoma City and remembered enough about the machine to get this one started and rolling in the right direction. The rest he would pick up as they went along.

With Vernon handcuffed in the passenger seat, he drove in a southeasterly direction across the open prairie. It was toward noon that he spied the line of telegraph poles. Like distant fence pickets at first, they rose out of the horizon and soon enough became the poles he knew them to be.

By that time he could see the railroad tracks and the road that ran parallel to the tracks on the other side. He eased the Ford up over the ballast and the rails and swung right onto the road and followed the tracks south. The road was a leftover from when the tracks were being put down and was old and unmaintained. Sometimes he would have to swerve to avoid a rotted crosstie that had been discarded by repair crews. He'd driven several miles before he began to see hayfields and knew that the Red River couldn't be much farther ahead.

When he saw the line of green and the treetops that marked the winding way of the Red, he sped up a little. But he had to slow down and finally braked to a stop when he came in sight of the river itself. There was no way he'd be able to ford it at this point. Instead he risked driving across on the trestle.

"I sure hope there ain't no train a-coming," Vernon yelled, midway across, the whites of his eyeballs like boiled eggs.

But either luck or God was with them, and they got across without so much as the whistle of an approaching engine. He swung off the tracks and rolled down the ballast embankment, the crushed rock crunching under the Ford's tires, and turned onto the road again. He'd taken a risk, yes, but one worth taking, with his friend's life at stake. Ham was fading, and Tom was afraid he might not last long enough to make it to a doctor. In fact, he was hardly breathing by the time Tom caught sight of Quanah up ahead.

"Ain't that a water tower I see?" Vernon asked.

"It is for a fact," Tom said.

They rolled past a few outlying houses and soon enough rumbled over the tracks of the Fort Worth and Denver City where they intersected with the tracks they'd followed, the Acme and Pacific. The dirt road into town became First Street, and Tom slowed and stopped in front of the Acme and Pacific depot, a white stucco building with a red-tile roof located across the street from the tracks.

A black porter was loading boxes off a freight wagon onto a

green iron-wheeled trolley. Tom called to him: "Hey you, boy, come over here. I got a question."

The porter placed the box he held on the baggage trolley and sidled over.

"Yes, sir?"

"I'm Deputy U.S. Marshal Tom Starrett, and I'm looking for a doctor. I got a wounded lawman here that needs medical attention."

The porter glanced into the back seat, then looked at Tom. "Yes, sir. That street there is Mercer." He pointed. "You go to the next corner, that'll be Second Street. You turn right and go three blocks to Earle. The doctor lives in the white house on the right with the picket fence. There's a sign with his name on it. You cain't miss it, sir."

Tom said, "Thanks," and drove on.

He turned right at the corner and drove quickly past a freight wagon being off-loaded by workmen, who paused to stare as they motored by.

Near the end of the third block, Vernon said, "Ain't that it?"

It was, and Tom pulled to the curb out front. The sign looked professional and hung from a white post beside the gate: "Dr. Graham Evens, MD."

He considered leaving Vernon with the car but decided against it.

"You'd best come with me." Tom got out and uncuffed Vernon from the seat. Then recuffed him and told him to stay close, and Vernon trailed after him, his manacled hands held close to his belly.

The pine-plank porch of the house was painted a light gray, and there was a swing with cushions that hung on chains behind a lattice thick with vines and flowers. Tom knocked on the screen door. From inside came the sound of a chair being scooted. A few moments later a man in his mid-fifties, trim, medium height, white shirt, gray vest, and black trousers, opened the door and looked through the screen. Behind him Tom saw, in the adjoining room, a lovely young woman seated at the dinner-room table, her hand at rest on the napkin beside her plate.

"Are you Doc Evens?"

"I am. How may I help you?"

"I have a wounded lawman in that motorcar behind me. He needs doctoring bad."

The doctor turned back toward the woman and sighed. "My apologies, dear, but it would seem our dinner will have to wait." When he turned back to Tom, he was smiling somewhat wearily. "Let us have a look at your friend, then."

Tom noted a rabbity look in Vernon's eye, and to stay on the safe side he gestured for Vernon to lead the way and followed them both out to the car. As soon as the doc saw Ham, he went to work. He drew a watch from his vest, popped it open, and, with the tip of his index fingers held against Ham's neck, stared at the watch for several moments. The watch snapped closed, and he looked at Tom.

"How long ago was he shot?"

"Late last night. He took a load of buckshot."

"Let's get him inside. I'll need your help. Wait here."

Doctor Evens hurried back to the house and quickly returned with a stretcher. They lifted Ham out of the back seat and eased him onto it. Tom unlocked one of Vernon's cuffs, ordered him to take hold in front, then grabbed the stretcher handles near Ham's feet. Together they lifted and carried him through the house and into perhaps the whitest room Tom had ever seen.

"Where do you want him?" Tom asked.

The doc was standing at a sink, a water tap turned on and his hands lathered with soap. He gestured with an elbow. "Next to the operating table, the one with the clean sheet."

They carried the stretcher across the room and eased it down.

They both stepped back, and Tom relocked the cuff to Vernon's freed wrist. Of a sudden, he began to tremble. He'd done all he could, but somehow it didn't seem enough.

The doctor called out, "Charlotte, where are you?"

"In the kitchen putting water on to heat," she called back.

"I need this man's clothing cut away."

"I'm on my way."

Within moments the woman hurried into the room, her genteel air now replaced by a no-nonsense quality that Tom found somewhat intimidating. She had slipped on a white full-length apron, and the cuffs of her long-sleeved dress were turned back to reveal slender, strong-looking arms. Her hands were still wet from washing as she opened a drawer and brought out a set of heavy shears. She crossed to where Ham lay and, with quick, deft moves, cut away his shirt and trousers, and was about to take the shears to Ham's new-looking stovepipe boots when Tom stepped forward and worked them off his big feet. Ham's socks were full of holes.

Tom said, "He'd skin me if I let you cut these off him, ma'am."

The doc, meanwhile, had prepared a syringe.

Tom tossed the boots to Vernon, studied the syringe. "What are you giving him?"

"Morphine, for the pain."

"You got any extra, I'll try some," Vernon said, the boots clutched to his chest.

Tom shot him a hard look, intending to shut him up.

The doctor gave Ham the injection and looked at Tom. "That should do it."

Tom nodded and watched the visible tension in his friend's rigid body ease.

The doctor ordered Tom and Vernon to take hold of Ham's shoulders while he and Mrs. Evens grasped his legs, and together the four of them lifted Ham off the bloodstained stretcher and placed him on the operating table.

"Gentlemen, you've done all you can. This is where we go to work. If you'll go through that door, you'll find the parlor. You can wait there."

"How long you reckon this is going to take, Doc?"

"I'm doing a surgical procedure, not shoeing a horse. I'll call you when we're done."

They waited in the parlor, Vernon staring out of predatory eyes across the room at Tom, while Tom, staring back, thought about the man who had shot his friend and killed all those others. Somebody would have to do something about that, and as he sat in the straight-backed chair with the sunlight fading in the parlor, he reckoned that that somebody was going to be him. As the last light faded and the room darkened, Vernon Cotton eased up out of his chair and took a cautious step on his tiptoes, but stopped as he heard the hammer on Tom's Colt click back a notch. He backed up a step and sat down again and, after a long moment, cleared his throat.

"Just wanted to stretch my legs."

"You can stretch your legs when they stretch your neck."

"You don't think they're actually going to hang me?"

"Yes, I do."

"Well, that ain't right, Marshal. Them's my own kids, not the property of no damned government."

"Tell it to the judge. He's bound to take that into consideration."

"You think he will?"

"Oh yeah."

Mrs. Evens came into the room and lit a lamp. Vernon Cotton blinked and smiled, his remaining teeth like rotted swamp stumps in his bleeding gums.

"The doctor is dressing your friend's wounds," Mrs. Evens

said. "He had a close brush, but the doctor believes you got him here soon enough. He's heavily sedated, and I expect he'll sleep out the night. You can look in on him in the morning. We'll want to keep him here for a while."

Tom was on his feet, hat in hand. "I can't thank you enough, ma'am. Can we help move him to a bed or anyplace like that?"

"No, Graham and I have everything in hand, but thank you. I believe there are rooms at the hotel across from the station."

"Yes, ma'am. Might I ask you a question?"

"You may."

"Can I assume you have a jailhouse in this town?"

"Why yes, of course we do. It's located on the courthouse square. Why?"

"It's my prisoner here. I need a place to lock him up, ma'am."

Vernon smiled and shrugged. "It's a misunderstanding, ma'am."

"I see," she said, and refocused on Tom. "I'll not detain you longer, Marshal. Good evening." She turned and walked out of the room.

"I'll check in on Ham come morning, ma'am," Tom called after her, annoyed at being snubbed on account of his prisoner.

42

The Hardeman County deputy shook Tom's extended hand, said, "Pleasure to meet you, Marshal Starrett. I'm Buck Carey, the night watchman."

Tom frowned. "Watchman?" The man was on the skinny side and kind of unkempt; he was in his midforties and wore a silver badge with the word "Deputy" stamped into it.

"Yes, sir," the watchman explained. "See, the sheriff, he don't want me to get no daylight-job ideals. He likes to have someone on duty at night. So that's what he calls me, but I'm actually a deputy."

"Well, Deputy Carey, I have a prisoner here with two counts of murder against him. Both murders were of children under the age of twelve. I need you to lock him up and hold him until I can arrange for his transport back to Oklahoma City." Tom was fully aware of the paperwork nightmare he was about to create by parking his prisoner here, but he couldn't worry about that, even if it cost him his job.

Deputy Carey lifted his hat and scratched behind his ear. "Well, Marshal, I'd have to call the sheriff about something like that."

"You call him, but do it after we get this gentleman locked up in a cell."

"Maybe I better telephone him first."

"Listen, son, I'm a federal marshal, and this man is a murderer. What you're going to do is lock him up first and then call your boss." Tom was running out of patience. It didn't matter he was putting Deputy Carey on the spot. At this point it was either get Vernon in a cell, or take him out on the prairie somewhere, put a bullet in his head, and write it off as an attempted escape. He sighed; even as pleasant as that happy prospect might be, it wasn't his preference.

The deputy allowed himself a quick glance at Vernon and got a big grin for his troubles.

"Howdy." Vernon extended one of his cuffed hands.

To the deputy's credit, he caught himself before he actually shook it. He studied Vernon for a long moment. Then turned back to Tom. "I guess we can lock him up. But I got to telephone the sheriff right after."

"Lead the way."

"The cells are back here."

Carey hurried out ahead of them to an iron door in the back wall. It groaned on rusty hinges. The rectangular room beyond had brick walls with barred windows high up. The cells were located in the center of the room and were made of plate iron and riveted flat bars, with a walkway all the way around. The deputy opened the door of the middle cell and stood back as Tom shoved Vernon through. Vernon staggered a couple of steps and turned around as the deputy closed and locked the heavy door.

"Stick your hands between them bars." Tom held up the handcuff key.

Vernon extended his wrists through a narrow gap between the

bars, and Tom unlocked and removed the cuffs. Vernon massaged his wrists as he looked around the cell.

"Is this what they mean when they say not a pot to piss in or a lid to cover it with?"

"I'll bring you a slop jar," the deputy said, and stared dubiously at Tom. "I got to say it, Marshal. He don't seem like a man who'd kill a kid."

"Who does? But, trust me, he did. Don't get too comfortable around this one."

"If you say so, Marshal."

Vernon was holding on to the bars now. "Hey, you wasn't lying about that advice you give me, was you, Marshal?"

"Advice?"

"About what to tell the judge?"

"Save yourself some money, Vernon. Tell the judge you want to be your own lawyer. You're a smart guy. I wouldn't trust no court-appointed attorney if I was as smart as you."

Vernon nodded. "Thanks, Marshal."

"You're welcome, Vernon."

The deputy followed Tom out of the cellblock, slammed and locked the iron door. Then crossed the office to the wall phone and lifted the receiver off the hook. He looked back at Tom.

"Is that guy as dumb as he acts?"

"Watch yourself with that one. He's dangerous. He'll kill you the first mistake you make and be gone quick as a snake."

There was nothing more to say, and he left the deputy cranking the wall phone, walked out of the jail and the courthouse, crossed the lawn to the Ford, and cranked the engine. He drove back along Mercer Street to the train station, parked near the "Whites Only" entrance, and went in. There were a couple of benches in the lobby. The waiting area was empty. He crossed to the telegrapher's office, opened the door marked "No Admittance," and stepped inside. The operator, a thin man wearing a visor, looked up from his key.

"I assume you can't read? But in case you do, the sign on the door means what it says: no unauthorized personnel allowed in here."

Tom showed his badge. "I'm sending telegrams to Lawton and Oklahoma City."

"Oklahoma City maybe, but not Lawton. That line is still down."

Tom frowned. "The line is down?"

"That's what I said. It's been down a couple of days. There's a break they haven't been able to locate yet."

Tom scratched at the stubble on his chin. "That makes sense."

"What makes sense?"

Tom went over to the barred customer window and plucked one of the yellow telegraph forms from the holder. He broke the string that held the stub of a pencil, and walked back to the telegrapher's desk, placed the form on the desk, and wrote a short message to his boss in Oklahoma City in neat block letters. At the end of the message, he added a series of code letters. Then he straightened and reread the telegram, marked through three unnecessary words, and handed the yellow form to the operator.

"Send that, and make damned certain you get the letters at the end exactly right."

The telegrapher read the message. His eyes widened.

"Right away, Marshal."

Tom stood behind the operator and listened to the quick dots and dashes. The telegram informed his boss that Sheriff McKnight was holding the murderer, Vernon Cotton, in Quanah, Texas. That he himself was in pursuit of another murderer who had killed six Comanche County deputies and all but fatally wounded Sheriff Hamilton Jones, who at present was under the care of a surgeon. Six code letters attached to the end requested another deputy marshal be sent to collect Vernon Cotton, as his own situation remained fluid. The telegrapher tapped out the correct code letters, signed off, and looked up at Tom.

"You know Morse code, don't you?"

Tom nodded. "I do."

"I can usually tell," the telegrapher said.

A train whistle sounded in the near distance. They both turned.

"That'll be the evening run out of Lawton," the telegrapher said, rising out of his chair and crossing to a window that looked onto the rail-side platform. "If you want to get that message to Lawton, Marshal, it'll probably get there faster if you send it by letter. That train will go back to Lawton come morning."

Tom crossed to the window as the engine rolled into the station followed by a line of cars. Behind him the telegraph key began to click. The operator hurried back to his key as the engine vanished momentarily in a cloud of exhaust steam. Couplings slammed together like the cracking of a long iron spine. A conductor stepped down from the lead Pullman hardly a moment ahead of an army officer—a captain wearing a flapped sidearm and khaki trousers, bloused inside canvas leggings, his field jacket buttoned to the throat against the cold. The chinstrap of his campaign hat was drawn tight against the back of his close-cropped head. The captain turned back toward the Pullman and began to shout orders. Soldiers came rushing off the train and began to form up on the platform. There were about twenty of them, and every man wore a backpack and carried an '03 rifle slung over his shoulder on its leather sling. A sergeant took up position in front of the formation, and when the soldiers were well formed he did an about-face and saluted the captain.

"Sir."

Behind Tom the telegrapher said, "Any other messages you want to send out, Marshal?"

"How's the line west of here?"

"Far as I know, it's operational all the way to California."

"Then send this: 'To all stations between here and Amarillo, keep a lookout for a—'"

"Hold on a minute, Marshal. You got to write all messages down. That's how Western Union gets reimbursed from the Marshals Service. You have to write it and sign it."

"You write it, I'll sign it, but right now what I want is for you to send it."

The telegrapher drew a yellow form toward him and took up a pencil. He looked at Tom and nodded.

Tom sighed. Then began dictating: "'To all law officers and concerned citizens,' stop. 'Keep a lookout for an armed, extremely dangerous murderer traveling west in a motorcar,' stop." Tom gave the telegrapher a little time to catch up, then said, "'This fugitive killed six Comanche County deputies and wounded the Comanche County sheriff at a location sixty miles northwest of Quanah,' stop."

The telegrapher looked up, disbelief on his slack features. "You're saying one man did all that?"

Tom nodded. "I reckon so. Let's get this done," he said. "'Repeat: This man is armed and extremely dangerous,' stop. 'Report any sightings immediately to U.S. Marshal Tom Starrett in Quanah, Texas,' full stop."

"That's it?"

Tom nodded.

"Then I got it."

"Good. Send that telegram word for word, and I'll want confirmation from every operator up the line that they got that message and proof that they relayed it to their local law enforcement."

"I'm going to need you to sign on these telegrams, Marshal."

"I'll be at the hotel. Don't bother me unless there's been a sighting. If you get one of those, then you come get me double-quick, understand?"

"I can't leave my station, Marshal. It would mean my job."

"Trust me, it won't. Keep up with the word count, and make the bill out to Deputy U.S. Marshal Tom Starrett, U.S. Marshals Service, and I'll sign the pay chit when I pick up those confirmations in the morning."

The "No Admittance" door slammed open, and the captain rushed in.

"I have a telegram that I . . . ," he began, but then saw Tom. The captain frowned. "The name is Banyan, Captain Banyan. Are you the sheriff or a deputy in this burg?"

"Deputy U.S. Marshal, Starrett's the name." Tom reached for the extended hand.

43

"I'm Sheriff Leigh," the man said to Chaco as he drew back the lapel of his coat, displayed a badge pinned to his white shirt. "Like I said, son, you're covered by my deputies and under arrest."

Chaco swiveled his head. Saw men with rifles tight against their shoulders moving out from the deep shadow of doorways across the street.

"Every one of those boys is a crack shot."

The Sharps lay ready to hand, but he didn't grab for it. Instead he watched the deputies advance with their rifles up and pointed at him, the jangle of their spurs and jinglebobs musical in the heavy silence. They wore dark vests over white shirts, sweat-stained felt hats, the barrels of their rifles unsteady. They were nervous, and that gave Chaco reason to be nervous, too.

"We're going to take you up to the jail," the sheriff said, his voice deeper now and full of regained confidence. "Slow and easy, I want you to climb down from that automobile and . . . please . . . move slow."

Chaco swung his legs out of the car and stepped down. He raised his hands and hoped that Bui was using the spyglass now, watching all of this. The sheriff drew his pistol and moved around behind him. He pressed the muzzle into Chaco's side, reached around, and unbuckled the heavy cartridge belt and tossed it into the back seat. He then patted Chaco's hips, pulled the pistol tucked in close to his spine, and shoved it under his own belt. He removed the clasp knife from Chaco's front pocket and tossed it into the car with the cartridge belt. Then he checked Chaco's boot tops for weapons and ran his hands up his sides to his armpits. This one mostly knew what he was doing.

The deputies were standing in a semicircle around them, their rifles at the ready.

"My Gawd," said one, "it's a Meskin and dressed up like a marine, too. Where'd you steal them clothes from, Pancho?"

The sheriff stepped back and blanched irritably. "Woodruff, for Christ's sake, lower that gun—the rest of you, too. Cain't you see we've done took him?"

Reluctantly the deputies lowered their rifles.

"You said to keep him covered," one of them grumbled.

The sheriff stepped behind Chaco, grabbed him by the shirt collar. "Put your hands behind your back, son."

Chaco brought his wrists together behind him, felt the bite of the handcuffs and then the sheriff's rough grip as he spun him around.

"If you got anything to say, now would be a good time. It'll go easier on you."

"He's your man, Sheriff," the hatchet-faced deputy said. "How many Meskins you figure to catch driving a motorcar?" He pointed his rifle toward the Model T.

"We'll see," the sheriff said. "Al, you stay here with the car. I'll add an extra dollar to the two dollars the county owes. You'll stand guard until I get this straightened out."

"Ain't nobody going to mess with this car, Sheriff. Heck, I kindly wanted to see—"

"You on the county payroll or not?"

"Yes, sir, I am," Al admitted dejectedly, stuck and aware of it. The man who got stuck with a reputation for unreliability, earned or not, had just as well clear out of the country.

"Then do the job." The sheriff prodded Chaco with his pistol. "Walk ahead."

He set out. A chill gust of wind sent a scrap of newspaper skittering along the street.

"Feels like a blue norther a-coming," Hatchetface said.

Woodruff looked up into the night. "It's a norther blowing in."

"Didn't I just say that?"

Chaco kept moving in the direction the sheriff shoved him. "Go left here," he said at the corner.

He turned the corner and walked north on South Jefferson. Deputy Woodruff came a few quick steps forward and fell in beside Chaco.

"What's your name, Pancho?"

So far Chaco had seen no point in speaking, and he saw none now. He stared straight ahead, gaze seemingly fixed on an invisible point, the way he'd been taught in basic training. Deputy Woodruff jogged a couple of steps ahead, turned, and walked backward, the grin on his face confident, if not that bright.

"You can tell me. What's your name? No? Won't talk, huh? How about a little whack upside the head? Bet that'll get you talking—"

"Hit my prisoner, Woodruff, and you'll share the next cell," the sheriff said.

The hard look in Woodruff's eyes quailed. "He's a murderer," he complained.

"He's my prisoner, and we're doing this by the book. We clear on that?"

Chaco kept walking. He could see the deputy wanted to punch him.

"Maybe he don't *habla* no English, Lem," one of the others said.

The sheriff scoffed. "Oh, yeah, he *hablas* okay."

"He looks more Injun than Meskin to me."

"How would you know, Bill?" Woodruff quipped. "You ain't never even seen one."

"No more than you. Besides, I seen pictures in a book. And this here feller looks Injun."

Chaco, listening as he walked, knew that whatever move he made, it would have to be after the sheriff removed the cuffs. He thought about Bui. Hoped she would be able to do as he'd instructed: use the dark to her advantage and get as far away from this town as she could before daylight. It would be left to her to carry his father's bones home to the mountains, to bury him where he belonged.

The sheriff shoved him again. He realized he'd been drifting.

I can't think about what she should do, he thought. I have to think about what I can do. A chance will present itself, and when it does I must be ready.

"Keep to the middle of the street," the sheriff said behind him. "No sidewalks for you, bub." He emphasized the order with another shove.

Chaco stumbled deliberately, his intent to establish in the sheriff a sense of ineptitude in him as a prisoner; give these men confidence of the kind that might lower their defenses.

Woodruff lagged off and came up beside Chaco, turned, and stepped along backward, his gaze fixed half-mockingly on the sheriff. "So this runt is the famous killer that marshal is after?"

"Come morning," the sheriff said, "we'll know one way or the other."

At the town square, on Sully Street, two and a half blocks

south of the rails, they came in sight of a brick, three-story, castlelike courthouse. The jailhouse was positioned on the corner of the square, and as they approached, Chaco studied the two-story stucco with its brick corbellings, iron bars in the glassless second-story windows, and the wood-framed front and back porches that appeared to have been added on.

"Here's your new home, son," the sheriff said.

The rising wind swirled dust out of a side street. Lightning flickered, and in the electric glow an owl swooped out of the darkness, snatched up a scurrying rodent, and with a screech disappeared into the night.

Woodruff snorted. "Lord, did everybody see that?"

The first drops of rain splattered dust in the street—big, cold drops that fell at first like a scattering of windblown acorns and then came in earnest. They hurried him along now. Chaco mounted the jailhouse steps, crossed the rain-splattered porch to the door, and waited for the sheriff to open it. He stepped through with the deputies crowding one another in their efforts to get out of the rain. This would have been his moment had his hands not been cuffed behind him.

He studied the sparsely furnished office: a scarred oak desk cluttered with papers, a spring chair behind it, the walls wainscoted beneath raw-looking plaster, a printed-tin ceiling.

"Is that you, Wilbur?" a woman called.

The voice came from down a hallway that led farther into the building.

Sheriff Leigh crossed to the door. "I'll be there soon as I put this prisoner up."

"Shall I fix an extra plate for him?"

"Not now, we'll feed him later."

The sheriff closed the door and crossed to another, this one made of riveted iron and hung from heavy forged strap hinges.

There was a big brass key in the lock that he didn't turn before he pushed the door open.

"Let's go, son."

Woodruff gripped Chaco's arm and squeezed it as they went around the scarred desk and stepped through the opening. The sheriff lit a candle lamp and led the way up to the second floor. He opened another iron door, and Chaco stepped through. The jail was a large brick-walled space with six iron cages located down the middle, three on either side, a walk space between the cells and the external walls. The cells were made of riveted, flat iron bars and welded steel plates. Rain had blown through the barred windows and puddled on the concrete floor.

"Which cell you want him in, Sheriff?" Deputy Woodruff asked.

"The first one will do."

Woodruff lifted a ring of keys off an iron peg set in the brick wall and unlocked the cell. It had a multiple-lock design and looked escape-proof. The deputy opened the second of two iron doors, slammed it back hard enough to shiver the rest of the cells in the block.

"What the heck's that about?" the sheriff demanded.

"I want him to know he's about to get locked up."

Chaco stepped through the opening, turned, and looked out at the sheriff.

"You can remove the handcuffs now."

Sheriff Leigh grinned. "I knew at some point I'd get you to say something."

"You will get more than something out of Mr. Goodnight if anything happens to his motorcar," Chaco said, dropping the name of one of the ranchers the store owner back in Olympia had mentioned. The sheriff blanched . . . as did his deputies.

"Stick them out here," the sheriff said gruffly but with less confidence.

Chaco extended his wrists between the bars. The lawman was gentler removing the cuffs than he'd been putting them on, and Chaco knew he'd planted a seed of doubt.

"I'll check out your story in the morning, son. It's raining out, so you're better off sleeping here, anyway," the sheriff said, the hard edge in his voice softened. "Best step away from the cell door. You don't want to get any part of you caught when I lock it down."

With a nod Chaco eased back from the door. The sheriff pulled down on a long lever that locked the second cell door, and then closed the outer cell door, inserted the big brass key, and locked it.

"Hey," a voice called hoarsely from the other end of the cellblock. "Why didn't you put that feller down here where a man could talk to him without having to yell?"

"Hank Smith, is that you?" Woodruff called.

"It sure is. And I'm hungry. When's my supper, Wilbur?"

"Here you go, Lem." The sheriff tossed Woodruff the key ring. "Go let him out."

Bill looked at the sheriff in disbelief. "You're letting Hank out after what he done on the courthouse steps?"

"Yes, I am. Go on, Lem. Let him out."

Lem Woodruff grinned. "The judge ain't going to like it. But . . . you're the boss."

The sheriff didn't appear to hear the warning. He was staring hard between the strap-iron bars at Chaco.

"I'll telegraph the deputy at Goodnight station first thing in the morning, get him to ride out to Mr. Goodnight's place to verify your story." He studied Chaco as if trying to gauge his reaction to that prospect.

Chaco massaged his wrists. He looked out as the cell door at the far end clanged open and a chunky, gray-haired man of medium height limped into view, with Woodruff a step behind.

"Did I hear right, Wilbur? You're a-letting me go early?" He pulled on a battered range hat and squinted at the sheriff.

"That's Sheriff Leigh to you, Hank."

"Till you start addressing me as Mr. Hank Smith, it'll stay Wilbur. And I'll tell you something else, Wilbur: I ain't leaving the comforts of my unlawful confinement in the middle of a rainstorm without I get my supper first."

"You want to stay locked up with a man who's likely a murderer?" Lem Woodruff asked.

"You meet a better class of people in jail." Hank squinted through the bars at Chaco. "Howdy, my name's Hank. You wouldn't be the murderer these fellas think you are, would you? I'm just asking, mind you."

"No, sir, Mr. Smith. That wouldn't be me."

"Sir and Mr.?" Hank Smith grinned and turned toward the sheriff. "Hey, I like that. This here is a young man that's got respect for his elders, not like some I could mention."

"Pancho there come into town loaded for bear," said Woodruff, "and driving a Ford motorcar."

"Sounds like all the proof you need to hang a man in this country," Hank Smith said, and winked at Chaco. "You're going to love the victuals here, son. If you're ever down on your luck and need something to eat and a place to sleep in this here burg, all you got to do is take a piss on the courthouse steps. Works every time."

———

44

The rain fell steadily and hard. The roll of thunder died, and Bui adjusted the collar of her brother's field jacket closer to her neck. She stared at the jailhouse from the cover of a doorway almost directly across the street from the structure. Beyond the jail the courthouse loomed like a darkened palace. She could just make out the dim flicker of light beyond the barred windows of the jail's second story. The men who had arrested Chaco would certainly be up there with him now. She slipped the canvas bundle from her shoulders, sat it near to hand, and waited. She carried the spyglass Chaco had given her, her rifle, an extra gun belt besides the one she had taken for herself. It was the nickel-plated pistol with the fancy sheath knife that her brother had taken off one of the deputies. She had also brought along the shotgun, broken down and tightly wrapped inside the blanket roll, and a canteen of water and four cans of beef stew. That had been all she felt able to manage. She'd gulped down a bottle of Coca-Cola and filled the left-side pocket of the field jacket with the last bottles of laudanum. Now she stood in the dark with a brace of pistol holsters crisscrossed over her shoulders and across her body—both belts too long to buckle about her gaunt waist.

She had no plan, no idea how she might get Chaco out of that jail, but she knew she must try.

45

Tom Starrett pushed his plate toward the center of the table. For the past half hour he'd listened without comment as Banyan obligingly filled in most of the blanks. Wrongheaded as the captain was, the details were pretty much straightforward. The captain was in pursuit of a young Apache who'd gone off the reservation. A short—maybe five foot six or seven—twenty-two-year-old named Frank Kidd. This Kidd had kidnapped one of Lawton's leading citizens, a man named Alton McDonnell, who also happened to be Banyan's brother-in-law. That answered one question. This Frank Kidd had also stolen McDonnell's motorcar, which answered another. According to Banyan, Frank Kidd was a decorated corporal who'd spent four years in Cuba fighting with the Marine Corps. That answered another question. The problem Tom had was with Banyan, and it had to do with jurisdiction. Renegade Indians, even one who kidnaps your brother-in-law and steals his car, currently fell under the aegis and responsibility of the U.S. Marshals Service, a change in policy for which the Army had only itself to blame. Renegade Indians had ceased to be a military concern after the political shit storm the Wounded Knee massacre had kicked up.

That had been—what—nineteen years back? The country had changed. But regardless, renegades were the responsibility of the U.S. Marshals Service these days—a fact Tom was about to point out to the captain, when his sergeant quickstepped into the dining room and snapped to attention.

"Sir."

Banyan removed the cigar from his mouth. "Report."

"As per your orders, the men are bivouacked in the vacant lot and the watch set."

"Have the men formed up at the station and ready to move out at oh seven hundred."

"Yes, sir."

"That will be all, Sergeant. Good evening."

Tom touched the corners of his mouth with his napkin and draped it over the uneaten portion of his steak and scrambled eggs. The sergeant was a beet-faced man of forty with a solid waistline, barrel chest, and cannonball shoulders. He snapped a salute, turned on his heels, and quick-marched out of the dining room.

"Good man. Obtuse, but then good noncoms ought to be, don't you think?"

"Tell me more about this Corporal Frank Kidd?" Tom asked. "This Apache ex-marine war hero, who all of a sudden decides to rob a store and kidnap its owner?" He reached for the coffeepot, and as he refilled his cup, glanced out the window of the café in time to spot the telegrapher midway across the street, hurrying toward the hotel.

"I hope that's what I think it is."

Banyan twisted around in his chair. Then he and Tom turned toward the cased opening, through which they could see the front desk in the hotel lobby. They heard the entrance door open and slam shut. A moment later the telegrapher rushed breathless into the dining room.

"Urgent telegram just in, Marshal: The sheriff at Clarendon —that's about halfway to Amarillo from here—he just sent down word. He believes he's got your man in custody."

Tom said, "When's the next westbound due?"

The telegrapher blinked owlishly. "At around three fifteen, if it's on time."

"I'll assemble my men," Banyan muttered, and scooted his chair back from the table.

46

H ank Smith was into a second slice of Miss Millie's apple pie and eyeing the third and last, when he heard the sputter of the motorcar. Wilbur, overconcerned about his long-term prospects as sheriff in the event he'd been wrong about the Mexican, had walked over in the rain to relieve Al and fetch the motorcar back to the jailhouse.

"Miz Millie, I'm an unredeemable hog for your cooking. You think I might have that last slice of your wonderful pie?" He displayed his teeth in an appealing smile, but Miss Millie was already out of her chair, oblivious to his charms, as she rushed to the window.

"Oh, good, it's him."

Hank washed down the last mouthful of pie with a swallow of coffee. He heard the front door as it swung open and slammed shut. A few moments later Wilbur came stomping down the hall into the kitchen.

"What took you so long?" Miss Millie asked.

Wilbur, shaking the rain off his slicker, hung it on the hat tree. "Had to get a telegram off to that U.S. marshal," he said, frowning with disapproval at what was left of dinner. "I also sent

Charlie Goodnight a telegram. Come morning we'll know what's what. I hadn't never fooled with a motorcar before, and we had a hell of a . . . a heck of a time getting it started." He shrugged apologetically. His wife was frowning; she disapproved in the strongest manner the use of foul language. "I was beginning to think Al and me was going to have to push the darn thing over here, but then she fired up." He slapped his rain-wet Stetson against his leg and hung it over the slicker, came to the table, and plopped down in his chair. "I expected you'd try and eat all the pie before I got back, and you danged near did."

"If I'd a had another five minutes, I'd of got it, too." Hank batted his eyes up at Miss Millie.

"You're a pie hog if there ever was one," Wilbur said as his wife set a plate in front of him. "Thanks, hon." He bowed his head and dutifully mumbled a few prayerful words. Miss Millie looked on approvingly. The sheriff finished up and helped himself to an extra portion of turnip greens. He stuffed a fork load into his mouth and looked across the table. "What you need is a good wife, Hank. But the thing you need in order to get a good one is a good job. Hard work and a good woman would straighten you right out."

"You think that'd do it, huh?"

"Yeah, it would, but she'd have to be strong as tiger's breath, I reckon, to put up with the likes of you."

Hank grinned and sipped his coffee.

"You're a pie hog, Hank, and that malady requires wifely skills to rectify."

"I been considering my options," Hank said, and batted his eyes at Miss Millie. She smiled sweetly, the implication sailing right over her head, as he'd known it would. "Miz Millie," he said, raising his cup in salute, "I'm afraid that your good cooking is the last refuge of my rapidly advancing years."

"Oh, you're not old," she fluttered. "Why, you can't be more than fifty-five?"

That one stung Wilbur enough to earn Hank a jealous glare. Hank plucked a biscuit off the diminished pile in the center of the table. "You know, Miz Millie," he said, watching Wilbur out the corner of his eye, "these biscuits kindly remind me of the ones my pa used to bake back when I was just a spud and still picking cotton in East Texas." The biscuits his pa had cooked were crusty as mud-clods and heavy enough you could have flung one right through Miss Millie's kitchen window and screen both; but he left that part out as Miss Millie fluttered happily. Wilbur stuffed a slice of pork chop in his mouth and pointed his fork pistol-fashion at Hank across the table.

"I allowed you could eat with us, Hank. I don't remember nothing in the deal about pie."

"Now, Wilbur," Miss Millie said.

Wilbur snorted. "Well, some people don't know where to turn around."

Hank leaned back in his chair. The fun was all over. He dabbed at his mouth with the napkin Miss Millie had provided, aware he'd ribbed Wilbur about as much as he dared. It was time to go. He stood and slid his chair close to the table.

"My compliments, ma'am," Hank said, and with a nod toward the sideboard, added, "If you'd like, I'd be proud to take that plate of food up to your prisoner before I head out. It'd save him the trouble." He sent an apologetic nod toward Wilbur. "That okay by you, Sheriff?"

Wilbur grunted and kept eating. Miss Millie hurried to the sideboard in that feminine way she had and returned with a napkin-covered plate.

"Thank you, Mr. Smith."

"My pleasure, Miz Leigh." He made a ceremonial show of taking the plate from her hands. "And many thanks to you for all your kindnesses during my all-too-brief vacation in your husband's crossbar hotel."

Wilbur choked on his food as Hank turned and crossed to the hat tree. He retrieved his hat, hung his coat over his arm, and without a backward look made his way down the hall. The scent of linseed oil and wax was replaced by the odor of stale tobacco and sweat as he stepped through the door into Wilbur's office.

Then froze in place.

On the other side of the office was a rain soaked Mexican woman standing just inside the partially open entrance door. Seeing her, he very nearly dropped the plate. She was short and sickly looking, and her eyes burned, either with fever or determination—he couldn't tell which. The one thing he could tell: her intentions were serious. In her hand was a fully cocked .45, and it was aimed at him.

"Close that door," she whispered, almost too softly to be heard.

47

Hank reached back for the doorknob, saw Miss Millie rubbing Wilbur's shoulders, and, gripping the knob, pulled the door closed. Turned and faced the woman holding the gun. Her features were drawn, her eyes dark and feverish. She looked utterly desperate.

"Open the iron door."

"If you shoot me, the sheriff will come a-running."

"Then I'll shoot him. The woman, too, if I have to."

You could never tell with a woman if she was bluffing or not. This one, though, she looked about half-crazy. It wasn't worth the risk, not to him. He bumped the iron door with his shoulder, and it creaked softly inward. She gestured with the .45 for him to lead the way, and he went up the narrow flight of stairs, reached the landing, opened the door, and stepped into the cellblock. The Mexican, if Mexican he was, stood in almost the exact position he'd been when they'd left him.

"I brung you a plate of food, mister," Hank said, and extended the covered plate.

Chaco saw Bui behind him in the doorway. He stepped up to the bars, slid his arm between them, and pointed. "The keys are hanging there," he said, looking at the old man and wishing she'd caught the one called Woodruff instead.

"Put the plate on the floor," Bui said. "Get the keys, and open the jail door."

The plate clattered a little as he set it down. The old man's hands were shaking. Bui kept the pistol pointed at him as he retrieved the key ring off the iron peg. He fumbled nervously with the lock mechanisms, but then the key went in and turned. The lockbox came open, and Hank lifted the lever.

Chaco stepped out of the larger cell into the entrance cell and waited for Hank to unlock the outer door. The lock clicked, and Chaco pushed the strap-iron door outward, stepped clear of the cell, and went around the old man. Bui handed him the pistol belt, and he buckled it on, drew the revolver, checked the chambers, turned, and looked at the one they called Hank Smith.

"If you want to live, do what I tell you when I tell you."

"Whatever you say, mister." Hank brought his hands up to shoulder level.

"What you need to remember is, I have nothing to lose." Hank swallowed loud enough that Chaco heard it. "What we are going to do is go out of this jail without any trouble. Understand?"

Hank nodded. "Will you tell me when it's okay to move?" There was resignation in his old eyes, a slight tremor in his hands.

"This is how it will be," Chaco said. "We all go down to the office together."

"Okay."

He looked at Bui, jerked his chin toward the door. "Any men downstairs?"

"*No men. The sheriff and a woman live here. They were eating when we came up.*"

He turned back to this Hank Smith. "What happened to the deputies?"

"Wilbur paid them off. They're gone. Nobody's down there but him and his wife. You're an Injun, ain't you?" Hank blurted and instantly clamped his lips shut, as if he'd let slip something best left unsaid.

"Remember this: every chance is your last chance. Where are the deputies?"

"I told you, they was paid off. Ain't nobody down there but Wilbur and Miz Millie."

"Where did they go, these deputies?"

"I ain't got a notion. I reckon Wilbur must have rounded that bunch up and deputized them when he heard you might be a-coming this way. As you might guess, I ain't exactly one of his confidants."

Chaco gestured toward the cellblock door. "Let's go. Don't make a lot of noise."

The three of them descended the stairway and went through the iron door and into the sheriff's office. Chaco saw that the door to the sheriff's living quarters was closed. He caught Hank staring at the sheriff's desk—the Sharps .50 with the heavy cartridge belt on top.

"Don't even think about it."

"I wasn't," he said, and busied himself pulling on his coat.

Yeah, you were, Chaco thought, and crossed to the desk, took up the cartridge belt, and strapped it on over the pistol belt. He took up the Sharps, checked the breech. There was a round in the chamber. He looked at Bui, nodded. Turned to Smith and gestured toward the front door. The old man went out ahead of them. Rain fell steady through the misty glow of the streetlamps on the square. The Ford was parked at the curb close to the jail.

"*Are we going to take that* motorcar?" Bui asked.

"Yes."

"*Good. I put Goyaalé's bones in the back before I came in.*"

Chaco looked around and saw the square was deserted. That

was good. Better if he didn't have to kill anyone. Rain drummed softly against the crown of his hat as thunder rumbled in the distance, the storm moving east. He checked the back seat of the Ford, verified that his father's bones were there. Noted the rain soaked blanket roll with the 'Takedown' Model '97 inside. The other firearms didn't matter. Someone would discover them, but not before they were far away from this place.

Hank Smith turned up his collar. "I got a question."

"Ask it."

"You plan to let me go or kill me?"

"Let you go, but not yet. You look strong. You think you can push this motorcar?"

"I can push a Studebaker wagon, and these things don't weigh much more."

"Get on the other side. We'll push her up the street a couple of blocks. No tricks."

Chaco signaled for Bui to get behind the steering wheel. Then handed her the Sharps, and, adjusting the handbrake-gearshift into the neutral position, he looked across the seat at the old man. "Time to push it. Let's go."

With Bui steering, they pushed together and rolled the car west along Third Street, Chaco telling Bui to adjust their direction as needed. She caught on quickly, how it was done. From somewhere out on the prairie came the faint howl and yap of a coyote. Chaco could hear Hank's labored breath as they crossed another street.

"How far you aim to push this thing?" Hank asked.

"A little farther."

Chaco kept the car rolling another block before he judged they'd gone far enough the sound of the engine wouldn't carry back to the jail. The old fellow was gasping by that time. They were still rolling as Chaco ordered Bui to scoot over into the passenger seat. He gave the car another hard shove, then sprang up behind the steering wheel, switched on the ignition, engaged first forward, and popped the clutch. The engine sputtered, caught, and ran. He stopped the car, drew the Colt, and waved Hank up to the motorcar.

Chaco looked at his sister and gestured toward the back seat. "I need you to sit back there, Sally." He'd never thought of her by any name but Bui, but he remembered from when they were kids that she'd liked her whiteeye name. He wondered if she still did.

She glanced at the old man, nodded she understood, and climbed over the front seat. Chaco, with a gesture, summoned Hank Smith closer. He approached, full of apprehension.

"Get in."

"I'll just slow you down, son."

He was wheezing and maybe putting it on a bit—enough so that under lesser circumstances Chaco might have smiled. This was a likable old rogue. "Get in," he said again.

"You'd best let me go. I'll tell you this much: There's a federal marshal a-coming to Clarendon after you. Wilbur sent a telegram to him not more than an hour ago."

"Get in."

"You're not going to let me go, are you?"

Chaco heard the controlled fear in his voice. "I'll let you go when I can."

"Yeah, you bet."

Hank Smith stepped up on the running board and situated himself in the passenger seat. Chaco handed the Sharps over the seat to Bui and shot her a quick look.

"You're shivering."

What they needed was shelter and a fire, but that wasn't going to happen. Somewhere he'd read that soft country bred soft men. He supposed the same could be said of a soft life. Bui had lived in the way of the Indah far too long. And there was nothing for it.

"I need gasoline," he said to the old man. "Do you know where I can get some?"

"At the drugstore, but it don't open till morning."

The gasoline they needed wasn't worth the time or the risk getting it would require. Not at this point. He'd have to find another way.

He engaged the transmission, drove to the next corner, turned right, and motored three city blocks to the rail yard. Swung left and followed the service road that ran parallel to the tracks away from the train station. Off to the right he heard the ring of a smithy's hammer above the general night crew noise of the roundhouse. He shifted gears. They rolled past the ammonia reek of the cattle pens and out past the edge of town, the rear axle fishtailing in the freshly muddied road, tires splashing. He put the car in neutral and idled down the engine, and the car rolled to a halt.

"You going to kill me now?"

"No, I'm not going to kill you." He looked at Bui, said, "*Watch him*," and set the hand brake and left the engine idling, stepped out of the Ford, and got the acetylene generator going. He managed to strike a match and lit the headlights, got behind the wheel again, and drove on.

The service road ran more or less parallel to the tracks, and a mile out of town the road dipped through a wet-weather creek beside the span of a rail trestle. There was a foot of swiftly rushing water in the creek, and midway across the Ford lost traction. For a moment it seemed they might be swept away. But then the tires found purchase, and, driving at a slightly upstream angle, they got across.

The engine labored as they climbed away from the rushing water, and, starved for gas, it sounded as if it would quit. But at that point the road leveled off, and the engine perked up again.

He drove on.

He hoped the map he'd given Bui hadn't got so wet it would come apart, when the time came to remove it from her pocket. He would like to have studied it a few more times, but for the present that was out of the question.

Another thing to remember, he thought. Never assume that you will have time or opportunity to study or learn something later.

He summoned a mental picture of the map. If memory served, Rowe would be the next whistle-stop up the line, then Goodnight, a place evidently named for Mr. Charlie Goodnight, and then Claude. The problem was, they didn't have enough fuel to even reach Rowe, much less any of those other stops up the line.

"If I get out of this alive," Hank mumbled, under his breath, "I'm going back to Blanco Canyon. I hunted buffalo in that country back when there was still buffs to hunt."

The engine of the Ford was pulling well and strong, but, with so little fuel, he was left with only a couple of choices, neither of them good. A quarter mile beyond the creek, he disengaged the engine and allowed the Ford to roll to a stop. He set the hand brake and stepped out of the motorcar and closed the valve on the acetylene generator, Hank looking at him as the headlights faded and his face became a black silhouette against the rainy night.

"Get out of the car, and come here."

The shadow shape hesitated. Chaco heard the old man's sigh above the patter of the rain against the engine cowling. Hank climbed out, came around the front end, and faced him.

"You can go," Chaco said. He was inclined to say something apologetic, because he liked this old man, but before he could say the words Hank turned and raced away at a dead run.

"*I would not have thought a man of his years could run that fast,*" Bui said.

"Me, either."

Chaco stepped up onto the running board and watched the retreating shape fade into the rainy dark. Spider lightning lit the sky, and in the gray moment he saw the town and Hank running headlong toward it.

In English, Bui said, "You think he will drown in that creek?"

"If he does, we won't get away."

Clarendon was less than a mile back, but as hard as the old fellow was running, Chaco didn't think it would take him long to get there. He hoped Mr. Smith could run that far without suffering heart failure. Of course he would sound the alarm. The question was, would they follow immediately, or wait for the federal marshal? Chaco, thinking now of that time the gunny and he had been pinned down above Sagua la Grande, remembering the gunny's laughter, the saying, "No battle plan ever survives first contact."

This plan probably wouldn't, either.

Bui climbed over from the back and settled into the passenger seat as Chaco dropped behind the wheel, engaged first forward, gunned the engine, and got the Ford turned around. He eased back on the throttle to conserve fuel, the Ford certainly running on fumes now, and gambled that the sheriff hadn't checked the fuel level in the tank.

The creek was a half-mile back, but they made it. He braked to a stop where the trestle ended on level ground and the road slanted down to the creek. He turned his head, looked across the car at his sister. She appeared to be listening. He could hear the rush of water below. It sounded swifter and like there was more of it.

The engine sputtered, galloped a few times, and died.

"*Did it quit by itself?*" Bui asked.

"Yes. They do that when they run out of gasoline."

"*What now?*"

"Can you swim?"

"No. Can you?"

"The Corps taught me, but I'm not very good."

"You think we're going to drown in that?" she asked, with a gesture toward the rushing sound below.

He set the hand brake, stepped out of the car, looked up as a spiderweb of lightning lit the swirling sky. Rain pelted his face, and for some disconnected reason he remembered the day he had walked with his father through the snow back at Carlisle. "*You look like her.*" It would have cost him nothing to acknowledge him as his son. He lowered his face, and the rain pelted against the brim of his hat.

"What happens next will decide everything."

For the first time he felt close to Lozen, the mother who had given him life—a secretive woman, a woman of fire, of the unspoken longings of her blood. He thought maybe he understood the reason she had lain with Goyaałé to beget him. Saw that through him she might strike at her enemy from the grave, and he saw the living of his life and his death to come, and knew that, like Aná Liluy and Lozen and Goyaałé, he must from this moment forward count himself among the dead.

48

T he fence pliers were still under the seat. Chaco slipped them into his back pocket, told Bui to stay with the motorcar. He scrambled up the crushed-rock ballast onto the tracks and jogged west between the rails a distance of perhaps a hundred yards. He stopped at a point where the parallel road curved away from the track to avoid a rock outcropping. Then went off the tracks here and shinnied up one of the telegraph poles, reached with the fence pliers, and cut the wire. The pole shivered as the wire shot away. He shinnied down and, jogging back along the tracks, thought about the marshal who would come on the train. The marshal would recognize this tactic as the one he'd used leaving Lawton. But if his plan worked, this marshal would not be around to point out that fact.

He came to the trestle, went off the tracks, and walked over to the motorcar.

"*What did you do?*" Bui asked.

"Cut the telegraph wire." He studied the dark outline of her. "You ready for this?"

"*I will go with you to the end.*"

Again he looked up into the night. The pelting rain had let

up some. He lowered his gaze and squinted through the rain at the town, the barking of dogs faint from that direction. He could just make out the train station, the building lit in the misty glow of several streetlamps. Something was going on in the street out front.

"Do you have the spyglass I gave you?"

Bui fished it from a pocket of the field jacket and extended it to him. He took the glass, raised it to his eye. The shadowy images of men and horses appeared in the optic circle in the street outside the station. He saw buggies with paraffin lamps attached to them: a posse was being made up.

He collapsed the glass and turned his attention back on the flooded creek. It rushed north under the trestle, toward the river a few miles away, the dark surface of the water smooth and swift where it swept across the ford. He heard the rumble of falling water downstream. Not good, but they were out of options.

"I want you to take Goyaałé's bones and the rifles and the blanket roll and cross over on the trestle."

"*What are you going to do?*"

"I'm going to roll this car into that creek and hide it."

"*But it is not deep enough.*"

"Trust me, and do what I tell you. Once you are across the trestle, follow the creek downstream to where you hear the waterfall and wait for me there. I'll get out before it goes over."

With her rifle slung barrel-down over one shoulder, her arms through the carrying loops of the canvas backpack, the heavy blanket roll tucked under one arm, and the Sharps carried low in the other hand, she looked at him. It seemed like a heavy load to him, but he sent her ahead and waited watchfully by the car until she was across the trestle and out of sight. Only then did he release the hand brake. He leaned against the Ford and got it moving. Then jumped in and steered it toward the rushing creek.

At the last moment he hauled back on the hand brake. The rear wheels locked, and the car skidded to a stop.

The creek had risen more than a foot since they had crossed. With no fuel he would have to hazard this part without the benefit of an engine. The Ford had gun-carriage wheels that were tall and strong, but not strong enough to withstand a waterfall of more than a few feet.

He slipped behind the wheel and released the hand brake. The tires crunched audibly as the Ford rolled forward. He swung the car into the rushing current, felt a moment of buoyancy as the wheels lost traction. Then the car slewed into the rush of the current and was swept under the trestle. Brush scraped the undercarriage. A limb cracked against the front fender. Then screeched along the car's side. The front tires found purchase, and he righted the vehicle. Impelled by the current, the car gathered speed, rumbled along. He heard the roar of a waterfall. The banks rose as swiftly as they narrowed. There was no place for him to jump. A gap appeared, and the car, accelerated by the current, went over a lip of rock. He was airborne. In a flicker of lightning, he saw a swirling pool of debris, as the front end splashed and the tires slammed against the bottom. Chaco was catapulted from his seat, yet, somehow, held on to the steering wheel as the car came down. The car careened in the swirling current, was washed up against something beneath the rampant surface, and stopped and held.

The floorboard of the car was underwater. In another flicker of lightning, he saw Bui making her way down to the creek. Apparently the Ford had come to rest in a swirling eddy in the cup of an overhang. When he stepped out of the motorcar, he found the water shallow enough, and the current mild enough because of the eddy, he was able to wade across to where Bui waited on a shelf of rock.

She touched his shoulder as he waded up out of the creek. *"Are you injured?"*

"No." He looked back, the black silhouette of the Ford all but invisible. That had gone better than he had any right to hope. Sometimes it was better to be lucky than smart. The car was far enough downstream from the trestle it might not be discovered for days. He hoped not as he took the pack from Bui, slipped his arms into the loops, took up the Sharps and the blanket roll with the shotgun inside.

"I can carry my share," Bui said.

"You have a wound. The rifle you carry is enough."

They turned simultaneously toward the sound of approaching riders.

"Come," he whispered, and climbed the bank.

Bui came up behind him as he paused and looked back toward the trestle: the squeal of horses, the shouts of men, the posse forcing their mounts into the rushing water. He placed a hand on Bui's shoulder.

"Stay close."

They set off at a jog back toward Clarendon. They went through several barbed-wire fences, Chaco stepping on the lower wire and lifting the upper while Bui ducked through—cutting through would tell the sheriff they'd passed this way. In town the dogs still barked. From a quarter mile out, he heard an angry voice shout "Shut up," followed by the slam of a door. The yell served only to increase the barking, which was a good outcome for their purposes.

The rain tapered off as they approached the first houses. The storm front with its constant lightning was east of the town now and moving away. Chaco adjusted his shoulders into the rope straps of the bundle and kept moving—the weight of his father's bones negligible, less than the lightest combat pack he'd carried in Cuba. They moved down the middle of a muddy street, a few houses here and there, and mostly vacant, weed-grown lots at the edge of town. Bui kept pace at his side. In a flicker of lightning, he read the pain in her face. The dogs had settled down. Only a few still barked here and there. No light in the houses they passed. The rifles they carried gave them the look of wilderness bums. Ahead on the right was a vacant city block, not even a toolshed on it, and across it he saw the silhouette of the cattle pens. He changed direction, and they crossed the vacant block from corner to corner and walked toward the configured shadows of two lines of freight cars and gondolas parked on the stockyard siding. They walked between the lines of empty cars toward the cattle pens, most of the cargo doors open. The smell of cattle dung and stale rail-yard oil was strong here.

They came to the last cars. Ahead the rails forked: one set curved right back to the main road; the other went straight ahead and disappeared through a set of gates into the stockyard. The cattle pens were dark and empty. No sound of cattle or humans came from them—and no movement, other than the dark flashes of hunting bats—as they darted through the swirls of insects buzzing near a single electric lamp on the far side of the stockyard. He heard the whistle of a steam engine followed by the slam of railcar couplings: likely a switch engine putting together a train of cars.

He jerked his chin for Bui to follow, and set out across the open ground. They reached the rough-planked outer pens. The dung smell was overpowering here. He peered between the boards. No movement of cattle in that dark warren of posts, planks, and barbed wire. Bui followed him to the rail gate. It opened onto a long chute that traversed the yard. They followed the chute. There were ramps to the left and right for loading cattle out of the holding pens. The last chutes on his right led them to another loading ramp with double-hung gates and a view of the railway station a short distance up the main trunk.

He eased the canvas pack from his shoulders and leaned it against the battered planks, placed the blanket roll on top. He looked at Bui as she leaned her back against the chute, slid down, and sat with a wedge of light from the station on her exhausted face. There was nothing he could do to make this easier for her. They were in a hard place. He peered out between the rough-cut boards. They were about seventy yards from the train station. Uniformed porters were loitering on the platform beside a baggage cart, apparently waiting for the westbound. He assumed the marshal would be on that train.

One of the porters straightened and looked east, apparently hearing what Chaco heard: the distant and mournful shrill of a train. The sound set the dogs of the town to barking again.

Chaco opened the breech of the Sharps, withdrew the heavy cartridge, and blew down the barrel. Then blew the moisture from the cartridge and rechambered it, closed the breech, and stared out between the slats of the gate at the train station.

"*If you shoot one of them, how will we get away?*" Bui asked.

49

The conductor leaned out from the Pullman. "I've never seen Clarendon this lit up before," he remarked, and looked up at the stern-faced captain, behind him on the rain-slick vestibule.

"Not surprising. I doubt the local constabulary catches all that many mass murderers."

Banyan turned and reentered the Pullman. He was shivering. This country, it never ceased to amaze: one day so dried up it seemed ready to blow away, and the next, like tonight, it would rain like Noah's flood. He hated the blazing days and the all-but-freezing nights. Once he'd foolishly complained of the conditions over brandy and cigars to his commanding officer.

"You're too thin blooded for this country, Banyan," the colonel had said—the implication being he was too thin blooded for the service itself.

Unfit, he fumed. They can have it back, the Army and this whole damnable country. The money; that was my ticket out; our ticket; so close, we were so close, Melissa and me. A new life, we were almost there. With Alton's wife in Kansas City, all we needed was another day or two and . . .

He saw it all slipping away, the life they'd planned, a life together in a part of the world with four distinct seasons. Frank Kidd had taken all that from him, and for what? A stupid Indian whore.

I'll kill that little bastard.

He drove his fist into the palm of his other hand and grimaced against the angry knots in his gut.

A flash of lightning momentarily lit the slanting rain pelting the Pullman's windows. He grimaced. Thought, God, how I hate this country. And moved up to the potbellied stove in the center of the car and chafed his arms against an abrupt chill. His sergeant, slumped on a bench snoring, cheek rested against the sill of a partly open window, hair damp from the blowing rain, was another of those half-wits who loved this life. An idiot with an imagination too limited to imagine any other. He stepped across the aisle and kicked at his boot.

"Wake up."

The sergeant's eyes snapped open, full of anger. But, seeing the captain, came to his feet. "Sir?"

"We're coming into Clarendon. I'll want the men off this train and assembled at once."

"Yes, sir."

"We'll be taking custody of Corporal Kidd within the hour."

"Begging the captain's pardon, but you don't really think it's him, do you?"

"I'm afraid I do."

"I mean, sir, I saw him get that decoration."

"As did I, Sergeant, as did I. But not every war hero is a patriot, it would seem."

Tom Starrett, roused by their conversation, stretched and sat up and blinked from behind grainy eyelids, irritated at having been wakened. God, he was tired. He pulled the flask from his coat and rinsed the sour taste from his mouth. There was no spittoon handy, so he swallowed.

He hadn't worked this hard since his Ranger days. And he'd been a lot younger back then. The only good news was, they were about to bring this mess to a close. That is, if this sheriff was holding the right man. His telegram had been full of equivocation. But if the sheriff had doubts, Banyan had none.

"It's Corporal Frank Kidd, all right," he'd blurted loud enough they'd heard him in the Harvey House kitchen back in Quanah.

Tom, staring calmly across the dinner table at him, had said, "Are you that sure?"

"To a moral certainty."

He had assumed Banyan was holding back information he wasn't willing to share; either that or he was foolishly overconfident.

Tom rose to his feet and stepped out into the aisle. He studied the captain, who for the present was operating under the erroneous assumption that the prisoner they were about to take possession of would be his. The Army's claim against this Frank Kidd—if indeed it was Frank Kidd the sheriff had locked up—was about to become a jurisdictional question. Tom was fairly confident the murder of six deputies and the attempted murder of Sheriff Jones pretty much trumped any claim the Army might have. That is, unless this Kidd had shot an American soldier, which as far as he knew at this point he hadn't.

Tom moved down the aisle and stepped out onto the vestibule as the train huffed into the station. On the platform, waiting beside a baggage cart, were black porters wearing billed caps and blue uniforms. The engine whistle sounded twice, and Tom grabbed the handrail against the abrupt stop as iron couplings came together down the length of the train.

Inside the Pullman, the conductor shouted, "Clarendon, five minutes."

Then the sergeant was yelling, "Get up, get out, move your asses."

As the train slowed into the station, Tom swung off on the platform and quickly got out of the way ahead of the sergeant, who hustled his men out of the car, backpacks on their backs, '03s slung over their shoulders. The troops hurriedly formed up in ranks. Tom watched the captain stride purposefully across the rough-plank platform, saw him greeted by a cowboy, who stepped out of the station door. They shook hands, and now the cowboy was telling Banyan something, something that angered him enough he yanked the hat off his head and threw it down on the rain-drenched planks.

Trouble, Tom thought, and hurried toward them. Whatever it was, he needed to know.

50

"I have seen that one before," Bui whispered, focused on the officer who, after throwing down his hat, stomped off a few paces and stood, face livid, fists bunched at his sides, like a man at odds with himself.

Chaco lowered the spyglass and looked at her. "Which one?"

"*The one who threw his hat down.*"

Banyan, he thought, and remembered the captain's wife in bed with McDonnell. The only way Banyan could have gotten here this quick was if she'd told him. Apparently there were things about the white way he would never understand. He raised the glass to his eye as the engine huffed and advanced a few yards, bringing the coalbunker with its water reservoir under the downpipe of the water tower. His view of the platform was blocked. He might not be able to see the soldiers, but he knew they were on the train by the shouts he was hearing: a noncom ordering men to fall in and form up. Soldiers, Captain Banyan, and this U.S. marshal.

A brakeman had climbed the ladder to the water tower and now lowered the standpipe. Water gurgled down from the tower into the water reservoir in the back end of the coalbunker and mixed with the sound of the fireman's shovel scooping coal and stoking the fire under the boiler.

With the soldiers and the captain on the train, shooting the marshal would serve no purpose. He ejected the heavy round from the Sharps, slid it into an empty loop of the cartridge belt, and closed the breech. He watched as the engineman descended from the cab and began to lubricate the linkages of the complicated drive.

Chaco looked at Bui and found she was staring back at him.

"*Which one were you going to shoot?*"

"We'd better eat," he whispered. "There won't be time later. What did you bring?"

She handed him a can. He drew the sheath knife from his pistol belt and used it to cut open the lid. He raised the can and sniffed.

"Smells like beef stew. Toss me another, I'll open one for you?"

"I'll eat a bit from yours."

Oily chunks of fat floated on top. He drank from the can and used the blade of his knife to ladle up bits of soggy meat and potato. Chewed them slowly, listening absently to the sound of the switch engine at work east of the cattle pens somewhere close to the roundhouse in the rail yard. When he'd eaten about half, he passed the can to Bui. Then stood up and watched the switch engine huff into view behind a block of freight cars and gondolas. Watched a yardman with a lantern swing the iron lever of a switching arm that redirected the block of cars onto the main track. The switch engine slowed as yet another yardman swung his own signal lamp from his position beside the westbound's caboose. The train shuddered down its length as the hookup was made.

"We have to go," he said, and reached for the canvas pack. Bui set the can aside and stood as he shouldered Goyaałé's bones onto his back, took up the Sharps, and reached for the blanket roll.

"I'll carry that," she whispered.

"You sure?"

She nodded.

The whistle of the switch engine shrilled; the engine uncoupled and backed away.

"We must hurry."

They made their way back to the traversing chute, turned, jogged to the east-facing gate, and looked between the planks. Directly across the yard was the roundhouse, the building surrounded by sidings crowded with freight cars. They opened the gate and hurried toward the line of cars situated closest to the main track. The twenty yards across were fully exposed to any yardman who happened to be looking their way. Then they were in the shadow of a line of cars. They moved parallel to the train —Chaco's boots soaked through, water squishing between his toes. He snatched glimpses of the westbound between the cars as they went along, and when they were far enough back, he ducked between two cars, went under the coupling, and straightened as Bui came up beside him. He noted her grimace of pain.

"How's your side?"

"*It's well enough.*"

She was lying, of course, but there was nothing for it.

From this new position he could see the engineman leaning out of the locomotive and saw that the soldiers had reboarded the train, some of them already seated at the windows of the foremost Pullman, while others were still removing their backpacks. All of them carried rifles. Altogether there were about twenty men. He saw Captain Banyan through one of the windows; he was talking to a red-faced sergeant.

"All aboard," a voice called. The engine whistle sounded and

its great iron drive wheels turned and spun on the tracks and
caught. The train began to move.

He turned to Bui, said, "Follow me," and broke from cover.

Bui jogged up beside him. They angled toward the moving
line of freight cars. He picked one with an open door that would
come up as they reached the moving train. He was not at all
certain Bui would have the strength to do this. He tossed the rifle
into the car, swung the canvas pack from his shoulder, and tossed
it in after the rifle. Grabbed the forward end of the doorframe
and used the train's momentum to swing up and aboard. He
scrambled around, got to his belly, and reached out for Bui. She
tossed in the blanket roll, reached for his outstretched hand. He
lunged and caught her wrist and swung her up into the car. It was
awkwardly done, but she was aboard, lying on her back, a hand
pressed against her side.

"This is only an educated guess, mind you," a voice rumbled
out of the dark from the forward end of the car, "but I'd say
you're both new at this."

The voice was gruff, but friendly. Chaco came to his feet as a
match flared in the dark. The flame revealed the face of an old
man, maybe sixty-five or seventy, a curved-stemmed pipe
clamped between his teeth. He puffed the tobacco in the bowl to
life. A cheerful face with mocking eyes that shone out of a well-
lived-in face. He wore a battered hat, and it was only when he
rolled up onto his feet that Chaco realized the man was a dwarf.
He came toward them drawing on the pipe, leaned against the
cargo door, and flipped the match in a red arc into the night.
"We'll be in Amarillo before sunup."

Bui sat staring up at the imp in stunned silence.

Chaco said, "Any stops between here and there?"

"Stations, but I wouldn't know about stops. My first hobo
experience, I'm afraid."

Chaco took up the canvas bundle, the rifle, and the blanket

roll, and carried them to the forward end of the car. He arranged the gear in a corner and sat down. What he needed was sleep, but he could not risk it yet. He watched Bui come to her feet, hand still pressed against her side. Hopefully she hadn't pulled any of the stitches. He could smell the canvas bundle, the faint odor of rot and sour whiskey. The car filled with the quickening click of iron wheels over rails.

"Come up here out of the wind," Chaco called, and Bui came away from the imp and settled on the deck beside him.

"*What kind of man is he?*" she whispered.

"He is a whiteeye."

"*How can that be?*"

"The ones born like this among our own people used to be left to die. Truly, you don't know what he is?"

"*No. I have never seen such a man.*"

There was a sudden thump on the roof of the car. Chaco looked up and listened. Someone on the catwalk walking toward the rear of the train, but then the walker stopped. Then came scuffing sounds, and, moments later, legs appeared through the cargo door, followed by a man who swung down and inward, let go, and landed in a crouch. The imp stepped back a pace as the man straightened. He was tall and thin. A billy club hung by a thong attached to his wrist. He looked around, and, for a lone moment, studied the imp.

"Where are you bound, friend?" asked the man with the billy.

"To the mountains of the west, I hope. And you, friend?"

"You looked taller running across the yard. Where's the other one?"

"Oh my," the imp muttered. "You're Amarillo Slim."

"Have we met before?"

"Your reputation precedes you, sir. But surely you would not deny passage to an admirer on such a night?"

"That's what they pay me for, friend," Amarillo Slim said, and swung the club.

It landed with a meaty *whunk*. The imp went down. Amarillo Slim positioned himself to strike again. And Chaco shot him—drew his Colt and shot the tall man—and, as he went down, Chaco came to his feet. The railroad bull had sat down hard, and Chaco, pistol in hand, walked over to the man. The bull was yanking frantically at a revolver that had snagged in his coat pocket. Chaco pressed the muzzle of the Colt against the bull's skull.

"Let go of the pistol."

He let go.

"Give me that club."

He extended the billy. Chaco took it. Stepped around behind the bull, moved in close, and swung the club in a roundhouse arc and heard the snap of the man's collarbone. The bull gasped and slumped forward. He raised the club, prepared to strike again, and for an uncertain moment stood with the billy club held quivering above his head. But at length he dominated the darker urge and lowered the club. He breathed out against the dark, holding on to the ragged edge of the world he wanted and not to the world that was. He tossed the billy through the open cargo door; it disappeared into the night, and he realized it had begun to rain again. He holstered the Colt, bent, and grabbed the railroad bull by his coat collar and dragged him to the cargo door and rolled him out. Heard the gravelly impact as he landed, and watched the man's black shape bounce and tumble and fade from view.

When he turned back, Bui was kneeling over the imp, his head in her lap.

"Is he alive?"

She looked up at him. "*He still breathes.*"

Chaco leaned on the doorjamb, tasted the wind-driven rain

against his face. I have to keep a clear head, he thought. In war, anger leads to error and error to early death. Ahead he saw the engine rumble onto the trestle, and beyond the trestle saw a cluster of firefly-like lights.

He seized the doorframe and leaned out. Firefly lights resolved into hurricane lamps and flashlights held in the hands of men—the posse. The beams directed toward a single man standing on the saddle of a horse held close to a telegraph pole by a man on the ground. The man standing on the horse was reconnecting the telegraph wires Chaco had cut. Lariats had been affixed to the cut ends of the wires, and the wires were drawn together over the glass insulator affixed to the pole—a neatly done and inventive bit of repair work.

As the car approached the cluster of men, Chaco stepped back from the cargo door and knelt beside the imp and touched his throat. "His pulse is strong."

"*He should be dead.*"

"Maybe imps are tougher than other men."

"Maybe they have to be," Bui muttered in English.

Chaco caught the dwarf under the arms and lifted him as their car rolled past the posse. The three of them were momentarily caught in the light of the posse's torches. A hoarse voice shouted something unintelligible, and then the car was dark again.

I am making mistake after mistake, he allowed, aware he was too tired to think clearly. At some point I got to sleep.

He carried the imp to the forward end of the car, flicked on the Eveready, and located the man's belongings: a ball-like bundle attached to a walking stick.

"Use his goods for a pillow under his head," he said to Bui.

She retrieved the bundle, slipped it under the small man's head. She straightened his limbs and loosened his belt while

Chaco retrieved their canteen and the blanket roll. The engine whistle sounded, and Chaco switched off the Eveready.

"*That was them back there, wasn't it?*" Bui said.

"Yes."

"*They saw us.*"

"Yes."

"*Do you think they know it is us they saw?*"

"They will as soon as they discover the motorcar."

Bui made a thoughtful sound in her throat, said, "*How long before that?*"

"I don't know. I didn't expect them to find the break in the telegraph line until morning. That sheriff is better at his work than I'd have guessed."

They sat silent in the dark as the train clicked onward, and watched the lights of the whistle-stops flicker between the slats in the car as the train rolled past them without slowing. When Chaco thought enough time had passed, he flicked the Eveready on and removed the bandana from around the old imp's neck. He dampened the sweat-stained cloth with water from the canteen and wiped some of the blood from his scalp.

"I'll do that," Bui said.

He gave her the bandana and canteen. Then took up one of the imp's thick hands and chafed it between his own. At length the man moaned and began to come around.

"Ellen? Where—"

"You're okay," Chaco said.

The imp blinked and then seemed to remember where he was. "Amarillo Slim." He turned his head a little and looked around. "Where is he?"

"He decided to get off."

The imp groaned and attempted to sit up but couldn't. "Left me with a bit of a headache," he muttered.

"You should lie quiet for a while," Bui said.

"I really should, shouldn't I?"

Chaco placed the canteen on the deck beside him, placed the imp's sturdy hand on top. "Drink some water," he said. "It will help." He switched off the Eveready and in the dark heard the gurgling slurp of him drinking.

"Before I left the jungle in Fort Worth, they told me to watch for that man."

"I think he intended to kill you," Bui said.

The old man chuckled. "Kill me? I suppose I have you to thank for my life."

"No. Thank my brother."

"Thanks."

The imp drank again and sighed audibly. "Nothing like water. I should have drunk more of it. Oh well. You do realize that there will be trouble waiting for us up the line? But never worry. I'm rather a novice at this, but I've picked up a trick or two." He fell silent for a moment. "You a marine?"

"I was."

"I was an army man myself, in the bloody Civil War. *Civil* War," he scoffed. "Nothing bloody civil about it. Or any war, for that matter, I imagine. Wrap it up in the flag and glory, but it's never anything but a bloody tragedy. Man's favorite sport, if you want the truth of it. If men didn't love the circus, they wouldn't bloody well go to it. I was a doctor, a surgeon—a butcher, actually. Cut off enough arms and legs to sink a four-master. Cut them off boys hardly old enough to shave—little more than babies, really, and so damned brave and, God, so goddamned bloody brave. The best part of me died in that war. Didn't realize it at the time, you know? Who does?" He fell silent for a few moments. "Sorry. Nobody wants to hear. Never have. Never will. Can't say that I blame them." And after another moment he looked at each of them. "Where are you bound?"

"Wherever this train takes us," Chaco said.

"It's the Rockies for me, if I make it that far."

"Why wouldn't you?" Bui asked.

The imp's laugh was soft and humorless. "According to my prognosis, I should have died about three weeks ago. Bloody cancer gobbling up my bloody insides. Six months, they gave me. I'd love to cheat the old devil, mind you, but no, it's not in the cards. But I'm done with worry. It's actually my poor sweet Ellen I feel sorry for."

"Ellen?" Bui murmured. It was the name he'd said as he woke.

"I told her I was going out for a drink. Lovely girl. Loyal. True blue. Everything a man could want in a wife or a Boy Scout. Couldn't do it to her. Decided to go it on my own."

"You mean die?" Bui said.

"The noble death of a hobo. Nobler than that of a failed surgeon, which I am. I had to do it, mind you, even though Ellen would never understand. She's a darling girl, my wife. Too good for me by half. Always was. I married above my station and she beneath hers. The only child of Brian Whit, of the Baltimore Whits. He referred to me as the runt, and I to him as the dim Whit. But with Ellen it was never about money or station or family name."

"That bull hit you pretty hard. Maybe you better stop talking for a while."

The doc coughed, and Chaco heard him spit, heard him mutter, "God, my head hurts." Heard the gritty sound of something being unscrewed and smelled whiskey. He heard the doc swallow and heard him sigh.

"I needed that. You know, I think I'm ready to stand up."

"You sure?" Bui asked.

"Better if I do it now than try and fail later."

Chaco hoisted the imp to his feet. He hung on to Chaco's wrist for a moment, then let go and tottered toward the cargo door. Chaco leaned his back against the wall of the forward end of the car and studied the shadow shape of the small man, outlined against the lighter darkness of the prairie. Spider lightning lit the night. He thought about the soldiers on this train, about the U.S. marshal. Throwing the railroad bull off the train had been a mistake. The sheriff would find his body, and if he hadn't already he'd telegraph ahead. Somewhere up the line other lawmen would stop the train. They would search the cars, and they would have the help of the soldiers and that marshal.

He had to think about that.

51

W hen the railcar shuddered, Chaco woke with a start and sat up. Gray light spilled through the open cargo doors. Bui lay on her side, curled up beside him. He blinked against the urge to close his eyes again, to go back to sleep. The train was slowing. He came to his feet. Saw the doc standing at the cargo door, on watch as promised. He shook Bui's shoulder.

Her eyes opened, and she was awake.

"*Time to go,*" he said.

She sat up, rubbed her face, and nodded. He left her and walked to the open cargo door. Doc looked up at him and nodded. "You look better."

"How long did I sleep?"

"About three hours."

Chaco leaned out into the chill wind. The morning air smelled clean after the rain.

"That will be Amarillo up there," Doc said, "unless I'm mistaken."

The train was slowing toward a low cluster of lights about a mile ahead. But there was something about those lights that didn't look quite right.

"The rails divide in Amarillo," Doc said. "One road will take you to Albuquerque and the other on to Denver. Now that's a lovely town."

Chaco wasn't really listening. The lights ahead held his attention. The locomotive sounded its whistle and was answered by the *ooh-gaa* of a dozen automobile horns, and as Chaco blinked the lights he was staring at resolved themselves into the headlamps of automobiles.

The locomotive was slowing toward a line of motorcars situated on either side of the tracks, their headlamps directed toward the oncoming train. A man stepped into the headlights and began to swing a red lantern from side to side.

Doc gripped the doorframe and leaned out of the car. "It would appear the Amarillo constabulary has arranged a reception committee."

Chaco hurried to the forward end of the car, took up the Sharps, shouldered the canvas bundle, and pulled Bui to her feet.

"We've got to jump."

She needed no explanation.

"Bring everything," he said, and hurried back to the cargo door, looked out, and crossed to the other side and looked out again. "We'll go out on this side."

The doc collected his bundle and came up beside them. He looked down. The train had slowed but nevertheless was still clipping along.

"We're moving a little fast, don't you think?"

"They're not after you, Doc. They're here for us. You don't want any part of this."

"It may comfort you to think that, but like it or not, I've bought into this jackpot."

Chaco shrugged. "It's your life."

"Damned right, what's left of it."

Chaco secured the leather safety loop over the hammer of his Colt, tightened the chinstrap of his wet campaign hat, and looked at his sister. Her bright eyes were hard as flint.

The train was slowing steadily. It was now or never. He sat down, with his legs extended through the door. Looked up at Bui, said, "Watch what I do," gripped the doorframe at its base and swung away. His boot-heels struck the gravel ballast in running bounds; he let go and leaned back, decelerating in long, heel-driven strides until he slowed to a stop. Ahead of him Bui and Doc picked themselves up and limped back toward him.

The engine whistle sounded as they joined up and moved away from the slowing train, Chaco expecting to hear "There they are," as they ran stooped over across the open ground. Somehow they reached the fence line without being seen, and, within the relative concealment of scrub and cedars that had grown up along the fence line, Chaco stepped on the lower wire and pulled up on the one above while Bui and Doc ducked through. He climbed the wire like a ladder where it was stapled to a fence post and jumped to the ground.

Cattle, wakened from sleep in the half-light, lurched to their feet and moved off—making noises he hoped the train would cover. He heard shouted orders and peered out from the covering cedars as men with lanterns advanced toward the train. Soldiers came off the lead Pullman, and a few moments later he heard Captain Banyan shouting commands.

"We need to move while they're occupied," Doc whispered.

Chaco nodded, and the old imp led out. They followed the fence line westward, taking advantage of the cover there was. When they came abreast of the line of motorcars parked on a wagon road, Doc paused behind the relative shelter of a plank gate. Chaco peered between the weathered slats. There were a few automobiles as well as wagons, and there were saddle horses tethered to several of the wagons.

Someone shouted "Over here," above the frustrated cries of the searching men, and then came the crack of a rifle and a shrill voice yelling, "I think I got him, Captain."

Bui gripped Chaco's arm.

"Don't shoot," another voice shouted. "I'm coming out."

"Keep going," Chaco whispered, and they jogged on, and scarcely a hundred yards beyond the gate came to a windmill turning in the first stirs of morning wind. Its wood frame was like a church steeple under construction, water dribbling feebly from an iron pipe into a mossy concrete trough, the well's sucker rods rasping and the wooden blades of the fan turning slowly in the broken silence.

Chaco refilled their canteens, then followed Doc back to the fence line; they eased between the wires and crossed some open ground to a lone juniper near the tracks and there hunkered down to wait.

Over the next half hour, the posse, with the assistance of the soldiers, removed eight men from the train: hobos and free riders they held under guard in front of the locomotive.

"Why are they after you?" Doc whispered.

"I took my sister away from a powerful man."

"And he wants her back?" Doc asked.

"Not anymore."

"I see." The doc was breathing hard, on one knee, a hand pressed against the wall of his chest. "Most of the time I still feel like I'm thirty. Then I spoil it by doing something like this."

"You okay?" Bui asked.

"I'll make it, sweet lady. And if I don't, well, what the hell, right?"

Chaco decided he liked this little man. He had courage. "Can you get on the train when it is moving?"

"It will be moving fast by the time it reaches this point," Doc said, worry in his voice. "I'll have to try for the ladders, climb up, and ride on top." He tilted his head back and studied the graying sky, already turning blue along the eastern horizon. "At least it isn't raining."

"I wish it were," Bui said.

They heard a man shout, "You lie to me again and I'll see you jailed for a year."

Chaco, recognizing the voice, peered through the juniper. Captain Banyan was standing over one of the hobos from the train; it looked as if he'd knocked the man down. "I know damned well he was on this train. Where'd he get off? Tell me, dammit, or I swear—"

"Four or five miles back," the hobo wailed, pointing toward the brightening horizon. "I seen this feller jump off."

"How many of them?" the captain demanded. "Two, three?"

"Yeah, there was two or three of 'em."

Now came more shouts. The posse had a direction. The automobiles were cranked. The soldiers climbed into the cars and wagons. Riders mounted. The locomotive sounded its whistle and huffed as its drive wheels turned. The train rattled down its length and moved west as the line of automobiles broke ranks and rolled eastward along the railroad right-of-way. Behind the cars came mounted riders and a number of wagons in a race to keep up.

When the locomotive rolled past their position, Chaco said, "We better go."

"Maybe we better give that bunch a little more time," Doc said.

"If we don't go now, we'll end up walking," Chaco said.

Doc nodded. "Okay. You lead the way."

Chaco looked at Bui. "Stay close."

She nodded.

They ran straight for the train, then turned and ran alongside it, the cars moving past them faster than Doc could run. Somehow Bui was keeping up. He heard Doc's labored breath. "Grab the next ladder," Chaco called, pointing to the front end of the next car as it rolled toward them.

Doc grabbed and was snatched off his feet and carried forward as he pulled himself up and planted a boot on the bottom rung. He looked back, a surprised grin on his face, as Chaco fell back, allowed Bui to get out ahead of him, and when the end of the next car moved by, she grabbed a lower rung on the iron ladder. Like Doc, she was snatched off her feet. She dropped the blanket roll, but she managed to hang on. Chaco snatched it from the ground on the run, wiggled his hand up to the forearm under the carry loop. Bui was climbing toward the roof of the car. When the next car rolled past, he grabbed the ladder with his left hand, swung forward, and got a boot onto the bottom rung. He climbed and was near the top when Bui reached down and took the blanket roll from him. He looked forward and saw Doc midway up the ladder of the next car.

"*I was afraid he wouldn't make it,*" Bui said.

"I didn't think he would, either. But he did."

Chaco came up the last few rungs and moved to where Bui sat on the catwalk that ran the centerline length of the car and sat beside her. He slipped the canvas bundle from his shoulders and watched Doc as he made his awkward way toward them.

"I think he's hurt," Bui said, concern in her voice.

Strange, Chaco thought. She feels an attachment for this small man. Somewhere he had read . . . or perhaps it was Mr. McGregor who'd read him the words, "There is no plumbing the depth of the human heart." Mr. McGregor, who swore that if the world of men could be saved, it would be poetry that saved it.

He untied one of the shoulder straps on the canvas bundle

and used it to secure the bundle to the catwalk as Doc came up and sat beside them.

"For a moment there I thought you might not make it," Doc joked, winded but happy.

"Are you hurt?" Bui said.

"Pulled a muscle, but otherwise sound." Doc winked at her. "This is the life."

The engine was slowing along a gentle downgrade toward the skyline of Amarillo. Chaco saw a six-story brick building near the northern edge of town that looked like it might be a hotel. He saw the rooftops and upper windows of several Victorian homes. There were people out and about, hurrying along on the sidewalks that flanked the muddy streets. The downtown area was made up of single-story and two-story brick buildings. Electric lamp poles and telephone poles with dozens of wires lined the streets. The engine swung in a long curve into an active rail yard with many sidings and a huge roundhouse. From their vantage on the roof of the freight car, Chaco saw that there was more than one railroad station here. The train appeared to be moving toward the smallest. Beyond the stations, as in Clarendon, there were holding pens for cattle.

"What do you think?" Doc said. "Bail off, or try to ghost our way through the yard?"

"There's too much activity," Chaco said. "We'll do it bold, ride straight through."

He saw switch engines moving cars, saw yardmen in overalls and billed caps working the yard.

"We should lie down," Doc said, and, without waiting for a response, got down on his belly.

Chaco looked at Bui and nodded. They flattened themselves against the roof. The engine rolled past the station and came to a full stop. Chaco heard the conductor shout:

"Five minutes. Sorry folks, but we're behind schedule. Five minutes."

By chance their car was far enough back that they escaped notice. Chaco watched a yardman climb the ladder of the water tower and lower the downpipe. Water poured into the engine's reservoir. Several passengers got off; a few others boarded. The engine whistle blew, the conductor called, "All aboard," and they were moving again.

Doc sat up as they rolled by the station, and Chaco grabbed for his shoulder to pull him down but was too late. A man leaning against the wall outside the express office saw them, drew a pistol, and ran along the platform.

"Hey, you," he shouted, and fired.

The bullet thunked into the catwalk as Chaco swung the Sharps off his shoulder. The man fired again as Chaco slid a cartridge into the breech, brought the weapon to his shoulder, and fired a snap shot. The fifty-caliber round caught the shooter in midstride and slammed him back. Chaco was on his feet. He looked at Bui. "Stay here," he ordered, turned and ran along the catwalk toward the engine.

Doc looked at Bui. "Sweet Jesus, I believe he just killed that man."

The train was slowing as Chaco leapt from car to car, running toward the engine.

52

Hank Smith jerked the lead rope of the reluctant pack mule as he hurried the claybank along First Street. The morning was still young, but, even so, a sizable crowd had gathered outside the Fort Worth and Denver station to gawk at the recovered Ford automobile that Wilbur had ordered dragged up from the creek and left on display. Wilbur had his reasons, the likeliest being the upcoming reelection. The automobile was a sideshow. A way to divert voters away from thinking too much about the murderer who'd managed to escape from the county's supposedly escape-proof jailhouse.

Clarendon hadn't seen this much excitement in a while. As for his part of it, Hank was ready to chunk it to 'em. They could have it all. He had looked into that Apache kid's eyes and seen his own mortality. He felt lucky to be alive. Last night Wilbur had obliged him to ride out with the posse. As a result Hank had been there when they reconnected the telegraph wires. And he'd been with Wilbur when a rider galloped up to report the automobile had been found jammed up in the creek downstream from the trestle, not a hundred yards from where Wilbur had ordered that break in the telegraph line spliced. That was the point at which Hank realized that he was alive only because he happened to fit into that Injun kid's plan. And he'd done exactly what that kid fully expected.

That shriveled his pod.

He bunched his shoulders against the chill morning and thought about his place in Blanco Canyon. What he'd do was plant a few beans and maybe some squash and other such. Buy a dozen cows or rustle up a few mavericks—enough for jerked beef and to keep the taxes paid on the place, if the place hadn't already been taken on account of him never having paid any. There was an overlook above his one-room adobe, a high rock that looked out over the canyon and the empty country beyond. He intended to sit out his years on that rock and listen to the wind.

He'd had all the fun he could take.

They'd found Amarillo Slim Johnson crawling in the road on their way back to town. He'd been back-shot and had several broken bones. There was no way to be easy with him. They'd heaved him up onto the saddle of Wilbur's horse and carried him back to Doc's place, where they soon enough had him shot full of morphine.

Once the railroad bull's pain was eased, Wilbur got his story. Slim had been doing the evening run up to Amarillo, like normal. He'd seen a couple of hobos running to catch the train as it rolled out. As soon as they were beyond the rail yards, he swung down into the freight car he'd seen them climb into. He'd had this hobo down, a dwarf, when the other one shot him. A runt not much taller than the dwarf took his billy away from him at gunpoint and used it to work him over. The next thing Slim remembered, he woke up rain soaked and in terrible pain alongside the tracks. He was pretty much stove up: broken collarbone, broken leg, shot through the side, several broken ribs, and a concussion.

Amarillo Slim's days as a railroad bull were done. Word was

he'd already been fired. The railroad was run by a practical bunch of fellows who had no use for a disabled man. It couldn't have happened to a nicer guy, as far as Hank was concerned.

Hank reined the claybank to a halt near the crowd milling about the recovered motorcar as Wilbur stepped out of the telegraph office. The sheriff waved and walked out to the street.

"So you're really going?"

"I told you I was. I might come back for some of your wife's good biscuits, though."

Wilbur extended his hand, and they shook.

"I won't say it's been a pleasure, Hank, because it ain't."

"Did they catch that Injun in Amarillo?"

"They searched the train, but he got past them somehow. A Pinkerton man spotted him on the roof of a freight car at the station in Amarillo. He got off a few shots before he got shot himself."

"Is he alive?"

"Barely," the sheriff said. "Makes you kinda wonder, don't it? You don't see too many smart killers."

"I don't see too many killers at all, period. Leastwise, not these days."

"They'll get him sooner or later. I've half a mind to head up that way and join the hunt. Want to come along?"

"No, I don't. And if you got any regard for Miz Millie, you'll let that one go. Getting rid of the Injuns is what went wrong with this country." Hank sat his saddle for a thoughtful moment. Then added, "They keep after him like they been, they'll get what they're after."

"They intend to kill him, I think."

"Well, that's an even better reason not to go, ain't it? But I got a question."

"Yeah, what's that?"

"What if they get fooled? I bet they ain't figured it could go the other way, have they?"

"Goodbye, Hank."

53

Chaco was standing on top of the coalbunker, rifle aimed down at the engine crew. Doc and Bui were seated on the catwalk, with the rolling country around them falling away toward the Canadian somewhere out ahead. They had been moving steadily for better than an hour now, and the land had begun to change. Bui stared at a low saddleback mesa off to their left. The country here was made up of shallow swales and low ridges marked by broken flags of sandstone, a sandy land covered with wispy grass, mesquite scrub, and cactus. Smoke curled back from the engine. She studied her brother. He looked tall standing on the high perch of the coalbunker. The tracks curved into view of a line of willows and cottonwoods that marked the course of the river they were fast approaching.

"We should see Tascosa coming up soon," Doc said.

"What kind of place is it?"

"Up and coming, or so I've heard. In the old days it was a gathering place for Comancheros. They rendezvoused there to trade with Comanches and Kiowas. The town named its graveyard Boot Hill, for the one in Dodge City. They say the only man buried there that wasn't shot was a Negro cook. The epitaph on his marker says, 'Just Died.'"

Bui laughed and then blinked as if realizing she hadn't done so in some time.

The river came in sight, and the tracks swung left and ran west parallel to it. The engine began to slow and sounded its whistle. There were buildings up ahead. Apparently Chaco had ordered the driver to stop. On the other side of the river, she caught sight of rooftops, a town over there, and in the shallow flow of the river the wreckage of a washed-out bridge. Its timbers scattered and half-buried in and along the river's sandy bottom. The train slowed steadily toward a small clapboard building painted railroad yellow, an open platform faced the tracks with two adjacent warehouses.

The cars began to rack, and the train came to a full stop. Bui untied Goyaałé's bundle, retied the shoulder rope, and got it slung onto her back.

"I assume we're getting off here," Doc said.

"He is," Bui said, and pointed.

Doc turned and saw Chaco on the ground, looking up at the men in the cab of the engine.

"Okay, then," he said, and got to his feet and extended his arm. "Lead the way, fair maiden."

Bui went off the roof of the car. She dropped the last couple of feet onto the ballast and looked in Chaco's direction. He stood, the Sharps rifle in hand, gaze fixed on the driver and fireman, apparently giving them instructions.

Doc came up beside her. There was a metallic thump on the roof of one of the cars. They turned and saw a black man climbing through the roof hatch of an ice car. Hoarfrost formed in his hair as he slapped his arms against his body.

"Where is we at?" he called.

Doc grinned. "Looks like we aren't the only ones they

missed." He winked at Bui and called up to the black man. "You'd better stay on this train, young man. There is going to be a trainload of trouble arriving here shortly."

The black man gestured with his hand, mimicking a tip of the hat. "Much obliged, mister, and I thank you kindly." He quickly descended from the roof of the ice car and had scarcely swung up into an open freight car before the train started up again. He waved to them and Bui waved back. Passengers in the Pullmans stared out at them from behind the closed windows of their cars as the train gathered speed.

Chaco jogged over to them. He looked at Doc. "You should have gone on to Denver."

"And miss the circus? Not on your life."

The little man had an unhealthy pallor.

"You think you can ride?" Chaco asked.

"I can ride."

"I don't tell people what to do, but the trouble we had back there with those men—they will come after us, and they won't give up."

"I assumed as much after you shot that man."

"You'd be smarter to go see those mountains you wanted to see."

Doc's pleasant expression soured. "I thought you weren't going to tell me what to do."

"You could lose your life, you know?"

"That's already lost. All I'm doing is picking my own place and my own time."

"*Let him come with us,*" Bui said. "*I like this man.*"

Chaco spared her a fleeting glance. He studied the old dwarf, seeing him, really seeing him, for the first time. They were in some way much alike, he realized: men born into a world to which they would never belong. "What do you know about horses, Doc?"

"Enough to know I prefer a buggy. Why?"

"Because I'm going to buy some for us now," he said.

They walked down to the river, which flowed shallower at this point. On the opposite bank a clear-water creek emptied into the river below an old bridge abutment. They waded across, climbed the bank, and followed the flowing creek toward several adobe houses. They came to a footbridge and crossed it into the town, then made their way up the main street through what was left of Tascosa. The buildings were mostly abandoned; the place was practically a ghost town.

They walked up the center of the sandy street side by side to a livery stable. The doors of the low-roofed barn stood open, and they walked through the building and out the other side. There were four holding pens in back, several horses in one of them, and a woman in the corral with the horses. Chaco leaned his forearms against one of the upper rails, looked between the poles, and watched as she removed a halter from one of the horses. The animal moved away and rejoined the little herd as the woman draped the halter over her shoulder and walked toward them, drawing up and coiling a lariat. Doc waved to her.

"Top of the morning to you."

"Mickey ain't around this morning, gents," the woman said. "Anything I can do for you?"

"I want to buy horses," Chaco said. "Can you help us with that, ma'am?"

"The name's Miss Thomas, no 'ma'am' or 'lady' to it," she said. "Yes, I can help you. These are my animals." She jerked the thumb of her gloved hand toward the milling horses. "They're green-broke mustangs, but I wouldn't give a dollar for an animal that wasn't wild raised."

"We'll need outfits, saddles, and bridles." Chaco squinted at her through the fence: a tall, full-bodied woman, handsome, strong, and proud. No nonsense in her manner, yet something of mystery in the way her gray eyes looked back at him. She moved with a swagger, like a cat in her dusty range clothes and down-at-the-heel boots. There were gray streaks in her hair, and it hung down in a long single braid from under a battered Stetson to the middle of her back.

She came out of the pen, and they hunkered down and bargained. She knew horses and was shrewd. She told Chaco that the saddles belonged to Mickey McCormick, a local hanger-on, so she couldn't come down any on the asking price for those. They went over to have a look at them. The saddles were old, with neatly stitched leather patches, but Doc said that all three were serviceable. "You'll not have to worry about a cinch giving out on you."

Thomas studied Chaco for a long moment. "It's none of my business, but mind telling me where you're headed?"

"North," he said.

"With three extra horses for remounts, you'd better carry along extra water. You'll need it." She aimed a finger at a stand-alone mule in the corral. "That animal can carry four five-gallon tins of water all day. You buy her at the asking price, and I'll throw in the packsaddle and four five-gallon water cans."

"You have any canned goods or food you could sell us?" Bui asked.

"I might," Miss Thomas said, and showed them what she had.

She lived in a one-room adobe next door. The floor was cleanly swept sandstone flags set in adobe mud. There was a sideboard against the wall, a table with four chairs tucked under it, a rusty, cast-iron, four-lid cook stove. There was a shelf beside a narrow bunk on which lay a neatly folded change of jeans and an extra shirt. On a low table beside the bunk were an oil lamp and several well-thumbed books. Against the opposite wall a blanket covered the pantry door. She pushed the blanket aside, went in, and came out a few moments later carrying a case of canned pot roast, a skillet, a coffeepot, and a pound sack of Arbuckles' coffee beans.

"You cook the coffee beans dry in the skillet and hammer them with the butt of your pistol," Doc said. "That's the best way to make good coffee."

Miss Thomas grinned at him and told Chaco what it all came to, the six horses Doc had picked, the three outfits, the mule, packsaddle, water cans, and the grub.

"My sister carries the money," he said.

"Now, there's a man after my own heart."

Chaco offered to carry the case of canned goods, but she waved him off and walked ahead of them out of the cabin. Bui, in the meantime, had saddles on two of the horses and was cinching up the third. They crossed the yard, and Chaco stepped through the corral poles and went to his sister. He unbuttoned the field jacket she wore, slipped his hand through the slit in the lining, and plucked out one of the packets of money. He peeled off several bills and tucked the rest of the money back in place. Bui stared at him wordlessly.

He ducked between the corral poles again and counted the bills into Miss Thomas's calloused palm and told her to keep the extra five dollars when she said she'd have to go down to the Equity Saloon for change.

"Tell you what," she said, and left them standing while she fetched a canvas satchel. "To carry these canned goods in," she said, and almost as an afterthought tossed Chaco a boot for his rifle. She helped them fill the water cans at the creek and helped strap the cans to the packsaddle, and Chaco lashed Goyaałé's bones and the canvas satchel full of canned meat on top.

Bui, ready to mount her horse, caught the saddle horn with both hands and with a grimace of pain pulled up as she jumped a foot into the stirrup and swung her leg over and sat the saddle.

Doc led his horse over to a bench and got aboard that way.

Smiling, Miss Thomas gave Doc a little salute. "Pleasure doing business with you."

"Likewise, Miss Thomas." Doc swept the battered hat from his head. "I've always admired tall women."

She grinned up at him. "You're kind of cute yourself."

They heard the shrill of the steam whistle and, turning, looked toward the river. Chaco brought his mount around. A locomotive was slowing into the station on the other side of the river. Their pursuers would most assuredly be on that train. He looked at Bui and Doc and, with a wave to the woman, led out at a high trot.

"Any delay of yon constabulary, dear lady," Doc called back as he kicked his mount into a high lope, "will be most heartily appreciated."

They left Tascosa at the gallop. A mile north of town, crossing a sandy ridge, Chaco drew up and looked back. The rooftops of the town were visible among the cottonwoods, a drift of coal smoke from the train across the river. The captain would be across by now. His men would be searching the town. They'd discover soon enough that they'd missed them again. At that point Banyan and the marshal would think about horses and seek out Miss Thomas. Figure another hour to obtain horses and gear before they got into their track. Unless he misjudged the town, some of the soldiers would ride out on barebacked animals. There couldn't be twenty usable saddles in what was left of Tascosa. And riding bareback, that would slow them down some.

I should have bought Miss Thomas's entire remuda. He grimaced. You keep thinking about what you should have done. What good did four years in the Corps do you if you keep making these kinds of mistakes?

With the Sharps in the saddle boot and the reassembled shotgun slung from his saddle horn, he rode on, Bui, Doc, and the spare horses and mule lined out behind. The morning chill soon burned off. By noon the sun blazed hot, yet the heat was tolerable. They moved across a sandy, almost treeless country. The greening grass of spring was sparse. Scrubby, foot-high mesquite grew in scattered patches across the rolling country out to the horizon. The land itself spoke of killing heat, of long droughts.

By early afternoon they were many miles north of the Canadian breaks. Chaco pulled up, brought the spyglass to his eye, and studied the country out of which they'd ridden. He judged they'd traveled far enough in the wrong direction. It was time: he swung west and now alternately trotted and walked their mounts at a mile-eating pace. They moved over the short-grass barrens toward a distant butte. At one point he turned in the saddle and saw, several miles behind them, a feather of telltale dust, like a yellow shadow against the fading sky—that would be the soldiers and the marshal.

The country through which they rode was not empty, only waterless and peopleless. It was a land that stood against the customary measure of the world: it did not lend itself to accurate judgments. He couldn't tell if the men who followed were ten miles back or twenty.

Late in the afternoon, with the horses tiring, they happened upon a spring-fed trickle, a kind of freak of nature, its location marked on the high prairie by several cottonwoods. A hand-width flow of water burbled up from under a rock, flowed forty yards along a tree-lined trench, and collected in a pool, the overflow of which disappeared into a gurgling suckhole.

"We'll rest the horses awhile," Chaco said.

Bui stood in her stirrups and studied the country behind them. "*We should keep going.*"

"The animals must have water and grain. And they must rest. We've come near fifty miles. We'll give them a couple of hours."

"*They could catch up by then.*"

The doc cut lengths of rope and made up rope hobbles while Chaco stripped the saddles. The horses rolled and drank and grazed. Doc opened one of the cans of roast beef, and they used their knives for spoons and ate while the animals nipped at patches of gamma and green watercress along the narrow flow.

Although Doc wore a look of good cheer, his face had turned even more ashen. Bui studied him out of worried eyes. She noticed how Chaco would glance at the old man now and then. Doc pulled up a double handful of the watercress and sat on a rock and began to methodically eat the crisp green leaves—looking around, clearly exhausted, yet somehow content.

Bui went to her brother. *"How much more time will you give the horses?"* This kindness to horses seemed strange to her.

For an answer Chaco came to his feet, retrieved the Sharps from the saddle scabbard, and walked up from the creek to a bit of high ground and there stood with the Sharps cradled in the crook of his arm, unmoved and unmoving, as he watched their back trail.

The light slowly faded.

Bui spent the time listening to Doc as he told her about his life. When he mentioned he was the fifth son of an English earl, she nodded as if she understood what an earl was. She listened as only women can listen, and he talked as men will talk, telling her the story of his life. None of it made much sense to her. Time slipped away, and when the light was almost gone she went up and stood beside her brother.

The first stars winked in the darkening sky.

"Can you see their dust?" she asked.

"Only just a little now. I think it's time to go."

They went down to the horses and saddled the spare mounts, Chaco cinching his onto the back of a short-coupled gelding that looked like it might have bottom and speed.

"They're close, aren't they?" Doc said.

"They are closer."

"*We should have kept going,*" Bui said.

"I don't know enough about horses to make that call," Chaco said.

While he reloaded the pack animals, Bui led one of the spare horses to the place where the spring bubbled from under the ledge of rock. She formed a loop in the animal's neck rope and slipped it into the horse's mouth and looped it around its lower jaw. She threw the other end of the rope over the animal's back and pulled it up under its belly. Then she lifted a forefoot and took a turn on the rope and pulled the animal's head toward her until it was forced to lie down in the water. She tied the rope off, then stabbed the animal in the throat several times. The horse squealed in terror and fought to rise. The squeals quickly subsided, and the horse died. She opened its belly then, drew out its intestines, and slashed them and mixed their contents with the animal's blood in the now-tainted water flowing away from the spring.

Chaco and Doc, who hurried over at the first scream of the dying horse, stared at Bui as she walked back toward them.

"You wasted a good horse," Chaco said. "The water will wash it all away."

"*Their horses will not think so. They will smell the blood and refuse to drink. This will hold them here for a while.*" She walked on to the horses.

He watched her mount and jerk her nervous horse around. She has iron in her, he thought, following Doc back to the waiting horses. He boosted Doc into the saddle before he swung up onto his own mount. Then leaned out of the saddle to grab the lead rope. With a kick of his heels, he rode up out of the little spring creek and continued west.

Doc trotted up and fell in alongside him. "It's too dark to see their dust."

"And too dark for them to see ours," he answered.

"How far back do you think they are, five miles?"

"Less."

"That's cutting it close. Four miles at the gallop, they could cover that in a few minutes."

"They might yet. I'd hoped they would hang back at the water long enough to water and rest their animals, but they will come on now."

"But Bui said—"

"She's wrong."

"That's the reason you waited here, isn't it—to tempt them with this water?"

"It would have worked, too," he said, and lifted the gelding to a trot.

They covered ground now. At one point, looking back, Chaco saw the black silhouettes of the soldiers as they crested a long rise. Then he lost sight of them as they dropped from view behind a swale of ground. He rode at the trot for a full hour, pushing the claybank hard enough to sweat him in the chill evening. When he finally eased back to a quick walk, Doc moved up and rode abreast of him.

"That was foolish back there," Doc said. "I caught a glimpse of light. They must have a few Eveready torches with them. That means they'll be able to track in the dark."

"Their horses will begin to cave on them soon."

"These are mustangs. Don't count on it. For an Indian you don't seem to know much."

"I don't. I was raised white."

"Miss Thomas had some solid-looking stock," Doc said, almost ruefully.

"We're riding the best of it," Chaco said, and quickened the pace again.

He alternately trotted and walked the animals, Doc and his

sister lined out behind. The horizon announced that the moon would soon rise. He had indeed waited too long. Now was the time to do it, if he was going to do it. Abruptly he swung southward and within the hour, under the risen moon, spied a shadowy black line of telegraph poles, and, as they approached, a set of tracks came in sight.

"Is that the Fort Worth and Denver City line?" Doc asked.

"It is." Chaco leaned on his saddle horn.

"You could follow these right back to Tascosa."

"You could."

"Then we're somewhere between Tascosa and Dalhart?"

"Closer to Tascosa," Chaco said.

"*Why this?*" Bui asked.

"*The Gila River country is that way.*" He pointed south.

"*Then why did you ride the other way?*"

"*To fool them,*" he said.

They walked their mounts ginger-footed over the rails and kept going, Chaco ignoring the telegraph lines this time. To cut the line here would draw out a repair crew. And that went against his purpose.

Trotting southward, he anticipated the captain's anger, his frustration. The captain would reach the tracks leading men on thirsty, exhausted horses. Unless he misjudged, the captain would have no practical means with him by which to make use of the wires. His men would almost certainly be low on water and most of them raw from riding bareback. And, of course, they would have used up any water they'd transported for the horses. Seeing the tracks, the captain might recognize two serious tactical failures: that of having left Amarillo without mounts for his men, but more important, neglecting to attach a freight car to the short train, the means necessary to transport fresh remounts forward to his present position.

The moon climbed past its zenith as they pressed on. Toward

morning Chaco called a halt. They watered the animals out of their hats, four full hats of water for each, and, with cinches kept tight, he allowed them a brief rest during which they grazed.

Beside the moon, like an ivory smile above the western horizon, a single star burned brightly in the blue-black sky. He read the hour by the position of the fading handle of the Big Dipper and located Polaris before he caught his horse, took up the lead ropes, remounted, and led out.

Bui helped Doc mount, then climbed aboard her horse. She galloped forward and pulled up abreast of her brother. "*You changed direction, you know?*"

"*Yes.*"

"*We are going back to the river, you know that?*"

"*Yes.*"

"*They can water their horses if we go that way.*"

"It cannot be avoided."

"*We may have to fight them.*"

"*That is a fight we cannot win,*" he said, and rode on.

54

Even before they reached the rails, Tom Starrett knew they were beaten. They were out of water, the horses were played out, and he doubted there was a gallon of water left in the canteens of the entire outfit. He damned sure wasn't going to share the little left he had. The best and only real option they had was to send a galloper back to Tascosa.

He conferred with Banyan. After which the captain called up his sergeant, told him to pick his lightest man. The trooper, an Italian immigrant, five foot four, with only a rudimentary command of English, tended to answer any and all questions put to him, whether he understood them or not, with a smart "Yes, sir." A translator was sought out. And while the sergeant selected three of their soundest mounts, a fellow Italian private with a better command of English explained to his shorter countryman what the captain expected of him. Captain Banyan, in the meantime, wrote out a set of orders and signed them. The private was authorized to commandeer and return with as many barrels of water as possible, plus all the hay, grain, and any foodstuff he found ready to hand and hire any help needed to load it all on the waiting train.

"If that train's still there," Tom interjected.

"It'll be there," Banyan growled.

Tom shrugged, and the captain turned back to his translator.

"He must return within seventy-two hours, and sooner if possible."

The order was translated, the soldier snapped to attention, said, "Yes, sir," leapt into the saddle, and galloped away with a set of spare mounts on lead.

Tom watched after the boy, quickly fading from sight, while behind him the private's fellow soldiers went about setting up dry camp. No fires, the captain ordered—not that it mattered, there being nothing to cook anyway. The sergeant set the watch, which Tom considered a waste of energy, but that was the Army's business. He was spreading his blanket when the captain sauntered over.

"What do you think, Starrett?" Banyan asked. "Back here by noon?" He was chewing his lip and looked mighty worried.

"Not likely."

"I hope you're wrong." The captain looked south and drove his fist into his palm. "I thought we had him."

"We'll get him. Sure as sunrise, we'll get him." Tom stretched out on the blanket and pulled part of it over him. "I'll get him."

The captain's eyes narrowed. "The Army has first claim, Marshal."

Tom tilted his hat over his eyes. There'd be time enough for a pissing contest once they caught him.

55

They rode down the sandy, unforgiving land, long night hours in the saddle behind them, the horses weary and wind scoured. Chaco reined to a halt. To their left a rose line marked the ink-black horizon. He dismounted.

"We'll water them here and let them blow for a while."

As Doc slid from the saddle, he grunted and clung to the stirrup, his cheek pressed against the leather fender.

Bui went to him. "If the pain is bad, I have something for it."

Doc looked at her, the corners of his mouth turned up in the semblance of a smile. "Mostly out of practice, I'm afraid. Give me a minute. I'll be fine."

Chaco was unlashing the water cans, taking them off the pack mule, and lining them up on the ground.

"*I can help,*" Bui said.

"I've got it. You and Doc should rest while you can."

"*We should have bought* nose bags *and grain from that woman.*"

"The next town we come to we'll get both." He ran his hands over the mule, felt the tremble in its muscles. "They won't hold up much longer if we keep up this pace."

"*I know,*" she said.

Chaco walked away, looked back across the empty country out of which they had ridden. "The horses need rest, but if they overtake us here, we'll have no chance at all."

So far his plan had worked almost exactly. But he knew too little about horses, how much they could do, what their limits were—things he would need to learn in the days and years ahead, if there were any. He regarded Doc for a moment and turned back to Bui and saw that she was also staring at the little man.

Doc began to cough; within moments he was leaning over his knees, gagging between rasping breaths. He coughed like the ones from the Indian school, spitting up the blood of their lives—the graveyard behind the school filled with their forgotten bones. Now, as then, there was nothing to be done. Not even whiskey to ease this man's suffering.

The coughing fit subsided. "Oh God," he muttered, and looked up watery eyed.

"You going to be okay?"

He shook his head. "This is nothing," he wheezed, and with the back of his hand wiped a fleck of blood-pink phlegm from his mouth. He straightened, and squared his narrow shoulders. "I'm ready to go if you are."

They watered the animals and relashed the empty water cans to the packsaddle. Bui gave Doc a boost into the saddle before she swung aboard her own horse. Chaco took up the lead ropes and mounted. The mule began to act up, and he yanked hard on the rope and brought her along.

They followed the descending remnant of an old buffalo trail. A mile or so on, they heard a lobo moan in the distance.

"How about that," Doc said. "I thought those old boys had been cleaned out."

Ravens cawed from the thorny branches of mesquite.

Overhead a solitary vulture drifted on the wind. Ahead the dark, meandering green of a tree line marked the river the Indah called the Canadian, the mule hee-hawing as they rode down to and in among the trees. Here the air smelled faintly of woodsmoke. They rode out of the trees and down to the sandy riverbank, and Chaco reined to a halt.

His thirsty mount walked a couple of steps forward and lowered its mouth into the clear, shallow channel. He sat in his saddle as the other animals lined up along the shallow flow of the first channel, lowered their heads, and sucked at the clear water. The river was fifty yards across: a red-sand bottom as flat as a table, with three shallow channels. On the far side he saw the source of the smoke, the embers of several burned-out fires. Beyond the fires was a camp with several wagons and at least three cabin tents. As he considered whether to cross here or go around, a man from the camp stepped out from behind one of the wagons and a moment later was joined by another.

"What do you think?" Doc said.

The riverbanks at this point retained the ancient signs left by the now all but extinct buffalo. This was an established crossing. There was a marked chance of quicksand patches at any point along this kind of sandy river course. They hadn't the time to look for a better crossing than this.

"They've already seen us," Chaco said, and lifted the Model '97 off his saddle horn. He jacked a round into the chamber, lowered the hammer to quarter cock, and rested the shotgun across his thighs.

On the other side three more men stepped out from behind the wagons. Now five men stared across the river at them.

"Looks like they're expecting trouble," Doc said.

"I need my field jacket," Chaco said to Bui.

She lifted her mount's head from the water and eased over

beside him, removed the jacket, and passed it to him. He slipped his arms into the sleeves, rolled down the cuffs she'd folded back, took up the shotgun, and fished a round of double-aught out of the jacket's side pocket, thumbed the shell into the Winchester's tube, and looked questioningly at his sister and Doc.

"It's your party," Doc said.

Chaco led out. He followed the riverbank upstream a little way, watching the men on the other side, looking for any others. The claybank waded into the slow flow of the first channel, and at midstream Chaco caught a whiff of the not-unpleasant odor of sour mash, and at that point he understood the setup, the reason for the wagons and this isolated location by the river—a reliable source of water.

"Moonshiners," Doc said under his breath. "They'll be nervous."

"I expect they will."

"Watch yourself."

"What are moonshiners?" Bui asked.

Chaco rode up out of the river at an angle, his gaze fixed on the men, yet alert against any peripheral threat. The men wore pistols tied down like they knew what to do with them. The one on the right was the one to watch, the way he wore his pistols, one on each hip, the butts pushed out. He carried a third in a shoulder scabbard and had black button eyes in a whiskey-ravaged face. The corners of his wide mustached mouth were pulled down in a dangerously stupid sneer. The claybank snorted as Chaco swung him sideways to a halt, the shotgun muzzle aimed casually in their general direction.

Doc reined up beside Chaco and gave the five a friendly wave. "Top of the morning to you, gentlemen, and are we too late or too early for breakfast? Or perhaps just in time for it, then?" Doc said, mimicking a more than passably Irish brogue.

"You ain't revenue marshals, are ya?" the one with three pistols said.

"Do I look like someone who would take up a career in the Marshals Service?"

"No, you look like a midget."

"Dwarf, my good man, I'm officially a dwarf. And I've never actually checked the qualifications, mind you, but I am morally certain that there are no dwarfs employed by the revenuer branch of the Marshals Service, or, for that matter, any other branch of that service. We are what we seem: weary travelers on the long road of life, and if that wondrous aroma I smell is what I believe it is, I'll be asking you gentlemen if you'd be willing to part with a dram? Of course, I'll pay, mind you. My flask has gone empty and needs a refill. We may look like wilderness bums, but I assure you that I, at least, can pay."

"What's a dram?" Three Guns asked.

"A drink, my good man," Doc said.

"I told you they weren't revenuers, Harlan," one of the others said.

Three Guns said, "Shut up, Dale."

The one called Dale stepped forward a pace. "Howdy, I'm Dale Brown These here are my brothers, all except Harlan, there. He's our cousin." Dale gestured to Harlan, the three-gun man. "And Sanchez, that's him there on the end. He works for us. He ain't kin to nobody."

"It is my great pleasure, gentlemen," Doc said, and swept off his hat.

Chaco spared Doc a quick glance. The old boy was putting it on bold, though the evidence of their long ride was written on his pale, gray-seamed face. Bui, he noted, had slipped the rifle from her shoulder; it rested across her thighs, her face stony, her eyes hard as obsidian.

"What's wrong with them Meskins?" Harlan asked. "They nervous or something?"

"Why, come to think of it, sir, they are the nervous type." Doc turned, looked at Chaco, winked on the side turned away from the men. "But I can't ask them any questions, I'm afraid. They don't appear to speak any English."

"I wouldn't hire a Meskin couldn't speak American, would I, Sanchez?"

The Mexican shrugged, the others laughed, and Harlan, who had asked the question, blinked indecisively.

"I figure that one for a full-blanket Injun," one of the others said.

"Injun?" Dale scoffed. "Are you blind? You can see by his clothes he used to be a soldier. The Army ain't had no use for Injuns since they whipped the last of them." Dale turned away from Harlan and looked up at Doc. "Step down, mister. Fact is we was about to have us a bite of breakfast when Sanchez here heard you a-coming. And I believe we got enough who-shot-John to wash it all down with, and enough to fill your flask, too." He swiveled his head toward the others. "Ain't that right, boys?"

The brothers shrugged in tacit approval; Harlan scowled and shook his head.

"Tell them Meskins they're welcome to come eat at the table with us," Harlan said, "but they got to leave them guns with the horses. A Meskin with a shotgun makes me nervous."

"Well, sir, that may be a problem. I'm afraid he's rather fond of that shotgun. Sleeps with it, you see." Doc was grinning good-naturedly.

Chaco watched and waited.

Finally the one called Harlan cleared his throat. "Well then, you can come eat at the table with us, but not neither one of them two. I'll have the cook bring a couple of plates out to them."

Doc swung his leg over the saddle, hung from the horn, and dropped to the ground. When he passed his reins up to Bui, his smile faded. The look in his eyes said he understood the situation. "I hope you have eggs," he said happily. "I do love eggs," he added, assuming the smile again, as he turned back to the others.

"We got scrambled beans, and we got beans over easy, either way you like them," Dale said.

The others laughed, the sound of it forced, and Doc waved farewell without looking back and moved off with the whiskey makers. Sanchez and Harlan, the crazy-eyed cousin, were the last to turn away.

Chaco sat the claybank and watched after them until they disappeared behind a wagon. From here the tents and other wagons, farther back under the shade of the cottonwoods, were made misty by the smoke that rose from what he assumed was their cook fire.

"*The water*," Bui said. "*We should fill the containers.*"

While Chaco watched, she led the mule down to the river, removed the cans, and filled them; then she watched while he reloaded them. He remounted and nudged the gelding up out of the river bottom, and they followed a track that climbed through a wind-quaked stand of saplings. They came out in a meadow of patchy gamma grass. The meadow was grazed down, but enough feed was left for the animals to make out. They stepped down and in quick order had the horses and the mule hobbled. He loosened the claybank's cinch, stripped the saddles from Bui's and Doc's mounts, then resaddled their two remaining remounts and left their cinches loose.

The animals drifted as they grazed out into the meadow. Chaco had left the Sharps in the saddle scabbard, but, out of regard for the one they called Harlan, he kept the shotgun at hand.

Bui had settled on a log in a bit of shade on the far side of the meadow.

He crossed over and joined her.

"*We should have kept going,*" she said as he sat beside her.

"I agree. I was about to say that, but then Doc said that about not speaking English."

"*So?*"

"So it would have caused trouble. The one called Harlan, the one with the crazy eyes, he would have done something foolish."

For a moment she seemed to consider the possibility. "*I think yes, that one would see it as a trick.*"

The log was an uprooted tree that had been deposited along the edge of the meadow by some distant flood. It was barkless and sun bleached. Chaco rested the shotgun across his knees and watched the grazing animals. It seemed to him he must soon find a safe place for them to graze and recover. How far would Banyan and the marshal take this thing? If they kept coming, he would be forced to turn and fight. He didn't want that, but he would have to before the horses began to die.

Doc had slept in the saddle for much of the night, but it was clear to him that some vital part in him had been used up. It was a troublesome thing, for he liked Doc. So did Bui, maybe more than she should. He studied her still face. She was watching the horses. He saw that at some point last night her wound had bled through. It was dried now. Her cheeks were gaunt and her eyes bloodshot. She didn't look much better than the horses.

A movement among the cottonwoods caught his attention, and he straightened. A woman walked into the clearing, paused, and stared at the horses. She came toward them, a round-faced woman with solemn black eyes. He recognized the tattered ankle-length skirt and purple blouse. A Navajo woman, he thought, and wondered how she had ended up in a moonshiners' camp. He'd seen the Navajo girls who arrived at Carlisle similarly dressed . . . before the matrons issued them the school uniforms. She carried two plates of food in one hand and gripped the handles of two tin cups in the other. Her skin was dark and her hair long and raven black and bound at the base of her neck with a white cloth.

"*Yat-ta-hey,*" he called.

"*Yat-ta-hey,*" she answered, the plates of food extended toward them. But as she came closer, she hissed, "Don't eat. The beans are poisoned—don't eat them."

Chaco leaned the shotgun against the log and accepted both plates, turned, and placed them on the log. "Is the coffee poisoned too?"

"It is safe to drink."

Her English was good. He took the cups and placed them on the log beside the tin plates. When Bui reached for one of the cups, he shook his head slightly. He looked at the Navajo woman, said, "Who is watching?"

"The Mexican. Harlan sent him."

"Why do you betray them?"

"*You are N'dé,*" the Navajo woman said in the tongue of the Diné, a language similar enough to his own that Chaco understood her, if imperfectly.

"Speak English," he said. "Tell me, why do you betray these men?"

"I must get away from them." She gestured toward the camp. "They don't know I speak English."

He came at the question differently. "Why are you with these whiskey makers?"

"*They killed my man three moons ago and took me for a slave,*" she said in the Navajo.

"In English," he said again.

And in English she told them about the murder of her husband. How she'd ordered her children to run away and hide before they took her. "They will kill you and take this one for a slave. They meant to shoot you as you rode out of the river, but Harlan saw the shotgun and told the others to wait. It was Harlan who put the rat poison in the beans. Sanchez laughed about it."

"Have they killed the little man?"

"He was alive when I came, but Harlan had put poison in his beans, too."

Chaco looked past her at the stand of saplings on the far side of the meadow, said, "How were you supposed to do this?"

"When the poison begins to work, I am to grab this one and yell to him. Sanchez will come and check on you. He will tie this one to a tree and go back to tell the others."

"Altogether how many of them are there?"

"What you saw."

"How many horses do they have?"

"Eight horses to ride, six mules for the wagons."

Chaco took up the shotgun, jacked the slide back an inch to verify the chambered shell, racked the slide forward, looked at his sister, then at the Navajo woman. "What is your name?"

"Sally Begay."

Sally, the same name the Indah had given Bui. He nodded, said, "Wait here," and set out at a jog toward the camp. As he came to the tree line, he caught sight of the Mexican running away, but not in the direction of the camp. Chaco kept running and now was in sight of the camp. Off to his left he heard a horse stumble and gallop away. He jogged past a wagon filled with oak barrels, past an iron grille over a fire pit beside a chuck wagon. Then he saw them seated at a plank table under a brush arbor, Doc situated in a chair at the head of it. Their plates were shoved to the middle, all of them laughing and drinking, Harlan with a clay jug hiked up over one elbow, pouring clear liquor into a tin cup.

Doc saw him before any of the others. His eyes went wide as Chaco raised the shotgun.

"Jesus," he screamed, and threw himself sideways.

Harlan dropped the jug and clawed at his shoulder rig.

Chaco shot him, the blast pattern turning his shirtfront red at the same moment the round took two others out of the fight. He swung the barrel and shot Dale as he stood out of his chair, his pistol half-drawn. Jacked in another round and walked toward Dale, the man on his back screaming "Oh God, oh God, have mercy," as Chaco fired and his face disappeared.

He drew the Colt and went around the table, found two still breathing, and shot them in the head. In the ringing silence he ejected the spent brass hulls from the Colt and reloaded. Holstered the revolver and was reloading the shotgun when a camp dog howled. He looked around for the dog.

"You killed them all," Doc said. He had struggled to his feet and was looking around in disbelief. "I don't understand, son. They were just simple, honest moonshiners."

"They poisoned you, Doc. You need to make yourself throw up right now. They put poison in your beans."

"Poison?"

"Stick your finger down your throat."

"But they ate the same beans as I . . ." Doc hesitated, his voice trailing off as his disbelieving eyes registered a memory.

He took a couple of steps, bent over, and inserted his index finger deep into his throat. He gagged and gagged again, but nothing came up. He shoved his finger into his throat in another attempt and began to cough—an uncontrollable cough that lasted too long and left him wheezing and watery eyed. When he straightened, he looked at Chaco out of hopeless eyes.

The camp dog howled again, and Chaco looked around. This time he saw it. The animal was penned in an iron cage. But the dog was no dog. The moonshiners had somehow captured a wolf. He turned back to Doc and saw blood in the man's palm.

Doc spit, and there was blood—a lot of it. He looked up at Chaco out of bloodshot eyes and righted the chair he'd used and sat on it. He looked around and aimed a finger at a clay jug lying in the sand.

"Bring me that, if you wouldn't mind."

Chaco picked up the whiskey jug, wiped the sand off, and handed it to him.

"Thank you." Doc raised the jug to his lips; his Adam's apple bobbed as he swallowed and swallowed again. He drained the jug, threw it away, stood up again, leaned over, and stuck an index finger deep inside his throat. But again nothing came up. He sighed, straightened, and grinned, self-mocking and hopeless. "It's what I get for being such a damned good drinker in my youth. It would appear my past has caught up with me. It would seem I'm too well practiced a drunk."

"Keep trying."

Doc wiped his mouth with his sleeve, looked at the smear of blood on it. "You know . . . I'd hoped for something a little more heroic." He smiled sadly. "You're certain about the poison?"

"The woman who cooks for them told me. You should keep trying, Doc. A man shouldn't give up when there's a chance."

Doc shook his head. "Another day on that horse would have finished me anyway."

Chaco pointed north to the haze of dust rising out of the breaks. "The soldiers are coming. You know that, don't you?"

Doc nodded. "Anything you want me to tell them?"

"I'm sorry, Doc. We should've gone around."

"Ah, lad, sweet lad, no, I wouldn't have picked this end, but it's the one fate dealt me." He sat down on the chair again. "Any messages for our relentless representatives of the law?"

"Tell them what happened here. Tell them if they turn back, this thing between us can be over."

"You just killed four more white men, worthy of death though they most certainly were. I fear they'll not care about poisoned food."

"You should have gone on to Denver."

"I imagine you're right, my boy." He smiled; blood on his teeth.

Chaco turned toward the rumble of approaching horses as Bui and Sally Begay rode out from the trees into the camp, the horses and mules of the men he had killed mixed in on lead with their own. As they reined to a halt, the horses and mules bunched up. Bui looked down at the men Chaco had killed and gave him a satisfied nod. She jerked her chin toward the Navajo woman, said, "She goes with us."

Chaco turned back to Doc. "I must leave you, my friend. You will tell them what I said?"

"I will tell them. But listen, I want to say something." Doc extended a hand, and Chaco went to him and they clasped hands. "I'm glad we met. I'm glad I came along . . ." Doc's voice cracked a little. There was more in him to say, but he couldn't say it, and at length he simply nodded.

"It's been an honor, sir."

A wave of pain cut at Doc. He grimaced but managed the semblance of a smile.

"Well, at least I'll not die cold sober." He shrugged. "Would you mind bringing me that jug? I can't seem to feel my legs."

Chaco went around the table and brought back a fresh jug of whiskey. He gave it to Doc and looked around. Bui had gotten down and was hurrying toward Doc. Flies were already buzzing the bodies. Doc took another drink, then leaned to the side and finally vomited. He straightened and looked up at Chaco out of watery eyes. Ran the back of his hand across his mouth and grinned.

"Now, that's encouraging. Who knows, huh?"

Chaco turned toward Sally Begay. "Get some more whiskey, and bring it to him."

She dropped lightly to the ground and ran toward one of the wagons as Bui reached Doc's side. She knelt beside him, clasped his hand, and looked searchingly into his eyes.

"Ah, lass," he whispered, and rested his hand affectionately against her upturned face.

Chaco walked toward the caged wolf. The wolf snarled and backed away. It looked young and appeared to be underfed. Its muzzle was scarred; it had obviously been abused. How a wolf had come to be caged in a moonshiners' camp he could not imagine. To trap a wolf without injury seemed to Chaco a thing next to impossible. Perhaps the whiskey makers had found it as a pup. Perhaps this cage was the only world this wolf had ever known. As he stared at the young wolf, it occurred to him that the Indian school had never been about education. It had been about domestication.

Keep the wolf in a cage long enough, and he becomes a dog.

Kill the Indian and save the man.

He went around to the door of the cage. Pulled the iron bolt from the hasp and swung the gate open. Moved away from the cage and hunkered down with the shotgun across his knees and waited.

"We should go now," Bui called.

He knew she was right, but he waited. The wolf was huddled in the corner of the cage. It looked out at freedom, there for the taking, yet it hesitated. Chaco saw that the cage was both a prison and a safe, familiar place. But then the wildness in the wolf won out. It moved hesitantly toward the opening, extended its nose beyond that invisible barrier into a wider, dangerous world, and finally stepped tentatively out and away from the cage. It moved off then, shying this way and that, until it reached the edge of the camp. It stopped then, turned, and stared back as Chaco rose to his feet, his shoulders drawn back. The wolf looked directly at him, a reckoning between one wolf and one man set against a world with no place left in it for either of them.

"Go, brother. Drink the wind."

Tom Starrett smelled the river long before they rode within sight of it: a meandering ribbon of cottonwoods that marked the flow of the Canadian. He saw smoke down there, a grayish black column above the tree line off to their right. They'd heard the report of gunfire a few miles back, and the captain had quickened the pace.

Banyan moved up and came abreast of him. "What do you think?"

"Whatever it is on fire down there, my money's on Frank Kidd having something to do with it."

The captain nodded. "We got him now."

"You've said that before."

They altered direction, and the column swung in behind them. To a man the troops were mounted on fresh horses, thanks to Private Giani, and the generous assistance of Mr. G. W. Peters, president and CEO of the Fort Worth and Denver City. Nobody had been more surprised than Tom when Private Giani, now Corporal Giani, showed up a scant six hours after he'd ridden away. The skinny private had stepped out of Peters's palace car, puffing a fat cigar, with Mr. Peters's hand clapped collegially on his shoulder. The railroad man had held up the westbound long enough to empty a freight car and refill it with fresh mounts and supplies. He had declared it an act of public service, and as the train pulled away from Banyan's replenished troop, had called from the steps of his private car, "I'd love to come along, boys. Sounds like a great party."

Quite a man, Tom Starrett thought, riding beside Banyan toward the smoke that hung over the river forest. He spotted an old buffalo trail off to their right and swung toward it.

"There's the easy way down," Tom called.

Banyan swung his lathered horse right and led his troop behind Starrett right down to the trail. It wasn't a single path, but many trails that crisscrossed one another. Almost at once Tom saw hoof prints in the powdery dust.

He swung down and studied them—straightened and looked at Banyan. "Fresh."

The captain nodded and led out at the gallop.

Up to this point Tom had held back, but something took hold of him now: an all but irrational anger. He climbed into the saddle and put the spurs to his mount and in short order galloped past Banyan, heard the captain curse and yell out. What Tom wanted was Frank Kidd for himself. He didn't want some army private getting off a lucky shot, cheating him. Frank Kidd had killed a good man in Deputy Jim Travis. And he'd damn near killed another in his friend Sheriff Hamilton Jones. This wasn't to do with the law anymore. This had to do with what was right, with everything he stood for, who he was, what he believed, with personal justice.

The pounding of his horse's hooves blotted out all sound. Now the tree line was just ahead. He rode in amongst the willows and cottonwoods, galloped along a trail, and now saw the river.

Try not to get yourself killed, he heard himself think.

And taking hold of his anger, he reined his heaving mount to a halt. He crossed his trembling hands on the apple of his saddle horn and leaned on his arms. Soon enough came the sound of galloping horses, and then the captain shouting the order to halt.

Banyan rode up alongside him. "You want to tell me what the hell that was about?"

"About getting someplace," Tom said for want of any useful excuse. "The fire is on the far side of the river. I won't tell you your business, Banyan, but I'd spread my men out on line now, say a hundred yards in either direction from this point out, and cross them all in one move."

"It may come as a surprise to you, Marshal, but I do know what I'm doing."

"I never said you didn't."

The captain signaled the troop to move out and kicked straight for the river. Tom fully expected Frank Kidd to shoot Banyan right out of the saddle. But that didn't happen, and it surprised Tom. Frank Kidd was never going to get a better setup. The troop waded across in column behind Banyan, and by the time Tom waded his horse out of the river on the other side, he knew that they'd missed their man again.

He knew another thing, too: Banyan was either stupidly brave or oblivious to danger.

No question about it: Kidd had stopped here. The camp was completely burned out.

Tom dismounted, as Banyan shouted, "Sergeant, deploy the men. Search for survivors. Post a guard on the horses."

Tom heard the buzz of flies before he saw the brush arbor and the table under it. He saw the bodies sprawled at odd angles on the ground around the table and paused. There was one man left alive, a dwarf seated at the table, drinking from a glazed clay jug.

Tom walked toward him, his mount made nervous by the smell of blood. The dwarf was old and looked sick-drunk.

"Well, thank God you finally got here," the dwarf said. "There was something important I promised to tell you before I go."

57

P rivate Joe Parker leaned on the fire-scorched handle of the shovel and watched as the Mexican rode into the illegal whiskey camp, waving a white handkerchief tied to a stick.

"What now, I wonder?"

"If you're asking me what I think," Hans said, looking up unhappy from the grave they'd been detailed to dig, "I don't much give a shit. Why in hell we got to bury these bums, anyway? Buzzards got to eat same as worms."

Parker, who'd been put in charge of the burial, turned back to the job. He hooked the toe of his boot under the body of the old dwarf and rolled him into the mass grave on top of the others. "Best get to shoveling, Hans. The captain don't like slackers."

"The hell with him."

"Better not let the sergeant hear you say that." Joe Parker looked over Hans's shoulder like maybe there might be somebody listening behind him.

Hans whirled around, realized he'd been tricked, and angrily set to shoveling again. In truth, Hans's quip pretty much summed up Parker's own outlook. His hitch would be up in three months, and he'd be going home to Indiana. Over the past three and a half years he'd puzzled many a time over the temporary lunacy that had led him to join up. Adventure my foot. When he'd put his John Hancock on the dotted line, he'd imagined exotic places with palm trees and white-sand beaches. The only sand he'd seen so far was Oklahoma sand. And as far as palm trees went, he was still waiting to see his first one. That recruiter, the one who sold him on the idea, he ought to go to work for Sears Roebuck; a man like that could sell dirt to a dirt farmer. Joe Parker had left home thinking he'd be a career soldier, a man of the world. Not once in that picture had he seen himself on a barren, burned-over prairie in pursuit of a renegade Apache.

Hans, who had gotten over his temper, was leaning on his shovel again. "What do you think they're talking about with that Mexican?"

"I thought you didn't give a shit."

"Mostly I don't, but I wonder what they're saying."

Lewis stopped shoveling and looked at them. "You guys want to get back to flinging your share of this dirt?"

The Mexican had dismounted and was now in a kind of huddle with the captain and that deputy marshal, the Mexican pointing south and then upriver, like he was telling them something. Whatever it was, it must have stirred the captain some, 'cause the next thing Lewis knew the captain was up off his haunches and calling out to the sergeant.

"Assemble the men."

"Jesus," Joe Parker muttered. "Here we go again."

"I hope we catch up to that son of a bitch," Lewis said.

"Why?" Hans asked.

"It'll make us famous."

"I don't want to be famous," Hans said, "I just want to rest for a while."

"You can rest when you're dead," Lewis said.

"Did anybody ever tell you what a dumb ass you are?"

"Yeah, my daddy. He did it pretty regular."

Joe Parker laughed at the joke and threw another shovelful of dirt into the grave.

Fifty years later, he'd tell his grandson how getting put on this shit detail probably saved his life.

58

They'd climbed steadily as they rode south away from the river and their climb brought them to a low, mesa-like shelf of sandstone: a hard pan that was flat as a table and extended straight ahead a quarter mile and to their left and right as far as Chaco could see. He pulled up there and transferred the packsaddle with the water to one of the fresh mules. He stripped the saddles from their weary horses and slapped them on the best of the whiskey makers' horses.

"From here we ride west," he said, and set off at a trot.

The Navajo woman carried a Remington slide-action Model 14 slung by a leather strap across her back. Bui had made the sling for it. She carried the rifle opposite a bandolier of .30-06 cartridges she'd taken from one of the wagons before Chaco set them afire. She wore the pistol belt and pistols of the one called Harlan, and she'd taken his hat as well. It looked better on her than it had on him. She kept the wind string drawn tight under her chin and looked straight ahead as she rode.

Bui rode beside her.

Chaco became conscious of how the three of them must look.

Like warriors in that time before, perhaps riding back from a successful horse raid. He caught himself looking at the Navajo woman and remembered some of the things his mother had told him about Lozen. She'd been a medicine woman, and the warrior sister of the great Victorio, and she had carried Aná and Bui to safety across a dangerous, enemy-filled country eight years before he was born. He wondered whether Lozen, his mother, would have liked this Sally Begay. He grimaced and looked back at the trailing pack mule on which his father's bones were lashed.

Chaco had always known there was something unstated in the way his honored uncle looked at him. Like he had something he should say to him but somehow knew it would be better for him, his son, if it was left unsaid.

Toward evening they swung northward and rode down to the river and allowed the horses to water and graze there for an hour. Sally Begay killed a pair of prairie hens with a throwing stick, and Bui cooked them over a smokeless fire pit. They ate in silence and afterward buried the fire. Then rode a few miles west, made camp, and lay down for a few hours of rest.

Sally Begay came to him in the dark, naked and warm. "Bui sent me," she whispered.

No other words passed between them. They shared a kind of desperate need. Her moans stirred fire in him. Later, much later, looking up at the bright stars, he said, "If things go wrong at some point, I want you to take something to the Gila River country for me."

"I will stay with you now."

"Yes, but if something happens to me, you must do this thing for me."

"What?"

"Do you know the Gila River country?"

"Yes, I know it."

"Have you ever been to Turkey Creek?"

"I know where it is."

"If something happens to me, this is what you must do," he said. And he then told her.

59

S̲ally Begay woke him well before dawn. "Time to go," she whispered, a warmth and happiness in eyes that before last night had been filled with sorrow. She touched his cheek, smiled down at him and moved off.

As Chaco dressed he could hear her and Bui at work among the animals. He heard the sound of a saddle being swung into place, and heard their soft laughter, and felt his face heat with embarrassment. He shook out a boot and crushed the black scorpion that fell from it. Shook it again and ran his hand around inside. Shook out the other and pulled them both on and laced and double-knotted them.

They rode west with the river and had traveled a few miles when Sally Begay pulled up abreast of him. She held out a strip of jerked meat.

"Eat," she said.

He bit off a piece and chewed slowly as he followed an old buffalo trail that was now used by cattle. The horse climbed for a time, and he reined to a halt at the crest of the rise and saw where the old trail slanted down to the river. He glassed their back trail, saw no indication of pursuit, and rode on. From time to time he turned in the saddle to watch for dust, for any unexplainable flush of roosting birds, for any sign of pursuit. But he saw no sign of them back there, and yet he could not shake the warning sense that they were. Riding the river like this, the captain and his soldiers and the marshal might be fifteen miles behind or just beyond the next rise. Of one thing he was certain: they were still coming. They would not stop. He'd known last night that they should keep moving, but Bui was only flesh and blood. So was he. The body must have rest, must have sleep.

Their winding way brought them to a fork in the river. The cool morning had burned away, and the sun smoldered white against the pale, unsheltering sky. Sally Begay rode close behind him. He liked the feeling it gave him to look into her eyes. She is a strong woman, he thought, remembering last night. He thought about her dead husband and her children. The children she believed were dead. When this was done, if they made it through, they would go to her country and look for her children. It was only right that he should do this thing for her.

Sally gestured toward the fork in the river. "Which of these is the Canadian, I wonder? They both have water, but it will be that one, I think."

"Whichever one we follow we must soon come to the headwater," Chaco said, and dismounted. "We'll let them drink here."

Sally Begay dropped to the ground beside Bui. The animals shuffled forward and dipped their mouths into the slow current of the shrunken river, reduced at this point to a narrow stream scarcely wide as Chaco's palm—flowing from semi-stagnant pool to semi-stagnant pool.

"Look." Bui pointed.

There was a board nailed to a cottonwood a little distance upstream. Chaco saw it, too, and stepped across the fork and climbed the low bank. It was gray as cigar ash and had at one time been a wagon plank. The words "Trujillo Ck" had been burned into the plank, and below the words was an arrow that pointed left.

He walked back. "There's water in this creek on the left. I think we'll follow the river a little way and look for a place to swing back."

Sally Begay nodded approval.

Bui said, "You think they still follow?"

"Without doubt." Chaco stepped into the saddle and led out.

Sally and Bui remounted and followed, the pack animals strung out behind. They followed the trickle of water that was the Canadian for about a mile before they came to a bit of rocky ground, flinty gravel that was overgrown with scrub mesquite and prickly pears. The three of them swung south and soon came to the creek again. They crossed over and followed the climbing flow of the creek toward its headwater. He suspected they would come to a spring at some point, beyond which they would face the waterless prairie. There was a surprising amount of good grass. As they rode they spied little gatherings of branded Herefords and here and there a few spotted mixed breeds.

Hours later they came in sight of a lonely windmill beside the creek and startled a herd of pronghorns watering at a mossy concrete trough. The antelope bounded away and soon were lost from sight. Cattle lolled under the shade of scattered mesquites. The blades of the windmill squeaked as they spun in the late-afternoon wind. Cow dung littered the barren ground near the water-trough. They watered the horses and the mules, topped off their canteens and a waterskin, and rode on.

Beyond the windmill there was no water in the creek. The land rose gently toward a vast mesa—or what at first appeared to be a mesa. Chaco reined to a halt, pulled the map from his shirt pocket, cocked a leg across his saddle, and smoothed the map across his knee.

The mesa toward which they rode was not marked on the map. The map did, however, indicate that there was another set of rails maybe thirty miles ahead. Steam engines were thirsty machines, and there would be water stations along the line.

They rode on. The closer they got to the low mesa, the wider it grew, until finally the line of rock that marked the mesa's summit extended beyond sight to the east and the west.

Chaco turned in the saddle and looked back. There was no dust. No indication of pursuit. There'd been none since they'd ridden away from the whiskey camp yesterday. But he could feel them back there, the captain and the marshal. He'd never thought this would be easy, never doubted there would be consequences. He'd done what had to be done. He felt bad about Doc, a little man tall as a mountain. It was always the good ones . . .

One of the mules squealed and went down. Chaco stood in the stirrups, came around in the saddle. A rifle report echoed up from behind them. The other animals, tethered to the fallen mule, were jerked to a halt. Three hundred yards back sunlight glinted off something. No drift of gun smoke, which meant smokeless powder.

Sally Begay and Bui galloped past him, riding for the summit. The wounded mule lay on its side kicking. Goyaałé's bundle was on one of the other mules tethered to the one on the ground, and it and all the other animals were bucking. Another mule went down a moment before the rifle report reached them.

Chaco wheeled his mount and galloped after the women. The slope steepened toward the summit. Ahead of him the women were plunging their mounts upward at too steep an angle. A bullet spit up a chunk of ground ahead of Chaco's lunging animal. Another scratched the air above him, and the horse under Sally Begay squealed and went down, and Bui's mount tripped over it and tumbled. She leapt clear, landed on her feet, and ran to a stop. And as his horse lunged past her, he extended a hand, but she waved him off.

"Go," she called, then swung the rifle off her shoulder, ran back to Sally Begay, and got down beside her behind her fallen horse.

Bullets were now kicking up dirt on every side of Chaco as he hung off the saddle. If he could make it to the summit, they'd at least have a chance.

60

The troopers were spreading out and bellying down into prone firing positions. The best of them were already working the bolts of their rifles, firing at the fleeing riders high on the ascending slope. Banyan strode back and forth behind them, shouting encouragements. Tom and the Mexican dismounted in a depression beside a wind-gnarled juniper. Tom went down on one knee and held the front sight of his Winchester steady on Kidd's lunging horse. All he could see of Kidd was his leg hooked over the saddle. The rest of him hung off the animal's uphill side. The horse was lunging ever nearer the summit. He squeezed off the shot and missed. Hard to tell whether his aim was low or high with the soldiers firing so wildly. He chambered another cartridge, aimed higher and off the nose of the lunging horse, and fired again.

"These soldiers can't shoot," Sanchez said.

"The Army doesn't waste a lot of ammo teaching them."

"You ain't no good, either."

"You noticed."

"If you want, I can shoot him."

Tom fired again, missed again. He turned to Sanchez. "Fire

away, if you're that good."

"How much you pay me, one hundred dollars?"

Tom jacked another round into the chamber. "Yeah, that's what I thought." He snapped off the shot, and this time the horse buckled and went down.

"You got him, boys," Banyan shouted. "Don't stop. Keep firing."

The rider jumped clear as the horse tumbled. Landed on his feet and ran back to the fallen animal. He was pulling something from the saddle. A rifle? No, two of them. And now he was running. He wasn't going to fort up behind the animal like the other two. Tom saw the rocky outcrop he was making for, higher up under the rim of the caprock. Tom brought his Winchester to his shoulder and fired—and kept firing. The ground around the Apache was spitting up in chunks, and then he disappeared behind the outcrop, the bullets of the soldiers slamming uselessly at that point against the blackened crag.

"Cease fire, cease fire," Banyan shouted, and stopped his pacing. He turned, fists on hips, and grinned at Tom.

"We've got the son of a bitch now."

His expression froze as a rifle report ratcheted down from the heights. He staggered a half step, disbelief in his eyes as he looked down at a bloody exit hole through his shirt.

Tom dropped to the ground as Banyan crumpled.

"They've shot the captain," one of the soldiers yelled.

One of the others fired a round at the stone outcropping. And then all the soldiers were firing. The sergeant was yelling something, but Tom couldn't make it out. Banyan lay on the ground, his mouth working like a guppy's. Tom crawled over to him, rolled him over. There was a hole through his belly big enough to put his fist in. Above the relentless crack of the rifles, the sergeant was yelling, "Cease fire, cease fire." Tom removed the bandana from around his neck, sweat soaked and dust caked, and stuffed it into the exit wound in an effort to staunch the bleeding.

The captain's eyes moved aimlessly behind half-closed eyelids. Tom took hold of his arm and, crawling and pulling, dragged him foot by foot toward the relative shelter of the depression. At the last moment the Mexican reached out, grabbed one of the captain's arms, and helped pull him the last few feet into the depression. They managed, working together, to get the captain straightened around.

Sanchez, studying Tom the way he might a curiosity, said, "That was a foolish risk."

It certainly had been. He didn't even like the captain. Tom rolled Banyan onto his side, pulled his shirttail out of his trousers, ripped it open, and located the entrance wound. The hole was no larger than the tip of his index finger and bled hardly at all. The bandana he'd stuffed into the exit wound had soaked through, and blood was seeping from the wound again. The Mexican scooped up a handful of dirt and applied it to the blood-soaked bandana. The soil mixed with Banyan's blood and formed a kind of bloody clay. Tom looked on in disbelief. But the treatment accomplished what the bandana had failed to do: it stopped the bleeding.

He looked at the Mexican, and the Mexican looked back at him and shrugged.

"He'll probably get an infection and die," Tom said.

"Man, what is the difference if he bleeds to death?"

Tom studied Banyan's face as the Mexican raised a canteen to the captain's lips, forced a couple of swallows down his throat, the gesture almost womanly in its outward compassion.

"That son of a bitch can shoot," Tom said.

"The bullet that bit this one, it didn't come from the shotgun man," Sanchez said. "It come from one of them women up there."

"You've got to be kidding me."

"I think the Navajo woman. I didn't even know she could shoot." He shook his head. "Good thing they never let her get hold of a gun."

Tom didn't believe him; that shot had to have been made by Frank Kidd. He made a move to rise up for a look see, and Sanchez placed a hand on his shoulder.

"What are you trying to prove, man?"

"Prove?"

"What do you think about that woman?" He gestured toward Captain Banyan.

"I don't get you."

"The way she waited for this one to stand still before she shot him."

"Waited?"

"You stick your head up, she's going to shoot it off for you, you can bet on it. Look at him, man." Sanchez jerked his chin toward the captain.

They both looked at Banyan, the whites of his eyes rolling behind half-closed eyelids.

The sergeant came low crawling toward them. Tom scooted over, made room in the depression, as the sergeant, who'd lost his hat, bellied in beside them, breathing in short, hot gasps. He blinked up at Tom, wallowed around and studied the captain's bloodless face.

"If the Army didn't have no business here before," he allowed, "it sure as hell does now."

Tom pointed to another outcropping of rock to the left and above the position held by Frank Kidd. "You need to get a man up there who can shoot."

"Great idea, Marshal, but it'll have to wait till dark. I haven't enough men to provide cover fire." The sergeant shook his head. "I warned the captain not to split his command."

"But he did," Tom said.

Banyan had divided his troop yesterday before they'd ridden out of the whiskey camp. Half of them he'd set out afoot with orders to follow the Canadian back to Tascosa and wait there for his return. Every man who'd ridden on with Banyan had brought along a spare mount on lead. The plan was risky, but it achieved its end: they'd covered twice as much ground and had overtaken the Apache.

The sergeant scowled. "I guess we got him where the captain wanted."

Sanchez grinned. "They kept this wolf in a cage that they liked to play a game with."

The sergeant turned, studied him. "What?"

"In this game all of them crazy brothers would get around that cage and one would reach in and grab that wolf by the tail. You had to let go before it could bite you, and you had to be quick, I can tell you that."

"What's that got to do with this?"

"That *brujo* up there, he ain't in no cage, *'mano*. You got him by the tail, but I don't think you can let him go."

"We've got him pinned down," the sergeant said.

The Mexican gestured toward the captain. "That's what he said. Your captain, he don't look too good."

The sergeant grimaced. "The bastard better not die on me."

They heard the passage of the bullet through the windless air and then the *whunk*.

"Jesus," one of the privates yelled. "He got Lewis. He's shot—"

The yelling private was cut off by another *whunk*.

"Holy shit, stay down, stay down," another yelled.

Sanchez shrugged philosophically. "That's two more. This is a witch-man, I can tell you. I knew it the first time I look at him. That's why I don't say nothing to him. Or to them. They think maybe they can fool this *brujo*." He shook his head. "They make good whiskey, but they was stupid. He's a *brujo*, this one. You can't see that?"

A rifleman yelled from cover, "Hans just tried to help Lewis, and the son of a bitch shot him."

"Took the top of his head right off," another shouted.

"Keep your faces in the dirt," the sergeant called back. "Stay low."

"What in hell's he shooting with," another yelled. "Some kind of cannon?"

The Mexican grinned at Tom. "That Navajo woman, she shot that last one. I know the sound of that rifle. It belonged to Harlan."

The captain muttered something, then gasped and was silent again. Tom pressed a finger against Banyan's throat. A weak pulse, but his heart still beat.

"Stay down," the sergeant shouted again. He looked up at the fading sky, then looked at Tom. "If we can hold out until dark, I'll take one man and try to flank him."

"With this one that trick won't work," Tom said. "If we don't do something before sundown, we're all dead men."

"The hell you talking about?"

"I've seen his work. He's better at this than anybody I ever come across."

They heard the inbound bullet ahead of the *whunk*.

Then another alarmed cry: "He got McIntyre."

Tom risked a quick look, saw the drift of smoke from the rocky outcrop, and ducked an instant ahead of a bullet that cracked the air where his head had been.

The Mexican grinned. "I done told you that woman can shoot, man."

"I believe you." Tom shook his head, said, "This ain't the result I was looking for."

"Me, either," the sergeant said. "The son of a bitch got us cut down to six men."

"He got you cut down to five, *'mano.*"

The sergeant turned, looked a question at the Mexican.

"The captain, I think maybe he's dead now."

Tom touched a finger to Banyan's throat, held it there. He sighed, looked at the Mexican and then the sergeant. "Gone."

The sergeant, in disbelief, stared at the captain. "Jesus."

Banyan's half-open eyes, reposed in death, had taken on a poetic almost soulful look. Tom stretched out a hand and with his fingertips closed them.

"How the hell we going to get out of this one?" the sergeant asked of no one in particular.

"I wonder if he'd recognize a flag of truce?" Tom said.

"I don't think you can surrender to this one," the Mexican said.

"No, not surrender."

"Well then, what?" the sergeant asked. "Don't look like he's going to surrender to us."

Tom lowered the hammer on his Winchester. He didn't like what he was thinking, but they were out of options. He was like many of his generation, men born during the last days of the Indian wars, and like some of his generation he'd come up resenting the way so many treaties with the Indians had been broken by the government in the name of the American people. Now he was about to join that long line of lying bastards, and he hated it. It just happened to be the only choice left, if he hoped to come out of this alive. He looked at the sergeant.

"We got one option left."

"What?" the sergeant asked.

"Treachery," Tom said. "If I can get within fifty feet of him, I can beat him."

61

T he surface of the rock had gotten uncomfortably warm. The air around Chaco shimmered. If he crawled forward, he knew the extra height would position him at a vantage from which he could finish off the four to the right. But the move would expose him to the marshal's fire as well. He assumed that it was the marshal down there with the Mexican. He thought maybe he would make the move in a while, before he lost the light. He looked down at the wound through his thigh. It hurt, and for it to hurt this much it couldn't be that serious . . . At least, that was what men claimed who had suffered such wounds. He'd stopped the bleeding, but he had lost some blood, and now the inside of his head had begun to turn.

Don't pass out, he thought, and swallowed in a dry throat. I should have grabbed the canteen instead of the shotgun, he thought, then chided himself: Don't think about the things you should have done. That's your whole life: all the things you should have done. But next time I'll remember about the water . . . if there is a next time.

He had stuffed the exit wound with his bandana and plugged the entrance with a bit of cloth he'd cut from his shirttail. He'd cut away his pant leg, ripped the material into strips, and used one of them to bind the compress bandages in place.

To his left and lower on the slope, he could see Sally Begay and his sister. They were hunkered down behind Sally's horse. When Sally wasn't looking down the barrel of her rifle at the soldiers, she would look up at him. He liked the feeling that gave him. The position they were in was not good. The body of a horse could not stop a smokeless .30-06 round. But for whatever reason the soldiers down there didn't seem to know that. Perhaps poor training; who could say? The soldiers had stopped firing altogether. Sally had shot several of them already, including Captain Banyan, and it occurred to him that the rest of the soldiers might be afraid to stick their heads up to shoot. She hadn't missed yet.

A trickle of sweat stung his eyes. He wiped his shirtsleeve across his face and checked the position of the sun: less than an hour until dark. If they could hold out that long, he would go down and finish this business. He didn't mind about the captain or the marshal, though it did bother him about the soldiers. He wondered what they were thinking down there, now that they had the fight they wanted.

Downslope about twenty yards the horses and mules stood tethered to the carcass of the animals the soldiers had shot. So far they hadn't shot any of the others. That was good. He studied the mule that carried his father's bones.

He heard his father's voice inside his head: "*I wish I had kept fighting until I was the last man left alive.*" And hearing it, he blinked and looked around, half expecting to see him.

The sun turned from golden to red, and the light was softer now. Everything below him lay in the mellow rose of fading day. He thought about the opiates Bui had taken from McDonnell's store and wished he had some of them now. He felt the pockets of the field jacket: nothing in them but bullets and shotgun shells. Bui must have stuffed the last of the drugs into her pockets before giving the jacket back.

Think about something else you want but don't have, he thought, and, with a kind of hard resolve, told himself he was glad he did not have the drug. He knew he would use it now if he had it, and at this moment he must be strong. He needed a clear head if he was to fight. The drug had the power to unman even the strongest. And if this was to be his last hour, he wanted to feel everything.

He studied the women where they lay crouched behind the horse. Sally Begay with the rifle resting across the saddle, aimed downslope at the soldiers, ready in the event any one of them foolishly raised his head. This Sally Begay, she was a woman he wanted to know better, the kind of woman to be a man's best friend if he was true or his worst enemy if he was false.

He studied the positions of the soldiers again. He knew there should be about twenty soldiers altogether. But so far he'd been able to account for only about half that number. There were about seven or eight left down there. Though it had surprised him to see the Mexican with them.

It occurred to him that the missing soldiers might be circling into a position above them, and if that was so and they got above them before the sun went down, then they were done for.

He looked up at the sky, muttered, "Usen," and blinked as an answering voice called out to him. It called out again, not from Usen; it was someone yelling up to him from below. One of the men down there was waving a rifle with a piece of white cloth attached to the barrel.

"Hey up there, we need to parlay. Hold your fire."

Chaco smiled. Of course it was a trick.

"Go ahead and talk," he called down to them. He saw now that the one waving the white flag was the marshal.

"I want to come up and talk."

The sun was just above the blackening horizon now. Soon darkness would settle over this place. Chaco swallowed dryly. He didn't really have anything to say to this marshal. Everything was settled now. The marshal and the soldiers would kill him, or he would kill them. That was the only outcome left for either side. He knew that this moment had been written before the rocks were hard, that this moment had happened before and would happen again and again down the ages. He turned and looked at Bui and Sally Begay and saw that both of them were looking up at him from behind the dead horse. The marshal wanted to talk, and it occurred to him that he might at least be able to use this situation to get them out of this.

"One of you can come up," he called down to the marshal, "but only one and no tricks."

"I'm coming," the marshal called.

Good, he thought. If this goes wrong, at least I'll have you. He signaled Sally Begay not to shoot. She nodded and looked down the barrel of her rifle but held her fire as the marshal, waving the flag attached to his rifle, slowly came to his feet. The fading sun showed the gray at his temples.

"Leave the rifle," Chaco called.

The marshal hesitated. Then he placed the rifle on the ground, straightened, and came on. Chaco noted the positions of the soldiers and saw that they were all still in place. When the marshal was far enough from cover that there was no way for him to make it back, Chaco drew the hammer back to full cock on the Sharps and came to his feet.

Everything would be good now. The marshal was almost where he wanted him. The soldiers, fearing him, would hesitate to open fire. He watched the marshal as he climbed steadily toward him, and in the marshal he saw everything he had hated since that day they took him away from his mother with their legal papers.

"That's far enough," Chaco called.

The marshal stopped. "Anything wrong?" he called.

"Nothing wrong. Everything is as it should be. Call down to the soldiers. Tell them if they fire one shot, you die first, then they die next . . . all of them."

"I think they hear you," the marshal yelled. But he turned and dutifully shouted down to them, "Did you hear that, Sergeant?"

"I heard," a voice called back. "You heard him, boys. Hold your fire till I say different."

Chaco shifted his gaze to Bui. "Take the horses and the mules, and go."

Bui came to her feet and went downslope to the animals, cut the lead ropes of the dead mules. The three mules on the end broke free and trotted away, and she let them go, swung up on a horse, and brought the other animals along with the mule that carried his father's bones.

He called to Sally Begay, "Go with her."

"I stay with you."

"Do what I say, woman."

She frowned, but as Bui rode past, Sally came up in a quick move and swung up onto one of the horses. "I will wait for you," she called as they rode past.

Chaco watched the marshal and listened to the sound of the climbing horses and felt at ease in his heart. Whatever else happened here, he knew that once Bui and Sally Begay reached the summit that they would be in the clear and would see to it his father's bones got back to his own country. He believed Bui would have a friend in Sally Begay, as strong a friend as Lozen had been to Aná, the mother of his heart. Bui would be safe with this strong woman. He would like to have done this thing himself, but they would do this for him and for his father if this didn't go the way he hoped.

There were things he wished he had told Sally Begay last night, things he had never known before. He was a little light-headed at the moment, but not like before, not like the time in Cuba when the rebel bullet bit him. This time he saw everything about his life in a light as clear as the shooting-light between him and the marshal, and he knew now what was important. He wished he'd had time to talk to her, to explain it all to her. To say all the words to her he had held inside him all these years. He thought that maybe Lozen was something his father could not explain to him. The mother who bore me was a warrior, he thought, as fierce in battle and as able as any man. I am Lozen's son and the son of Goyaałé, known to his enemies as Geronimo. He had believed for most of his life that he was alone in the world. And he had lived inside himself alone. But now, maybe too late now, he saw that he was not alone. That he never had been. He was a man of the People, free in his heart.

He heard his sister and Sally call to him from the summit in a trilling yodel he'd heard only a few times in his life. They were letting him know they were in the clear. Now was the end, the hour he had moved toward from the moment his mother said take him, see that he lives. Chaco drew a long breath and focused on the marshal, aware that this hadn't gone the way the lawman hoped. Behind him the sound of horses and mules had faded, and now there was only the whispering voice of the wind.

"What now?" the marshal called.

"You should have turned back."

"That's not how it works, Kidd."

"I know."

"Even if you kill me, even if you kill us all, you can't win."

"I know."

"I didn't come up here to yell back and forth. I'm coming up."

"One step and I shoot you."

The marshal grimaced, glanced behind him as if weighing his chances, but then turned to face Chaco again, the red sun now quickly fading beneath a distant blackened horizon.

Be strong, Aná's voice echoed down the lonely corridor of his life. His gaze lifted to the sky, and he thought: Thank you, Usen, for my life, for my mother's life and the life of my sister; for Goyaałé, my father, and for Lozen, who gave me life, and for Sally Begay. Now comes the night. Deliver my enemies into my hands this one last time that I may be revenged.

He stood, defiant as a tattered flag against the wind. High in the fading sky a red hawk cried. It was a good omen, a sign from Usen, given when a great spirit enters or leaves the world.

ACKNOWLEDGMENTS

Writing is a solitary affair, but seldom entirely so. Thanks to Stephen and Susan Rain-Fox for the loan of a cabin and great Colorado evening conversations during the writing of this work. To Hal Reames and Ana Carvalho for their friendship and support. Thanks to Jodi Koumalats, steady friend of many years; and thanks to XErnie, brother of the heart. SPECIAL THANKS to longtime friend and fellow writer, Laura Resnick Chavez, and many thanks to Tosh McIntosh, fellow wordsmith and the guy I want in the cockpit when the engines give out; and Tiffany Yates Martin, and Matthew Patin for their help and input in this work. And thanks to all fellow NIPpers, past and present, to include Susan Rockhold, John Burch (ALS/RIP), Deanna Roy, and so many others, unnamed herein. A singular nod goes out to fellow writer and past traveler into the dark heart of Mexico, Señor John Jones. Lastly for my sons, John Ernest and Charles Edward, both wise beyond their years.

ABOUT THE AUTHOR

Darrel Bryant, a fifth generation Texan, brings to his writing a decade of military service in both the U.S. Navy and U.S. Army (airborne), to include Special Forces training. An early taste for adventure led to treks across the Yukon and Alaska, hikes into the Grand Canyon, up the Appalachian Trail, and along Hadrian's Wall in the north of England. A Hemingway summer lived in Paris. Five years as a riding hand on a 27,000-acre Montana cattle ranch, and crewman aboard the yawl *Open Return* on her homeward voyage from Long Island, NY to Galveston, TX. With a half-dozen novels in finished form tucked away in a file, he lives alone in a house he built with his own hands, from mostly recycled lumber, on the outskirts of his hometown, Austin. *Geronimo's Bones* is his first published novel.